"MY LOVE
WILL DESTROY YOU. . . ."

"Force me from you. Fight to be away. If you have an ounce of self-preservation, you will do this, Brienne."

"I cannot," she pleaded, wanting him with every inch of her body and soul.

"If you stay here tonight, my mark will be permanent. I'll have it no other way." He took her face into his powerful hands, searching for her answer.

And she gave it, not with words but with her lips. Deep inside him she heard a moan, and soon she felt her laces being severed one by one with the sharp edge of his knife. His hands slid the dress apart, and it fell in satin folds around them as they both half-sat and half-lay on the floor. He kissed her as he took off her green satin slippers and then pulled down her silk hose from her creamy thighs. He paused only to instruct her to untie his sash, then stood, leading her to the state bedchamber—and his ornately domed bed.

"NO CHOICE BUT SURRENDER is highly entertaining. . . . It captures your heart with a poignancy reminiscent of Judith McNaught's romances."
                                              —*Romantic Times*

NO CHOICE BUT SURRENDER

Meagan McKinney

Island
B O O K S

ISLAND BOOKS
Published by
Dell Publishing
a division of
Bantam Doubleday Dell Publishing Group, Inc.
666 Fifth Avenue
New York, New York 10103

ISBN: 0-440-16412-5

Printed in the United States of America

Published simultaneously in Canada

May 1992

10   9   8   7   6   5   4

RAD

For my two best friends:
Thomas Young Roberson,
my husband,
and
Richard John Goodman,
my father.
I love you both.

PROLOGUE

He loved England
as an Athenian loved the city of the violet crown,
as a Roman loved the city of the seven hills.
—Lord Macaulay

St. Mary Parish, Maryland
November 1780

The house was considered old, even though the United States had declared its freedom only four years before. It stood up from the Patuxent River, and its tall roof and gothic dormers gave its exterior an appearance of grandeur that the modest rooms inside could not attain.

Robert Staples sat discontentedly by the keeping-room fire. Being a boy of thirteen, he couldn't help but peek now and again into the next room, where his father and four men had gathered. There was an air of secrecy about these four men. They sat around a small table playing cards.

It was odd that they were gambling at the run-down manor when they could have been playing more comfortably at Satterlee Mansion, where there were many ornate rooms with fine Georgian carvings and elaborate card tables made by the finest cabinetmakers in Salem.

But there they sat, four strangers at a small cherry butterfly table, while the owner and his son watched anxiously from the side.

"I say, Avenel," one of the younger gamblers commented as he gazed about the small wainscoted room, "it's a rather dismal place you've brought us to."

The dark, bearded man with the medieval-sounding name merely glanced at the young lord; that was enough to quiet him completely. But Avenel added, "Would you have us play at the Satterlee Harbor house and be recognized for the Tories we are?"

"I have no opinions on this silly war! I need not be labeled a Tory! My only hope is to leave this rustic land behind and never return. The lure of tobacco fortunes is not great enough to withstand the sacrifice of my position." The young man wiped his brow.

"Perhaps you do not take sides. But one look at that vermilion satin waistcoat leaves no doubt that you are of the British nobility." Avenel looked at the young lord in disgust. "And need I remind you that there is no nobility here in America? 'Tis one of the things the damned war is about."

"Well, for one who was born here in America, you don't seem particularly enthusiastic about your freedom. What say you, Avenel? Are you a Tory sympathizer?" Squire Justice spoke up. That older man was annoyed that he was losing, but he found some consolation in the fact that the young lord and the ill-fated Lord Oliver were even doing worse than he was. They were betting way over their means—especially Lord Oliver, who had wagered his estate, Osterley Park. He had to admit that he was shocked that anyone could gamble so compulsively. But he'd seen it before. Unfortunately, it was a common practice among the peerage, one that had ruined more families than he could name.

"I shall be leaving for England tomorrow, so I have forced myself to remain uninvolved in politics." Avenel Slane shook himself, seemingly to ease his fatigue, and

then finished, "But enough of this. We must continue."
He looked straight at the man across from him, Oliver
Morrow, who had yet to speak since the game began. He
was about Avenel's size and stature, but the resemblance
ended there. Where Avenel was dead calm yet bold in his
approach, Morrow was nervous; his hand shook as he
shifted around the five cards in his possession. And the
cautiousness about Lord Oliver said only one thing: He
had a lot to lose.

"Besides," Avenel added enigmatically, "I have my
own war to fight."

"I think 'tis time we called it a draw, gentlemen." The
young lord wiped his brow with a heavily scented hanky.
"There's too much at stake here. Of course, I can afford
to cover my losses," he said, and then he coughed as he
remembered the sizable sum he owed already—and
mostly to that bastard Avenel Slane, he thought, feeling
bitterly emasculated. "But I think we should see that this
is bordering on the absurd. After all, Lord Oliver is the
Earl of Laborde. Surely you cannot let him gamble away
his very estate. It's outright criminal!"

"This is no fops' diversion, my lord," Avenel said, each
syllable hanging disdainfully on his tongue. "You all
came here knowing this was a man's game."

"But the stakes are getting to be too high. You have
taken advantage of us in our boredom and fear. This wait
for the ship to arrive at Satterlee Harbor to take us back
to England has been hellish. Why," he exclaimed, "every
time some Whig bluecoat stops at the mansion for tea or
to inform the supposed supporters of the Revolution
how the war is coming along, we've had to play hide and
seek among the wall panels. I say, you took advantage of
us. You knew we'd jump at the chance to ride out to the
neighboring estate for a game of cards. Inhumane cir-

cumstance is what we've been put through. And now this—it's too much!"

"There would have been no need to hide if you had renounced your social standing—at least until you were on the ship for England." Avenel closed the fan of cards in his hand and placed them facedown onto the nicked surface of the table. "All that would have involved is a mere change of clothes."

"I was not born to dress as a peasant like you Americans!" The young lord put his cards down on the table and straightened his heavily greased and powdered wig. After preening himself, he looked at Avenel and felt suddenly quite superior. He noticed every detail of the man's dress, from the plain doeskin breeches to the dark blue worsted waistcoat. The man sported not one ruffle on his white cambric shirt; not an inch of expensive lace edged his cravat. Nor did he wear anything on his head. He relied instead on the appearance of his neatly tied queue of natural dark hair.

"'Tis your choice," Avenel said, and then added slowly, "my lord."

Now the young lord felt the man was laughing at him. His air of superiority started to dissipate. "I'll not continue with this charade any longer! Man, you will take me back to Satterlee now." He motioned to Robert's father as he would to a servant.

"Surely, my lord, you don't mean to stop in the middle of the hand." Master Staples tried to reason with him. He moved forward and then looked back at Robert in the confines of the keeping room. "Nob," he said, using the boy's nickname, "be a good boy and quit gaping. Go fetch the men some of that ham cured at the mansion and some more spirits."

Quickly the young fellow left for the keeping room, where he made up a large tray with ham, apples, and bread. Stepping humbly from the dirt and straw floors of the keeping room up to the new pine boards that had just been fitted into the parlor, Nob brought the tray to his father. After placing it on an ancient walnut William and Mary lowboy, the boy stepped back from the men, heeding the warning in his father's eyes. The men were playing the last hand now, and he knew there were to be no disturbances.

"I'll bring the ale now, Father," Nob whispered in the same semi-British accent as his father, which proved his Maryland ancestry. But instead of giving him an approving nod, his father shook his head forebodingly and gave him a look that said to go back to the keeping room. Before the young boy could turn around and retreat, there was a terrible banging sound as the cherry table crashed to the ground. All its contents scattered over the immaculate knotty pine boards.

"I warn you, Avenel, if you insist on taking Osterley Park, there will be no end to my vindictiveness!" shouted the Earl of Laborde. That older man with the tall build suddenly stood over the mess. His long, bloodless white hands were balled into fists, and his face became red in contrast to his finely groomed dark gray hair.

Secretly Nob was glad Oliver Morrow had lost. There was something about the earl that he had instantly disliked.

"In fact," the earl continued ominously, "I'll see you dead before you walk about my home!" With that, the man reached for a knife in the waistband of his breeches. Suddenly he lurched toward Avenel, which made Nob scream in terror.

As the fight escalated, the other men stood about watching stupidly from the perimeter of the room. Nob and his father tried to stop Oliver Morrow, but he was so quick, they floundered about; each tried to control the earl without making himself a target for the steel blade. Finally they, too, stood back and watched as Avenel swiftly moved out of the way of the knife. He kicked out at the earl's arm, and the knife flew out of the older man's grasp, skidding along the floor out of reach.

"If you think I am afraid of a knife, then think again. I have experienced its sharpness before, and I daresay my hide is too thick to be cut further." Avenel looked at the earl and reveled in the frightened look of recognition in the man's visage. The earl gasped in horror.

"I should have known you from your eyes, *gelding!* But I'll keep you down, Slane. You'll not ruin me! I've always found a way in the past. I have never been defeated—"

"Say no more!" Avenel laughed and picked up the cream-colored vellum that had fallen off the overturned table. "All your threats are meaningless now. You face the consequences of carelessly wagering a magnificent house. Your greed has gotten the better of you. Your very desire to win at all costs has been your downfall. Now I own Osterley Park. And I have won it fairly. 'Tis back where it belongs, and in better hands than yours." He placed the heavy paper in the inside pocket of his blue waistcoat. "If I'm not mistaken, you haven't the coin to get off this continent, let alone to buy Osterley back from me. So set your mind to other matters than revenge."

Avenel walked over to the cherry table and righted it. He smiled at Nob, whose thin adolescent body was quaking from excitement and fear. The boy immediately knew to bring him his coat and the three-cornered hat that had been placed on a chair. Avenel slipped on his coat and started out the door to his waiting horse. Nob stared after him, hero worship lighting up his face. His father started out the door, too, ignoring for the moment his other guests.

"Slane! Have you not forgotten your winnings?" He ran to where Avenel was mounting his horse.

"I have what I want." He turned to look at Staples. "You've done more than I could have asked for," Avenel said gratefully.

"I couldn't have done less. I wouldn't have a roof over my head if you hadn't given me the land to build on."

"My father was returning to England. He had no use for the land."

"Perhaps. But where tobacco can be grown, there's money to be made."

Avenel mounted the finely bred animal and bent down to shake Staples's hand. He laughed and said, "Watch your tongue! You speak too kindly of a Tory!"

"I suppose we shall always be speaking kindly of Tories, now that you are determined to go back to London."

"When the war is over, perhaps I'll come back." Avenel turned thoughtful and looked ahead to the blue Patuxent River as it wound its way through the glorious ambers and burgundies of the fall foliage. "I've been here all my life. I admit 'twill be difficult to be an Englishman." A slow smile twisted on his lips suddenly. "But you should see Cumberland! He's already planning his new wardrobe—dressing gowns and all!"

Both men laughed this time. Avenel took the reins in his hands and began a slow trot to Satterlee Harbor.

"You'd best return to the house, lest you find all my winnings back in their pockets!" he called over his shoulder.

"Godspeed, Avenel!" said Staples, watching him take off at a canter. He left behind a most pleased man.

Dinbych-y-pysgod
Tenby, Wales
December 1780

The auburn-haired girl took one last glimpse of her empty house as her coach drove by it, headed for London. Several pigs squealed and ran from the road into another abandoned Tudor home nearby. This one, however, stood roofless; its jettied-out top floors were now filled with rainsoaked debris.

Her homeplace, the small fortressed medieval town of Tenby, was not the least bit fashionable. Not for hundreds of years had the town flourished. But it had made a perfect home for her and her mother. In Tenby, people hadn't cast probing looks at a husbandless woman, nor at her daughter, the beautiful dark-haired girl. No one had ever bluntly put questions to them—questions the mother and daughter would have been loath to answer, such as where had they come from years before, and who they were.

The old distressed town welcomed all who came there. It unconditionally offered a beautiful view of Carmarthen Bay from its embattlements and fresh prawns and oysters from the Llangwm fish sellers, as if in thanks for the pleasure of the company.

But now yet another home was being left empty. A new lease seemed doubtful in light of the town's dwindling population. The girl's old home settled back quietly, accepting its fate. The scurries of small gray mice running across the dirt floor in the design-painted merchant's room would soon drown out the echoes of past laughter.

The girl was one of the town's own. She had played there as a child and had dreamed there as a young woman. Now she stared off to St. Catherine's Island and Castle Hill. She was now lost to Tenby. And as if mourning her departure, the town looked sadder than usual—a bit more squalid and a little more deserted. Not a soul was in attendance to see the girl off. But still, she looked back at the small coastal town from her worn leather seat in the coach and curled her fingers as if waving good-bye to an old friend, one that had protected her and helped her make her way. How she would miss it! She turned back in the coach, as if not wanting the fragile old place to see tears of homesickness already welling up in her soft violet-blue eyes.

Crossing her arms in front of her, she seemed a dismal little creature. There was no one to divert her sad thoughts—she was the coach's only passenger. They would pick up others on the way to London, but not until they reached the larger town of Carmarthen.

Sitting back in her seat, she looked out the dirty window of the coach at the hilly Welsh countryside. For the time being, she allowed herself to fret and imagine what life would be like where she was going.

I

OSTERLEY PARK

. . . worthy of Eve before the Fall.

—Horace Walpole

CHAPTER ONE

Osterley Park
January 1781

Brienne Morrow recalled the sight of Osterley as she'd seen it when she walked past its brick gatehouse a month ago. The great portico was alive with white griffons plastered on the pediment. Large stone eagles, each holding an adder in its beak, loomed fearlessly over the steps; their gray granite eyes forever watchful.

But now as she sat on the cold stone bench and looked at the house, she found it much more powerful now in contrast to the neglected landscape. There were no hills or stately elms to soften its effect. Rather, it sat on an immense flat plain by a long finger lake and completely overwhelmed even the largest of the trees nearby, a tall spindly oak.

She eyed the withering tree. The harsh winter was taking its toll on it. She had started on a melancholy walk about the grounds for the comfort found in the desolate landscape. Its very bleakness offered the respite she needed from the opulence of the house.

From the marble bench near the pebbled carriage drive, she allowed the house to take over her thoughts. She watched the pair of white griffons, noting the stance of their lifted paws and thinking that they looked as if they had been raised a bit since the day before. The Elizabethan turrets on all four corners were incongruous with the neoclassical facade. Brienne wondered if long ago there had been a comfortable, happy house where the portentous one now stood.

But she only had a few memories of Osterley at an earlier time, because she'd moved from it as a child of five. She remembered the coldness of the gallery, in which the great Venetian windows at each end had never seemed to break the drafts. Now the windows were bricked up. And she remembered her mother's room, which had been the exact color of sunshine and had always smelled of orange blossom. Brienne had an unpleasant memory of that room. She had had a nightmare and had run to find her mother, but her mother hadn't been in her room. The maid had come to put Brienne to bed again, but the servant's explanation that her mother had duties in another room had left her feeling even more frightened and alone.

Brienne looked down at her mended brown mitts and shook her head. Despite her memories and her mother's accounts of Osterley, she had still been unprepared for its greatness. She had been overwhelmed by the magnificent house as soon as she entered its gates. The very fact that she was its only resident, aside from the servants, gave it that much more command over her. Day after day, she walked through the elaborate rooms, more as a servant than as the daughter of Lord Oliver, the eighth Earl of Laborde. She found it ironic that she, small and shabby, was his only claim to manhood and the only bearer of his name.

Her mother's stories hadn't always been truthful. She twisted uncomfortably on the cold marble bench. Her thoughts turned to a miniature stowed in a secret panel of her bedroom chest of drawers. She had found the miniature in a trunk at an old merchant's house in Tenby right after her mother had died. It was a picture of a man's angelic profile, painted neatly on a thin sheet of ivory. He was young and very handsome, but his beauty had not made her gasp. Rather, what the miniature had seemed to imply was a greater shock.

It was something Brienne had wondered about for years. Had her mother ever been in love? She knew her mother had never loved the earl. Brienne's father had proven himself unworthy of love. So who was this beautiful man in the miniature? she had asked herself. Was he a distant cousin who even now pined for her mother? Or was he a sea captain who kept Grace Morrow in his thoughts even though he might be clear on the other side of the world?

Holding the miniature to her breast, Brienne had clung to her romantic fancies. There was comfort in believing her mother had known love after all. That she hadn't gone through her short life having known only one man, Oliver Morrow, who had treated her more as an ornament for his precious Osterley than as a woman who could be hurt by harsh words and rough hands. Though Brienne knew there would have been consequences had her mother had a relationship with another man, she chose not to dwell on those. In the distant corners of her mind, she thought she herself bore a likeness to the gentleman in the picture. But then, she told herself sternly, perhaps she was reading more into the picture than was warranted. The only thing she knew for sure was that the miniature had meant a lot to her mother. It had been important enough to keep all these years, and for that reason it had been a precious find.

That search for valuables had been necessary for more than just personal reasons. The creditors had come to call. A tuppence pending for a long-ago-worn-out bolt of cloth and a shilling owed for a long-ago-eaten side of pork had added up. Not long after that, she realized she would have to leave Wales.

There had been long sleepless nights when she'd been overwhelmed with doubts and fears. She'd lain awake in the top room and stared at the arched rafters, holding the precious miniature in her cold palm. Now and then she'd risen, only to find small relief in opening the leaden mullioned windows to the night air. Finally she'd made a decision. There would be no joy in her new home. She had shuddered at the thought of a chance meeting with the man she knew as her father. But she really had no choice. She had nowhere else to go.

Being forced to move, she had had to part with many of their treasured belongings—several of her mother's pearl pins, all her mother's gowns and most of her own, and all their wonderful books, including volumes of Shakespeare and Chaucer. But there had been two things Brienne had refused to part with, no matter how urgent her need for money. One was a gold and amethyst comb that she'd found with the tiny portrait. It was a bitter-sweet reminder of her mother's kind eyes, the same shade of blue-violet as her own. And the other precious possession was the miniature.

Brienne sat very still on the bench. Her mind was flooded with memories. They left a bad taste in her mouth and gave her a deep, lonely ache inside her belly.

But she'd enjoyed one bit of good fortune in the recent past: Her father had been blessedly absent from Osterley in the month she'd been there. And from what she could gather from the servants' gossip, he was not expected back anytime soon.

So absorbed was she in her thoughts that she didn't notice a fashionable coach-and-four enter the grounds until it was almost in front of the house. Before she could rise from her bench, the familiar figure of her father's solicitor sprang from the vehicle and made his way toward her. His gait was impatient.

"Good day," Brienne said from her position on the bench. Warily, she wondered what had inspired this unwelcome visit.

"Good day, Lady Brienne. No, please do not rise. I won't be staying long." The dour man stood over her and continued in an arrogant manner. "I have come to inform you that I am no longer your father's solicitor. He hasn't the funds for my services." He looked as if he expected a reaction of some sort from her, but she disappointed him by not giving him one.

"Excuse me for my candor," she finally spoke up, "but I don't see the necessity to inform me of that. I have never had any need of your services."

"There is something else. Your father has been in America for some time now. He has been found to have gambled excessively." The solicitor eyed her; this time he was hoping to provoke a reaction from her. "He has had heavy losses."

"Yes?" Brienne looked up at him. Her eyes held no apprehension whatsoever.

"In fact, he has lost everything. He gambled and lost Osterley entirely."

"I see." She thought about this bit of news for a second or two and then brushed it aside. "I shall inform the servants. Is there anything in particular they need to be told?"

"Excuse me, Lady Brienne. I don't know if you heard me correctly. I said the earl has lost Osterley. You are in effect homeless."

"Yes, I heard you correctly the first time. And I'm not surprised. How very like my father—by the mere draw of a card, to lose such a magnificent home, not caring whose livelihood he has ruined."

"The new master has requested the servants to remain here. In his letter he asked me to inform them that he will choose who is to go once he has arrived."

"And when do you expect that will be?" She was nonchalant, reasoning that she would be far away from Osterley by that time.

"It's hard to say, but my guess would be the end of the week at the latest, perhaps even tomorrow, according to the dates he stated in the letter."

Finally the solicitor got the reaction he'd been waiting for. Gasping out loud, she stared at him in disbelief. "Surely you are jesting! Why was I not given notice?"

"Letters from the Colonies more often than not arrive with the senders, my lady. This was the best I could do. I myself just received notice of your father's impoverished state." The bony solicitor couldn't hide his look of distaste. "He has relieved me of my services and informed me of his difficulty in returning to England. I fear that the war and his lack of funds for passage have found him in dire straits."

"Well, at least that is good news," she murmured under her breath.

The solicitor cleared his throat. "Though I have not yet been paid for my past services for the earl, I nonetheless did find it my duty to drive here and offer you my assistance. If I may make one suggestion, my lady, the place in Bath is still in your father's possession, I believe. And I know he still has a small, modest town house in London. I expect that when he returns to England, he will arrive there. I'm certain, as he is your father, that he would not find it objectionable if you were to take up residence there in the meantime."

"Perhaps he would not find it objectionable, but I would. I've come to Osterley only for a short time while I find a more suitable place to live. My stay here will just have to be cut."

"The new master seems very charitable. I'm certain he would not be disagreeable if you remained here until further arrangements were made. Of course, anyone would understand your humiliation at accepting such an indecent offer."

"Humiliation? Why should I feel humiliated by accepting the kindness of a stranger? The true humiliation is living under my father's 'kindness.' My mother could have told you about that." She mumbled these last words, not willing to elaborate on the subject.

"Well, if it does not bother you, Lady Brienne, I'm sure Master Avenel Slane would bid you to stay until it is comfortable for you to leave. The situation's lack of propriety is shocking, but if you are not bothered by it, then I shall offer no further advice."

"You can tell my father, if by chance you see him, that not only will I accept the kind Master Slane's offer, should he extend it, but to avoid the earl's company, I would even consider taking up a position permanently in the new master's household." She laughed and then added, "Yes, do inform him of that. Tell him I would prefer being a scullery maid at Osterley than living with

him in London. You will tell him, won't you?" She
looked up at the man; her beautiful eyes were alive with
merriment.

"Yes, my lady. If that is what you wish." He looked at
her as if she were crazed. Then, perhaps because he
thought her daftness made her vulnerable to him, his
eyes wandered over her rich auburn hair. It was so dark
it could pass for magenta. Her figure was petite and
young, and its only fullness was found in her chest and
her hips. There was an invitation in his small, squinty
eyes, but Brienne dealt with it by staring at him with a
stony expression until he realized his flirtation was hopeless. She had told him she was willing to stay on in a
stranger's house rather than live "respectably" with her
father, but she would never take a lover, not one of her
choosing or anyone else's. She watched determinedly as
the solicitor swiftly took his leave without offering her
pity or solace.

She knew she had to inform the army of servants and
make her own plans before Avenel Slane showed up.
Brienne dejectedly got off the bench. Making her way
through the grand portico and across the uncovered
courtyard, she noticed that all was eerily silent—too silent for such an immense and well-furbished house. It
was a testament to the fact that there was no owner in
residence—yet.

CHAPTER TWO

"She's been sitting there for days." The footman eyed the scroll end stool, covered in dark blue leather, on which Brienne sat quietly. The fireplaces crackled with warmth in the two opposite apses. Their fires contrasted with the cold marble hall that was filled with Roman statues, now white from age. With no more hospitable place to go, she sat watching the flames, waiting for the new owner perhaps more anxiously than the two footmen who watched her.

She'd had little luck in trying to leave. No coach would be hired for the amount she was able to pay. She had yet even to figure out where to go. London held little appeal for her; it was too big and she knew not a soul there. At her father's town house she would encounter him should he return from the Colonies, so she had ruled that out right away. Then there was Bath. She knew there were bound to be old friends of her mother's there, taking the waters and enjoying the social whirl. But how would she get there? She had come to a grand stumbling block. And then she had run out of time.

She got up, wrapped her cloak around her, and smiled at the two elderly footmen as she went out the door. The sting of freezing rain met her face, and she wrapped the cloak even more tightly around her. She ran across the courtyard to the great portico and stood there watching the drive. Leaning on one of the smooth Ionic columns that loomed over her, she felt as if the house watched her even more closely than the two griffons as she made her way under their pediment.

Then she caught an observing eye. Suddenly she laughed as she saw the upstairs maid, Annie, whip the yellow taffeta curtains closed from a bedroom on the second floor.

They all think I'm daft, she said to herself and smiled bitterly. *And why shouldn't they? They've had the pleasure of living with my father. They must think madness runs in the family.* With that she let out a low laugh and wiped some of the rain from her face.

She stood very quietly, too agitated to wait in her room. Despite her ladylike manners, she sought the rain and the cold as a buffer from the house. Soon she spied a large coach making its way through the gates. Her stomach spinned and then tightened as she watched the elaborately japanned, sleek green vehicle move closer. Its gold and red crest shone brilliantly, despite the dark, dismal day.

"So he's here!" she exclaimed in a small voice.

Nervously she ran into the great hall, which was now bustling in anticipation of the new owner. Up in her bedroom she shed her wet cloak and grabbed some hairpins from her dressing table. She haphazardly placed these into her damp auburn hair while contemplating which of her gowns would be best for such a situation. She took little time to decide; she remembered one of her favorites, a pink polonaise that was rather out of style but still in good condition. She went to the tall satinwood wardrobe to get it, but to her surprise she saw an edge of glowing pink silk moving just around the corner to her dressing room.

"Annie, whatever are you doing?" she asked. Arriving in the dressing room, she saw the maid prancing about in front of the looking glass with the pink polonaise half on and half off. Brienne wasn't sure if this was because Annie had not pulled the dress on fully or because the dress was too small in the waistline.

Annie jerked around, caught off guard. She mumbled something, but Brienne could not make out what she was saying.

"Do speak up, Annie! I would like to know the meaning of this," she said sternly.

"I won't be waitin' on you anymore, milady."

"That's fine," Brienne answered, wondering what had gotten into the girl. It was unusual to see such insubordination in a servant, and she worried about its meaning. "You know I have not grown up with servants, Annie. I have not asked much of you during my stay here. Still, it is reproachable for you to try one of my dresses on. Whatever is going on?"

"You aren't the master's daughter anymore."

"Perhaps not." A few delicate lines appeared on Brienne's brow. The consternation she felt was all too clear. "But that still doesn't explain why you're wearing my dress." She watched Annie's stomach. Her stays were so tightly laced that she knew the gown would be torn before too long. "Please take it off."

"Oh, my lady, it's just that I've heard that the new owner is something of a man. And I'll be wantin' to show him that I can be useful,'' the maid whined, trying to play on her pity.

"You mean to let him trifle with you?'' Brienne asked naïvely.

"It'd be better than the stableboy. And with this dress he'll be thinkin' I'm a lady.''

"But you haven't my permission.'' Brienne looked at Annie, not trusting her. It had been clear to Brienne from the day she'd arrived at Osterley that Annie had begrudged her her appearance, even as shabby as it was.

"There's no harm done!'' the maid exclaimed with mock recrimination. "There!'' she said as she placed the gown back in the yellow taffeta room. Then she pulled her own dress back over her linen shift and stays. " 'Twill not happen again, milady. At least I can promise you that!'' Annie abruptly left the room without apologizing. She wore a smug smile on her lips, which she was sure Brienne had not noticed. But Brienne had noticed, and she stared after the maid in disbelief, knowing there was something afoot—and that she was somehow going to get the worst of it.

Musing over the reasons for Annie's strange performance, she walked over to her inlaid wardrobe, which was exquisite with marquetry and cross-banded with rosewood. She studied its diminished contents; her dresses were far outnumbered by the pegs fitted in its interior. The polonaise was now too wrinkled to be of any use to her, so she took out a dark violet wool and placed it on the bedstead. She combed her long hair at the pierglass of carved and gilded ribbons, husks, and bellflowers, then she set its length once again within the confines of the amethyst comb. She pulled the violet dress over her linen shift and stays, noting wryly that her own ladies' maid had had finer stays than she.

Hoping she presented a plain but not impoverished appearance, she nervously ventured from her room. She wasn't sure how to go about approaching the new owner in this awkward situation. She knew that the best she could hope for would be extra time to find a new place to live. She prayed the new owner would be charitable enough to allow that.

She left her yellow bedroom and was making her way down the hall when she heard voices coming from another bedroom. Unconcerned by servants' gossip, she continued down the hall, but then she stopped when she heard one of the women mention her name.

"Lady Brienne Morrow will not be needin' those dresses where she'll be going. She's a homeless creature now, and a good candidate for Bedlam, too. I mean to see that the new master gets our point of view. Why, not even her own father will 'ave anything to do with her." Annie's voice sounded clear through the bedroom door as she spoke to another servant.

"Bedlam," Brienne whispered to herself, recalling the horrible stories she had heard about the madhouse—the filth, the decay, and the punishment that the patients were forced to endure. She smiled grimly. "They *do* think I am mad."

"She 'as the devil in her," Annie continued, unaware that she was being overheard. "Her hair reeks of it, and her strange eyes—When I'm the master's mistress, I'll 'ave 'em come and take her away. You'll see. I've cursed her since the day she came to Osterley. There's not a man's eye that she's not captured."

"But none of the men have even touched Lady Brienne! There's no need to be jealous. Besides, I think you're in over your head, Annie. After all, the new master has just arrived. And already you're thinkin' yourself to be his mistress! And telling him what to do!" The other maid, whose voice Brienne recognized, spoke up.

"She's a bewitcher! Even my poor ol' Jack never had a chance with her, and it drove him mad!"

"There's no such thing as witches, Annie."

"You'll not say otherwise, I know that. But I also know the truth, and I'll not be swayed from it. She is mad, with her walks in the rain and her readin' all night long. It will not be hard to convince the new owner."

"Perhaps, but before you can be the new master's mistress, we must make ourselves presentable. I'm sure he'll be calling for all of us sometime tonight. Let's be off." The other maid pulled open the servants' jib door in the back of the bedroom, both girls disappeared down the steps that led to their quarters.

At first amused by Annie's presumptuous talk, Brienne was now a bit shaken. Things were bad enough for her, and this gossip about Bedlam angered her. She knew it was unusual for women to read, but not for those of her class. And her ability did not make her crazy. If she was mad for reading until the late hours because she was bored and lonely, then so be it. But feeling rather defeated, she started once again down the hallway, wondering who the new owner would believe—herself or Annie.

The pale blue walls of the grand staircase provided a magnificent backdrop to the Rubens painting on the octagon-shaped ceiling. Brienne stopped and looked up as always, taking in the beauty of the picture, "Apotheosis of a Hero." This and the griffons were the features she truly liked about the house. She sometimes found comfort in her enjoyment of them.

"Oh!" Brienne turned around on the steps, only to

find a small man watching her from the bottom of the staircase. He was middle-aged and had kind periwinkle eyes, and he was adorned in the most magnificent embroidered waistcoat she had ever seen. It was canary yellow and had gold thread sewn so heavily into it that one could only see small patches of satin.

"And who might you be, my dear?" The older man bowed to her and showed his leg.

"I—I am Brienne." She stared at the man's rich waistcoat and instantly thought he was the new owner.

"Now, lovely Brienne, you wouldn't be the upstairs maid, would you?" The man took her hand and led her to the landing, seemingly enchanted with her. "I am looking for the earl's daughter and was told I could find her upstairs. You wouldn't know where Lord Oliver's daughter is, now would you?"

She quickly put her hands on her arms to hide the woolen material thinning at the elbows. She was embarrassed that her appearance had proved to be so impoverished that the new owner had mistaken her for Annie.

"I am the earl's daughter," she said solemnly. "I am Brienne Morrow."

Suddenly the gentleman looked at her sharply; a worry line furrowed his brow. "You are the earl's daughter?"

"Yes, but I can explain my appearance. You see, I—" She was not allowed to finish.

"No, I am afraid, my lady, that nothing can explain your appearance." The man gave her a grim smile and looked at her violet eyes and her deep auburn hair. She kept her hands crossed over her arms, wishing desperately that she had had a more appropriate gown to wear. "Well, child, there is nothing we can do about it, now is there?" The man smiled at her in a sad, enigmatic way.

She thought he meant to throw her out, and she

started her prepared speech. "As you may already know, sir, I have been residing here. I expect to leave as soon as that can be arranged, but in the meantime I would not find it beneath me to work in your household. My mother taught me all—"

"My household!" the older man exclaimed. "My lady, this house does not belong to me!" He laughed as if she had made a joke.

"No?" Brienne stumbled on her words. "But I thought —I mean, I had guessed—"

"No, I am sorry." The older man shook his head almost with despair. "How I wish it were now. Dearly I do."

"Then where is the owner? I should speak with him about my position." She tried to regain some of her poise after this strange conversation with the little man.

"He is waiting in the gallery."

"I see," she said. "I suppose, since you have come to fetch me, that he knows of my situation?" She looked at him sharply.

"Yes, he found out that you were here from your father's solicitor."

"I had hoped to explain it myself." Her shoulders slumped visibly. Now that the owner had had time to think about the situation, she knew it would be hopeless. At best, it would be awkward to have the daughter of the previous owner in the house. But without the element of surprise, she knew there was little she could do to convince him to let her stay on. She would now be forced either to seek out her father or to be homeless. She would choose the latter.

"Would you show me to him? I suppose everyone would feel better if this matter were cleared up." She smiled at the kind gentleman and was sorry he had not turned out to be the owner.

"Of course!" His worried expression returned as he walked down the hallway to the gallery. She noticed that he was biting his lip, and she began to wonder if this new owner were someone she would be better off not meeting.

They entered the gallery through the south doors. Fires blazed in the two fireplaces, and in the middle of the long room a table was laid out with tea. Two footmen stood at all the doors, and petticoats flurried as one of the housekeepers bustled over the proceedings. But at the north end of the room, a man stood as far away from the activity as he could. His back was turned to them, but Brienne could tell he was staring at a portrait of Oliver Morrow—a portrait she had wanted to burn on many occasions.

The older gentleman took her arm and seemed to gather courage. He brought her down the long gallery, but she could feel his hand shake as they made their way. His nervousness was beginning to infect her, and she slowed as they came closer to the man.

The first thing she noticed before the man turned around was his magnificent size. Not that he was fat; on the contrary, she knew instinctively that only hard muscle would be found underneath the man's expensive clothing. But he was tall, and his shoulders spanned the cloth of his blue-black silk brocade waistcoat almost to the point of splitting it. And his legs that fit so leanly into his breeches had no need for the pads that many men found useful.

"Slane," her escort began in a shaky voice, "I have found the earl's daughter."

The man continued to stare at the portrait. "Bring her

to me. We've got our agreement. I trust you won't inter-
fere."

"She's here with me now, Slane." The older man let
go of her arm and stepped back from her. Brienne felt
her mouth grow dry; she dreaded the man's turning
around.

But the man did not turn around instantly. First he
took his eyes from the portrait and bent his head as if he
too feared to see her. Then he raised his dark head and
faced her.

The man who greeted her did not look like the monster she had expected. He was dark, and there was a
cruel slant to his fine lips, but his features were aristocratic and well bred, from his chiseled nose to his high
forehead. And then there were his eyes. They were like
two blue diamonds shining out from thick black lashes.
Their hardness was hidden temporarily by their bril-
liance, and she found them hypnotic.

He seemed almost startled by her appearance, as if he
found her as surprising as she found him. He stared at
her for such a long time that she found her hands go
once again to her elbows to hide the shabbiness of her
dress. When he looked away for a brief second, she
pulled at her bodice, hoping to present as neat an appearance as possible.

"Cumberland, would you please see that we are left
alone?" the man stated baldly.

"Listen, Slane, I've—"

"What is done is done, Cumberland!" He almost yelled
at her escort; the man's rudeness angered her.

Finding himself useless, Cumberland agreed to leave.
Turning to her, he asked, "Will you be all right if I leave
you two alone for the moment, my child?"

She nodded and gave the man a warm smile. He was

trying to look after her, and she appreciated it. The man could not have known that she had taken care of herself for a long time before coming to Osterley. And he could not know that worse fates surely lay before her when she would have to leave.

CHAPTER THREE

"Sit down," the man said to her. When she did not comply, he eyed her judiciously. "Lady Brienne, if you insist on standing, then so must I. However, I prefer to sit while I drink my tea, so if you would be so kind?" He motioned to a large mahogany elbow seat that was covered in pea green silk damask.

She sat down and waited for the housekeeper to bring them their tea. After she had poured out, the woman wheeled the cart near to them and left the gallery. They were completely alone now, and she was nervous.

"I wasn't aware until recently that the earl had a daughter."

"I do not socialize," she answered, trying very hard to hide her nervousness behind a facade of self-possession.

"And why is that? Surely you have the means." The man's crystalline eyes fell to her bosom, and she found it very hard to meet them once they were raised.

"But not the desire," she said. A blush crept up her throat.

"Have you no thoughts of snaring a husband?"

"None."

"So what are your plans for the future, my lady?"

Brienne cleared her throat and slowly sipped her tea. It was strong and hot, and it gave her strength. "I was hoping to leave for Bath, sir, but I have been temporarily waylaid."

"At Osterley?" He smiled wickedly, or so she thought. "And what are you planning to do here to earn your keep? I am not your father, and he is no longer the owner."

"I realize that, sir. But at the moment I have no means to go elsewhere. There is a coach that leaves next week. But until then the situation has, shall I say, caught me unawares. My father cannot be reached, and I have no other relatives."

"Your mother?"

"She's dead."

"I see. But your father—surely he would not allow his only child to stay here? Wouldn't he rather you went to him? I don't understand this."

She was quick with her wits. To get around her father's negligence she made things up as she went along.

"My father has given up on me, since I do not favor his way of living. My mother shared my feelings, and I stayed with her until she died."

"At Osterley?"

"No, she died in Wales, where we had another estate." She looked down at her teacup and then took a deep sip of the brew. She was not sure he believed her, but it was the best she could do under the circumstances. There was no point in telling him the truth, for then he would either force her father to claim her or kick her out onto the streets without mercy. This way she at least had a small chance of biding her time in decent surroundings until the next coach passed through. She would worry about the fare later.

The man studied her for a very long time. He was obviously displeased with her answer, and she couldn't account for it.

"You are lying."

She caught her breath at his bold statement. "What makes you think that, sir?"

Suddenly without warning, she was grabbed from the elbow seat, and her arms were thrust forward.

"There," he said, pointing to her threadbare elbows. "Does a man like Oliver Morrow allow his daughter to run about in rags solely because she disapproves of the way he carries on?"

"I've not seen my father in a long time. He does not know of my state." He let her go, and she sank back down into the seat. After she had caught her breath, she began again. "I do not want to burden you with my family's eccentricities. I merely would like to stay on at Osterley until I have made other arrangements. It is my home. I am very attached to it."

"Again, I say that you are lying. I know for a fact that you have been here no longer than a month. Before that, your very existence was unknown to the servants here. Explain that if you can."

Owing him no explanations, she angrily stood and faced the man. "I would merely like a respite from this turmoil you and my father have thrust upon me. If this is not possible, just tell me so, and I shall move on at once. But my past and my relationship with my father is no one's business but my own." Her amethyst eyes flared, and she knew her cheeks were hot and flushed from annoyance.

"There is no need for anger, Lady Brienne." He sat back down in his elbow seat. His long legs were stretched in front of him in relaxation that belied the power and agitation beneath the man's surface. "You may stay here if you like. In fact, I insist upon it."

"Thank you." She eyed him guardedly. The unexpected change in his attitude caught her off guard. "Let me assure you that in the meantime I plan to keep myself busy. I know how to care for a house such as Osterley. My mother was a wonderful teacher."

"Yes. Marie Antoinette is fond of the rustic life, too. I suppose your mother was just like her?"

"Yes, she enjoyed running a household. She found it . . . amusing."

"But there is a difference, my lady, is there not? I am surprised that you have not noticed."

"And what is that?"

"The good queen does not dress in rags; nor does she callous her hands with work—not even for amusement."

Angrily she closed her palms from his view. "I will not be backed into a corner. If you seek to appease your curiosity, I shall leave now." She turned to go. She would not be tricked into telling this man about her father. She would not! She started to walk away, but his voice boomed out from behind her.

"You shall not leave, Lady Brienne. As I said before, I insist you stay. You will get to know Osterley before this is through, for you are not leaving until we have a visit from your father."

She blanched at this last statement. Why would he want the earl to come to Osterley Park? Oliver Morrow must be furious about losing the estate. She would stake her life that a meeting between him and this man, Avenel Slane, would be bloody. She turned to face him, but could not decipher the veiled look he gave her. In a blind moment of panic spawned by confusion, she found her tongue.

"I will not stay here. And you may not insist. You are forgetting that I'm the daughter of an earl, and you are not even a lowly squire. There is nothing that you can do to induce me to stay here." She could not let him know that she feared her father's arrival, so she spewed excuses at him. "I will not stay in the same household with one such as you."

"And why is that, my lady?" he asked, baiting her with his smile.

"You have no manners." She blurted out the first thing that came to mind. She saw the ridiculousness of her answer, but it was too late to take back the words.

He started to laugh. "I have no manners?" He laughed again even harder this time. "Now, whatever makes you say that?"

"You—you—" She fumbled for the most effective words. "You have failed to introduce yourself, and you have called me a liar!"

He stopped laughing and looked at her brilliant eyes and at the disdain in her sweet rose-colored lips. "But you are a liar, my lady," he stated simply. "But for what reasons, I haven't the time or the desire to expose at the present."

He moved forward, took her by the arm, and guided her to his seat. She pulled to be free of his grasp, but it was like an iron shackle. In the next instant she found herself sitting intimately upon his lap; his arm had taken her unrelentingly by the waist.

"Let me go this instant!" she demanded; her anger overwhelmed her fear. She struggled, but that only made the arm hold her waist that much more tightly.

"But I was remiss in our introduction, Lady Brienne."
She felt his arm relax somewhat after she stopped twisting. She was amazed that it could hold her with such
power and yet with such gentleness.

"I am Avenel Slane," he said. His other hand moved
along her smooth cheek and slowly made its way down
along the fragile column of her neck. Its soothing
warmth was unexpected, and she found herself unbelievably complaisant under its caress. Her senses overwhelmed, however, she attempted to regain control and
again to move out of his grasp. But when she turned to
confront him, his eyes caught hers with such intensity
that she was suddenly still. Gazing into the frozen depths
of his eyes, she tried to discern what was in them. What
was it? Pain, desire, hatred? Almost unconsciously she
felt both his hands, warm and strong, grasp her delicate
face until she was completely in his power. His face was
very close, and she could feel his breath on her cheek.

"And you, my strange, beautiful one, are Brienne Morrow." With that his lips descended on hers. Their
warmth was intoxicating, and for a moment they made
her dignity and even taking her next breath seem unim-
portant.

But as quickly as it began, it was over. He pulled his
lips away and stared down at her with eyes as cold and
uncaring as the North Atlantic. It took her a moment to
get her bearings, but as soon as she realized what had
happened, she resumed her struggle to be free, noting
with endless embarrassment that he had dared to do
what she had been determined never to let happen.

That was the final insult. She took her free hand, and
despite his quickness she cracked it hard across his
cheek. Tears sprang to her violet eyes, and she tried to
escape from him. But once again she was pulled, this

time viciously, to his side. He looked murderously at her; his cold, dispassionate eyes now gleamed silver with wrath.

"You have done it once, my lady. But you will never do it again. I'll not be struck by a Morrow." With that he flung her across the room. Her tears had no effect on him.

"There will not be a second time!" she shouted, thinking of the kiss. Wiping the tears off her soft cheeks, she berated herself for being so weak. "I would sooner live in a stable than here with you!" With that she turned and fled, wanting only her few belongings so she could leave Osterley Park and Avenel Slane behind forever.

But before she departed, he left her with the haunting words, "You may just get that chance, my lady."

CHAPTER FOUR

"She is not what I expected her to be." Cumberland wiped his forehead with a square of linen. In spite of the cold damp day, he was sweating. He coughed as he examined Avenel, who was steadfastly looking out the window of the gallery. Avenel stood perfectly still except for the twitch of a muscle in his jaw, and he did not look at Cumberland. "I'm not quite sure I approve," Cumberland continued. "She's not the woman I expected. I've talked with her, Slane. She has a gentle spirit."

"She has her father's blood," Avenel retorted as his crystalline eyes stared off into the far misty fields of Osterley. In the distance a doe foraged for her dinner behind the garden house. He seemed entranced with its gentle movement across the lawn and thus gave Cumberland little of his attention.

"Yes, but she has her mother's blood in her, too. And I daresay the lass hardly looks like her father. Such coloring I've never seen. I never would have guessed her to be the earl's daughter."

"Damn her mother! Damn her beauty!" Avenel finally faced Cumberland. "As long as her name is Morrow, I'll curse her."

Hearing this, Cumberland sat down in one of the elbow seats and stared hard at the floorboards, deep in thought. Finally he spoke, saying each word carefully and with much thought.

"I've been with you now for twenty years, Slane. We've been through thick and through thin, riches and rags. You know I was just a bosun on that ship. But you, you were nobility. Your brother was a viscount, and your father . . . The point is, damn it, that I trust you more than my own mother, but I'm not sure you're right this time."

Avenel spun around and looked at him sharply. "It does not concern me whether I have your loyalty."

"You have my loyalty," Cumberland answered simply, mopping his forehead again. "I haven't forgotten what we've been through. And I'll not forget as long as I live. It's not a question of loyalty, Slane. It's just that she's so young."

"And what of Christopher? He was young, younger still than she is now. That bastard gave no thought to sparing my brother." Avenel turned to the portrait of Oliver Morrow. His eyes blazed violently at the image of the man in the giltwood frame. "What makes me so divine as to think of sparing her? All children must pay for the sins of their fathers. She will at least have her life to live when I am through. 'Tis more than he gave to us, my good friend. And much more still than he gave to Christopher." He turned to look at Cumberland again. "You should be lauding me for what I have come to do, but yet you sit there like a reproachful old man."

"It's not that I have forgotten! I bear the same scars!"

Cumberland stood up to him. "But I have a forgiving nature. I'll never forgive the earl, mind you. But what does his daughter know of his treacheries? Why must she bring about the means to his end?"

"I did not know he had a daughter when I won Osterley! I did not plan this! But she exists, and she is here. 'Tis the opportunity we have waited for, and we shall make the most of it. 'Twill make the end come about sooner than we ever dreamed possible." Avenel let out a long, tired sigh and looked at his friend. "As you said, 'tis been twenty long years. Years of backbreaking work in the tobacco fields of Maryland. Years of honing our skills and hoarding our money to be able to take on the beast who has made every day of our lives a living hell. Any reason I can find to end this charade will be well worth the cost. I am tired, my friend."

"Yes, I'm tired also. I shan't oppose you, Slane." Cumberland shook his head wearily. "We've been through too much together, and I feel for you what I would feel for a son. But I tell you now, I'll not be a part of it. I'll not aid you in the lass's downfall."

Avenel looked at his oldest friend. It was obvious he felt betrayed. "Already she has won you over?"

"It's not just beauty she has, Slane. She has a kind spirit. She's innocent of her father's wrongdoing."

"She's a Morrow." Avenel turned to watch the doe make its way closer to the house.

"She has a good heart."

"Yes," he retorted cynically, "and if we were able to cut it out, you would see that it is as mad and wicked as her father's."

In the background there was a loud banging of pots. A man's voice was heard shouting Gaelic profanities at the doe from the ground-floor kitchen. Both men watched as the doe pricked her fine buff ears. There was further cursing, and she wasted no more time. She disappeared in an instant, leaving only the memory of a twitching white puffed tail.

Cumberland smoothed his vest and stuffed the damp linen handkerchief under his sleeve. "Where is she now?"

"Packing to leave, no doubt." Avenel still stared out the window after the doe.

"I see. I suppose that doesn't mean you've had a change of heart and will let her go?" He looked at Avenel but did not expect an answer. When there was none, he walked to the door of the gallery, saying, "I won't cross you on this, Slane. You've been right so many times, I dare not act on my own judgment. But I will not participate. I want to make that clear. There's going to be a time when you are wrong, and I pray to God this is not the day."

He paused by the door and looked at his friend. Avenel stood silently at the window; his tall frame was rigid with repressed anger.

Shuddering to think that the sweet, violet-eyed beauty upstairs would be the recipient of his rage, Cumberland left a parting comment. "Would that she could outrun you, my friend." But Avenel only stared out the window at the bleak, darkening grounds.

Furiously, Brienne threw her possessions into the woven bag, not caring about their disarray. Her extra shifts and stockings were balled up and tossed with no regard for their expense into her sack. She swung around to the honey-colored wardrobe and threw open the doors to gather her sparse apparel and be out within the hour.

But she stopped dead in her tracks. She saw only one dress standing out from the rest. The pink polonaise hung wretchedly on its hook; its strange new form was limp and tattered. Slowly she pulled it down from the large wardrobe and examined the rips and tears in the soft pink silk. She knew without a doubt who had ruined it. Annie had feared her too much to steal the dress but not enough to make sure she never wore it again. She threw the dress onto the yellow taffeta coverlet of the bed.

Sadly Brienne thought of the day she had first worn the gown. She and her mother had gone to the fair in the center of Tenby. They had sipped a drink made of lemon juice and sugar and had chatted gaily with their elderly neighbors, the Thomases. The day had ended with a walk down to the ancient walls of the small town, where swimmers dove into the blue sea from the battlements of the old ruined castle. With innocent eyes, she had stared at the naked, sun-bronzed boys until her mother bade her look away.

With reborn fury, Brienne stuffed her belongings into the bag and then went to retrieve her valuables. Opening the third drawer of the satinwood commode, she saw the small hinge in the back that she had discovered at the beginning of her stay. With a slight twist of her hand, she sprang open the secret panel, revealing the hiding place for her miniature and her amethyst comb. Pulling the comb from the cubbyhole, she looked at it, knowing that she could get a fine price for it.

Besides the death of her mother, the comb dredged up another bitter memory as well. Placing the bejeweled piece into a kerchief, she recalled the day the earl had arrived unannounced at the neat little house near London where she and her mother had first lived after their flight from Osterley. Despite her mother's precaution of refusing funds from Oliver Morrow and despite the passage of years, he had found them.

At first, she had been enchanted with her father, who was tall and strong. Her mother's anxiety had not affected her, and she was happy to have even for a few hours what most children took for granted: a father. But after the visit wore on, her father had taken her to his lap and he had touched her—simply, at first—on her shoulders. Then he had placed a mild kiss on her cheek.

But there had been something wrong with his affection, and soon she shared her mother's uneasiness. To her horror, his hand had begun to enclose one of her small, developing breasts. Her mother shrieked, and the earl had thrown Brienne from his lap. Then he rose from his seat and proceeded to slap her mother almost senseless.

"You've stolen it from me. Would you exchange it for your daughter's innocence?" Oliver Morrow had demanded.

"I haven't got it," her mother had pleaded.

"My proof! It's my only proof!" He had slapped her mother again. In the end he had taken Grace Morrow upstairs. Brienne could sometimes still hear the quiet, desperate sobs that had come from that bedroom. She had crawled into a space behind one of the cabinets to hide. Even after the earl came down the stairs and told his driver to head back to London, she had stayed there, unwilling to move until her mother had coaxed her out. They had moved again and again until they found peace in Tenby. But a knock on the door still made Brienne's nerves jangle, and the earl's last words still rang horrifyingly in her ears: "Brienne love, someday I'll have you both."

She was now nineteen, old enough to know about husbandly rights. However, every time she recalled that day, she thought of rape. Her mother had been raped because of the comb she now held in her hand. It was the same old-fashioned comb that she had found with the miniature so long ago in Tenby. Brienne turned it over and over again in her palm, as if by doing so, its mystical power would finally be revealed. But it was of no use. It would be worth a few pounds, especially with the seal of the Labordes stamped into its back, the initials QE, and then the crossed fasces. But she would never understand the price her mother had paid to keep it from the earl's clutches. In many ways she felt she would be well rid of it.

Hating these terrible memories, Brienne vehemently wrapped both articles in her embroidered kerchief and placed them carefully at the top of her bag so they would not be crushed. She then wasted no time in leaving Osterley. She was out the front doors before even a footman saw her, and she made good time down the carriage drive, hearing only the crunch of the pebbles beneath her pattens. She found it a happy sound, for it told her that she was putting Osterley and its foul past behind her.

Already she was making plans for her new life. Perhaps once she sold the comb, she would have enough money to make her way to Bath after all. If she had any luck, she might be able to find a job at one of the booksellers. Her thoughts centered pleasantly on her new freedom. She didn't notice the two new men who manned the gatehouse. She stopped at the closed gates, eyeing both distrustfully.

"I have need to be leaving here. Please open the gates," she called to the man nearest her. She pulled her cloak closer to her figure to ward off the cold and the men's stares.

"She wouldn't be the one with the purple eyes, would she, Hans?" The man, a blond giant, stepped from the gatehouse and walked up to her. Brienne lowered her eyes and moved from his path, but the giant bade her look at him. He gave a sharp whistle between the gap in his front teeth.

"If I wasn't here to see it myself, I wouldn't believe 'twas true. Hans!" the giant called to his mate.

Another large man walked out of the gatehouse. This one was also blond but was bearded, with a slight tint of red in his whiskers.

"She's got 'em, just as Slane said." The man named Hans peered into her eyes and then took a step backward.

" 'Tis like nothing I've ever seen. So where are you off to, Brienne Morrow?"

She tried to hide her dismay that they knew her name.

"I shall be leaving Osterley. Please open the gates." She spoke in a brusque manner, not knowing quite what to make of the two Nordic giants.

"Master Slane gave orders to the contrary." The giant with the smooth chin moved back to the gatehouse.

" 'Tis of no consequence. I ask you again, open the gates." She was not yet intimidated by the still-closed gates. Her freedom was too close at hand for her to worry that the guards would not open them. When neither of them made a move to comply with her wishes, she walked over to the heavy wrought-iron gates and tried to open them herself. But they would not budge.

"I will not stay here!" she cried out as she placed her bag on the damp ground and put all her strength into pulling the gates open.

After watching her tug futilely for several minutes, the giant with the reddish whiskers came over to her.

"There be no point, my lady. The Master Slane bids you not leave, and we follow his orders."

"The Master Slane, is it?" she spat at him, now furious. "Well, there are other ways of leaving than through the gates!" With that, she walked over to the side of the wrought-iron fence and tried to swing her bag over the ten-foot height of it. Her first attempt missed, but her second succeeded. The tan woven bag landed with a thump on the other side of the fence.

She eyed the two giants, who had left the gatehouse and were now timidly watching her; both were obviously unaccustomed to female rage. It was then that she took her chance. Swiftly she ran along the fence and through the open doors of the gatehouse. She had almost gotten to her bag and was about to disappear into the underbrush when she felt herself being picked up off the ground. Two gigantic hands wound themselves around her waist, and she knew without a doubt that there was no way she could struggle out of them.

It was Hans who carried her back through the gatehouse, but both giants walked her back to the house. Neither one of them dared to speak. Throughout the guarded journey she shot quelling looks at both of them; her fiery jewellike eyes sent off sparks of purple fury.

By the time they reached the house, her cloak clung damply to her chilled body, and her hem flopped around her ankles, wet and muddy. Even her hair was soaked from the pervading mist that blanketed the English countryside. And like this, soaked and bedraggled, she was deposited in Osterley's gallery like so much baggage.

With a nod from Avenel Slane, the two blond giants left Brienne and himself alone. He was sitting comfortably by the south fireplace, very close to the portrait of the earl that she hated so much, and she stood before him feeling like a half-drowned cat.

"I will not stay here with you, so accept that fact and let me go. I can imagine no reason for your wanting to keep me here except to use me as some kind of perverted bait for my father. And I must tell you now," she said, taking a deep breath, "it will not work. I refuse to stay, and my father will refuse to come." She spoke through clenched teeth—whether from anger or to keep them from chattering, she wasn't sure.

"Why don't you come closer to the fire, Lady Brienne, and warm yourself? You seem to be catching a chill."

"Your gigantic cohorts can't be everywhere all the time. I shall find a way to leave if you refuse to be rational about this." She stood where she was, making threats but not daring to move closer to him.

"Now calm yourself. There is a fine bedroom for you upstairs. I have offered you a place to stay. Why must you get yourself so upset?" He stretched out his long legs before the fire and leisurely sipped a crystal glass of brandy. As she observed all this luxury, an image of the very man before her came involuntarily to mind. She saw him placing his lips intimately upon hers and making her feel things she permanently wanted to avoid.

The image made her fingers move unconsciously across her lips to stop them from tingling. She moved away from the culprit who had caused the sensation.

"I will not share a house with you, no matter how large and grand it is. I must leave!"

"You shall not leave!" Suddenly he stood up and started over to her. What he lacked in size compared to the two giants, he made up in fierceness. Brienne knew she had to stand up to him, but she wasn't sure how to.

Since she could not possibly overpower him physically, she looked defiantly into his cold, silver eyes and repeated, "I will not stay in this house with you!"

"Then you will stay in the stables." He looked at her and then motioned to a dark corner of the room. "Cumberland will show you your new room, Cinderella."

Cumberland arose from his seat in the corner and walked over to her. His eyes were full of sadness.

"And don't forget your ball gown." With that, Avenel picked up her tattered pink polonaise from a nearby stool. She had not noticed it there before. "You see, Cumberland, she walks about in a threadbare dress because she has taken a knife to the one decent gown she owns." He flung the useless pink silk at her and gave a deep malicious laugh. "Perhaps she is as mad as they say."

Incredulous, she found herself about to be led away. It was difficult to find her tongue after Cumberland had taken her arm, but she looked back and said, "Perhaps 'tis a better thing to be in with the horses. At least they are warm-blooded creatures, unlike you. God has yet to make the thing that could warm your cold carcass!"

She allowed Cumberland to put his arm around her shaking shoulders and walked out of the gallery. She was unaware that Avenel was watching the wet, clinging wool of her cloak curve around her buttocks as she left. Nor did she hear his words.

"Perhaps there *is* one thing, my lady," he whispered sarcastically as he watched her go.

CHAPTER FIVE

"**W**hy is he doing this?" Brienne hung on to Cumberland's arm as they walked toward the stable block in the darkness. The huge structure lay empty and silent before them except for the lonely whinnies of the few horses that had arrived today. "What use am I to him?" She stumbled on a stray brick from the ancient building and clutched her companion tightly. "You must tell me what he wants."

"He wants for nothing, my lady." He guided her over a small puddle from the day's rain. "For if there is something he wants, he merely takes it and appeases his desire. That is something you will learn of him."

"I will not learn anything of the sort! I shall leave tonight. The new master is crazed. Surely you see that?" She looked at the small man. Finding no agreement in his eyes, she pleaded, "You can help me leave. We could take the coach and the horses. And then in the morning you could bring them back. It wouldn't be stealing."

"Nay, my lady" was all he said as he brought their lantern through the main doors.

"Is it difficult to harness up? Perhaps you could help me with that. I could don a disguise, and the two giants would think me a stableboy."

"It will not work. They're aware that the stable lads haven't arrived yet."

"But you could drive it just to the other side of the gates."

Cumberland shook his head gravely. "This comes to no good, Lady Brienne. I'll not help you."

Suddenly she jerked her arm from his grasp and looked at him as if he'd struck her. "You are on his side then? I thought you were a gentleman, a man of breeding."

"I'll not betray his friendship. I don't condone his actions, but I won't contradict them, either. He is doing what he must."

"Whatever his plans are, they don't involve me. Why not let me go? You don't know what he did when we were in the gallery. It was unspeakable."

Suddenly the older man laughed. "Kissed you, did he?"

She felt warmth spread over her face and was relieved that the darkness hid her blush. "No man has ever touched me like that. It disgusts me," she replied vehemently.

"Not all women agree with you there. I've known them to swoon merely from having Slane look upon them. Such a way he has when he wants it."

"The ladies were faint from fear, not desire! He is a beast!" Again she stumbled in the darkness, but this time the obstacle moved, and she let out a cry.

A large creature backed into the corner and gave a low growl. When Cumberland brought the lantern around, she saw a large dog; its hackled white fur bristled along his back.

"There you are, Orillion!" Cumberland's voice was re-assuring. "Here is your new mistress. Come and introduce yourself."

Responding to the familiar voice, the dog walked up to her and began to inspect her with his nose. Finally, when he was satisfied that she posed no threat, the large white animal went back to its corner and lay down to watch the proceedings more leisurely.

"Is it your dog?" she asked, her knees still quivering from her scare.

"Orillion belongs to Slane. He picked him up on the streets of Annapolis. Such a cur he was! But now he's rather tamed."

"Only a beast can love another beast." She followed Cumberland up the stairs, looking over her shoulder lest the large animal decide to follow them. But Orillion stayed in his corner looking arrogant and rather bored. His half-closed blue-white eyes reminded Brienne of his master's, and she felt a small tingle of what she thought to be dislike run down her spine.

The door to the room at the very top of the stairs was open, and the two of them walked in. The old, crumbling stable block had once been in much finer shape; its extra space had sometimes been used for the overflow of male guests on a romping weekend. But now the immense structure was in a sad state of disrepair. It was at the very best a pitiful place to retire to.

Looking around the dust-laden room, she saw a few hooks along one wall and a crude oaken stool stood near a bed. The ropes on the bed frame were in such desperate need of tightening that the thin feather mattress sagged almost to the ground.

She walked over to one of the huge leaded windows and looked down at the old tower spire below it. "A fine room! Fit for a madwoman, to be sure." She found her lower lip trembling, and she bit it to keep it still.

"Don't be saying such things! Why, Slane has not put you here because he thinks you mad."

"He is not the first one." She threw her pink dress onto the mildewed bed.

Cumberland looked at the polonaise and asked softly, "Did you rip the dress in an accident?"

"It was no accident." She smiled bitterly.

"Oh" was all he said, and silence cloaked the dismal room.

Finally she could bear his doubts no longer. She said glumly, "It was not done by my hand. Annie, the maid you had taken me for, was playing a prank. She has a jealous nature." She looked at him; her eyes were a soft velvety hue. "If you would but believe me—"

"I believe you," Cumberland answered steadily. "And you mustn't think Slane considers you mad, either. We've heard the stories. It's unusual to find a woman who reads, but not in your peerage. As for the walking about" —he gave her a fatherly wink—"well, a pretty young thing like yourself cannot live in such solitude as Osterley offers without becoming bored."

After hearing his words of gentle reassurance, she couldn't help but give her new friend a hug. Not since her mother died had she been treated with kindness or understanding. And even though Cumberland was a friend of Avenel Slane, she couldn't hide her gratitude.

"Thank you," she said solemnly after the embrace. "I have been restless. My mother passed away only two months ago, you see. She was my only friend." Brienne sat down on a small oak stool that was so old, its bottom stretchers had been completely worn away. She looked around the room. "It's a bit dreary, it's true. In contrast to Osterley, that is."

She heard Cumberland sigh, and once again they both fell silent, each with their own thoughts.

"You need not stay here, Lady Brienne," Cumberland eventually said.

"No gentleman would make me stay here." She turned to face him, hoping that he was starting to doubt Avenel Slane's wisdom. "And I know you are a gentleman, Cumberland. You would never touch me the way your master did." Believing she had paid her friend a compliment, she looked at him expectantly, waiting for him to relent and help her leave. But instead he stared at her. What she had just said troubled him greatly.

"I behave like a gentleman because I have no choice in the matter. If fate had treated me differently, you would be no safer in my company than in Slane's."

There was no mistaking the bitterness in his voice. Brienne, unsure what she had said to make him feel that way, frowned in confusion.

Cumberland watched her steadily for a long minute and then he parted with only a brief, "Good night, my lady."

After he shut the door behind him, she felt terribly confused. An overwhelming panic rushed through her veins, and she ran to the closed door and flung it open, wanting only to leave the dusty, abandoned stable room behind. But before she could take a step outside, she was stopped by a mass of immovable snowy fur. At the threshold lay the white dog, Orillion. His head was raised to the sudden commotion, and his teeth were bared. They were as white as his coat.

"I see you have already offended Cumberland." A voice boomed out from the darkness below. Standing at the bottom of the stairs was Avenel Slane. She peered down at him from her door, not daring to move any farther.

"I said nothing but that he was a gentleman—and very much unlike you." Brienne made a slight movement with her leg, but Orillion was quick to notice and snarled ominously. "Call off your beast. I have no need to be guarded," she demanded.

" 'Tis more for your protection." He leaned against a squared-off post, leisurely watching her. And she watched him despite the darkness, noticing that his rich, brocaded waistcoat was unfastened, which left his shirt open and revealed a fine sprinkling of dark hair on his chest.

"I need no protection. I'm more than capable of caring for myself," she said, looking away from him.

"Orillion shall stay. You wouldn't want some errant servant to wander into your bed." He looked at her, but she couldn't tell what his expression was because his face was cast in shadow.

She gave a sarcastic laugh. "Then do call him off! The only one I truly need protection from is you—and in that case the animal is useless."

He smiled and replied, "How astute of you, Lady Brienne. But nonetheless, Orillion shall stay." Changing the subject, he called up to her, "How do you find your quarters, my lady? Are they meager enough for you? I wouldn't want to ruin your game of playing the peasant by subjecting you to fine accommodations."

Anger built in her breast. So he thought she was play-acting? That she was the rich daughter of an earl whose only amusement was to pretend she was poor? Suddenly the thought of her mother selling her magnificent jewels and her heavy, embroidered court dresses one by one came into her mind. So that they would not have to live at the mercy and whim of the earl, her mother had done without. They had barely managed. Their shabby clothes and meager surroundings had not been an amusement!

"It was no game," she whispered with a vengeance, yet so softly she thought only she could have heard it.

"If that is so, you may come back to the house." Avenel started up the stairs. Orillion watched him; his tail thumped vigorously as his master approached.

"You have a beautiful bedroom to return to. Why stay here when all that magnificence is waiting for you?"

"Osterley is a horrible house." She spoke her thoughts aloud before she could catch herself.

"How can you say that?" He reached the top of the stairs, and there was no mistaking the mocking contempt in his voice. "They say 'tis the most beautiful house in all of England. I have paid dearly to own it." There was bitterness in his voice, and his face, now showing clearly from the light of her room, appeared to be lined with anguish.

"You did not pay for Osterley. You won it in an illicit card game. You gambled for it." She stressed the word *gambled,* remembering Tenby's Anglican minister's many lessons on the evils of gambling. That made her ignorance of contemporary gentry obvious.

"Spoken like a Puritan." He looked at her curiously and then bent nonchalantly to stroke Orillion's white-piled head. "Tell me, have you never played an innocent game of whist with your peers? I find it hard to believe that one of your station is completely unfamiliar with it. Even the young women in America are not immune to the pleasures of gambling."

"Never," she said. Her slightly pointed chin jutted out self-righteously.

"You're a strange one," he said, watching her closely. "You condemn gambling as if it were original sin, yet you show a remarkable lack of grief at your father's loss. Do you not resent the fact that I have won Osterley?"

"Riches do not make the man," she said simply. "Whether my father owns Osterley Park or not makes little difference to me. Except," she added, "for the inconvenience that now I am displaced and that you are preventing me from finding a new home." She stepped back into the stable room and walked over to the dead hearth, realizing how cold the empty stable block was at night.

He walked in behind her, and Orillion followed, looking glad to be with his master.

"Cumberland was right. You're not what we expected." He looked at her loosely bound auburn hair, which fell almost to her hips, and continued questioning her. "Did your mother have such coloring?"

"We did look alike." Warily she turned to face him. "And I have her eyes."

He stepped closer to her and took a thick lock of hair in his strong hand. Slowly he stroked it, admiring its rich magenta highlights.

"And your hair? Did she have your hair?"

She backed up against the carved oaken mantel, feeling trapped by the question and the hold he had on her hair. He came closer as if drawn to her, and she felt herself shaking, afraid. But her fear was not so much of the man before her. Despite his brooding looks and his leashed, mysterious anger, she somehow knew he would not harm her physically.

But she was afraid of what he was doing. As he looked at her hair, there was no mistaking the softening about his face; its usual tautness was displaced by a relaxed, almost sleepy sensuality. There was actually warmth in his eyes, cold as they were in color. They sparkled like snow melting in the sun. His desire became apparent with that gleam, and that frightened her more than any of the threats he'd made to confine her at Osterley or to exile her to the stable block.

Her mother's cries rang in her ears, just as they had when she'd been a little girl and Oliver Morrow had come to visit. Was it like that for all women? Would the strong, virile man before her who undoubtedly possessed a rare expertise in lovemaking behave the same way as the vile, crazed Earl of Laborde? Confusion abounded in her thoughts, but she knew she had to come to a conclusion before he pressed the issue. Yet however irrational it was, at that moment she could not differentiate between the act that had been forced upon her mother and the invitation that was so apparent in Avenel Slane's eyes. She started to moan from deep inside her, and before she could stop herself, she cried in a little girl's voice, "Please do not touch me!"

Quickly she retrieved her lock of hair from his palm and turned away, embarrassed by her fear and by the look of disbelief and guilt in his eyes.

"You find me unattractive?" He spoke to her rigid back. "I have my faults, but I didn't realize that that was one of them."

"I have no desire for a man's attentions, whether he be attractive or not. I thought I made that clear in the gallery." She was completely still and refused to look at him, hoping he would go away and leave her alone.

"I see." He sounded agitated. "Where did this unnatural abstention come from?"

"I need not answer to you," she retorted, still facing the mantel.

"No. But one day you'll wish you did, my lady. There has never been a woman who rejected my lovemaking. And I swear you will live to regret it."

"So you threaten me harm if I don't comply?" She spun around to face him, anger vivid in her face. "How like a man!"

"I have never harmed a woman. But there are other ways to make you suffer, ways that can be just as devastating. You deny your womanly feelings, but there is a weakness in your shaky armor. I shall find it. And when I do, I shall be merciless." He walked to the door and bade Orillion sit. He parted, saying only, "Sleep well, Lady Brienne. I hope you enjoy your chastity tonight." Then he looked about the dismal room and shut the door behind him.

When the door closed, she heard the thump of footsteps on the stairs. Satisfied that he had left the stable block, she cracked open the door, only to find Orillion still sitting sentinel on her threshold.

Not bothering to close the door again, she made a silent oath and walked back into the little room. How would she ever make it through the night?

She sat on the little oaken stool; her mind went over and over again all the day's strange occurrences. Unusual things were definitely going on at Osterley, but she was sure of only one thing: that she was a pawn in a game that this man, Avenel Slane, was playing with the earl. And she knew that she would have to get away from the estate at all costs, because whatever was going on, the end was bound to be catastrophic, with herself caught desperately in the middle.

Her body and mind were exhausted; sleep got the better of her, despite her denials. Resigning herself to the sagging bed, she used the pink polonaise as a pillow and as a barrier against the mattress's strong smell of mildew. She curled up in a ball, trying to fight off the cold and her loneliness, and found some small comfort in her determination to leave at the latest by tomorrow. She finally fell asleep by visualizing her old house in Tenby: the design-painted walls of the room off the street and the roaring fires that were always so cheerfully tended to ward off the chill.

She wasn't aware of the creature that came to join her later that night. Only slightly did she feel the thump when Orillion jumped up on the bed. But she did feel his blessed warmth as he curled up beside her; his canine instinct had decided there was no need for both of them to be cold.

The kitchen was like a madhouse that evening at Osterley. Not only was the cook busy over her fires, trying to make even the blandest of English fare memorable and appetizing, but every servant from liveryman to ladies' maid wandered in and out of the great room; each divulged the latest tidbit of information on the new owner and his desires. The lowliest scullery maids paid avid attention to small details because they knew that even they had to make Avenel Slane happy.

"You ha' be'er get tha' taken care oove, Annie. Orr ya might find tha' lazy arse o' yours ou' on the streets." Fergie McInnis brought in the heavy sack of stone-ground barley and placed it near the back of the kitchen. He stood silently and looked at Annie, who was slowly eating a huge Sally Lunn.

"And what concern is it of yours, Fergie?" Annie took another small mouthful and chewed the bread carelessly.

"The man made a special request, Annie." The cook spoke up, carefully peeling a pile of baby carrots. "We've all got a lot to lose. I myself have been a jittering bundle of nerves ever since he set afoot in the house. We've got to please the man—there's nothing more to it. But so far you're the only one he's asked to do anything. We just want to make sure it gets done."

"I'll be takin' my own time on it," Annie said, her voice full of rage. She threw the Sally Lunn into the fire nearby and stood watching as it smoked and burned. "How could he ask me to go and wait on her when she's living in the stables? 'Tis beneath me."

"She is Lady Brienne, the daughter of an earl. Waiting on her is not beneath anyone, except perhaps those of her peerage, of which you are not." The cook finished her peeling and changed the subject. She placed the carrots into a well-salted pot of water and cooed, "Fergie, love, 'tis mean I've been to you today, what with the cakes that burned and the bread that didn't rise. But I've a request for another pound or two of that sugar, if you would be so kind." The cook looked at her large Gaelic husband and lowered her lashes rather demurely for her three-and-fifty years. But Fergie merely blushed at her unusual affection and complied, obviously happy to please her.

"Perhaps not yet," Annie said smugly, puckering her upper lip, which to her pride and joy held three natural moles. She had been proclaimed a lusty sort because of them, but this never seemed to bother her; rather, she thrived on hearing herself described that way.

"Not ever, Annie Peters." The cook gave her a stern look. "I never have known where you've gotten such airs."

" 'Tis just that I know better than to lower myself."

"Well, you had better lower yourself now because the Lady Brienne is sitting in the block waiting for you, no doubt. I don't know what kind of game she and the Master Slane are playing, but there will be hell to pay if you don't heed his request." The cook gave her another foreboding stare and then turned busily to her carrots, which were just coming to a simmer.

"Who will miss the task left undone?" Annie whined. "The only one who will be the worse for it is the Lady Brienne herself. And as I see it, a less influential creature does not exist if she has been abandoned by Lord Oliver and taken up living quarters in the stable."

Getting no argument from the cook, who was too busy with meal preparations to listen to her any longer, Annie watched her for a few seconds more and then sullenly left the great room. Once in her own room, she shed her clothes and slid her body beneath the wool coverlet. She fell asleep instantly. Her thoughts were not on Brienne Morrow at all.

CHAPTER SIX

Early the next morning, as the mist still clung to the flat yellow fields, Brienne was rudely awakened by a loud banging on her door. When her eyes opened, she saw that Avenel had entered her room and was standing near the doorway watching her.

Tiredly, she pulled herself up to a more dignified sitting position. She wanted to reprimand him for his uncivil entrance. But then she noticed the stretched-out form of Orillion lying so close to her that her long, dark red tresses spilled over his sparkling white fur. Soon the dog's large tail began to thump as he watched her, sending clouds of gray dust into the air from the dirty feather mattress.

"Whatever is the meaning of this?" She looked at Avenel, her eyes still glassy and full of sleep. She could see that he was angry, but for what reason she could not be sure. She hadn't ventured or strayed from the block all night.

He didn't offer a word of explanation for his strange

behavior. He merely stood there looking furious. He noticed every detail of her appearance, from her bedmussed glistening hair and her loosened stays to the soot-colored smudge left on her cheek where it had rested on the mattress.

"Has anyone been here to see you?" he asked abruptly, his eyes flashing cold and white.

"I've had no visitors." She started to stand, pulling the sides of her violet wool dress as close together as she could, since fastening it would be impossible with her stays loosened. "Except, I might add, for your mangeridden cur. And I do believe that you've been here too frequently for my taste." She turned away from him and tried futilely to relace herself. Failing at that, she said crossly, "Haven't you the decency to leave me alone while I am in this state of dishabille?"

" 'Tis not often a man chances to see such sights." She heard him laugh, and she turned a cold eye on him.

"As I said last night, you are a beast and have absolutely no manners." She faced him, but feeling like a coward, she took two steps backward; she recovered the fallen shoulder of her dress that exposed the creamy skin of her shoulders and much too much of her full, curving breasts.

At this last comment, he laughed all the harder, saying, "I thought our kiss in the gallery was quite polite. But do you desire further proof of my manners?"

"No, for you would only prove your lack of them," she quipped hastily, hoping he would go and leave her in peace.

"Perhaps." He smiled and moved closer to her. "But then, an English maiden cannot expect courtly behavior from a colonial."

"A colonial? You? You're as English as I!" She spoke up from amazement.

" 'Tis true, I am a Brit. Perhaps even more than you," he said thoughtfully. "But I can truthfully say I am an American also, for I was born and raised in the beautiful colony of Maryland."

"Then it's no wonder you're a barbarian! Being raised in that war-mongering, savage, hell-begotten place! I've heard that even the richest of them live like peasants of the previous century, so ungracious and backward are they." She raised her head slightly in a superior manner; her heart was gladdened somewhat to know that she, despite all her misfortunes, at least had had the privilege of an English upbringing.

"Of course. 'Tis so ungracious they are, that you in your finery would put them all to the blush." He grabbed at the loose material of her dress and held it up to her, showing not more than one ragged flounce at the elbows and a worn, unembroidered petticoat of the same violet wool as her gown. "Do tell, Lady Brienne, what is your secret? I am sure your dowdy American cousins would like to know how you manage to stay atop the fashions of the *ton*."

"Stop this, I tell you!" she cried, pinkening all the way down to her breasts. "Perhaps I've not the most fashionable gowns, but at least I'm not a heathen American!" She grabbed the wool from his grasp and fought the urge once again to slap his arrogant face.

"Heathen!" he exclaimed incredulously. "You may call them that only if that's your name for beauty and heart! American women are not like these pale, insipid, whimpering little wallflowers you English call the fair sex. Why, I've seen better flesh on my Arabian mare!"

"Pale and insipid?" she whispered, too incensed to

shout. She looked at him and speechlessly tried to fight back with an expression of complete disdain. But once again he let out an inappropriate laugh.

"You, my little wildflower, I have forgotten. You are the exception. You put on airs as if you were a queen. But alas, what a wretched state your kingdom is in!" He ran a strong, work-worn hand over her knotted and tangled hair and gently touched her cheek where the dirt from her bed had smudged it. She pulled back from his touch; this seemed to make him grow thoughtful. "Ready yourself now. I'll have the maid draw you a bath and bring a tray to your room—your room back in the house."

"I'll not be going back to the house. I am leaving. As I said last night, you'll not be keeping me here." She looked at him defiantly. She knew she was small—especially in his presence—but she was determined that her stature would not make her remain a prisoner.

"And where are your funds—your means to get away?"

"I have the means. Not much, but enough to get me where I am going." She thought of her mother's comb and the pain of having to part with it. It would be difficult to sell it, but not as difficult as remaining at Osterley with this Colonial brute and her father's imminent arrival hanging over her head. She gave a small sigh and stated, "Now, if you will leave me so that I can complete my toilet—"

"Would this be part of your plans?" Avenel reached into his waistcoat pocket and held out a brilliant gold comb set with eight large square-cut amethysts, sprinkled with at least a score of tiny pinpoint diamonds. She could not stifle her gasp. Unmindful of her state of undress, she ran to her bag and shuffled through it, desperately searching for her mother's piece. When she could not find it, she searched for her miniature. She whispered a quiet prayer when she spied it among the folds of her handkerchief.

"Give that back! You have stolen it from me!" she cried in abject frustration.

"Stolen it? Why, one of my men found it on the other side of Osterley's gates, apparently lost by some thoughtless maiden. You don't mean to say that this lovely piece belongs to you?" he taunted.

"You know it does! Please give it back to me. It's all I have in this world."

"All the more reason to keep it then, my lady. 'Tis a valuable piece. More precious than you could know," he said enigmatically.

"You must give it back. It's mine!" She tried to keep despair out of her voice, but it was too difficult. He knew as well as she did that without her comb she would have no means to leave at all.

"Prove it."

When his command met a mute response, he looked her over; his mercurial meanness returned. She once again tried to pull her dress together with shaky fingers, but somehow she felt his eyes would have seen more than she wanted them to even if she had been properly laced.

"It's mine!" she gasped as she watched him leave.

Before he departed, he tucked the comb securely back into his waistcoat pocket, saying, "There will be a warm bath and some breakfast waiting for you in the yellow bedroom whenever you are ready to come back."

Leaving her behind, he walked out the door and down the steps to the stableyard. She cursed him silently as she watched him from the grimy leaded window make his way through the stable block. Finally he disappeared under the portico of the main house. But she continued to stare at the house until the sporadic morning sunshine burned off the last of the mists and then vanished itself under a heavy sky of gray.

The servants' quarters beneath the house were as quiet as the Roman catacombs when Avenel walked through them.

"A foin day to ya', Master Slane. And what biddin' may we do fer ya?" Among the silent crowd of servants, Fergie tipped his lambskin wig and waited for his master's answer.

"I've come to speak with Annie, the little ladies' maid," Avenel said, holding his anger at bay. He looked through the group but did not seem to find the one he was searching for.

"Well, now, she's a bad egg, tha' one."

"Shut your mouth, Fergie McInnis!" Annie cried out in her defense, finally coming forward. She was just vain enough to believe that Avenel wanted her for some reason other than to dismiss her.

"There you are, Annie. Will you please get your things and come with me?" Avenel took in the girl's buxom figure. With a trained eye, he noticed that soon all her curves would turn to fat.

"My pleasure." Snootily, she gave the cook a haughty smile and then turned to retrieve her belongings. The cook watched her with utter dismay on her face, hardly believing the chit could be so obtuse.

"She's got her faults, but deep down, she doesn't mean harm, Master Slane," the cook pleaded the girl's defense.

"She thinks highly of herself. She will get by," Avenel

answered tersely, obviously angered by the incident. "I will heed no disobedience in this household. That must be made clear."

"Yes, sir." She backed away as Annie once again pushed through the crowd of servants.

"I've come, sir." Annie looked up at him expectantly.

"Then you may go. Please follow Hans out to the gates. He has instructions to give you some funds and a fare-thee-well." Avenel turned to go.

"I'm not to become your—? Why, it's not fair!" Annie shrieked as soon as she realized what was happening. "I'm above all these others. Look there at Maura, will you, or Peg?" She motioned to the other little maids that stood with the group. "They're lower than me, just like the other dirty Irish that run about this place. You cannot mean to let me go!"

" 'Tis exactly what I mean to do. Good riddance. Hans?" Avenel looked at his hefty Nordic helper. When he nodded, Hans began to escort the maid out of the house—but not before she called out her revenge.

"Lord Oliver will hear of this! And when he retrieves Osterley, I shall return. He will not go easy on you for this! I was his favorite, you know. I was his favorite!"

"Aye, a bad egg, tha' one," Fergie was heard to whisper as soon as Annie's shrieks were no longer heard.

"I'm inclined to agree with you," Avenel murmured before he left their quarters.

It was late in the evening before Brienne finally gave up her vigil and returned to the comforts of Osterley. She had withstood her hunger and her worries, but it was the cold that finally forced her hand. When the crisp chill of twilight began to descend on the block, the thought of another night on the sagging rope bed was unbearable. So she gathered her bag—and, for some strange reason, the dirtied and tattered polonaise—and walked back to the house.

The two old footmen discreetly opened the large glass doors from the courtyard as if they had been awaiting her arrival. She merely glared at them as if to say that they too were the enemy. They both looked away and refused to challenge her stares. Satisfied, she made her way back upstairs to the taffeta bedroom, thankfully meeting no one else on her way there.

She entered her bedroom but was amazed at its transformation. All the articles in the room were the same, from the bed hangings and curtains of Chinese painted silk taffeta to the satinwood furniture with its green inlaid acanthus leaf motifs. But there was a new atmosphere that made it another world altogether. Where the hearth before lay cold and bare, there was now a crackling fire burning away in its depths. A copper-lined tub brimming with steaming water lay near it, and the room was filled with the scent of honeysuckle and jasmine. The Pembroke table was laid with a snowy linen cloth, and on top of it rested four covered salvers from the eating room; the well-polished silver cheerfully reflected the glow of the fireplace.

Brienne's first thought was that she had mistakenly walked into the bedroom that Avenel was using, but this conclusion was quickly overruled by the room's feminine colors and scents and by the realization that Osterley's new master would surely reside in the state bedroom on the first floor. Her confusion increased when a small, dark-haired young woman stepped out of the dressing room.

"Ah! *Vous êtes* Lady Brienne! I am Vivie. Ah"—the small Frenchwoman searched for words—*"je suis . . .*

ah . . . I am *votre nouvelle fille de chambre. Votre bonne de demoiselle.* Ah!" She gave a small sigh and continued in a heavily accented voice. "Forgive me, *ma demoiselle.* My English is sometimes slow."

With that the maid walked over to Brienne, took the bag from her hands, and placed it in one of the painted beechwood armchairs along the wall.

"You are the new maid? What happened to Annie?" Brienne asked in French. Her mother has insisted on teaching that language to her, claiming it was an essential part of a young lady's education.

"How wonderful that you can speak French, my lady! When I am nervous, my English is unrecognizable!" the little woman answered in French, smiling in gratitude. "But to answer your question, I have just arrived from London today. Master Slane has brought me here for you. And such a rush he was in this morning! I have never traveled so quickly! But as for this Annie, I do not know where she is. I have not met anyone by that name here. Would you like me to find her?"

"No! That is, I suppose she is busy with other matters now." Brienne felt a strange little jab inside her, and she wondered briefly if those other matters included warming the state bed.

"But, my lady! Enough of my chatter! We must think of you!" The little woman went to work, busily laying out linen towels by the bath, pouring steaming water into the tub from a brass kettle near the hearth, and then helping Brienne, who was rather dazed by all the attention, out of her soiled clothing.

Letting Vivie do everything, Brienne allowed herself to be whisked into the tub. Her icy fingers and feet luxuriated in the warm scented water as the little maid scrubbed her back and lathered her long, rich hair. Then

Vivie poured pans of deliciously warm water over
Brienne's head until all traces of the expensive soap
were removed from her hair and body.

Then she was wrapped in the linen towels, and Vivie
labored over her wet hair, combing it dry by the fireside;
only then did Brienne ask the questions that were hover-
ing in her mind.

"What did Master Slane say of me? I mean, what relationship did he propose we . . ." She spoke in perfect
French until she found it too awkward to continue.

"He has not said a word, my lady. Please do not concern yourself." Vivie stopped combing for a moment and
brought her a clean white night smock and her old slate
blue wool dressing gown. After helping her into these,
the maid moved to the Pembroke table. She took the
silver covers from the platters and discriminatingly filled
a Sèvres porcelain plate with the delicacies within.

"Vivie," Brienne said as she watched her dinner being
served, "I suppose you think I am here to—"

"No explanations are necessary, my lady. I am French.
These things are a way of life for a French girl. But for
you at least there is such a man! I have heard he is kind
and generous—and a true Adonis. What more could one
ask for? To be taken in and cared for by one such as he is
more than—"

"No! It is not like that! I am not his mistress! You see,
he is holding me . . ." *Here,* Brienne thought abruptly
to herself, her voice trailing off. *You see*—she recited the
speech to herself—*he is holding me here against my
will for some reason that I do not yet know. And even
though he may pay you well and is obviously one of
the most virile and handsome men a woman could
ever desire, he is really an ogre, and . . .*

She gave a heavy sigh of despair. There would be no

point in telling the sweet little Frenchwoman any of this, she knew. Either Vivie would think it a ghastly lie to cover up her role here as Avenel's mistress, or the little maid would believe she was as crazed as Annie did.

Vivie brought her a tray with her dinner, but Brienne found her appetite diminished by the strange circumstances in which she found herself.

"Please try to eat something, my lady." Vivie watched over her like a mother on her daughter's wedding night. "It will not be good if you get too thin." The maid gave her a sage look and then went into the dressing room to unpack Brienne's worn and muddied bag.

Brienne tried some of the roasted tripe but found the heavy red wine more to her liking. Finally she sat back in the settee, which had been moved nearer to the fire, with a full wineglass in her small hand. It did not take long for her to become drowsy. All day she had worn herself out with futile planning.

Thinking back to the morning, she recalled that she had paced furiously in the little stable block room, trying desperately to come up with a means to leave. She had considered using one of the horses as a means of escape, but she'd known she wouldn't get far, since she didn't know how to ride.

Later that afternoon, she'd tried just walking away, descending the steps to the stable yard and then, bag in hand, sauntering to the back of the house to head due west toward the woodlands. It was not a complete failure; no one had physically tried to stop her from going. But doubts had seized her when the cold winter wind whipped at her petticoat and reddened her cheeks with their sting. Where would she go? She had no money for even the most meager of lodgings; even returning to Tenby would cost her coach fare.

In that second of indecision she had turned around to look back at the house; its immense brick structure had beckoned her with at least a fireside and some food. Then she had seen him staring at her from the gallery windows that lined the entire back of the house. Avenel's face had had a hard expression on it as he watched her, and his mouth had formed a grim line. Their eyes met, and then she knew exactly why he was merely staring out the window at her and not coming forth into the cold to bring her back. It was not that he had suddenly been taken with a fit of compliance. He had simply known even before she had that she would not go. She was trapped at Osterley, more because of her lack of means than because of locks and threats and giants guarding the gates. She couldn't go anywhere without her comb. He had not doubted that she would come back to get it.

Scalding tears had burned her raw cheeks. In frustration she had turned from the house so that he would not see her defeat. She'd never been prone to tears and emotion. But then that had been before this man had shown up at Osterley. In one day her very insides had been turned inside out from the wonder, worry, doubt, and fear associated with his arrival.

All alone in the great field behind the house, she had stood rigidly still. When her tears had passed, with her head held high despite her feelings of hopelessness, she had returned to the stable block room, noting on her way that he had moved from the gallery windows. But she knew he was still watching her just the same.

Now, sleepily curled up on the pale yellow settee, she was still trying to figure out a plan. She knew the first thing she had to do was get her comb back. That had become crystal clear during her battle with her tears.

Only then, would she have the means to leave. But then her inexperience with spirits caught up with her as she imbibed the rich Burgundy; she told herself almost merrily she would soon have the pleasure of seeing Osterley Park and Avenel Slane for the last time.

With this comforting thought, she took one last sip of her wine and placed the glass on the Brussels carpet. Her thickly lashed eyelids closed in deepest slumber; she was completely unmindful of Vivie, who peeked into the room and then contentedly retired for the night.

CHAPTER SEVEN

Three days of waiting—that much time passed before Brienne saw Avenel leave the house. There had been no point in venturing forth from her room while he was in residence, for surely where her comb was, he would be, guarding it. But here was her chance.

Slyly she watched him through the painted taffeta curtains of her room. He walked arrogantly toward the stable block, looking completely unmindful of her and her troubles—or so it seemed, she thought irritably. It was a rare glorious winter day; but a few billowing clouds swept their way across an azure sky. Avenel obviously meant to take full advantage of the beautiful weather by spending it on horseback. From her room she saw the bright sun glinting off his well-sooted and shined black boots. Tied back with a dark silk cord, his natural hair glinted with blue shimmers. He saw the new stableboy bring his fully tacked up horse to him and flashed him an even white smile. Brienne's feminine instinct told her with little doubt that there were women on at least two continents thinking of him at that very moment. Looking at him now, relaxed and smiling, basking in the sunshine and anticipating his ride, he had a boyish quality about him that she begrudgingly admitted was very attractive.

But enough of this! She nervously stepped back from the window and let the curtains fall to their hanging position. She had to find her comb, and there would not be much time!

She crept stealthily out of her room and down the great staircase. In the hall the old footmen were as omnipresent as the ancient Roman statues lining the wall. They stared after her, but she dismissed their vacant, fixed gazes and swept purposefully toward the drawing room. There she bypassed the south passage and went instead through room after room to gain access to the state bedroom, thereby avoiding any servants who might be wandering the halls.

Ignoring the rich crimson Gobelins tapestries that hung like so much wallpaper in the magnificent antechamber, she quickly sought the door to his room. Her nerves were strung tight as she moved into the bedroom; she knew full well that she must not be caught. She closed the door firmly behind her and stood just inside the room, taking deep, calming breaths.

She had seen it many times, but the room's rich decoration still caught her by surprise. How oddly beautiful it seemed now that someone inhabited it, she mused. Whenever she'd come here in the past month, the room had appeared rather dark and oppressive; but now she was struck by how lovely the hues of pleated green velvet were that warmed and lined the walls, and how overwhelming and terribly unnerving the splendid domed bedstead was that boasted not less than eight painted and japanned columns with gilt capitals. But not wanting to waste one more precious minute, she made herself turn her gaze from the bed and pushed her wary thoughts of it to the back of her mind.

She swept over to the south passage door and pulled it closed to keep away the prying eyes of the servants. The japanned commode was the most logical place to start; she walked over to it, opened the top drawer, and rummaged through Slane's spare handkerchiefs, a plain pewter snuff box, several pairs of fine white silk hose, and his own tortoiseshell comb that still held two or three of his shiny, long black hairs. But she didn't come across the comb.

She opened drawer after drawer of white, immaculately pressed linen shirts. She rifled through these, not caring in what condition she left them, hoping desperately that her risk-taking wouldn't be for naught. But her sparkling purple and gold comb did not turn up among his shirts either. She groaned with nervousness and frustration and looked about the room, searching for possible hiding places for her comb. But the bedstead so dominated the chamber that there was no room for additional furnishings. Silently she cursed the huge structure; its very immensity possessed new meaning at the unbidden thought that Avenel had awakened in it that very morning. The bed loomed over her. It intensified her desire to get far away from him.

She forced her attention to his trunks, which were placed one on top of the other against the north wall. Apparently they had been emptied and were about to be removed for storage. Gladly moving away from the bed, she went to the leather trunk at the top of the stack and pulled it down. But quickly she found it too heavy for her, and the massive piece fell to the ground with a clamoring thud. Her heart pounded in her chest, for she was sure that an army of servants was going to descend upon the room and find her out. But a few minutes of silence passed, and the only sound she heard was the quiet, steady tick of the French clock on the mantel in the state bedroom.

Breathing an enormous sigh of relief, she sat cross-legged on the edge of the Thomas Moore carpet that had been made to outline the magnificent bed. She tapped and jiggled the undone locks of the trunk until it fell open. She could not hide her disappointment when she found the trunk empty.

Pushing it aside with disgust, she went for the next trunk, this time anticipating its weight and taking it more securely in her arms. But just as her arms had a firm, steady hold on it, she suddenly made out the faint, menacing sound of riding boots on the marble floor coming toward her from the passage. Fear jerked through her like a bolt of lightning, and the trunk fell from her arms with a loud crash and boom. Wild-eyed, she waited for the sound of running feet. But the footsteps did not quicken their pace; instead they confirmed her worst fears by merely continuing forward with maddening and dooming evenness. That was enough for Brienne.

Flying through the jumble of trunks and thankfully not tripping over any of the angled and open lids in her way, she knew she could reach the tapestry-room door before anyone entered the bedroom. But when she got to it, she found that it had somehow locked behind her. Despite her pushing and pulling on the arabesque-decorated door latch, it would not open. She was left with no way out.

"Looking for this?" Avenel filled the doorway to his

bedroom with his large frame and dangled the comb from his thumb and forefinger.

"Damn you! Why didn't you go riding?" she whispered from the locked door; her back hugged every board in it. Her mouth had gone dry, and she swallowed several times to moisten it.

"Now, how did you know I was going riding? You wouldn't be spying on me? And here I thought you were merely a thief!" He sauntered into the room and shut the passage door behind him with such finality that she had to close her eyes to keep from shrieking in terror. She had only seen the tip of this man's anger before, and then she had not provoked it. But now, caught searching his bedroom, she felt that he would surely kill her or worse. Forcing her eyes open, she saw to her horror that the bedstead which had seemed so large before now seemed to have grown to an overwhelming size.

If she had been weaker, she knew she would have fainted. But instead she met her foe, saying as steadily as she could, "I am not a thief. I have come to retrieve what is mine."

"This?" He held the comb up to her. "I told you before—this was found by one of my men." He walked toward her at a slow, steady pace, holding the brilliant bejeweled comb in front of him.

"It's mine. The comb is all I have in this world." She looked up at him as he came closer. Her face was pale, but she didn't know that this enhanced the dark, rich red of her hair and the full ripeness of her pink mouth. Her fear made her look like an enchanting wood nymph, clinging to the impassable doorway in high-strung anticipation.

"If this is all you possess, my lady, then you aren't worth much, surely." With that, he took the comb, and with precise calculation he threw it into the middle of the looming bedstead. She started for it almost immediately, but her arm was grabbed in a strong grip, and she felt herself being turned around to face him. Then his sensuous mouth, which had appeared to her boyish and smiling only an hour before, clamped down on hers in a way that only a man could know of. Her fear made her momentarily passive, and she stood there feeling his angry, demanding lips move over hers almost as if she were a spectator rather than a participant. Slowly she started to struggle with him; she pulled at his linen shirt until she had completely opened it, exposing a tantalizing amount of soft, curling black hair. But he would not let her go. Instead he moved closer, placed his hands around her tiny waist, and moved them upward along the side of her body. He rested them intimately under her arms, just to the sides of her breasts. She felt a growing hardness near her belly as he pressed himself against her. But in spite of his previous demanding and forceful manner, she found she was suddenly not afraid, nor, to her surprise, repulsed.

He was kissing her now with the softness of a lover. His lips took time to move over her face and slowed over her nose and her closed, relaxed eyelids. He made her feel something that did not seem terrible at all. In fact, it was like a floating sensation that she had felt before in one of her dreams. And the more she relaxed, the more heightened the sensation became. All thoughts of what she was actually doing seemed unreachably distant. Before she knew it, she had accepted his mouth willingly over hers. She then bade him enter her mouth as she opened it in an instinctual act that came from deep inside her. As his tongue moved inside her, her nerves flared and sparked. Wanting more of him, she took his dark head in her hands and pulled him to her, desiring the fiery, impending explosion that was wreaking turmoil in her body to go on and on.

Eventually he pulled his head up, and she knew she was panting just as hard as he. He looked down at her with his arms around her; there was an expression of mild disbelief in his visage. "So you aren't afraid of me after all."

She nodded her head, keeping her jewellike amethyst eyes so close to his that she could see the brilliant white flecks that burst from the cerulean ground in his irises.

"You're beautiful, little wildflower." He held her close and whispered into her faintly honeysuckle-scented hair, "Perhaps 'tis I who should be afraid of you. Your father must have created you just to bewitch me."

At the mention of her father, waves of reality lashed through her body. What was she doing? Had she lost all her reason? The man before her was entirely capable of doing to her what Oliver Morrow had done to her mother! But deep down, she realized that there was a difference between the two men. Her realization made Oliver Morrow that much more evil in his abuse, and it made Avenel Slane that much more powerful—and frightening.

Pulling away from his hold, she took several steps back from him; the warmth she had felt from his body was now gone, leaving her empty and unfulfilled. But she had to stop this. He obviously hated her for something her father had done to him, and he had made no effort to hide that fact. If she were not careful, he could inflict more than just physical pain on her.

"I'll have my comb now, if you don't mind." She tried to affect a cool tone, but it was hard when her pulse was drumming fiercely and her skin was pink and hot.

"By all means," he replied, giving her a wickedly beautiful smile. With his arm, he gestured at the towering domed bed with her comb nestled in the plush silk of the pale green coverlet.

"After you."

"I will not," she stated, nervously looking at the ornamented structure.

"Then you will have no comb." He leaned back against the tapestry-room door and watched her. She was again wearing the violet wool dress, but today she had donned a deep wine-colored petticoat of almost the same shade as her hair, whch was now piled becomingly into a large, loose chignon and covered with black netting.

"Tell me, Lady Brienne, what is it about this trinket that makes it so valuable to you? Why not steal some of the riches this house has to offer?" He walked over to the corner of the room, where an ancient lapis lazuli urn sat on a tripod pedestal. He unceremoniously picked up the Roman antiquity, jockeyed it between his hands, and then turned to her. "Why not take this, for example? I imagine 'tis thousands of years old. Surely it would bring you all the funds you need to get out of here. And you would also be doing your father a service by depriving me of some of his wealth. What say you? Why not give it a try?" He suddenly tossed it to her, and she barely caught the priceless object before it shattered on the ground. She clutched it to her bosom for safekeeping. At her near miss, he merely cocked one of his fine jet eyebrows, which made him look almost satanic; his eyes gleamed like silver coins.

"That would be stealing," she told him indignantly.

"Stealing! And what do you call this? Rifling through my belongings, knocking my trunks onto the floor. Come now, my lady, you need a better reason than that. Why not take the vase? In fact, 'tis yours. You may keep it."

"You know why I dare not take the vase!" She was suddenly furious at this game of cat and mouse that he was playing with her. "Whatever I could carry from this place would be unsellable, and you know it. Anyone could trace it back to magnificent Osterley Park. Everything in this house from the doorknobs to the firelogs has the mark of Robert Adam on it. I would be accused of stealing it by the authorities. And I sincerely doubt that you would aid my defense by revealing that you actually gave me one of the priceless treasures from its interior. The whole idea is ridiculous. I do not trust you nearly enough to take that chance; I am not such a fool."

At this he stepped up to her and took the dark blue urn from her hands. He placed it gently back onto its stand and laughed. "Then your only chance, as I see it, is the comb. Am I correct?" He continued without her answer. "So there it is. All you have to do is pick it up, and 'tis yours." He stood back and eyed her, crossing his muscular arms over his powerful, broad chest.

She watched him through lowered lashes. There was no trusting him, but she wanted her comb. It lay tantalizingly within her reach. She looked up and judged the distance they each would be required to move to reach the bed. She was by far the closer. The nagging doubt in the back of her mind that he was swifter seemed small when she judged that he stood far across the room by the gilded tripod pedestal. Agonizing in her mind whether to take the risk, she took one step nearer the bed and looked at him to see if he had moved. Not a muscle twitched in the man's entire body, and that was reassuring. But then again, he was standing almost too calmly, like a jaguar viewing an antelope, pausing to choose not how to catch one but which one.

She decided to take the chance. With her comb in her possession, she could be in Bath in less than three days, and this strange, dark adventure would be just a memory. Her mind made up, she started to run as fast as her healthy young legs could take her. She had her comb within inches of her grasp. But then with a cry it was gone, and she was being pulled onto the huge jade coverlet completely against her will. Avenel's body came down heavily upon hers, and she struggled to free herself as she had never struggled before.

"Hush! Be still! I'll not hurt you." He grabbed her flailing arms and held them firmly over her head. After that, nary a muscle in her body could move beneath the enormous strength of the man on top of her. She silently cursed herself for being so easily baited, and she glared at him with flashing violet eyes. He spoke softly to her: "You must be still. I remind you that you came here of your own free will."

"I did not come here to be raped," she spat at him.

But he merely cocked that infuriating eyebrow and started kissing her, licking and nibbling at the creamy skin that was exposed at the top of her bodice. He smiled and tenderly moved up to kiss her temple and hairline. "I shan't rape you. Why would I deny myself the pleasure of seeing you groan and plead for my lovemaking?" He removed his grip from her arms and she started to struggle again, but he quickly ended it by taking both of her delicate wrists into one masculine hand. He gave her a warning look, and once again he let her arms go. But this time she held them quietly, not wanting him to hold her so fiercely.

"You know," he said, "you should be more kind to

me." His lips touched her temple, and he again made a maddening assault on her senses. "I could keep you in here and take away all your clothes." He kissed her. "Make you my concubine and let you wear nothing at all except for that ridiculous little comb . . . and me." He kissed her now full on the lips; she couldn't help releasing a soft groan as a melting, drifting sensation made its way up to her belly. God, what was happening to her?

His kiss was long and full, and after it was over she looked up at him with a sleepy, almost drugged expression on her face. Her lips were stained a deep, moist pink from his touch, and her cheeks were hot and flushed. She felt him slip off the net binding her hair, and soon her auburn locks spilled over the green coverlet. He stroked her hair, as if sensing magic in its strange color, and then she felt him slide her coveted comb into her silken strands.

Instinctively she grabbed for it, but he held her back. "Be still—I just want to look at you," he whispered, gazing at her face and hair, not missing a detail. She lay back quiet and still, unsure what he was doing. "It suits you, strange as it seems," he said enigmatically. "I must allow you to wear it sometime. Perhaps at dinner, when we are alone."

"Give it to me now! You know it is mine," she pleaded.

"No," he said sharply. He got off the silk coverlet, took the comb from her hair, and stood over her while she groggily sat up. The intoxicating effect of his touch was slow to wear off, and she sat on the bed and watched him as he pulled open the top drawer of his commode. He placed her comb in it and locked it.

"Please!" she begged as she watched him shut the drawer.

"No," he said again, pulling the black silk cord that held his hair in a queue. He strung the drawer's key onto the cord and then knotted it around his neck. The brass key gleamed warm and yellow against his dark chest, which was visible due to his undone shirt; it was too enticing for her to bear.

"Now, if you want to leave Osterley, you will have to earn my favor," he said as if he were a commander reviewing the troops.

"You bastard!" she cursed, shocking even herself with the force of her anger.

"Now that," he said, taking her jaw into one of his hands, "that, my beautiful young maiden, will not do. But your good behavior will, and . . ." He looked at the bed that she was sitting on. "Would that you tried pleasing me here. I should give you the highest kind of privilege—perhaps even enough to gain this key."

"If by letting you bed me, I win my freedom, why not rape me now and be through with this?" She wanted to scream in vexation, but she kept her voice tame, trying not to anger him.

"Raping you would not please me. I must have you come to me. And when that time comes, if a single fair muscle in that woman's body of yours should flex with reluctance, it will not be good enough. Do you understand me?" He watched her face intently, waiting for her obedient reply.

"Yes," she mumbled.

"Good." He released her jaw from his grasp and allowed her to get off the bed. "I expect you to have dinner with me tonight. You can come to my bed tonight or the next or the one after that. But in the meantime there will be no snooping about my room."

She pulled her long hair into a semblance of order

before she left the room and thankfully started for the door. But this new twist in her struggle to leave weighed heavily on her mind.

"Lady Brienne"—he interrupted her exit—"I would have a kiss before you go."

She turned to glare at him, but he reminded her, "That would please me, wildflower, immeasurably." Standing in rebellion, she watched hypnotically as the golden key swung from his neck. Then she went to him, uncharacteristically cooperative. Raising on tiptoe, she pulled his dark head down to hers to give him a perfunctory brush on the lips. Just as her lips touched his, she moved her hand up his chest and pulled on the black cord around his neck. But her hand was quickly brushed aside; he wrapped his arms around her and pulled her up so that her feet could no longer touch the ground. With one hand grasping her waist and the other firmly beneath her buttocks, he crushed her to him as if she were merely a doll. Before she knew it, his tongue demanded entrance to her mouth. At that she felt the slow torturous pleasure of her body's betrayal.

Had she been standing at that moment, Brienne was sure the force of his persuasion would have knocked her over. But instead, being under his control and possessing no real choices, she relented and allowed him to deepen their kiss. With each thrust of his greedy tongue, she knew he claimed a victory. Yet it truly made her sick that she herself seemed to find perverse delight in her own defeat.

When he finally let her go, he took his time sliding her down the entire length of his body. It seemed she was introduced to his every supple muscle, as well as some that were not so lax, until she thought she would die from the very intimacy of it all. Finally separated, she found herself battling with such opposing emotions that she felt that they surely would rip her apart. Wonder and frustrated anger warred within her, and she stumbled almost blindly for the door and for some fresh air to clear her head.

"Remember, little one, please me here, and you will find I can be most generous."

"You arrogant colonial beast," she spat at him in the Welsh she'd learned as a child; she was too cowardly at the moment to use a language he could understand. "No wonder we English have been so provoked into war!" With that she fled from his look of surprise, but his full, deep laughter followed her through the hall and all the way back up the great staircase.

CHAPTER EIGHT

Vivie let out a great dissatisfied sigh. *"Ma demoiselle,* you have nothing suitable to wear. I have cleaned and pressed your dresses so many times! They are worn out!"

"Then we do not need to bother with it. I will not go." Brienne sat at the edge of the pale yellow settee. She stared into the fire that was now a regular feature of her bedroom hearth. In contrast, Vivie was cheerful and bright, flitting about the room in great anticipation of the task ahead: dressing her mistress for her first social occasion, dinner with Master Slane.

If her situation had not been so dire, Brienne knew she might have laughed at the little maid's antics. But it was such a ludicrous situation she was in. Upstairs, Vivie thought she was a country maiden who had been taken under Avenel's wing to be taught the finer points of how to please a man. But downstairs, she thought almost with a shudder, the real drama was taking place. She was fighting for her life, it seemed, with every new episode.

And now that the dictator in the play had complete control over every aspect of her life, she knew the climax was just behind the curtain.

"This one will have to do! I shall press it again." Brienne looked up as Vivie brought in her round gown, a closed robe that revealed no petticoat, of robin's-egg blue. The dress had a deep plum-colored *échelle,* whose small bows ran all the way down to the tip of her busk.

"Really, this is not necessary. I have no desire to—"

"Your maidenly reluctance suits you, my lady," Vivie said in French. "I have never seen you so beautiful. Your hair! Your eyes! The glow! I know Master Slane will be very happy with you. You must not fear!"

Not so! she thought to herself, smiling grimly. But it was too much to explain to the woman. Vivie was completely enamored with Avenel, and there was no speaking rationally to her about imagined trysts.

Seeing her mistress's smile, Vivie misinterpreted it and asked, "You have had a nice day today, yes?" She added slyly, "And if all goes well, perhaps you will have an even nicer night; is it not so?" She started to smile gaily now but saw Brienne's bewildered expression. "Do not fear, I will have the dress back soon, and I will do everything I can to make it look new again for your . . . ah . . ." She started to giggle and found she couldn't finish her sentence. *"Tout de suite, ma demoiselle!"* She laughed and then disappeared through the dressing-room door.

Letting out a long breath of disbelief, Brienne shook her head in frustration and then mutinously dropped her chin into the palm of her hand, staring back at the flames in the hearth. She might be called mad, but only because she was residing in a madhouse! It was all too much!

An hour later, she sat at her dressing table examining the fine work that Vivie had accomplished on her dark tresses. Vivie had loosely piled curl after curl onto the top of her head, allowing only one or two to fall free at the nape. Each strand of hair was shot with burgundy and pink highlights from the smoothing and brushing. Even Brienne had to admit that despite the occasion, it was wonderful to be pampered.

"Should you powder my hair?" Brienne asked, wondering if it was the lack of powder, and not her own lack of finery, that detracted from the entire effect.

"Perhaps I will powder it when you have guests. But for now, I know *les Américains* do not like it. You see, my brother, he is over there now in Virginia," Vivie confided in her. "He fight the war, *ma demoiselle*. I tell you this because Monsieur Slane, he was his friend there. That is how I have come to be here. My brother told him of my difficult position. There is hardness here now for the French, you see? I could not find anyone to take me. But then . . ." She gave a happy sigh and continued with her chatter. "But your hair! I am so easily sidetracked! You must forgive me."

Brienne only laughed and waited for her to finish. Vivie's revelation about her brother clarified a few things. The maid's gratitude to Avenel was now explained. Vivie's kind attentions to her mistress were simply an offshoot of her regard for her employer, which obviously ran very deep and strong.

"I think you leave it *au naturel.*" Vivie scrutinized her piled hair and then tried to explain. "You see, Monsieur Slane, he does not wear the wig. Because he is like *les Américains,* yes?"

"Yes, he is definitely like *les Américains.*" Brienne smiled at her again. She found herself liking Vivie more and more. In addition to her vivacious manner, Brienne appreciated the maid's genuine affection for her. Even their first evening, when she had shown up at the door dirty, tired, and miserable from the stable block, the young Frenchwoman had been considerate and kind. And she had never made Brienne feel inferior because of her outdated and worn fashions. Instead, Vivie chose to blame her mistress's circumstances. She became very serious when she delivered diatribes about what a sin it was that Brienne should have to wear the same dress more than once.

"How did your brother meet Avenel, Vivie?" Not wanting to appear as if she were prying, Brienne stood up from the dressing table, and in her sleeveless linen shift and stays she started to pull on a pair of her finest white hose; she rested her slim, shapely leg on the stool in front of her.

"Is a magnificent story!" Vivie exclaimed, and she started chattering just as Brienne had hoped she would. "My brother, Jean Claude, he was shot in the war. He had to walk very far to get rest from the fighting. He found a large plantation along a river. And at this beautiful, quiet plantation he was allowed to stay to heal. And there he met Monsieur Slane, who was . . . ah, *le* . . . houseguest! But that is not all.

"While he was still very sick, the owner of the house betrayed him. He brought the British to kill him and make him give them information! But the Monsieur had friends who came and took him away to Virginia to care for him. The plantation people never found out who it was that took their prize away. Monsieur Slane still laughs when he tells the story of how the cowards had to hide my brother's uniform in a hole in the paneling to keep from being found out as the American traitors they were. You cannot be on both sides of a war, *ma demoi-*

selle. Unless, of course, you are a coward." Vivie handed her her purple kid slippers.

"But Master Slane is playing both sides. Is he a coward, too?" Brienne slipped on her shoes, which regrettably did not match the gown, and then moved over to where her gown lay freshly pressed on the bed. She was trying very hard to be nonchalant. Finally she was obtaining some information about the mysterious man downstairs; she did not want Vivie to find her too eager.

"Mais non! He is the bravest of them all! He has done much for his country. He is not a traitor!" Vivie exclaimed.

"But how can that be? He has forsaken his country and moved to the enemy's!" *And how I wish he had stayed where he belongs,* Brienne thought.

"Yes, it seems so. But his family was originally from here. He has pulled away from the war for just that reason."

"Family? You mean he is married?" She could hardly breathe while she waited for Vivie to answer her.

"Mais non! He is very much unattached! What I mean to say is, his family came from here. The Monsieur knew he could not be a traitor to the British, so he came back here for his family and to leave the war behind him."

"And because he had other things on his mind besides that colonial war." Brienne suddenly shivered at the thought of seeing the earl at Osterley. Whatever was between these two men was far more important to Avenel than even that war for independence. She certainly did not want to get caught in the middle!

"Lady Brienne! You are shivering! Come stand by the fire while I dress you! We must not let you catch a chill!" The little woman's voice pulled her out of her thoughts.

Obediently, Brienne moved to the fire and stood patiently as Vivie dressed her, tying each of the ribbons along her bodice into a perfect bow. "There!" Vivie stood back and examined her work. Exclaiming in French, she said, "Oh my lady, there is not a more beautiful woman anywhere! You are truly ravishing!"

Brienne looked expectantly at herself in the pier mirror hung across from the fireplace. Disappointed, she saw only the same old girl staring back at her. Her blue dress, although painstakingly pressed to a fine finish, was as it had always been. And although the new hairstyle gave her an older and more womanly appearance, the heart-shaped face was still hers, despite the dusky glow cast on her cheeks from the fire and the sparkling plum shine in her eyes.

She laughed at herself. Had she really expected to see someone different? Perhaps to see a woman better dressed than she, with magnificent white hair piled high on her head and a patch dotted alluringly over one crimson lip, like a picture she had seen in one of her mother's precious magazines? Why did she care? There was no one here that she wanted to impress.

Shaking herself, she watched Vivie in the mirror. The maid was very proud of herself. She had turned her drab churchmouse mistress into the semblance of a lady; she had so wanted to please her.

"Thank you, Vivie," Brienne said as she turned from the mirror. "If I look good, it is all your work. You have done miracles with what little you had." She gave her a grateful little smile.

"*Mais non, ma demoiselle*. You underestimate yourself. A beauty cannot be made from satin and powder. The woman herself must be beautiful, or there is nothing but artifice. And you are a beauty, both here," Vivie said, sweeping a hand across her face, "and here." The maid placed a palm over her heart.

"You are too generous, Vivie. You hardly know me, and yet you say such nice things."

"I know the Monsieur. He would have his woman no other way."

"Perhaps I am not his woman, Vivie. What then?" Brienne frowned a little as she said this, not wanting to lose Vivie's friendship. But she knew she owed the maid as much of the truth as she would accept.

"Not yet, *peut-être*. But it is only a matter of time with you two. I have seen the look when he speaks of you, and I have seen his eyes. His eyes, *ma demoiselle*—they will never be warmer! You are the one for him. Once he knows he has your heart, he will want no other."

My heart, she thought to herself, *is the one thing he will never have.* But there was no more time for that determined thought, for she was quickly ushered out the door to her waiting dinner partner.

As she made her way down the stairs, she was pleased to find Cumberland waiting for her. She smiled down at him, heartened to see that he had forgiven her for whatever had bothered him in the stable block.

"Lady Brienne, may I say that never before have I escorted so beautiful a woman to dinner?"

Brienne took his outstretched arm. "And may I say that I have never been in such distinguished company?" Laughing, she felt relieved that he would be joining them for the evening. Cumberland looked dignified in his silver-gray velvet breeches and coat, along with his fringed cobalt satin waistcoat. He almost made her look like a pauper in her old blue tabby, but she was pleased to be on his arm.

They walked down the north passage, where the eating room joined the gallery, but when she saw it was completely dark, without even one candle, she cried, "What is this now? I thought we were to dine—"

"Yes, yes, my dear. Don't be overly alarmed." Cumberland patted her arm reassuringly.

But she did not like surprises if they even remotely involved Avenel Slane. Anything out of the ordinary with him was to be suspected. She looked at him sharply. "But then where—?"

"In the gallery, my dear. Slane thought it would be more intimate."

"More intimate? The gallery is four times the size of the eating room!"

"Well, then, let us just say that it is his favorite room. And he prefers it." Again he patted her arm; there was a twinkle in his faded blue eyes. "He's eccentric, to be sure; but Americans will be no other way!"

"Well, at least one of his colleagues has been blessed with some British sense." She smiled back at him and let him lead her to the gallery; the two walked in quiet camaraderie.

When they reached the gallery, she noticed that one of the three mahogany tables from the north passage had been placed at the far end of the room. The early Georgian gateleg table had been set with a creamy tablecloth and celadon green *Sèvres* porcelain. A silver candelabrum with eight burning candles provided the only light, except that from the large fire in the hearth, which was vigorously burning the chill from the evening air. By the fireplace she saw the rugged form of Avenel as he leaned on the mantel, casually holding a glass of amber liquid.

"I say, Slane, we've been favored with gracious company tonight." Cumberland led her to the table. She gave an involuntary shudder at the picture of the earl looking down upon them from the mantel. Morrow's dull, muddy eyes stared at her and followed her, clinging to her every movement until she had to look away.

"Good evening, Lady Brienne." Avenel took her hand and bent down to place a kiss on the back. She was shocked by the sensuous warmth of his lips as they touched her skin, and she pulled her hand away quickly. "As always, you are unspeakably lovely." He pulled up to his full height, and she found herself staring at the fabric of his coat; her eyes were barely level with his shoulders, so much more taller was he than she. She noted that his coat was of some dark-colored satin, but whether it was green or blue she couldn't be sure in the soft glow of the fire.

"Lady Brienne, do allow me!" Cumberland eagerly pulled one of the three ornately carved elbow chairs from the table. She sat down in it, grateful that her back was to the fireplace and the portrait of Oliver Morrow.

She looked up just in time to see Avenel cock one of his infuriating jet eyebrows in Cumberland's direction; he was no doubt amused by the elderly gentleman's behavior. Flustered and perhaps a bit embarrassed, Cumberland took the chair to her left, mumbling to himself about the unchivalrous behavior of certain individuals.

"Thank you, Master Cumberland. Only in your company am I treated so well." She shot Avenel a daring look of distaste, but she was met with one of his most charming smiles, and she felt cheated out of a proper reaction.

"You certainly like this room." She looked down to the far end of the long gallery and could not even make out the long, delicately curved sofa that lined the far wall, so obscured in darkness was it.

"*Like* it, Lady Brienne? You are mistaken! I *love* this

room. Being in this room means everything to me. I can gaze at your father and laugh, relishing his return." Avenel snapped his fingers, and two footmen appeared, one with the wine, the other with the first course.

Suddenly Brienne lost her ravenous appetite. The earl's arrival was something she dreaded with every fiber in her body. The thought of seeing him in the flesh sickened her. *"I'll have you both!"* The words echoed in her mind until she grasped the edge of the table. She looked down at the thin strips of canard and sections of orange. Forcing herself to take one mouthful, she picked some up on her silver fork. She tried very hard to be casual when she asked, "How soon do you expect the earl?" She placed the utensil delicately in her mouth.

"Oh, 'tis hard to say. If he should chance have some good luck, we should see him sooner than expected, eh, Cumberland?" With that both men had a hearty chuckle, unmindful of Brienne, who had lost her appetite.

"You mean you have no idea when he might arrive?" She tried to get down her food with a sip of claret. Her mouth felt so dry that each morsel seemed to stick against the back of her throat. However, she eventually found her courage, and she glowered at Avenel. "He could show up at the door right now and find us all communing at the table. I tell you, I will not be part of this!"

"You are part of this, my lady, whether it pleases you or not." He gave her a stern look.

"I will do no such thing." She refused. "Why, the complete audacity—"

"I say, the cook has really outdone herself tonight. And to think she was here when we arrived!" Cumberland took a relishing bite of his food and then gave Avenel a reproachful stare.

Avenel leaned back in his elbow seat and took a healthy swallow of the wine. Mutely he stared at Brienne, who for Cumberland's sake refused to even look back at him. Fuming, she begrudgingly took another bite of the delicious duck, but she was too angry to enjoy her meal. The awful realization that Oliver Morrow might be standing in the courtyard at that very minute, anxious to get back his house and discipline her, made her stomach curl into a hard, unyielding knot. And there was no relief in sight, for if he did not show up tonight, there was always tomorrow or the day after that. Slowly she bit into her soft lower lip, unmindful of those at the table.

Looking up, she found both men staring at her; then they switched their gaze to the painting that hung in back of her.

" 'Tis remarkable how little you resemble your father." Avenel leaned forward and examined her. "Seeing you both in comparison, why, no hair on your head is even remotely like his."

Nervously she looked down at the long burgundy curl that swept over her neck and bosom. "Many children do not look like their fathers."

"Perhaps."

"The earl claims me as his." She defended herself.

"Of course—he would. But in a case such as yours, my guess would be that only your mother would know for sure."

"What are you implying, sir?" She tried to look her most insulted and squelch the terrifying anxiety that threatened her.

"I mean nothing by it. Let us just say that your mother must have been terribly beautiful, and we all three know what the earl is like. It would not be hard to imagine—"

"Well, do not!" She stood up from her seat. "There

would be consequences for me if the earl should wonder
about my parentage. But if he believes I am his, then I am
his. I have not been informed otherwise!"

"Please, Lady Brienne, be seated." Cumberland stood
up. "It does you no good to get upset. We do not doubt
what you believe, do we, Slane?" He shot him another
reproachful look.

"I did not mean to offend you, my lady. Please rejoin
us." Avenel, still seated, pulled her chair out farther, and
Cumberland took the lead in seating her once more.

She gave in simply because she did not want to make
too much of the situation. *The less said, the more easily
it would be forgotten,* she thought. She resumed nibbling on the orange slices. More wine was poured, and
she gratefully took hers to her lips, seeking the soothing
effect it offered.

After the second course of fish in cream, the wine
helped her find her tongue once more. "Why are you
both so sure the earl will show up at all? It seems that he
lost Osterley fairly. What reason would he have for returning here? I can't let you continue to believe that he
would return for me. The truth is that he has not seen
me for years, and I daresay he does not even know I have
been at Osterley at all."

"He will show up." Avenel's face looked as if it were
chiseled from solid granite. "Do not think you are the
bait, Lady Brienne, for that gives you too much power.
You see, the earl will come here, but I can assure you,
not for you." At her puzzled expression, he started to
laugh. "Never fear, little one. We shall all be around here
long enough that you may come to find our company not
so distasteful."

"It's not Cumberland's company that I find distasteful,
sir." She slowly sipped her wine from the heavy crystal

glass and let her artless dark eyes toy with him. "And I daresay it will take a longer time than we have on this earth for me to find your company pleasurable." She heartily bit into a small roll made of white flour; her teeth showed clean and pearly as they pulled on it.

"You may change your mind. I have found 'tis not unusual for a woman to do so."

"Yes, but then, I am not like other women," she said smugly.

" 'Tis so." Avenel leaned toward her, speaking quietly and for her ears only. "And you may come to wish it were otherwise. For it may prove to be your downfall." He looked at her now; his silver-blue eyes did not miss a detail. They wandered ruthlessly across her sweetly tied *échelle* and finally rested at a point just below her shoulders, where the creamy tops of her breasts were exposed from the shallow lace edging her bodice.

Wishing she were provincial enough to don a concealing fichu and not have to remain under the dominion of his stares, she took another casual sip of wine and redirected her attention to Cumberland; she refused to please Avenel with so much as a blush.

"Tell me, how did you meet this . . . American, sir? Especially when you are so wonderfully British, I might add." She smiled at him beguilingly and was glad to see a faint, happy blush on the older man's lined cheeks.

"I suppose we seem an odd pair, eh, Slane?" Cumberland laughed and then tried to brush off her question. "We met on a ship, my lady. It was such a long time ago, I have completely forgotten how we started our friendship. But I fear I must correct you, my lady, for you could call me an American, also. For although I was born and raised here in merry old England, I have lived this past score of years in the Colonies. In Maryland, to be exact."

"Well, at least it does not show in you. If all Mary-landers were like him, they would have to keep you all in cages!" She knew the wine was making her rather bra-zen, but she liked its effect. Smiling at Avenel, she hoped to see a sign of anger, but there was none.

"Cumberland is not a . . . How did you put it?" he started in English. "Arrogant colonial beast," he finished in Welsh. He laughed out loud and placed some more raisin tart on his plate from the platter the footman of-fered him. "More, my comely Welsh lass?" He was infuri-atingly polite amidst her sputters as he made his offer.

"I suppose it would do me no good to tell you in French exactly what I think of you." She couldn't keep annoyance from showing on her face.

"Go ahead! I would love to know what you really think of me!"

"I shall decline then, thank you, for I have already heard the tale of you and Vivie's brother. I suspect it would be an exercise in futility." She stabbed at one of the tarts that the footman held out for her. Was there anything this overbearing man did not know?

The dinner was thankfully over soon after that. The men sipped brandy, while she was given tea in a large, wafer-thin porcelain cup. Soon her head started to droop; she was an early riser, and it was unusually late for her. She wanted to make her plans for tomorrow. Perhaps she would be able to get the key that lay un-reachable underneath Avenel's silver-embroidered waist-coat, she pondered. But at the moment she felt so over-whelmed by the claret she had drunk that her only real desire was for the cool, linen sheets that awaited her in the taffeta-hung room upstairs.

"I think she's done in, Avenel. We've worn her out," Cumberland could be heard whispering, but he seemed very distant, and she found she did not care what they had to say about her.

"I shall take her up, my friend. I'll rejoin you shortly." Avenel's chair legs squeaked as he stood up. Quietly he took her arm, and she allowed him to escort her out of the gallery. But before Brienne left, she kindly thanked Cumberland for his companionship throughout dinner.

"Why, it was my pleasure, truly." He bent and chivalrously brushed her hand with his lips. Then he watched them go and finally retook his seat as they neared the door of the gallery.

It was a short walk to the grand staircase and then up to her bedroom. They made it rather peacefully. She was unaware of how heavily she was leaning on Avenel's arm due to the wine she had drunk. Without really wanting to, she started to giggle.

"Methinks your friend Cumberland won't be dining with us again!" she spurted out, finding the whole situation at that moment very funny.

"And why not, you silly wench?" He took her by the waist, as they had reached her bedroom door, obviously determined to make the most of her jovial spirits.

"Why, his poor stomach must be churning from the bickering. It went on all evening long!" She laughed merrily.

"His stomach may be churning, but 'tis not from our bellicose ways. I believe he's quite taken with you, my wild one." He leaned closer to her and breathed in the clean scent of honeysuckle that lightly permeated her hair.

"He is so nice." Brienne was sincere. "He would be the father I wish for."

He looked at her for a long time after that, and her lids grew heavy as they stood by her door. But finally he spoke, asking in a gentle way, "Tomorrow, little one, I would like it very much if you would go riding with me."

She raised her heavy head to look at him in amazement. "I cannot believe my ears! You! Giving me a proper invitation to a proper activity and not to some lewd, licentious—"

"Will you?" He looked deeply into her eyes, and she felt that the wine must have affected him, too, for his eyes had warmed to a definite gray.

"All your gentlemanly courting is for naught, Master Slane, for I have never been on a horse in my life. I am sure that if I did, 'twould put the fear of God in me." She leaned her head back on the door to gaze up at him.

"I will teach you, then. You won't be afraid, and soon you will find it quite pleasurable. I have a very tame mare. She would not frighten a kitten."

She watched him as he spoke, then slitted her eyes suspiciously. "Master Slane, if I am reading you correctly, 'tis not only Cumberland is taken with me at the moment. I almost wouldn't know you."

He smiled at her; his teeth flashed white and brilliant, even in the candlelight of the hallway. Slowly he bent his head down to kiss her, but she quickly turned her head, somehow having anticipated his desire.

"I take it all back. 'Tis you after all," she stated after successfully dodging his advance.

He laughed and swung open her bedroom door behind her, making her almost lose her balance. Catching her firmly with both arms around her waist until she was steadied, he then let her go. But before he left her, he took her hand and bent over it, placing a soft, warm kiss directly in the middle of her sensitive palm.

He curled it up after he straightened, and she heard

him say as he was leaving, "Think of me, wildflower, when your head touches the pillow." Then he quickly descended the stairs, leaving her with no doubt at all that she would.

CHAPTER NINE

The largest bay stud Brienne had ever seen in her life loomed over her. His head nudged her playfully and rubbed his forehead across her stiff, frightened back.

"Ah! Stop that, you mawkish fool!" Avenel snapped at his mount and pulled his horse away from her. He handed the reins over to the young stableboy, Kelly, and then attended to her.

"I'm not sure they like me." She took a step back from the dappled mare, who was not as large as the stud but still as intimidating. "Perhaps we could do this another day?" She turned around, but much to her chagrin she found Avenel blocking her way.

"Are you a coward?" He looked down at her, and his eyes confirmed what he thought.

"Most certainly not! But I do not see the necessity of learning to ride." She shrugged her shoulders, tightly bound in a jacket that was too small for her. She hadn't had an occasion to wear the indigo-dyed wool jacket for

several years, and now she found it to be fitted for a
smaller girl than herself. The length was still fine, however; it fell well down to her knees and provided suffi-
cient protection to her violet wool dress. Still, she was
uncomfortably looped into it from the waist up, and she
was concerned that her movements on the horse would
cause the fabric to split. "Perhaps on another occasion?"
She twisted her shoulders once more, trying to find
some give in the weave.

"I would like a companion on my rides. That reason
alone should suffice." He tossed the reins on the mare's
bridle over the animal's head and placed them at the end
of the pulled black mane.

"Then could not Cumberland take these rides with
you?" She searched every avenue to avoid having to
perch atop that huge beast.

"Cumberland is not a young man, and I daresay he
would not find it pleasurable to jog in a saddle for hours
at a time."

"And you believe I will?" She looked doubtfully at
him.

He smiled; his lips curled with a boyish twist. "Perhaps not at first. But at least you are young enough to
weather the bumps and bruises well. Besides, the exercise will tire you out, so I won't have to listen to you
pace in your room when I visit the library in the evening."

"I have no need for exercise, nor for the accompany-
ing bumps and bruises," she said, her pretty lips curling
in disdain.

"It may not be so bad. I would think that, under that
bum roll you don, you're comfortably padded."

She gasped and glared at him like a startled, hissing
cat. How dare he be so crude as to mention her under-

things in the presence of a stablehand! She started to turn away from the horse, but Avenel blocked her way. He came just a little closer and rested his hands on the fine French leather of the mare's saddle. She was aware of the masculine scents of glycerine-rubbed saddlery and well-groomed horseflesh that clung to him. When he demanded her attention, Brienne made herself look at him so that her overcome senses could return to normality.

"If you would rather avoid testing out on the mare," he said, keeping her head caged between his arms. He then continued in Welsh, knowing full well that she was the only one in the stable block who could understand the dialect, "we could go back to my bedchamber and . . . you could ride me." He whispered this last statement, making her legs, which had seemed strong and mobile before, go weak. He bent down to her once again giving her a scent of that elusive masculinity that seemed to exude from his every pore.

Sputtering with embarrassment, she gave the stableboy Kelly an anxious glance to see if he had understood what Avenel had said. Gratefully, she saw that he was busy with Idle Dice, Avenel's large bay stallion. When she was free from that mortification, she turned on Avenel and said viciously, "You heathen! Speaking of such things to me!"

"Mayhap. But that still doesn't satisfy my curiosity. Is it the mare or me?" He gave her a cocky look that she fervently wished she could scratch off his face. But she knew there would be no way around his other offer if she refused the mare. So finally she complied and allowed him to give her a leg up onto the sidesaddle.

She quickly grabbed the reins but made them too short in her hands. The mare obediently started backing up, and there seemed to be no way to stop her from going all the way to London. Feeling terribly out of control, she didn't know what to do next, but Avenel comfortably took the lead, swinging easily into the saddle of his stud and taking a mild trot over toward the northwestern fields.

Much to her rising terror, the mare followed, progressing into a bouncing, jarring trot also. Brienne almost feared for her life, for she didn't have the vaguest idea how to go along with the miserable gait.

"Is it that you are trying to kill me now?" she screamed at Avenel when they finally stopped in a closely clipped pasture. She hung over the pommel of the saddle, relieved and grateful that the mount had stopped moving and was now standing calmly beside Idle Dice. "Is that the plan you've had all along?" Huffing, she tried to pull up her bodice, which had fallen during the uncomfortable ride. She then pulled the edges of her dark blue jacket closer together, noting that one of the frogs on it had become undone. Fastening this while she shot Avenel looks of molten rage, she firmly decided that learning to ride was utterly dispensable and that she would find another way to be free of the man.

"Just think of this, if it becomes too much for you Lady Brienne." He untied his shirt and pulled the shiny black cord from around his neck. He dangled the key seductively within her grasp, but she was not such a fool as to grab for it here. Balefully she tried to give the key and him her complete disregard.

"I will learn to ride, Master Slane," she conceded; the key held the power of persuasion, "if that will please you. Anyhow, riding is far better than anything else you've suggested, no matter how painful and awkward it is."

"Wonderful." He noted her forced compliance. "And to make it more comfortable, I will ask you to keep your hands loosely upon the reins and to hold them like so." He draped his reins over the right shoulder of his mount and then laced them through his little finger, holding his wrists at a relaxed angle.

"Good," he said when she begrudgingly emulated him. "Now, 'tis important for you to keep your hands down near her mane. You'll gain more control over her mouth, and it is more pleasing to the eye." He watched her lower her hands, and then he instructed, "Now walk her. Shift forward slightly in the saddle and nudge her with your calf."

She did as she was told, and miraculously the mare started to walk. "But how do I tell her where she should go?"

"A demure tightening on the left or right rein will suffice for now. You'll learn more effective ways later."

He sat on Idle Dice and watched as she and the mare went around him in circles. He showed her how to turn the mare around. Suddenly, feeling more in control, she wondered if she would like riding after all. It was a relief to be outside and away from Osterley. The day was a glorious repeat of yesterday; the blue azure sky provided lots of strong yellow sunshine. The air smelled of fresh grass, and it was truly a great spiritual uplift to be on horseback, looking at the faraway fields alternately of green alfalfa and bright gold flax.

"I think you've taken to her already," he said as she rode around him.

"What is her name?" She leaned forward and patted the side of the mare's dappled neck, forgetting her uncomfortable jacket and falling bodice in her pleasure.

"She has no name yet. You may name her."

"Me, name her? Then I will call her . . ." She bit on her lower lip with her gleaming front teeth, looking very much like a little girl trying to name her first doll. "I will name her . . . Queenie. She looks very much like a queen, don't you agree?" She looked up at him, her face full of happy anticipation. The sun had given her cheeks a pretty blush, and her eyes had never before seemed so full of light and so uncommonly purple.

Brienne was mildly puzzled by the way he watched her. It was as if she had done something extraordinary and he simply could not believe his eyes. But his look was quickly frozen over by his icy blue eyes, and he looked away, apparently finding something more interesting to gaze upon in one of the far-off clusters of oak trees.

The ride did not continue much longer after that. Gruffly, Avenel gathered his reins and bade her follow him back to the stable. He took off at another damnable trot, and Queenie instinctively followed him, despite the precarious seat of her rider. Inwardly, Brienne silently prayed that she would be able to stay in the back-twisting, awkward saddle. She tried with all her might to anticipate the next jolt and sway, knowing the embarrassment she would suffer if she fell off. It was with much relief and annoyance that she finally followed Idle Dice and his master back into the stable yard.

"Must I endure that maddening gait coming and going?" She shot him a sour look as his hands spanned her small waist and helped her to the ground.

" 'Tis the only way to learn to ride," he said abruptly. She watched as he handed Queenie's reins over to Kelly. Then Brienne almost stamped her foot in exasperation when he left for the house without saying another word.

She heard splashing from the Etruscan room and took this for a sure sign that the master of the house was bathing. Having fumed all day after their ride, Brienne had hoped for such a moment. Hiding in the niche between the state bed and the door to the south passage, she heard Avenel's voice excuse his manservant and finally the quiet splashing sounds of bathing.

Here was her last chance. The key lay as a gold temptation on the commode in the pier. She moved closer to it, hoping the firelight would not betray her. For through the cracked door to the elaborately painted dressing room beyond, Avenel sat just out of sight in a giant, oblong, copper tub. She pulled the hood from her cloak over her dark shining hair to lessen its reflection in the light. Then she quickly made her way across the bedroom to the key that lay enticingly bright atop the black japanned chest of drawers.

Taking her time, she took the key into her shaking hand and ever so slowly put it into the proper keyhole. There was an almost imperceptible click as the lock was sprung. Her heart beat so loudly in her chest that she was sure that even if Avenel had missed the sound of the drawer opening, he would not be deaf to the wild pounding in her chest. Hardly daring to breathe, she almost collapsed when the sound of trickling water from the Etruscan room stopped. She saw through the barely opened door of the dressing room that the shadows that had played with Avenel's movements along the opposite wall of the fireside were now still and cold.

But after a time, Avenel seemed to be assured that there was no sound from his bedchamber. His bath continued, and Brienne heard him scrubbing his chest with a sponge. Her lungs filled with badly needed air, and she trembled with relief. Returning to her task, she vowed to be even quieter, cursing the man in the other room for having an uncanny sense of hearing.

In complete silence she guided the drawer out far enough to spot the sparkling gems that encrusted her comb. She reached for it and enclosed it lovingly in her palm. She hid it among the folds of her cloak, smoothly rolled the drawer into its closed position, and placed the key back on the top, taking extra time to place the black silk cording around it in the same position as she had found it.

"That should fool him," she said to herself, happy with her work, "and give me some extra time." Slowly breathing in, she felt refreshed by the heavy, comforting burden of the comb near her side.

Turning to make her way out of the bedroom, she knew there would be one last obstacle to her freedom. That was once again getting by the slightly open door to the dressing room. Brienne knew he was finishing his bath by now, and she heard the water fall from his body as he stood up from the tub. Soon she heard him drying off with the household linens.

As she passed the dressing-room door, she saw that he stood with his back to her. The picture of him tall and naked before the fireplace lingered in her mind long after her eyes had passed it over. His wide, smooth shoulders rippled and flexed as he rubbed a towel over his damp hair, and his lean, powerful thighs tapered up to high, muscular buttocks that bunched with every motion. And then she saw that the hair on his legs seemed to become denser close to his groin. The very thought of that mysterious male flesh that almost appeared between his legs when he bent down to dry his legs made her blush.

Closing her eyes, she stumbled near the door to the

passage and grabbed at one of the columns on the bedstead to stop her fall. It was as if he had a sixth sense; she heard Avenel walk to the door of the dressing room and open it to see if something was amiss. Without even thinking, she pulled back against the darkened wall near the bedcurtains, hoping against hope that he would not come into the bedroom. She heard him pause uncertainly as he stood out of her sight in the doorway. Figuring he'd seen nothing out of place—particularly the gold key, which lay just as he had left it on the commode—she heard him start back into the dressing room to warm his naked body by the fire.

Moving like a timid rabbit, she went to the passage door and took an excruciating amount of time closing the lock behind her in an effort to be thorough. She would need all the time she could get, and she did not want to leave any traces of her having been in his room. Once in the south passage, she darted into the drawing room to hide from the old footmen in the hall. From there she peeked into the dimly lit long gallery. Finding it pleasingly empty, she found her way out the central door to the back of the house.

Once outside, she crept along the house to the stable block in the late twilight. There were no lights to be seen from any of its openings as it loomed before her, and she was amazed by her luck. Kelly was nowhere to be seen when she entered the stable, but Queenie stuck her gray head out from the closest stall to greet her.

Nervously patting the horse on her huge forehead, Brienne was momentarily stumped as to how to begin to tack the animal up. She walked over to where several saddles were stored against the wall, and seeing the only sidesaddle, she picked up the incredibly heavy leather piece and made her way back to Queenie's stall in the dark. She went back to the saddlery once again to search for the animal's bridle, but there she was completely confused: all the bridles and harnesses that lined the wall looked alike to her. Finally, exasperated, she took the closest one to her, thinking it would do just as well as any. She went back to Queenie and lugged the heavy saddle up onto her back, then went to the other side of the animal with the girth. After attaching this as tightly as she could, she examined the intricate bridle, losing several minutes of the precious dim twilight trying to figure out how to put it on the creature before her.

Turning the thing over in her hands until she thought she knew what to do with it, she slipped it over the mare's head. She was grateful that the animal took the bit automatically into her delicate mouth. But as she forced the crown piece over Queenie's attentive ears, Brienne was dismayed. She had gotten the wrong bridle after all; this one seemed horribly tight around the ears. But she congratulated herself for getting the confusing straps of leather onto the animal at all and silently led the mare out into the courtyard of the stable, thinking the tight bridle would do no harm.

Brienne was startled when Orillion ran up to her from the stable wagging his tail. Playfully, she scolded the dog for frightening her. They had become great friends since spending the night together in the stable block.

"Now, don't you tell that master of yours that you saw me, Orillion," she said as she bent down to pat him good-bye on the head. She stood up and gave one last look at the house; its enormous windows were lit up with the light of hundreds of candles. For a flashing, poignant moment, she stood in the darkness with Queenie's reins in her small hand.

A house like Osterley had much to offer a young girl

like herself who was starved for companionship and for a taste of the upper crust. But every time she found herself being seduced by the grandeur of Osterley, it wasn't the thought of Avenel that brought her out of the reverie, for he had yet to prove the ogre he seemed capable of being. But there was no relieving her mind of the imminent appearance of her father. She had much to fear from him. She wouldn't take the chance of meeting up with him, not even for the seductions of wealth and position.

Resigning herself to her fate, Brienne awkwardly managed to get into the saddle from the mounting block near the carriage drive. She took one last look at the Park as she turned her head toward the northwest woods. Then, with an uncomfortable feeling that there was still something left undone, she inexpertly guided Queenie into a steady walk.

Much too soon, however, she found that more skill was needed for horseback riding than one lesson could provide. Queenie's sensitive mouth rebelled against the tight bridle. The mare tossed her head constantly, chewing and salivating to ease her discomfort. The night noises—everything from an early hooting owl to a late-night gathering of squirrels among the tree branches—seemed to start the mare into an ungodly jog that left her passenger with absolutely no control.

They had hardly gotten past the first clump of trees when the animal calmed down. But then, as if seeing something utterly terrifying before her, Queenie came to a dead stop; her ears strained forward and her neck arched unnaturally.

"What is it?" Brienne whispered to the frightened mare. Becoming intimidated herself, Brienne nervously took the reins even more tightly in her hands, but there was no head response from the horse. Fearing what she could not see, she ungraciously kicked the animal's left flank, hoping to move her onward. Suddenly the animal reared forward in an effort to flee from whatever had scared her. Queenie wasted no time; she took off at a dead gallop toward a far clearing. In the mare's wild frenzy, Brienne was left terrified and, worse, completely unbalanced. There was nothing she could do to control her mount, and almost paralyzed with fear, she grabbed hold of the trim mane for dear life.

They reached the clearing in an impossibly short time; she was sure the crazed pace would be the end of them both. Rearing once again as they reached the darkened meadow, the terrified mare tested Brienne's ability to stay on her back. But she threw Brienne completely off balance, and the girl tumbled to the hard, black ground of the clearing, stunned and desperately trying to breathe with lungs that simply refused the air. Brienne watched as the mare, having disposed of her rider, galloped madly away into the dark surrounding forest, her tail held straight with fright.

Finally, when Brienne thought she would surely smother from lack of air, the cold night breeze swept into her chest. She sucked it in with terrifying quickness and lay there on her belly, panting and crying, until she heard hoofbeats behind her, coming from the opposite direction of where Queenie had gone. Not even daring a look behind her, all at once Brienne felt hopelessly frightened by the horseback ride, the threat of the earl, and the black rage that must surely be on the face of the man behind her.

"Damn you, woman!" Avenel whispered harshly as he dismounted. Swinging the reins angrily back into Idle Dice's face, the animal reared in fright as his master

threw a lather-covered whip to the ground behind her.
"You little fool! I should beat you senseless!" He stood
over her and looked down at her wracking shoulders; his
legs were slightly parted in an angry stance. He pulled
her up from the ground and tried to discover if she was
injured, but she violently turned away from his touch.

"If you have any decency at all, you will leave me
alone!" she cried out, her face muddied and stained with
tears. "Can't you see that I must get away from here?
Why must you continue to stop me?"

"We have been through this already. You may leave
when I am through with your father," he said sternly.

"My father! I'm no bait for my father! He hates me! He
abandoned me as a child! He will not come here for me
now," she said, trying not to reveal too much of her past.
Again those terrible parting words Lord Oliver had uttered echoed in her mind: *"I'll have you both, both,
both."* Brienne put her hands over her ears in an effort to
shut them out. How would she ever endure a visit from
her father? How had her mother been so brave?

"I have no need for you to entice the earl here. He will
show up whether you are here or not." Again Avenel
tried to pull her to her feet.

"Then you have another use for me in this demented
scheme? Pray tell, what is it?" She swerved from his
grasp and got up by herself, planning to run from him
and hide in the blackness of the surrounding woods. But
she did not get far, for her ankle had been wrenched and
was now swollen and weak. Falling squarely into his
waiting arms, they both fell to the ground; this time
Avenel's greater weight pinned her down.

"Where is the comb, Brienne?" He looked down at
her, his eyes glowing like two full moons despite the
dark, overcast sky.

"I don't have it." She tried to get up, but he wouldn't let her.

"Hand it over now, or I'll strip you naked as a babe in order to find it." He started with her cloak, pulling the hood from her back.

"No, please . . . wait!" He began on her bodice; the lace that edged her shift started to tear with his reckless-ness.

"Give it up, Brienne." He smiled a sinister smile and ran his hand lightly down the front of her chest.

"Oh . . . you're an absolute cad!" She wrestled with him, trying to keep him away.

But it was a futile exercise. Although her chest heaved from the exertion, he dominated her easily. With her hands held down, she groaned as she felt him loosen her laces. Her unsupported shift fell down to one shoulder, and then his warm, searching fingers roamed over the intimate swells and valleys within her bodice.

"Well, it's not in here," he murmured wickedly, his hand lingering over one of her breasts.

"Then stop touching me!" she demanded, blushing to the tips of her toes. But when he refused to comply, it was anger, not humiliation that drove her to the final rash act. Her teeth clamped down on his roving hand.

"Ugh!" Avenel grunted, and pulled his fingers from her teeth.

Angrier still now that he had forced her into such un-ladylike behavior, Brienne found new strength. While Avenel examined his bitten fingers, she wiggled from be-neath him, scrambled to her feet, and started to run.

"Use your teeth again, and I'll put you in a cage." With natural grace, his hand reached out and grabbed her pet-ticoats. There was a rending tear, and Brienne screamed as she felt several of her underskirts rip off in his grasp.

This tripped her up, and soon she was down again—but this time, on top of him.

"If you don't give up the comb, love, I'll be forced to rip everything off you. Shall I begin here?" He clutched the front edge of her bodice.

"Would you believe I've lost it? Perhaps it fell when Queenie bolted."

"A lady like you lose her only jewels? I think not." He swept the curtain of her hair away from her mouth. "Give me the comb, or suffer the consequences."

"I haven't . . ." Her words dwindled away as his mouth rose to capture hers. Violently she turned her head away. But by rejecting his advance, she only allowed him a better view of her gaping bodice as she lay over him. Eventually, however, her attention was called back to him—not because of the hungry stare that seemed to eat her alive, and not because of the grip that held her better than a ball and chain, but rather because of the roaming hand she felt on her backside. Beneath her ripped petticoats, Avenel's hand was ever so slowly sliding up her bare thigh.

"Is no place sacred to you? Dare you look even under my skirts?" she asked venomously.

"I dare" was all he said before his hand finally cupped her smooth, naked buttocks. The chill of the night on her skin, skin that was always warm and well protected under several layers of clothing, was a strange sensation. But the touch of his palm, like a brand on her flesh, shocked her to her very core. Yet as he fondled her, even her prudish core seemed to melt and grow hot with his expert caresses. Her unreliable body was betraying her again. She was so stunned that she hardly noticed that he'd begun to kiss her.

First her neck, then her chin, and finally her tear-stained cheeks accepted his gentle assault. Releasing an incoherent, shuddering plea, she felt his tongue, hot and enticing, in the hollows of her throat.

"Where is the comb, love? I fear, should we continue, that your first experience with a man will be in the cold, and on the ground," he whispered in her hair. His fiery hand still stroked the smooth flesh of her derriere.

"Damn you!" Half sobbing, she stood up and fumbled for her modesty. When her skirts were back down and her laces retightened, she slipped her hand into a hidden pocket in her cloak, and flung the comb at him. "May you rot in—!"

"Careful! We cannot have you talking like a lusty barmaid."

She watched through teary eyes as he took the jeweled hair ornament from the ground and placed it securely in the waistband of his breeches. She found bitter consolation in the fact that her escape had forced him to dress in a hurry. He'd obviously not even had time to tuck in his shirttails properly, nor to don a jacket, despite the coolness of the evening. Perhaps he'd freeze to death on his trip back to Osterley, she thought hopefully.

"How did you know I had gone?" she asked, not bothering to hide her hostility.

"I had a feeling that you were in my bedroom while I was bathing. I suppose that was when you got the comb. When you didn't appear for dinner, Cumberland went to fetch you and found you were missing. I guessed you had gone this way since the last time you tried to leave I saw you go in this direction from the gallery."

"Then the next time, I will try a different route." She backed away from him, wishing she could stop feeling so frightened of the future, but it loomed before her now, as dark and brooding as he was.

"There will be no next time." Without warning, he picked her up and placed her on Idle Dice's back.

"There *will* be a next time," she cried, beginning to dismount until he stopped her.

"There will not. I shall make sure of it." He shook his head and for once seemed to speak his mind. "You little fool, galloping off on Queenie in the middle of the night. Did you know you could have been dragged? As it is, you've injured your ankle getting it loose from the stirrup. I have seen it before—an inexperienced rider getting her leg caught and being dragged for miles. 'Tis not a pretty sight when they finally catch the horse." He snatched up her soiled cloak and swiftly mounted behind her. Quashing any further rebellion with the muscles of his arms, he wrapped the cloak tightly around her. He pressed himself so closely against her back that she was forced to ride on the pommel with her limbs resting on the animal's shoulder. They started back to Osterley, with Idle Dice taking a leisurely pace toward home.

"But what about Queenie? Hadn't we ought to fetch her?" she asked, looking back at him. His stony face made her heart stop.

"You should have thought of that when you stole her. The best we can hope for now is that she will make her own way back tomorrow and that we won't have to shoot her for a broken leg."

"I . . . meant to return her," she said softly, her voice trembling miserably.

"Did you, now?"

"I just cannot be here when the earl arrives. Why can't you understand that? All this would be unnecessary if you would just return my comb and let me go."

"Your fighting is for naught, Brienne. You run like a

panicked deer even though I have tried to make things pleasant for you during your wait.''

"But he will be here soon, and—''

"What makes you think Oliver Morrow will be here soon? He's been given so many handicaps, I should think it will take him a while to overcome them.''

"How long is a while?'' she persisted anxiously.

"He could arrive tomorrow; he could take several months. It all depends upon him.''

"Months!'' She was astounded. Her tears of frustration dried up in the wake of this new information.

"Perhaps,'' he added enigmatically, "so diminish this sense of urgency. I would think that if it takes him that long, you could become quite comfortable at Osterley— that is, if you would allow yourself to be.''

"I would know why you believe my father may take that long to arrive here?'' she demanded.

"He's in Maryland now,'' Avenel explained patiently. "With the war going on, he will be hard pressed to find a ship bound for the British Isles.'' He appeared to be enjoying his explanation, as if for some reason he were responsible for the earl's inconveniences. " 'Tis more than likely he will have to come up from St. Christopher in the West Indies, and that trip alone can take months. In all likelihood we have some waiting time, my wild-flower. Of that I can assure you.''

"But I cannot stay here overly long. It's not right.'' She raised her glossy auburn head. "What can you be thinking of?'' she asked, giving him a look of complete distrust.

"You don't want to know. 'Tis best,'' he said abruptly, and then changed the subject. "However, if leaving is your wish, you have the power to go at any time of the day or night. You may even have my coach at your disposal."

"Are you crazed? You tell me I'm your prisoner one second, and the next you tell me I may leave. Why did you follow me, then?"

"You did not earn the privilege to go, my love. Shall we again go through the motions that we wasted on the cold ground and reenact them in the warmth of my chambers?" He smiled and pressed against her; his hand went to her nape, as if in an effort to brush away her hair and ready her for a kiss.

"You have the comb. I see no further need to repeat that disgusting display." She grew stiff and pulled away from him as far as she could without taking another fall.

"Not even for your freedom? Of course, for that we would have to go further than we did this evening. We'd have to . . . shed that cloak of maidenhood, so to speak." His other arm tightened possessively beneath her breast. She was infuriated.

"If I were a snake, I wouldn't shed my scales for you." She tried to twist his arm from her waist but was grossly unsuccessful. He only laughed.

" 'Tis your choice. But in the meantime I've no appetite for racing around in the middle of the night to fetch you. If you persist in this vein, I warn you, I will keep you locked in your room." He looked down at her, but she could not read his expression at all. "Or better yet, locked in mine."

"How is it you think to get away with this? Despite my father's poverty, you still have no right to treat me, the daughter of an earl, this way, holding me prisoner, and then forcing me into . . . this evening's . . . activity." She found herself blushing, but this only made her that much more hostile. "There isn't a decent personage of the crown who would allow you to do this!"

"So where are all these noblemen? I must say, Brienne, you have an appalling lack of protectors. In fact, taking you has been the easiest task I've performed in the past twenty years," he mocked.

"You haven't taken me yet." The second she had uttered the words, she fervently wished she could take them back. It seemed she had all but dared him.

"True. But if you're anxious to start, we could play a game of hide and seek. You hide the comb, and I shall seek it. Only this time, I bid you to place it in a more provocative spot." She could feel his warm breath on her neck. His teeth nipped at the sensitive skin on the exposed part of her nape. When his tongue caressed her, her shoulders went up in self-protection.

He laughed. "How refreshingly naive you are, my love. Are you sure you do not want to gain your freedom tonight?"

No! she wanted to shout at him. Instead, she jerked her head toward Osterley's lights and watched them in bitter, stony silence. *How weak and naive I must appear to him,* she thought, hating herself. But at the very least she consoled herself with the fact that she hated him more.

CHAPTER TEN

When Queenie finally found her way home, she was not unscathed. Brienne watched on as the mare pranced about in the courtyard of the stable block with vines tangled in her usually impeccable mane and with many scratches on her finely boned legs, which seemed to spew dark red blood all over the alabaster pebbles lining the drive. Kelly calmed the animal down and soothed her by rubbing her silky neck with his palm until she could be brought into the stable to be treated. He did not cast any condemning looks at Brienne, but she almost wished that he had. She felt terrible that the mare had been so frightened and hurt. Brienne stared after the animal as she stood by the front steps to the house; her vision became blurred with tears of guilt.

"There, there, now. No occasion for tears." She turned to find Cumberland standing next to her, as he had been when Avenel brought the mare back. She could not stop tears from streaming hotly down her cheeks.

"It is because of me, you know. I suppose he has told you."

"Yes, he told me the entire story. But the mare will be all right. You'll see. She's just fussing now. She'll be like new soon." He took her by the shoulders.

"But she is bleeding." She hiccuped, feeling altogether miserable. "Avenel will never forgive me for hurting her." She turned her face from the older man's view. She didn't know why she should even want Avenel's forgiveness, but somehow it seemed very important.

"Horses are large animals. It seems like a lot of blood, but really it is not. She's back home now, and all in one piece. That's more than reason for you to be glad."

"But you saw Avenel's face when he led the mare home." Brienne shuddered, casting down her violet eyes that were reddened from crying and lack of sleep. "It was like the day we first met. He had that awful bloodthirsty look. Avenel hates me, I tell you. He absolutely hates me."

"There, there, love. He doesn't hate—" Cumberland tried to console her, but he was interrupted when she started to purge herself of all her horrible thoughts.

"I know. It's because of my father. Avenel somehow blames me for whatever has happened to him." She faltered. "Perhaps he is right. Perhaps there is something in my blood that makes me do the wrong thing. Things have never gone well for me, nor did they go well for my mother. It seems from as far back as I can remember, I have been running from my birth. Trying to avoid something that was terrible and obscene. Maybe I have Oliver Morrow's blood after all. I've always gotten curious looks wherever I've gone. People find me strange," she berated herself. "Perhaps I'm from the devil after all."

Flooded with self-pity, she ran down the steps, not wanting to hear Cumberland's words of reassurance.

Needing the fresh air and to be alone, she knew a long walk through the grounds would do her good. When she returned to the house later that evening, maybe she would find Queenie in an improved condition.

"How—how is she, Kelly?" It was dark by the time she finally appeared in the stable. Her hands felt like two clumps of ice, and her piquant face was chapped from the cold.

"Lady Brienne?" Kelly held the lantern up to see her small cloaked figure standing at the end of the stable.

"Is she still bleeding?" she asked tentatively.

"Why, that daft mare is doing just fine! But you must get yourself inside, my lady. It doesn't do to have you out here in the cold." His concern showed in his youthful blush; she guessed that Kelly could not be more than fifteen years of age.

"She will be all right, then? I—I saw her when he brought her back."

"She'll be stiff for a few days, but that serves her right —taking advantage of you like that. She ought to be whipped."

"No, really, it was all my fault. She's a lovely animal. It was a stupid mistake. I didn't know what I was doing." Brienne's lower lip trembled, and she knew she was getting herself upset all over again. She turned to leave, saying only, "Good night, Kelly. I'll check on her in the morning."

"Good night, Lady Brienne," Kelly called eagerly to her as she walked away. "And don't you be worrying over the mare. She'll be just fine—you'll see."

Brienne tried to smile and nod her head, but she found

she couldn't, so she walked back to the house in dismal silence.

When she went through the front door, she greeted the wizened footmen and then made her way wearily up to her room. All she wanted was to sleep and to stop her mind from going over and over again all the grim possibilities of her past. For a good part of the day she had sat on the marble bench near the house and wondered exactly what had caused all her troubles. She was Lady Brienne to all those around her, but she was dressed little better than a pauper and had no money of her own. She was homeless and had no relatives to speak of except the man who called himself her father. Yet he had never provided for her nor cared for her. And then there was the awful nagging question of her birth.

Her mind had flitted back and forth between the miniature in her chest of drawers and the portrait of the earl in the gallery. God, how she hated the thought of the earl's blood in her veins! She hated the man as much as Avenel Slane did. But to be illegitimate was too awful to think about. The shame that could be brought upon her was terrible to ponder. Her mother had always let her believe that the cruel man who had visited that time in London was her father. But perhaps that had been her mother's way of protecting her. If a man like the earl had reason to question her parentage, he could create grave consequences for both mother and child. Was she now learning the same lesson her mother had learned—that no matter how objectionable the earl was, she would have to accept him as her father? And that to do otherwise might prove fatal? Just thinking these thoughts made her head ache.

Now, up in her bedroom, she sat stiffly on the yellow settee wondering what she should do next. Vivie was nowhere to be found; she missed her cheerful companionship this evening. Glumly she stared down at her hands, which were now chafed and raw from the elements.

"Are you dining like that, my dear?"

She looked up and saw Cumberland standing timidly just outside the open door to her bedchamber. "Why, no. That is, I had not expected to go to dinner."

"I saw Vivie, and she is now pressing one of your dresses so that you can come downstairs for dinner." Cumberland made no move to enter her room. Instead, he stayed back at a proper distance.

"Well, I . . ." She shook her head. "Could you tell him that I am not feeling well? I just cannot tonight." She frowned and looked into the fire.

"If by 'him,' you are referring to Avenel, you need not worry. He won't be joining us tonight. He has just left."

"Left? Where has he gone?" She raised her eyes inquisitively.

"He's gone to London."

"Because of me? Because of what I did to Queenie?"

"No, no, my dear! He has been planning to renew some old friendships. I don't expect he will be back for some weeks."

"Weeks?" she repeated dumbly. Now, why did his going away bother her? She should be elated, but oddly enough, she felt even worse than she had before. She felt empty. Was she developing a liking for that cold, hard man? Was it possible? Then, as if to deny this, she said almost too brightly, "If it's to be just the two of us, then I shall be delighted to come downstairs to dine with you, if you will give me some time to make myself presentable."

"Why, of course. And you must excuse me for being

so forward as to come upstairs like this." He blushed, and his wrinkled, pink cheeks took on an iridescent glow. "I just was not sure if I would see you downstairs otherwise. Perhaps you can forgive me?"

"Of course. It need not be mentioned again." She smiled at him tenderly. Through all her troubles, he aways seemed to be the one who was on her side. She knew he cared for her despite his compliance with Avenel. His thoughtfulness at times was quite touching.

"Thank you, my lady. You are too gracious." He bowed and then said as he left, "We will dine in the breakfast room tonight, if that is all right with you. It's a smaller room, and I think it will be more suitable to both our temperaments."

"It sounds like a wonderful idea. I won't be long," she called to him and got up off the settee, feeling determined to have a pleasant evening.

She had just started to brush out her hair when Vivie came in with her freshly pressed dress. The two women chatted gaily about various things, but when Vivie mentioned Avenel's trip, Brienne once again grew quiet and thoughtful.

"He will be back before you realize it, *ma demoiselle.*" The little maid relaced her stays, which had become loosened during the day.

"It's none of my concern whether he comes or goes." Brienne tossed this off, trying to be light.

"I see. But perhaps you will change your mind when he returns. I am sure he will not come back empty handed," Vivie said mysteriously.

"He is bringing something back with him?" Brienne questioned. When the petite maid did not continue, her curiosity was roused. What was it? An awful thought occurred to her. Perhaps he was bringing back not something but someone. She ruled the earl out as a possibility after their conversation last night on Idle Dice. But then who else? Was it a woman? Was he going to humiliate her by parading her as his mistress in front of another woman—a woman he was courting? Was that what Vivie was speaking of? Brienne mentally shook herself. She was becoming obsessed. She concentrated on getting ready for dinner and refused to think of anything even remotely related to the master of Osterley.

"You are too lovely, my lady." Vivie smiled at her when she was ready to go downstairs. "Even that sad little dress cannot detract from your fairness. But perhaps we will get rid of it anyway."

"I'm afraid that by the time I can afford to buy another dress, this one will have so many holes it will resemble my polonaise." Brienne looked down at her tired violet wool gown and reminisced. "My mother had a wonderful gown once. It was woven entirely of silver threads. It had tarnished by the time she had to part with it. There were enormous hoops, much like those of an old-fashioned farthingale; they were worn with it to hold out the material. Then everyone could see how it sparkled in the light. She must have been so beautiful. My mother was even presented at Court, you know. Of course, that was before she married . . ." Brienne looked up and gave a little laugh. "It's funny the things you remember from the past. None of them seems to have any meaning."

"They have meaning. It just takes time to know what it is," Vivie said affectionately. Then, eyeing the clock on the mantel, she said rapidly in French, "Now you must go! The poor Monsieur Cumberland will be on his third brandy by now!"

When Brienne found her way to the breakfast room, she was pleasantly suprised by the cozy atmosphere created by the cheerful fire. It was reflected in the two particularly fine Adam pier glasses. The room was small enough to allow the candlelight to be reflected, creating a magical glow not otherwise possible. She entered the room, and Cumberland jumped up to seat her in one of the lyre-back chairs, covered in delicate needlework.

"Feeling better, are we?" He sat opposite her at the old gateleg mahogany table that had been brought in from the passage.

"Much. I should check on Queenie in the morning, but Kelly told me she will recover quickly." She smiled as the footman filled her footed glass with a heavy claret.

"Wonderful to hear that. I don't like to see you so distressed by half. I wanted Slane to stick around, thinking he could cheer you up, but he felt he had to go."

Hearing Avenel's name, she calmly took from the platter that the footman held out for her, not caring what it was she put on her plate. As she picked at the food, she inquired, "He was planning this trip?"

"In a matter of speaking. You see, he has a cousin on his mother's side of the family in London. He felt it was time to pay her his respects, you see."

"I see." She took a hearty sip of her wine.

"I expect he'll be bringing her back with him. He mentioned something about a ball he wanted her to help him with. To get reacquainted with the gentry, as it were." Cumberland seemed to be enjoying his meal; he took large, vigorous bites of the sauteed prawns.

She found this news strange. "Reacquainted? I was not under the impression he had been acquainted at all. I thought you both had just arrived here in England."

"Ah yes, that's true. But . . . ah . . ." He nervously twitched his brow, searching for words. "Well, it's a long story and much too tedious for me to tell at this time of the evening." He gulped down some claret and then abruptly said, "I think you will like Slane's cousin. Rose is a wonderful woman, as lovely as they come."

She saw Cumberland's eyes light up at the mention of the woman's name. "It's hard to think of Avenel as having relatives—especially nice onces." She knew she sounded bitter, but she couldn't help herself. If he had such a lovely cousin waiting for him in London, what was he doing at Osterley tormenting her?

But Cumberland merely laughed, finding her comment terribly amusing. "Yes, I suppose to you it does seem an impossibility. But she is a fine one, that Rose. I am sure that when you meet her you will agree. I expect you two ladies will get along famously."

"Yes. Especially when she learns that I am being held prisoner here. That should warm me to her heart." Brienne pushed away her food and stared angrily into her wineglass. An abysmal silence followed, and even Cumberland seemed to lose his appetite at her accusation.

"Listen, my child, you mustn't let yourself go on in this overwrought state."

"I cannot continue in this vein!" She pleaded with the elderly gentleman, "Can you at least tell me what he wants? Can't you tell me now so that I can give him—"

"I cannot. Do not ask me for that, because I cannot tell you anything without revealing what he has kept a dear secret." He reached over and took her smooth, young hand in his wrinkled one. "It's nothing as bad as you may fear."

"But he is living in a fantasy, thinking I can stay here indefinitely to wait for my father! It's pure folly. What will be the explanation for my presence here during all that time? His cousin is to arrive. What will he tell her? What can he tell her but that I am his mistress? And he will have to continue telling that story until it is so!" She stood up and walked over to the gilt pier glass and looked at herself. The girl who stared back looked tired. There were deep hollows in her cheeks, and her eyes had faint lavender smudges underneath them from worry. "But I tell you that will never be so. I will not be a man's plaything. I think it would be more pleasant to die first." She thought of the earl, and her mouth formed a grim, straight line.

"Do not say such things." There was heaviness in Cumberland's voice, and his guilt feelings were betrayed. "It will not come to that. Avenel is not one to force himself upon a woman. He can be quite the gentleman if he wishes. And I know he has tried to see to your comfort."

"Yes, he has." Once again she felt cheated out of her anger. "It's just that something is going to snap." She faced him and looked directly into his aged, understanding eyes. "I'm aware of how my situation must appear to you both. I have nowhere to go. I admit I have no home. I must seem terribly pathetic and helpless to you both in my threadbare gowns, which I wear night after night, and my sad lack of funds. But yet I am not so helpless as to go blindly along with this game we are playing. I know something is being set up here. And I know I am the one who will receive all the punishment."

"You admit you have nowhere to go." He shook his head in bewilderment. "Is it not better then that you remain here, where you will be taken care of and looked after?"

"But for how long? Until this charade has ended? Then what?"

"It's impossible to tell you what will be then." He walked up to the glass and watched her, and his voice softened. "I realize that Avenel is a terrifying man. He is filled with anger and hatred toward your father. And for the time being, he cannot always separate you from the earl. The times when he has been able to, he feels guilty —as if by accepting you as anything else but Oliver Morrow's daughter, he has betrayed his past and his purpose. But I also think that, given time, he could find you to be his salvation. He has a penchant for you, one that I have not seen in him before." He finished softly. "I know you better each day, my lady, and I know you could never resemble your father in any manner. As strange as this may sound, I think you can bring Avenel the peace he deserves."

"Tell me what he did," she whispered almost inaudibly. "What did the earl do? I want to understand this."

"It's not my story to tell." Cumberland backed away and placed his thumbs in his green brocade waistcoat. "But I would like to tell you this, if I may." He took a paternal stance and continued. "It is my wish that you try to be comfortable here, even if you have to take each day as it comes. That will be beneficial to all of us during these trying times. I cannot stand to see you so unbearably upset. Even if it is just to please a wizened old man, I hope that you could find this life agreeable enough to tolerate it, if only for a short amount of time."

She listened to him throughout his speech, and when he stopped speaking, she could not help but smile in a soft, affectionate way. He stood before her so anxious to please and yet so worried that she would not be. She actually got a feeling of what it must be like to have a father, one who absolutely doted on her.

"I suppose I can try, but only for a while," she said eventually. "I must say, it should be much easier if

Avenel is to be gone for a few days." She gave a wry little laugh, and soon Cumberland joined in.

"I promise to make it as enjoyable as possible, my dear." He held out her seat for her to return to the table. "So for now let us both try to forget your situation here and relax! How does that sound?".

"I can promise at least to try," she said reluctantly. Reclaiming her seat, she suddenly wished fervently that Cumberland were the owner of Osterley. She let out a small, undetected sigh. How much simpler things would be then, without that flinty-eyed man now in London.

CHAPTER ELEVEN

It was the most wonderful time of her life. Before Avenel returned to Osterley Park, the winter sky held the promise of snow, but miraculously none came. It seemed that this winter, February's Nordic winds and tedious white landscapes were destined never to materialize. Although Brienne still had to dress in her heaviest worsted petticoats and jackets, it was possible for her to continue the walks about the grounds that she enjoyed so much.

During one of these walks, she came upon the groundsbuildings that faced the lawn. The Temple of Pan, she had decided, would be the perfect place to read in blissful solitude. Entering another groundsbuilding, the Doric Orangery, she found to her delight that a few neglected trees were making a brave attempt to blossom. The other trees sat in their jardinieres withered and dead, but they provided a perfect foil for the wispy, gentle white blossoms of the more hearty plants. Brienne breathed deeply, filling her nostrils with the mineral scent of cold soil, the burned fragrance of dried wood branches, and then the overriding, sweet fragrance of orange blossoms reaching their peak. Before she returned to the house later that afternoon, she made a decision to take care of the trees herself. As long as she was being forced to stay at the park, she rationalized, she should have a respectable occupation to fill her time.

With her new hobby of keeping "springtime" astride at the Park, Brienne found that the days passed with wondrous speed. Her evenings, if not spent with Cumberland in the large, well-stocked library near the eating room, were whiled away quietly with Vivie in her room. The anxiety that had plagued her since her first encounter with Osterley's new master was less immediate now that Avenel was away in London. And this made her much more companionable. She and Vivie spent many an evening sharing reminiscences of their homes and their families, now so far away from them both. During their time together, they became more than servant and mistress; they became friends.

The memory of Avenel Slane and his dominating presence was becoming a dim specter in her mind. There were times when she forgot about him completely and failed to realize that his return was more likely with every passing day. Even now, as she walked through the frostbitten kitchen gardens to the neoclassical outbuildings, she was unaware of a procession that moved along the pebbled carriage drive at a dignified pace.

Her thoughts far from the goings-on at the front of the house, she walked over to the small Doric Temple of Pan and entered it through the unlocked door. There was a soft smile on her face as she peeked into the shabby, interior; her mind flooded with happy memories as she pictured her mother near her in the tiny, beautiful building. Brienne herself must have been only four years old at the time, and her memories of that day were just precious fragments in her mind. Unlike now, it had been a spring day, and the Doric building had been flooded with brilliant sunshine. The light had poured through the large eight-paned windows, and she and her mother had sat on brocade cushions as her mother read to her from a book.

Portraits of Sir Isaac Newton and Colen Campbell, the great architect, faced her as Brienne entered the doorway. She saw her mother pointing them out and telling her things about the studies of science and art. But now, more vivid than that image in her mind were the feelings that it aroused. Security, peacefulness, and the feeling of being loved were very strong in this little room. Brienne adored being there as her eyes feasted on the stuccoed elemental scroll frames of air, fire, earth, and water, and the medallion heads that represented spring, summer, autumn, and winter respectively.

She was drawn into the room. The servants, who had noted her penchant for the temple, kept it as warm as they could by attending to the small fireplace. Still, the floor was cold and dusty. But she piled the sadly faded brocade cushions upon it and sat as if it were once again springtime and not the gray middle of winter. With her body at ease, Brienne lifted her sweet, rose-colored lips, softly revealing a smile of remembrance. She had intended to read, but instead she pulled her loosely bound hair over her shoulder, took a thick plait into her hands, and untwisted it until it was undone. Feeling almost sleepy, she dropped her tresses from her hands and lay back on the cushions to gaze at the geometrics on the ceiling; her deep burgundy hair cascaded around her face like the most expensive and rare of furs. Coaxed and caressed by the remembrance of better times, her eyelids soon grew too heavy to keep open. Though she knew the room was no place for a nap, she let out a soft, inaudible sigh and fell into a deep, dream-filled sleep.

Two tender, warm lips made their way across her bare throat, taking an excruciating amount of time to find their mark. Brienne felt the full force of them on her mouth. Not daring even to breathe lest she wake up from the sensations burning within her, she allowed her lips to part so that the magical beast before her could seek his pleasure further, thus increasing hers to an intoxicating level. In the fog between sleep and reality, she imagined she was being kissed by Pan himself, who had wandered in from the woodlands and was playing upon her as if she were his flute, made from the reeds that grew along the lake.

Much too soon the kiss was over, and the warm mouth left her. She cried out to have it back, finding it as dear to her as the bread and wine that offered sustenance. But when her eyes opened, her cry quickly became one of alarm as she gazed up into Avenel's darkly lashed, cold, blue eyes. He laughed in a slow, relaxed manner, showing strong, even teeth and a clean-shaven jaw. Moving down on her once again, he leaned on his elbows and took her head in both his hands.

"I have found a wood nymph, it would seem. Are you from the forest, or did you arise from one of the far meadows?" He bent to kiss her once more, but this time she refused to comply and pulled her head from his grasp.

"Must you steal upon me like this?"

Undaunted by her rejection, he once again took her head into his palms and gazed into her eyes.

"Tell me you have missed me, wildflower. I have missed you." He bent down and placed a soft kiss on her slightly retroussé nose.

"I find that hard to believe—and harder still to believe that you have not sated your desires in London."

"Desire is a strange thing." He rolled from her and also lay on his back, gazing toward the ceiling. "Sometimes 'tis a very difficult thing to appease."

"As long as it is with someone else." Brienne sat up and pulled her hair to one shoulder so that it would be more manageable. She started to stand when one strong arm grabbed her by the waist, and she was pulled on top of him with her hair nearly covering his starkly white linen shirt. There was a distinct hardening of flesh between his thighs as she lay on top of him, and even his doeskin breeches, her petticoats, and the front of her bum roll could not sufficiently hide his maleness.

"Is that your wish, little one? Was there not one night among these many that you did not long for a man's attention? Is your lovely body so untried that you are blind to the pleasures before you?"

"Please, I don't want you to hurt me," she said softly, hoping he would not be induced to go further. "It's shameful what you speak of." She looked at him with heavy-lidded, watchful eyes.

"Always the lady, despite your rags." He pushed his hips even more intimately against her and said, "There will be no forceful gestures, my lady. But if you desire a liaison, I can promise you pleasure beyond your wildest imaginings. And there will be no pain except that which must be sacrificed in order to begin."

"You speak like a fool! I know it to be different. It's a horrible, painful ordeal that must be suffered through.

My mother ran from it, and she taught me to run from it. I will not succumb to your lovemaking." She gazed defiantly into his steely eyes, pursing her shapely lips as if to keep them from him.

" 'Tis understandable what your mother tried to avoid. But I do not believe she always ran away. There was one time when she wanted to be caught." As if in a trance, he palmed the long, auburn tresses hanging down from her shoulder, admiring their unusually rich color.

Squirming uncomfortably, she said, "The earl has shown me all I need to know of men and their ways. I have no need for either."

"All men are not the same. You wrong me by comparing me to your father. I have nothing in common with him, not even as a man."

"This is not something I want to find out—so if you will release me?" She pulled up from him, arching her back, but her breasts threatened to spill out from her round-necked bodice if she moved farther away. She distinctly distrusted the gleam that suddenly appeared in his eye.

"Give me a welcome kiss, wildflower. 'Tis what I have waited for and dreamed about." There was a deliciously wicked smile on his handsome face and she knew better than to comply.

"You're daft! You've been away from Osterley for so long, you've forgotten how it is between us."

"I have not forgotten the key. Or have you taken the opportunity while I was away to claw through the lock on my commode and retrieve your comb?" He raised one black eyebrow at her.

"So you admit it's my comb after all," she said smugly. "Perhaps then you will concede to giving it to me?"

"I admit nothing. 'Tis your comb when you have

earned it. Until then, I will call it your comb, for it is seemly to do so, and because the piece suits you so well."

"If it suits me, then give it to me. Surely you have given gifts to certain women in your doubtful career. Why must this be different?"

"You are not a trollop," he answered, looking strangely defensive.

"But I must behave like one to get it back."

"I suppose that is subject to different interpretations." In an instant she was tumbling to the floorboard as he abruptly got to his feet. He stood over her dazed and disheveled figure and then bent down to retrieve his topcoat from where he had discarded it earlier. "Have Vivie make you presentable. We have guests, and I expect you in the drawing room in less than an hour."

"Who?" she inquired, completely flustered.

"My cousin is here, and . . . some friends from London."

"I see. Cumberland mentioned you would bring her back. I suppose this is the test—to see if I can stand being humiliated as your whore—"

She found herself suddenly being grabbed from the floorboards and shaken so that she felt her head would spin off her shoulders. Finally when he took his hands from her, all he could do was shove on his wrinkled topcoat and say, " 'Tis not for you ever to say such things. It does not become you, and I will not have it."

She opened her mouth, but before she could get out a reply, he took her by the arm and started leading her out of the small groundsbuilding toward the house.

"Say no more, little one. Reality has slapped us both in the face once again."

"Venetia has gone upstairs with the rest of the guests. I suppose the journey has worn them out." A pretty, blond-haired woman spoke as Avenel entered the elaborate drawing room. He walked underneath the plastered ceiling with its writhing golden sunflower and rays of curling ostrich feathers. The pink, gold, and green ceiling motifs were echoed in the rich Thomas Moore carpeting underneath, and the entire room was so full of studied movement that even the dated rococo curves of the seat furniture seemed in place.

Avenel sat down in one of the gold serpentine chairs covered in swirling silk damask and hung his head tiredly before him. He ran an agitated hand across his jaw and began to speak. " 'Tis good. Let them rest. I'm afraid we will need this time to talk."

"Why, whatever is the matter, Avenel? I haven't seen you so worked up since Christopher died. And as you well know, I have been a widow now for almost twenty years." From the fading sunlight of the window, lines were seen on the beautiful woman's face, but it could not be discerned whether these were from worry or aging.

"In many ways, 'tis like when Christopher died, Rose."

She stood up from the tea table and walked toward him. "Whatever can be that bad? It was a brutal death that your brother and my husband suffered. But he is dead and has found his release."

"But it seems there is no release found for us."

"What is it, Avenel, that makes you speak so bitterly? You have Osterley back. And when Oliver Morrow shows his blackguard face here, you will have it all back.

It was worth fighting for. I can believe it was worth dying for."

He grabbed her hand and placed an affectionate kiss on its back. " 'Tis been hard for you all these years. So unnecessarily hard and lonely." He looked up into the older woman's face and then said, "I always knew Christopher would have the finest of women. You are the finest, Rose. My one comfort is that he was a happy man until the day he died."

"We were happy. But now I must continue without him. However, I confess that I haven't been quite as fortunate as you. I cannot imagine a lovelier room. With all his vile ways, Oliver Morrow certainly made Osterley into a palace. It's not the place we were told about as children, is it?"

"No, 'tis not the same place," Avenel said darkly. "There is something I must tell you, Rose. When I came back here, the house was not empty."

"He is not here, is he? You would not bring me here!" She gave him a sharp look of alarm.

"No, Oliver Morrow is well and away in America. Never fear that I will ever allow you to set those lovely eyes on him. You may rest easy."

"Then what are you trying to tell me, Avenel? What has gotten you so upset?"

"There were some things I did not know about him. He was married for a short while. There was a wife and apparently a child. They left him a long time ago. But when I arrived at the Park, the child had returned. His daughter was here . . . when I came back." He gave Rose a deep, probing look.

"My God, how awful!" She shuddered. "What did you have to do to get rid of her?"

"I have not gotten rid of her. I have made plans for her."

"Plans? But surely you cannot keep her here. Why, how can you even stand to look at her face day after day? That horrible reminder of—"

" 'Tis the damnedest part!" He kicked the chair out from him and walked over to a marble-topped mixing table to pour himself two stiff fingers of brandy. He took the liquor in one quick medicinal gulp and placed the glass down heavily on top of a demilune rosewood commode that pictured Diana and her hounds.

"I have never seen you so!" she exclaimed, walking over to him.

" 'Tis her face! She has the fairest face I have ever set eyes upon. She could bewitch anyone." A small, knotted muscle near his jaw started to twitch, and his eyes looked down solemnly. "Sometimes I think it must be the devil himself that has me by the throat. I have the earl's daughter right underneath my hand, and yet does she repulse me? On the contrary, I find that I am drawn to her. 'Tis as if Oliver Morrow had created her just to ensnare me."

"But no matter how comely the girl may be, surely the offspring of the earl—" Rose interjected, not knowing how to comfort him.

"I would have thought so. In the time we have been together, I have searched for that one gesture or expression that would show her paternity. Just one thing that would turn me away from her. But there is none, I tell you! Every smile, every laugh—even her tears bear no resemblance to the man! She is as winsome as they come. If it were not so foolhardy to believe otherwise, I would swear to you right now that she is not the daughter of Oliver Morrow." He sat down on a matching settee and held his head in his hands.

"Cast her from here then, Avenel. Make her leave. She has no rights upon this place. Not even the right to be here." She bent down to stroke his dark head, the one that so closely resembled his late brother's.

"But think of it. I must get Morrow to come here and make his confession to his peers. How much simpler it will be if I am holding his only child! His only offspring. I cannot let her fly the coop just when I need her the most."

Rose frowned. "But have you considered the possibility that she may not be his daughter? Perhaps that is why no one has heard of her. Then what have you? Merely more aggravation."

"She may not be his natural daughter. But the earl claims her as his. I have spoken to his solicitor. He has told me that in the earl's will she is named as heiress. So even if she is no relation, her downfall will be felt by Morrow. As long as he thinks she is his daughter, she is too valuable to let go."

"What have you planned for her?" There was a long moment of silence in the room, but when Avenel did speak, he evaded her question.

"There has been some difficulty with her trying to run away. However, I find I cannot keep her locked up as if in jail. I must start entertaining, because it is the only way we can recover our place here at the Park. Therefore, I will need your help for the next few days until the ball."

"What is it you want me to do?"

"I must find a plausible story for the girl. An explanation for her presence here. I cannot pass her off as a maid, and I am afraid with Venetia and the other guests here, she is going to be seen. There is no avoiding that. The only thing I have right now is that no one seems to know that the Earl of Laborde has a daughter. Thus her story, if she ever chose to tell it, would not be believed.'' He turned to his cousin and took her by the arm. "This may gall you at first. But I want you to pass her off as a relation from America.''

"You are jesting with me!''

" 'Tis the only way. If I claim her as a mistress, Venetia would be capable of anything. You know she has been coveting me and my purse since I arrived in London. I cannot handle any more unruly females.''

"But I have not seen the Colonies for twenty years! I came back to England after Christopher died. No one will believe me.''

He took her fragile, doe-eyed face in his hands and said, "Cousin, I'm afraid everyone would believe you. You see, that is your trouble. 'Tis just that way.''

"I won't be able to keep up the appearance. I shudder just thinking about that wretched girl. How can I look upon her and be civil, let alone pass her off as a loving relation?''

"It may take you time. But as I said before, she is winsome. I believe you may even come to like her, despite your feelings now.''

"Such blasphemy! How dare you say such things! She must be a witch for you to speak so.''

"Perhaps she is. Do not think the possibility has not occurred to me. Will you go along with me, Rose? I should not ask you to do such a thing, but I believe it will be worth it in the end.''

"Whatever you should ask of me, Avenel, I would do without a qualm.'' She softened further. "I have not wanted for anything since Christopher was taken from me, and I know there must have been times when you needed the coins more than I did." She sighed and took one of his hard hands into her own silken ones. "She can be my long-lost cousin from America, Master Slane. But do not ask me to like her. That I cannot do."

"Ah, Rose, 'tis not much I've left of my family. But what I have is more than enough!" He laughed, appearing very much relieved, and irreverently patted her behind.

"Avenel! Remember your place! We are not children anymore, playing on the harbor!" She laughed quite girlishly, and arm in arm they walked to the settee to have their refreshments.

CHAPTER TWELVE

Brienne sat on a stool while Vivie brushed out her hair with long luxurious strokes. Her nerves jangled at the thought of meeting the houseguests Avenel had told her to prepare for. She had donned the robin's-egg blue gown but she quickly tore it off in utter disgust. She would not wear it again! Even the ripped and torn polonaise was beginning to look good to her, if just for a change. Eventually she settled on the violet wool and her petticoat of burgundy red. She was sitting in this worn-out attire when there was a heavy knock on her door.

Without allowing her even a moment to consent to his entry, Avenel walked into her room and startled Vivie into a spurt of French.

"Mon dieu! Bonjour, Monsieur Slane! *Bonjour!"* Vivie greeted him in flustered speech.

"Vivie." He gave the small maid a nod and then turned his attention to Brienne. His eyes did not miss a single curve beneath her violet dress nor the luminescent gleam of her hair. She could not help but note that he looked splendid in breeches and coat made of lustrous slate blue satin. His waistcoast was of simple silk brocade, but the color was like molten silver. He cut an imposing figure as he stood towering over her.

He waited for Vivie to make a discreet departure and leave them alone; Vivie needed no prompting. She gave her mistress a concerned look and then swiftly left the yellow bedchamber through the jib door in the dressing room.

Gathering her unruly dark hair to one shoulder, Brienne stood up, feeling self-conscious. He had never presumed to enter her room before. She found she could do nothing but wait for him to address her.

"My cousin, Rose, has arrived. She is going to be your salvation during the next few days, so I'll not tolerate any disrespectful outbursts where she is concerned." He made himself comfortable on the yellow settee. "I also will be having other guests as the days progress, and I want you to understand that under no circumstances are you to reveal your relationship to Oliver Morrow. Not only will you not be believed, but it will cause me great embarrassment. If that should happen, you will then have my full wrath to deal with, and I will not tell you what that is like. I will simply leave it to your imagination. Do you understand all of this?"

"Thoroughly," she quipped.

"Good." He shot her a particularly wicked smile and continued. "I will not tolerate any bad behavior these next few weeks. If you make any attempt to run away now, I will tell my guests you are crazed, and I will send you to the nearest asylum. Am I making myself clear? I have no desire to keep you locked up here all the time, but if you cannot comply with my wishes, so be it."

"Perhaps the asylum is the better choice." She twisted her hair nervously as she baited him.

"If you're looking for degradation and abuse, I think we could hand it out here just as well. Now I ask you, will you comply?" His eyes had narrowed dangerously.

"Perhaps." She answered him with one stiff word. Once again he had the upper hand. In so many ways, Avenel Slane was the strangest of men. There were times when he was being especially kind that she felt as if she could forget her circumstances here at the Park. But now, just hearing his tone of voice made her sink back into anger and frustration.

"I hope so." He stood up after her ambiguous assent and pulled something from his coat. He walked over to her dressing table, where she stood, and flipped the article onto its satinwood top. She gave a small cry when she saw her comb gleaming in the firelight. She grabbed for it, but before she could take it, he took her hand in a viselike grip and made her turn to him. " 'Tis only for the evening, my lady. Remember, I'll be with you until it comes off tonight." He let her go and watched as she brushed out her hair and placed the comb in its upsweep.

It felt wonderful to have her mother's comb back, even if just for the evening. Her eyes sparkled like the very amethysts held in her hair. It made her feel not quite as shabby as she had before, and she held her head a bit higher when she turned to face Avenel. She was not, however, prepared to meet the diamond-hard eyes that were burning through her with what could only be called unveiled lust. Quickly she looked away, not knowing how to react.

"Come, they are waiting for us," he said after a long, painful pause.

As they entered the drawing room, Cumberland was sitting near the fireplace between two of the most beautiful women she had ever seen in her life. On his right sat an older woman, an angelic blonde attired in an ornate gown of figured silk. There was a serene, amiable quality about her, and Brienne felt drawn to her instantly.

The second woman could have stepped right out of *The Ladies' Magazine.* She was most fashionable in her ornamented powdered hair and ice pink tabby polonaise. Strands upon strands of diamonds were woven through her wig and dog-collared around her neck. She possessed tiny brown Pekingese eyes that bore an uncanny resemblance to those of the small pampered lapdog that looked up defensively from the folds of her quilted cream satin petticoat.

"Is this a new custom at Osterley? I thought scullery maids belonged in the kitchen." The white-haired woman gave her hand to Avenel, which he brushed with a perfunctory kiss.

Brienne's face burned from the woman's insult, but before she could even sputter in disbelief, the older blond woman stood up and breezed over to her.

"Brienne, darling, I cannot tell you how long it has been. The other guests will be down in a minute, but here, let me introduce you to Lady Venetia. Her father is the Earl of Culpepper." Brienne felt the woman's arm go around her waist as she led her over to the others.

"Lady Venetia, I would like to present my cousin, Brienne. She has come all the way from the Colonies, so you must excuse her provincial attire. She has not been in England long enough to attain a suitable wardrobe." The blond woman looked down at her, smiling like an old friend. But Brienne found herself too confused and startled to smile back. Instead she looked at Avenel for an explanation, yet he was not watching her. His eyes were riveted on the fashion plate, the Lady Venetia, who studied the American cousin with a keen but false eye.

Brienne soon discovered that this was the story they had contrived for the next few days. Thoughts of rebellion reared quickly in her mind, however. The scene was simply too absurd especially when she was forced to endure Lady Venetia's barbs.

"What a mistake I have made!" Lady Venetia turned to Brienne, looking anything but contrite. "Of course, one does hear such strange things about the Americans— their obsession with equality, you understand. But although I knew they desired to treat their servants as equals, I had no idea they aspired to dress like them also. How quaint!"

Brienne prickled and found that she could no longer bear the pretense. Interrupting Lady Venetia, she said, "I would have you know, I am no servant. I am the daughter of—!"

"Brienne!" Avenel cut off her words. Whipping her head around to face him, Brienne saw the message in his eyes. He was telling her to comply. *And if I don't?* she asked silently with a glittering stare. But his look told her with the utmost certainty that there would be terrible consequences. A promise lingered in his crystalline irises, a promise that was meant just for her. Noting it, Brienne abruptly backed down. That was Avenel Slane's unique ability, she thought; her cheeks flared with repressed fury and indignation. Not only would he give her all the abuse he had promised, but worse, he would make her want it—and from him alone.

Having no other recourse, Brienne forced herself to be docile. She murmured a stiff apology and took the seat Cumberland offered her, one unfortunately close to Lady

Venetia. Brienne resigned herself to being an onlooker for the rest of the evening. But this was not satisfactory to Lady Venetia, who seemed to bombard the room with chatter from the minute Brienne settled into her chair.

"How silly I must appear! What a faux pas! You see," Lady Venetia turned toward Avenel, who was standing above her, "the entire misconception began when I saw Brienne upstairs. It was after she came in from her walk. She appeared so disheveled—I just assumed she had been cleaning one of the flues or something of that sort. You must try to forgive me. I didn't think Rose's relative would be involved in such a messy undertaking." Venetia sipped on her claret, tilting her black patch provocatively on her upper lip. Then, staring possessively at Avenel, who had accepted a brandy from the footman and was easing himself into another brocade armchair, she added, "I believe you went for a walk also this afternoon, did you not, Avenel?" The woman's question hung in the air like lead.

"Only to retrieve Rose's cousin, my lady. She has a tendency to wander off." Avenel calmly took a sip of the golden brown liquor just as Cumberland was consumed by a fit of coughing.

It was a long, tedious evening. There were twenty-five guests staying at the Park for the upcoming ball, and Brienne knew not one topic of conversation to embark upon with any of them. There were women flounced and quilted in the best satins and men bejeweled as she had never seen before. The Duke and Duchess of Hardington were present, and she could only stand mutely in awe as she was introduced to them.

They were a magnificent pair. The duchess wore a gown of emerald green brocade with an elaborate petticoat of vivid red. The duke cut a fine figure in his gold topcoat and breeches; he had a bloodred ruby the size of a baby's fist stuck between the folds of his neckcloth. With the exception of Avenel, Brienne felt all others dimmed in comparison to the grand couple. Those who were only viscounts and squires were dressed in simple silks, but none seemed as dull as the little cousin from America. Brienne looked down at her violet wool and bemoaned its very existence as she sat near a woman in satin as white as her hair; embroidered vines twisted up and down the petticoat.

Dinner was served in the eating room, and Brienne sat between Cumberland and Lady Venetia, neither of whom said three words to her all evening. Not that she blamed Cumberland for ignoring her, for she could see that he was completely enamored of Rose. The two old friends spent the evening reliving a past that was years old, and they appeared to enjoy each other immensely. She had never seen Cumberland as blissfully starry-eyed nor looking quite as young as when he smiled at Rose's every look of fancy and laughed out loud at her hints of flirtation. Brienne was genuinely happy for him. If anyone deserved the companionship of a well-bred woman, in her mind, it was he.

Brienne herself had liked Rose almost from the first moment they had set eyes on each other. She appeared to be the essence of a lady, and Brienne could tell Rose was very fond of Cumberland, which made her that much more easy to like. There were a few moments during dinner, however, when she had unexpectedly looked up from her plate and seen a strange, disconcerting look on Rose's face as she stared at her from across the large table. Brienne had spent more than one unbearable moment under Rose's odd perusal, but Brienne had brushed it off, thinking that the woman felt as uncomfortable as she did about their play-acting.

Lady Venetia, on the other hand, did her best to engross Brienne in her conversation with Avenel. Not that she had actually included Brienne in any of it; on the contrary, she had pointedly left her out of her and Avenel's tête-à-tête. But every overly loud word Venetia uttered and every dramatic gesture she made seemed to be for Brienne's benefit alone. Never had Brienne seen a woman so frivolous and coy.

So soon after the last course was presented, Brienne announced she had a headache.

"Yes, darling, let the child go to bed," Venetia said to Avenel.

"So soon! It seems the evening has just begun!" Cumberland looked up from his dinner companion and gave Brienne a smart little wink. She couldn't help but smile at him. Seeing him so happy made her heavy heart a little lighter, but she quickly made her excuses.

"Please do not end the evening on my account. It was silly of me to take so much sun, and it has affected me. I'm the one who belongs upstairs, not the rest of you," Brienne said as she stood.

"I do hope you will be better tomorrow, dear. We have so much catching up to do! I don't know if we'll ever have enough time." Rose stood up and pecked her lightly on the cheek. She bade her good night and then returned to her seat, where Cumberland stood by.

Brienne started to leave, but before she could get out the door, she heard Avenel distinctly announce to his guests, "I will see you up, Brienne. If you will excuse me, ladies." The familiar footsteps could be heard across the floorboards, and then she felt his strong hand at her waist. From across the room, Venetia stared holes into

Avenel's broad back, but there was no disturbing Rose and Cumberland, for they were once again engrossed in their reminiscences.

"Let the child go to bed, Master Slane. Your kind escort is not needed for so young a babe," Brienne whispered to him through clenched teeth.

"But this particular young babe has something that I must retrieve. Preferably not in the presence of ladies," he whispered back, and she shot him a daring glance before they left the eating room entirely.

It did not take long to mount the stairs. Once in the yellow bedchamber, his hand fell to her crown and snatched the comb from her hair. Her loosened tresses rippled down her back and around her face in fluffy disarray, and her lips, reddened from the claret she had drunk, peeked out provocatively from the dark auburn mass.

"Now child, you may find your bed." He took his forefinger and held out her chin so that he could gaze at her beautiful face. "I take it by your silence tonight that you do not like my family or my friends."

"Rose is very much a lady. However, I'm afraid that other woman—"

"Careful! I will have you know that Lady Venetia's father, the Earl of Culpepper, could make for a very powerful neighbor one day," he said, and seemed to watch for her reaction.

She could not hide the spitefulness in her voice. "I too am the daughter of an earl. Or have you forgotten?"

"That remains to be seen, wildflower."

"I insist that Oliver Morrow is my father!"

"But is he an earl?" He brushed a thumb across her smooth cheek.

"Why, what else would he be?" She looked up at him with confusion on her face.

"As I said, my love, it remains to be seen. But I have guests to attend to, and I am afraid that, as painful as that may be to you, I am obliged to return to them."

"There's no pain for me to bear. I've had too much of your company for one day."

"One would not have thought so when I first came upon you in the Temple. You appeared rather starved for my company then."

"I was asleep! I thought I was dreaming."

"Of me?" He looked down into her face, keeping hold of it with only one strong finger.

"Of course not!" She spoke truthfully, remembering her vision of Pan just before she awoke. "I am sure Lady Venetia would dream of you if you would but ask her to." She pulled her face from his touch. "But I shall dream of what I wish. Despite being held here like a prisoner, you cannot control that."

" 'Tis true, I cannot control your thoughts." He seemed to brood for a long moment with this last statement as if he were thinking something through. He sat down on the yellow settee as if to ponder his idea. But when she passed him to fetch a ribbon for her unruly hair, he quickly pulled her onto his lap. Wild-eyed, she looked about the large room for Vivie, but the woman was nowhere to be seen. "But if I commanded your body, I imagine your thoughts would not be far behind. You talk a good game, little one. You lift your nose at me and say you have no use for my lovemaking. But if that's so, then I'll wager you. Kiss me now." He took her fingers of one hand and placed them on his lips. "You say you've been dreaming of someone else. Then kiss me, and I will wager that you will dream of no one else but me from then on."

"I will not kiss you, you self-serving beast!" She struggled against him in their age-old game.

"I am not asking you; 'tis more than that. I am daring you." He held her down effortlessly.

"It's not worth trying. You have no effect on me." She stopped momentarily to look at him. Had he gone mad? Was there not a woman downstairs who would gladly play his games? Why must he always taunt and trifle with her?

"Then kiss me. Prove me wrong." He slouched back on the settee and stretched out his long, powerful body so that her buttocks rested easily on his thighs.

She looked down at his cocky face and wished wholeheartedly that she could wipe that arrogant smile off his visage. She considered his proposition, seeing the ridiculousness of it, but finally she had to conclude that if, by kissing him this once, he would leave her alone for a while, then perhaps it was worth the risk. Vivie would be appearing soon, so that any scurrilous thoughts he might have of forcing her to go further than one kiss would soon be put to an end.

"What about your precious guests? I would hate for them to be kept waiting," she said, making one last attempt to avoid him.

"Cumberland and Rose have no desire for my company tonight. As for the others, none of them are sober enough to realize I have gone. Lady Venetia, of course, might have to wait longer than she would like, but if you're correct, this should not take very long. Just place those sweet lips on mine, Brienne. We will find out how dispassionate our relationship is."

"This will greatly disappoint you." She lowered her

thick lashes. Summoning her strength—for it seemed to go against her nature to kiss this man—she took a deep breath and bent down to where his head rested on the back of the settee. His black lashes lowered over the glowing silver of his irises when her lips touched his, and he was rigidly still as she kissed him fully on the mouth. Despite her self-control, she lingered in the kiss perhaps a little longer than was safe. Inhaling his warm, masculine scent, she felt herself lean limply against the broad muscular expanse of his chest. Before she could recover, his hands swept through her hair and held her head to his, not as a gesture of force but as a directive measure. Her thoughts became fogged as she felt a melting sensation between her legs. And that sensation was heightened almost uncontrollably when his tongue found its way into her beckoning mouth. She moaned deep within herself, but whether it was because of the battle she knew she was surely losing or from her exalted senses, she could not be sure.

They kissed until she thought she was surely losing her mind. When they parted, there was no smug, self-righteousness in his visage; rather, there was a desperate, hungry look that made his face appear lean and handsome and gave a wild blue spark to his snowy eyes.

He sat forward with her still on top of him, and he bent his dark, glistening head over the ivory flesh exposed at the top of her bodice. His lips felt so warm, it was as if their warmth went through to her heart, which was beating furiously. She moaned again but felt hopelessly complacent as he unpinned her stomacher. She watched the woolen triangle fall silently to the carpet as he started in on her laces. Slowly, inch by inch, her stays yielded the tantalizing flesh they held so securely. He laid her back onto the settee and grazed his sun-bronzed hand just over one rose-colored nipple. He looked her full in the face, and when she showed no fear, he placed his hand fully on her breast, possessing its every blossoming curve as he bent down to kiss her once more.

The sheer madness of the situation was intoxicant enough, but there was no containing the unbridled passion that burst forth from every part of her body. Her nipples grew taut underneath his warm, coaxing fingers, and even though her mind might have been saying, "Enough," her body cried and begged for him to go on. To find that ultimate release was the only salvation possible, for without it this was unbearable torture.

"Ah, my lady, is that you?" Vivie's voice could be heard coming through the dressing room. Avenel's head jerked up just as she entered the room bearing a large tray with a fresh pot of chocolate. Seeing the two of them, Avenel's face granite hard and Brienne's serene eyes glazed with desire, the Frenchwoman blanched and uttered apologies. Immediately she turned from them and fled the room, taking the tray with her.

The silence that followed was ominous. Slowly Brienne caught her breath, but it was some time before she could sit up and wrap her arms modestly around her chest to cover her bared flesh. She looked on as Avenel stood and scooped up his top coat and silver waistcoat from the floor. She was amazed that she could not remember his taking them off. She looked up as he towered over her; then he slowly bent down and placed a sensuous kiss on the overflowing flesh that her slender arm could not possibly cover all of. Shaken and confused, she watched Avenel go only after he stated the obvious in a deep, irreverent voice: "You lose, my lady." Then he left, and she stared at the closed door behind him for a long, long time.

CHAPTER THIRTEEN

The ball was three days away, and day after day Brienne watched in awe as preparations were made for the event. Rose had been the mastermind of the proceedings. Everything, from what the guests would drink with their salmon mousse to where they would place their cloaks when they came in from the courtyard, fell under her ultimate control.

Brienne couldn't help but admire Avenel's cousin. Often when Rose poured out tea in the late afternoon or as she directed a footman where to place a vase of pale pink tulips, Brienne pictured her mother doing exactly the same thing so many years before. Rose was actually very close to her mother's age, had Grace Morrow still been alive; many wistful thoughts entered Brienne's head on these occasions that echoed the same sentiment: "What if things had been different?" It was easy to picture herself with two loving parents at her side, growing up rich and spoiled at the Park, as Lady Venetia had at Culpepper House. Her mother would have been happily married to that mysterious person whose handsome face was painted on her miniature. There would have been proper suitors calling for her, chaperoned weekend visits, and balls to plan. And she would have known exactly what to expect at Avenel's ball.

Brienne had yet to tell anyone that this ball absolutely terrified her. She had been to few social events in her life and never one of this magnitude. How to behave and what to say in the presence of the ton were enigmas to her. The lively conversation that seemed to be an art with the well-bred guests was beyond her grasp. To make matters worse, she knew she would be questioned constantly about her "homeland," and she would have to fabricate replies all evening.

Lady Venetia had become the bane of Brienne's existence precisely because she'd developed an interest in her. She asked all sorts of confusing questions about her family and what life had been like in the war-torn Colonies, none of which Brienne could answer truthfully or knowledgeably. Even now, as the female guests were seated in the drawing room, Lady Venetia continued to pry from her information about her past.

"I have heard that in America there are so few women that most of them are married even as children. How is it that you were able to escape such a fate and not become shackled to a Colonial?" Lady Venetia's soft hand stroked her lapdog.

"I . . . ah . . ." Brienne started but was not quick enough with her answer. As she was doing with embarrassing frequency, Rose interjected an explanation.

"Brienne can afford to be choosy. Am I not correct?" The pretty woman looked at Brienne, who threw her another grateful look.

"I suppose that's a luxury not many women can afford." Venetia looked at Brienne's simple worsted round gown and then adjusted the satin *échelle* that ran along her own elaborately embroidered floral stomacher. "Especially one who is so obviously less endowed. But I suppose it is worth the sacrifice. Spinsterhood is a small price to pay to leave what must be a heathen land."

"A heathen land? Lady Venetia, you must be mistaken." Brienne could not swallow her anger this time. The woman's barbs were becoming sharper every day. Despite her lack of knowledge about the Colonies, she was determined to stand up for herself this time and not force Rose to pave the way. "Some of the finest palaces in the world are in Maryland! While I personally was not raised in such castles, I can tell you that there are very civilized and well-bred people in America who would be soundly shocked by the sad lack of manners found in many of the ton here in England."

"I never! How dare you speak to me that way!" Venetia's eyes rolled furiously, and even the Pekingese seemed to mimic her by jumping up and barking.

"Lady Venetia, you must calm yourself. Brienne was not implying—" Rose tried to soothe the ruffled feathers.

"She was, I tell you. Besides that, she is lying to me. There are no castles in the Colonies! Your cousin is a fool to think I would believe such nonsense! She is a fool and a liar!" Lady Venetia stood up and placed her pet on the floor.

"Perhaps we could go for a walk through the garden. This has gotten you upset and so unnecessarily." Rose stood up also, but despite her calming demeanor, Brienne was pleased to see her eyes twinkle with amusement when Venetia bent down to attend to her dog.

She watched on in unremorseful enjoyment as Rose

led Venetia away toward the gallery. As soon as the
carved mahogany door was shut behind them, Brienne
burst into laughter, feeling momentarily relieved.

" 'Tis very funny." Avenel's voice could be heard behind her, and she spun around to find him watching her
from the open door to the tapestry room.

She swallowed and was not sure how to approach
him. She had seen very little of him since that night in
her bedchamber. This arrangement seemed to suit both
of them, for she had gladly taken her meals in her room,
and he likewise had refrained from seeking out her company.

"You saw?" she asked impudently.

"Everything." He walked farther into the room.
" 'Twas a bad display, Brienne. I have warned you not to
do that."

"She deserved what she got! She has a mean streak in
her, and she continually directs it at me. I find her intol-
erable." She took a step away from him but held her
shoulders in an unyielding posture. "Whatever worth
you see in her escapes me completely."

"Women in her position need only to be virtuous and
beautiful. Since she is both, any other qualities she may
or may not possess are superfluous."

"I see," she said; his speech made her feel like a dusty
churchmouse. "I suppose that means that women in my
position need only to spread their thighs and keep their
mouths closed." She could not hide the bitterness in her
voice, and she hoped that what she had said had been
shockingly crude. After that last night in her bedchamber, she had felt toyed with. He had never mentioned the
episode, as if it had been a lark, a careless romp with a
tavern wench.

" 'Tis not what I said." He gave her a dark look and crossed his arms forebodingly over his chest.

"You don't even need to say it." She thought of yesterday, when she had looked out her bedroom window. There he and Lady Venetia had been walking to the Orangery. Lady Venetia had had her arm looped intimately through his, and Avenel had seemed to smile at her coquetry. Brienne had never seen him behave so charmingly. Before she could deny the feeling, she had started to begrudge the circumstances that prevented him from behaving that way with her.

Brienne turned from him now and started out the door to the passage. He did not attempt to stop her, and there were no more words between them. In her eyes, no more were needed.

She trudged up the great staircase, whisking her petticoats away angrily as she took each step. When she got to the hallway, she saw Rose across the way closing the door to Venetia's room. Brienne walked down to meet her. It was the first time an opportunity had arisen to speak to the kind woman alone.

"I am sorry if I embarrassed you by my outburst, Rose." Brienne touched her on the arm to get her attention and whispered to her, realizing Venetia must be napping beyond the door, "It was silly of me not to let you—"

Brienne immediately pulled back from the look of horror contorting the lovely woman's face. It was as if she had just slapped her full across the face. "What is it?" she murmured, not sure if she wanted to know.

"Don't ever touch me!" Rose rubbed her arm where Brienne had tapped her. "I've agreed with Avenel to go along with this charade, for I am deeply indebted to him, but I don't presume a friendship with you, and I don't want you to speak to me when we're away from the guests.''

Brienne felt a terrible stabbing pain in her chest. She knew it was hurt and betrayal. All of Rose's kindnesses had been an act that she performed at Avenel's request. All the appearances of friendliness that Brienne had mistaken for the genuine article were now gone. Brienne looked up at the abhorrence on the woman's face, and it pierced her through to the bone. Her eyes helplessly filled with tears, and she moved back, stumbling on a gilt chair that was standing against one wall. Suddenly she felt closed in, and all her thoughts centered on getting out of the hall and away from Rose's accusing delft blue eyes.

Brienne regained her balance as she sobbed, "I—I am so sorry," apologizing for something she instinctively knew the earl had been a part of, something that she was now being held accountable for. She needed to run away, to close her eyes to the horrific picture of Rose's rejection. But she felt herself being grabbed as she stumbled again, this time on a wrinkle in the French carpeting. She looked up and saw Avenel's questioning gaze staring down at her in consternation. Without really seeing him, she pulled free and ran wild-eyed to her bedchamber and to the badly needed solace it offered.

A tray was brought up to her and then returned with the food upon it untouched. Brienne sat on the bed and stared at the delicately painted bedcurtains and then dropped her head back to rest on the embroidered Deccan counterpane. Vivie had persuaded her to undress, and she lay now in her dressing gown. But the little maid had had to admit defeat when the tray was sent up from the kitchens. Quietly Vivie had left her, hoping that she would take a nap. Instead she merely stared ahead with her eyes wide open and blank, her thoughts dark and heavy.

The sound of the door opening did not disturb her black reverie, nor did the footsteps that moved to her bedstead.

"I really don't need anything, Vivie. Please go ahead and have your dinner." She turned on her side away from the door to gaze out the large windows to the darkening sky. She saw in the distance that several children from the township had gathered in the far grounds of the Park to play and scuffle. She had seen these children before; they were a motley bunch of ragamuffins that had succeeded in avoiding the caretakers of the estate; they knew all the openings along the fenceline through which a child could slip undetected. They loved to run along the grounds and taunt the visitors, but since they were little more than a nuisance, Avenel, unlike the earl before him, had never tried to expel them. Now she looked on almost enviously as they held each other's dirty hands and skipped around in a circle; their singing was all but silenced through the windowpanes. At least they were free to come and go, she thought, and then turned away from the window in disgust and despair.

"I cannot apologize for Rose, little one." The voice came out of the darkness of her room, and she immediately sat upright. Her eyes were too puffy from bouts of tears to make out the form. But that was unnecessary, for she knew the voice well enough.

"What did he do to her?" She spoke to the darkness. "I—I must know." Her voice trembled and wavered, but she was able to relay her conviction.

There was a deadened quality in Avenel's voice as he

spoke; it seemed at first that the words were going to catch in his throat. "He killed her husband."

"Oh, God! My God!" she heard herself say over and over again. It was like a horrible nightmare, but one that had no ending. "Why? How?" Her voice cracked. "Was there a duel?"

"No duel. Oliver Morrow does nothing as honorable as that."

"Tell me, why did he—?"

"More than likely, he did it out of pure enjoyment." This statement, spoken so coldly, rammed itself through her breast. She knew, even without seeing him, that his face had gone hard. Probably not even a lash quivered.

"There must have been some other reason. My father is quite calculating. Avenel, you know the reason. Tell me." She pleaded with him.

"I cannot." He was pointed.

"You know what it is. I've a right—" she began.

"You're at Osterley now. Your rights are gone." After tonight's ugly revelation, Brienne could almost believe for the first time that she deserved his cruelty.

"Please tell me," she murmured futilely, knowing all the while that after having fought so many battles with this man, he was not going to tell her tonight. "Rose thinks I'm some sort of monster. She probably thinks I'd be better off dead than—"

"She would not wish you harm." His voice was coming closer; soon she felt a heavy weight at the edge of her bed.

"I must be worse than a leper in her eyes," she moaned in self-recrimination. There was no answer for this, so she continued. "She had seemed so friendly. I didn't know! I never would have presumed . . . I never would have spoken to her." She started to cry. "Let me leave here, Avenel. I cannot face her again! I think I'd rather die than see that look of revulsion again. How she must hate me for being alive when her husband . . ." She could not go on. She sobbed into her hands. Avenel made no move to console her or accuse her. He appeared in outline, sitting on the far end of her mattress like a rigid soldier. He seemed to be battling something within himself that came to an absolute draw. It would not allow him to bend one way or another, so he had to remain perfectly still while she cried her heart out in remorse for the grief that her father caused Rose.

It seemed hours before she wore herself out. Eventually she lay back against the pillows, but still there was a stray sniffle or two as she felt herself, now bone tired, drift off into the void of a dreamless sleep. There was a point during the night when she felt herself being picked up and tenderly placed underneath the counterpane, yet in her state she'd not been sure if it was Avenel, who so gently swept the hair from her aching forehead, or Vivie, who had finally returned to put her mistress to bed.

"I cannot!" she said after several minutes of arguing. She looked around the taffeta bedroom at the mountains of dresses that had arrived that morning. It was the day of the ball, and the entire house was buzzing with last-minute preparations for the notables who would arrive that evening. Earlier there had been a knock at the door, and then footman after footman had entered bearing large trunks that held the exquisite gowns that were now spread over every available piece of furniture in the room. Vivie's eyes had become as round as saucers when she opened the trunks.

"*Ici! Ma demoiselle! Ici!*" She had pulled out a dark green serge riding habit with black embroidery around the cuffs and hemline of the coat. Next had come several round gowns of cotton sateen, and then several more of silk lutestring. But when Vivie pulled out a gold ball gown with a gleaming bronze-embroidered stomacher, Brienne had to voice her objections.

"This is madness! Vivie, you must put these back! I am sure they belong to Lady Venetia, or perhaps Lady Carlotta or Lady Anne. Nonetheless, whoever they belong to will be enormously angered to see that I have opened up the boxes."

"Mais non, ma demoiselle! This is not so!" Vivie had cried, still digging farther into a deep trunk.

"How do we know it isn't Lady Venetia's trousseau? Perhaps Avenel has asked her to marry him, and—"

"His eyes are for you, my lady. That other one"—Vivie made a moue of her small mouth—"she is only for show."

"Please put them back!" But by then it was too late. It seemed that all the dresses had been unpacked in an impossibly short amount of time. Vivie began her persuasions.

"You must try one on, *ma demoiselle!* See this?" The little maid held up a powder blue pair of satin stays. Brienne nodded dumbly, her eyes fixed on the exquisite workmanship of the piece. "Made by Cosins! Think of it, *ma demoiselle!* The finest staymaker in all the world has made this! Are you not curious?" Vivie went over to the gold ball gown. She held the dress to Brienne and made a display. "Come, you must want to know what this will feel like against your skin! You must!"

"Well," Brienne said as she indecisively bit her lower lip, "perhaps just one . . ."

Vivie was all smiles as she laid out a fine batiste sleeveless shift edged in French lace. She placed the blue satin stays alongside it, but Brienne put her foot down. "I cannot try on the underthings. I cannot, and I will not!"

"*Oui! Oui!* Then you must try on the dress! When you see how well it fits, then you will know that what I say is correct!" Vivie unhooked the beautiful gown and helped her out of her brown worsted. Pulling the yards upon yards of wonderful silk over her head, Brienne felt transformed even before she had the dress fully on. Vivie fussed and fitted, pinning the stomacher in place perfectly over Brienne's old off-white linen stays.

"There!" the French maid cried when she had finally dressed her. "You are a vision. He will not be able to take his eyes off you!"

Brienne moved to the pier glass that faced the fireplace. Slowly she turned around, watching every swirl and sway of the expensive fabric. The silk was as soft as a kitten's fur against her bare shoulders, and when she moved she heard an exquisite rustle near her feet. The gown fit so well, it was as if every curve of her body had been painstakingly measured and remeasured. She laughed out loud, feeling almost childlike in her awe of herself.

"I shudder to think what Lady Venetia would say about my wearing her gown!" Brienne spun around in it before the mirror once more and watched how pink her cheeks became and how clearly her eyes sparkled. She laughed again, turning to Vivie.

But Vivie was now facing away from her and looking toward the doorway. There was a slight smile on the servant's lips, and Vivie did not appear to be afraid. But Brienne felt her heart skip several beats when she heard the steady knock on her door.

"Do not open it!" She looked around the room for a

place to hide. But it was a futile exercise, for immediately
the door opened, and Avenel stood in the threshold.

" 'Twas a joyful sound to hear, little one. Was it laughter I heard? For if it was, it was well worth the expense."
He wandered into the room and circled her, taking in
every angle of the dress to where it skimmed the top of
her bosom and pinched in her waist, then fell in shim-
mering folds to the floor.

"I—I do not know what to say . . ." Brienne stammered; her face showed the first effects of a long, painful
blush.

"You need not say anything. Just let me hear you
laugh." He decided to watch her from the comfort of the
settee and dwarfed the piece with his large frame.

"Surely Lady Venetia will not find this a laughing matter." Brienne folded her arms modestly across her chest
and wished he would go so she could change back into
her own clothes.

"Ma demoiselle will not believe me when I tell her!"
Vivie turned to Brienne. "I said the Monsieur was bringing back a surprise from London, did I not, my lady?"

"I—I thought the surprise was Rose, and then too, the
houseguests." Brienne pulled the bed-curtains to and
then stood behind them to undress. She reappeared in
her brown worsted and placed the precious gold gown
back in the trunk whence it came. "But it doesn't matter," she said as she carefully packed the dress away. "If
you've gotten these dresses for me, I'm afraid I cannot
accept them. I haven't any coins to pay for them, as you
well know."

"It could be said that I've already been paid. You're
the one who insists I am keeping something that belongs
to you." Avenel seemed amused, and he sat back com-

fortably. *Too comfortably,* she thought, *for being in a lady's bedchamber.*

"The cost of that comb could never cover these expenses."

"What do you know of the comb's true value?"

"I know enough." She shuddered softly, thinking back to another time.

"Then you may consider the dresses a loan, for you will need one to wear tonight."

"I'm not going tonight." Brienne got down on her knees and began repacking the green riding habit.

"You will be there." He leaned back in the settee and closed his eyes complacently.

"I'm afraid I'll be incapacitated by the same illness that has been plaguing me these past few evenings." Brienne ignored him, enjoying the rich folds of a mint green cotton sateen polonaise. There was a pink one, too, much finer than her old one. Regrettably she began to pack that away as well.

"I've been lenient with you these past few evenings, wildflower. But you are going tonight, and that is my final word." Avenel's words were full of arrogance; her refusals didn't even make him open his eyes.

"I will not see Roşe again. I will not subject either of us to that strain." Brienne checked the anger rising in her voice.

"Rose expects to see you. She will not be upset."

"Then I would be upset. I am not going."

"You are going." His eyes flew open, and he got up off the settee.

"I am not," she replied, setting her jaw.

"Vivie, please leave us," Avenel commanded. The loyal maid complied; Brienne inwardly cursed her retreating back.

"So how are you going to force me into obedience this time, pray tell?" She stood and threw a quilted satin petticoat into the trunk, refusing to be intimidated by Avenel. "Are you planning to chase me around the room until I agree? Or will you be more subtle and merely rip off my garments one by one until I comply?"

"Ah, I think the latter would be a pleasure." His answer was low and soft, but the overriding anger in his tone made Brienne flinch almost as if he'd shouted at her.

"The perfect answer from a heathen." Vehemently she jammed another petticoat into the trunk.

"Stop packing," he growled.

Her taunts had made him furious, but she didn't care. Feeling reckless, she took several shifts from the bed and strode back to the trunks.

"I said stop packing!" He grabbed her wrist and made her halt.

"I'm not going to keep these gowns."

"Yes, you are."

"And why is that?" She tried to twist free from his grasp.

"You'll accept them because I want you to! And for the same reason, you'll go to my ball. Because I desire it!"

"*You* desire it? But I shall never do anything for you willingly. Not sleep in your bed, nor attend your ball!" She looked up, meaning to give him a belittling glance, but instead her face became etched with dismay. He towered over her, his arms crossed tightly over the great expanse of his chest. His face bore a grim, sardonic smile.

"There are certain activities for which I require your cooperation. However, concerning this ball, my pleasure will not be substantially increased by your desire to oblige me. Therefore, I say you are going. Tonight your feelings about the ball mean nothing."

"Why is my presence necessary? For the past few days all your guests seemed to enjoy talking about is Rose's shabby little cousin from America. I've become a novelty for them. But I daresay, by now their amusement has worn off." She hid the humiliation in her voice beneath a thick coat of vengeance.

"I'd rather they talked about you than wondered about you. If you're not at the ball, there will be speculation. That I prefer not to see. Do you understand me, little one?"

He watched her closely, but she just shrugged.

"Do you?" he repeated, his tone husky and ominous.

But instead of heeding the warning in his voice, she merely turned her back to him, proving her unwillingness to comply. This time, she vowed, she would not give in. She would not see Rose again, or his precious guests.

Suddenly his hand twisted through her hair. Her pins fell to the carpet like raindrops, and although he didn't hurt her, he forced her to face him.

"Perhaps my guests can be put off by that cool, quiet demeanor of yours, but I am not so easily thwarted." Releasing her tresses, he wrapped his arm around her waist. "You, my beautiful creature, are going to my ball, even if I have to dress you myself."

Her fury rose to a fever pitch. She ground her small, delicate fists against his chest in an effort to push him away, but he put his other hand around her waist and pulled her so close to him, she couldn't move her arms.

"God, why must you torment me so?" she said harshly, turning her face away.

"All I want is your compliance. All I want is a docile woman who will cooperate. But you fight me at every turn!"

"I don't want to go to your infernal ball. I want to leave!"

"You will leave when I want you to leave." He pulled her head up to face him.

"You despot!" she cried out. Her unbound auburn locks shimmered as she shook her head. "Why can't you see that you cannot treat me like this?"

Her accusation only served to raise his ire further. "What I am is of no concern to you. All I want is your answer. Will you come to the ball?"

"Yes! Yes! I'll go to your ball!" She smiled vengefully. "Go ahead and force me into one of the dresses you bought for me! But just know that when you come to pick me up, you'll have to drag me downstairs like a truant child! I'll kick and I'll scream! See if that doesn't give your precious guests something to wag their tongues about!" Her eyes sparkled with rebellion.

But soon she widened them in shock as Avenel violently pulled her to the bed. He sat on the edge among the billowing silk and satin gowns and whispered through clenched teeth, "Like a truant child, eh? And what does one do to a truant child, Brienne? A child who will not obey?" Although she struggled, he easily rolled her onto his knees and placed her in a prone position. An iron hand held her down while another controlled her flailing limbs.

"I won't let you do this, Avenel!" she cried out. "You will not lift my skirts again!"

"I'll give you a choice, Brienne. Which would you rather feel on your backside—the sting of my hand or the burn of my mouth?'' He laughed, obviously enjoying tormenting her.

"Oh," she moaned. "How unfair your tactics are! That you even speak such words to me—"

"Which is it?" he interrupted, already having stripped one leg of her stocking and garter. He nipped at the bare calf of her kicking leg, and as she boiled with rage, he only chuckled.

"Stop, you evil man!" she gasped out when she felt his tongue licking the sensitive area behind her knee. "I said stop!"

"For what?"

"For the ball. I'll go to your ball!"

"Willingly?" His fingers slid up her thigh, stroking her tender flesh.

"Willingly!" she screeched.

Abruptly and without ceremony he stood and dumped her at the foot of the bed. She swept down her skirts and gave him a look of pure hatred.

But without giving her a backward glance, he went to the jib door. Calling Vivie, he directed, "Have Lady Brienne ready at eight o'clock."

"*Oui*, Monsieur." Brienne heard Vivie's subdued voice and realized that the maid must have been listening at the door. Quickly Avenel departed in silence.

When Vivie entered, she began unpacking all the dresses Brienne had put back into the trunks. But Brienne merely looked on; every now and then she bestowed a baleful glance in the direction of the door.

"You *must* powder my hair, Vivie. I will not have the guests laughing at me another night." Brienne spied her own pale face in the looking glass by the dressing table. Her nerves were as raw and tight as chafed laces, and she wondered how she would ever get through the evening. Every time she closed her eyes, she envisioned a new situation to worry about. She saw Lady Venetia sneering at her unpowdered hair while her own soared gracefully high to the ceiling, carrying all kinds of trinkets such as artificial flowers, fruit, ribbons, and pearls among its waves. Brienne also had the awful thought that she would have to speak to Rose and again endure the horrific look that she'd seen on the woman's face. Thinking of Rose, Brienne's very soul felt pierced with unfounded guilt and remorse. She placed her head between her hands and moaned, "Oh, how I shall hate this evening!"

"Mais non! You will have a wonderful time. What is it that makes you fret so, *ma demoiselle?"* Vivie started up in French, which was common when the two women needed to speak intimately.

"You know I'm being forced to attend this mockery of a ball," Brienne answered Vivie in French, grateful to speak with someone about her mounting apprehensions. "I don't know why Avenel has insisted upon this charade —unless he knows I've little experience with these kinds of social functions. Unless he wants his friends to laugh at me!" Brienne angrily shoved aside several perfume bottles. "How I detest them all!"

"My lady! You must forget them! Their laughter is hollow, for they laugh out of envy!"

"Vivie, you must powder my hair! I don't care what Avenel said. Tonight I refuse to be the Colonial cousin. Tonight I will be who I am!" She looked at Vivie with fresh determination.

"Do not ask me!" Vivie seemed torn between loyalties.

"It's so important. I would not ask you to go against your master's wishes if it were not vital."

"All right. I will try." Vivie backed down and went to get the hair grease. After taking a small scoop of the thick, gray-brown fat into her hand, she palmed it until it was warm and liquid and then turned to Brienne's willing head with its shining, dark burgundy tresses.

"I cannot." Vivie looked down, whispering sheepishly in French. She instantly found a linen cloth and wiped the grease from her hands, shaking her head. "I cannot cover that beautiful color with this." She held the grease-laden linen up to show its dulling effect.

In frustration, Brienne rose from her dressing table and began to pace the carpet. "Is there no part of my life Avenel Slane doesn't control? Am I not even free to choose my own hairstyle?"

"Come, let me dress you. Then I can show you how successful you will be." Vivie sympathetically took her by the hand and led her to the settee. There she laid out a gown, one that Brienne hadn't yet seen. It was a purple brocaded satin, so deep in color that it could almost pass for black. With a matching petticoat and stomacher lightly embroidered with shining gold threads, the gown would become her, Brienne knew, but she had yet to see a dress so unfashionably dark.

"The color, is it not . . . ?"

"Monsieur Slane, he asked for this one. Could it be more exquisite?"

"No. All the gowns are beautiful beyond belief. I just can't understand how you were able to fit them."

"I took the measurements from your other gowns. But the master, he was the one who ordered them. As I understand it, he was very particular. There is not one article of clothing here that does not complement your coloring perfectly. He is to be congratulated, *non*?"

Brienne merely shrugged noncommittally and stepped

into the rich brocade. The stays were built into the gown so that only the thin cotton batiste of her shift came between her and the dress. This turned out to be a blessing, for the material was unbelievably heavy and would have been hot if not for the gown's ingenious design.

"You are ready, my lady." Vivie stood beside her, breathlessly awaiting her approval.

Brienne looked at herself in the gilt mirror and was shocked to find in it such a lovely woman. The gown was cut appealingly low; her shell pink skin was set off perfectly by the dark material. Her face had a dusky glow about it, and the eyes that looked back at her through thick, dark lashes were sultry and promising.

"Are you not most beautiful?" Vivie touched up a long auburn curl that was nestled in Brienne's bosom. "The master will find himself a jealous man tonight."

Brienne gave a wry laugh. "My only hope is that he will have his hands so full with Lady Venetia and his other *demoiselles* that he will not be able to spare me a glance."

"He will prove otherwise," Vivie said, resuming her English. "I must leave you now. But the Monsieur will be here soon." Quickly Vivie went about the bedchamber, picking up stray linens and straightening chairs. Going out through the dressing room, she whispered to Brienne, *"Vive l'amour!"* and left with a shining smile of confidence.

Brienne watched her go, and her nerves jangled as the first bars of music came up from the gallery. There was a bustling in the hallway as she heard Lady Venetia and Rose being escorted by Cumberland down the great staircase, but no one came to call for her. She sat down on a corner of her bedstead gingerly so as not to wrinkle her gown, and soon she grew edgy.

After several minutes, she began to wonder if the whole evening had been built up as some preposterous prank. Perhaps she was not expected to attend. Perhaps Venetia had insisted she not be present, or maybe Rose thought she would shame . . .

Suddenly there was a light knock on the door. Brienne stood up and then smoothed the rich satin over her new bum roll. Licking her lips, which had suddenly gone dry, she said in a suitably impersonal voice, "Come in."

The door opened, and Avenel appeared, dressed splendidly in black satin breeches and matching topcoat. There was a severe lack of decoration on his person; the only embroidery was found on his brilliant white-on-white waistcoat, which lent his eyes a crystalline gleam.

As she took in every aspect of his appearance, she noted that no detail of her own attire was lost on him. His gaze swept over her gown and hair, then rested on her face. Finally he was able to say, "As I expected, you're lovely, wildflower. I only wish it were possible to keep you to myself tonight."

"Then perhaps it would be best if I did not attend." She made one last effort to extract herself from the evening. However, she was wary of being too insistent, for she could still feel the tingle of his touch on her thigh.

"My decision is made. I'm glad you've had the sense to take it to heart." His eyes again took in her attire. He lingered on her dress, obviously appreciating the laced-up curves of her waist and the generous display of her bosom. After a full pause, he said, "Unfortunately, with you in that gown, I can see that there will be many inquiries about Rose's American cousin."

"I suppose I should have brushed up on the Colonies so that I can keep my story straight this time," she said coldly.

"Yes, particularly about the castles. I'm afraid to tell you, there are none." He laughed, but it was a harsh, uncomfortable laugh. Taking her hand, he placed on its back a gentlemanly kiss. His lips seemed to scald her flesh where they touched it, and Brienne quickly took her hand away. Unnerved, she started out the door. "Wait." He pulled her by the waist nearer to him and then placed a heavy silk purse in her hands.

"Whatever is this?" She looked up warily.

"Open it," he said. His eyes were hooded, and she could hardly fathom what emotion was in them. Was there a shimmer of regret in those icy depths? No, she told herself, she wouldn't believe it.

She opened the purse slowly and spilled the contents onto the seat of the settee. Her comb she recognized instantly, but it took a moment before she recognized the other item. It was a close-fitting necklace of large square-cut diamonds and pear-shaped amethysts, and it appeared to be as old as her comb. It was obvious that it matched the hairpiece, but she couldn't understand why Avenel would have such a thing made for her.

Avenel bent down and silently pulled the necklace around her delicate throat. He fastened it tenderly in the back, saying, "Tonight it will be your turn to look down upon everyone."

"It's lovely." She touched the jewels at her throat and looked up. "You had it made to match my comb. Why?"

"It does seem to have been made for you" was all he said.

Abruptly he handed her the matching comb and beckoned her to the looking glass. Avenel's eyes seemed to caress her as she looked at their reflection in the glass. With a trembling hand, she placed the comb in the waves of her dark auburn hair. Then, knowing her questions would have to wait until a more suitable time, she took the arm he extended to her and allowed him to lead her out the door to whatever the evening offered.

CHAPTER FOURTEEN

"After all the money he spent redecorating this place, can you believe that awful man sold it?"

"Well, I say good riddance! He was a nasty one, that Lord Oliver. I never trusted him, what with his abnormal *appetites,* shall we say."

"I heard finishing the Etruscan room nearly broke him. Of course, that could have forced him to give it up."

"But what do you think of the new master? He's not even among the peerage."

"A far cry from the old earl, at least! And Lady Venetia seems quite taken with him, I must say." With this last comment, all eyes at the table, including Brienne's, moved to where Avenel and his party were having their meal. Three tables had been set up in the eating room; the first had been set for the master of Osterley and his more distinguished guests. Lady Venetia sat at Avenel's right; the other notables at his table, besides Rose and Cumberland, included the Duke and Duchess of Hardington and the Earl of Culpepper.

Brienne had been sitting all evening at one of the other tables, having been abandoned by Avenel as soon as they entered the gallery. After descending from her bedchamber, his attention had been quickly taken up and jealously guarded by Venetia, who had walked up to them and bestowed only a curt nod of recognition on Brienne. Then, taking his arm, Venetia bade Avenel get her a claret. Brienne watched them go and felt a sudden panic at being left alone in the large gallery with so many strangers. But soon Cumberland joined her, and she felt a little better. Always the gentleman, Cumberland introduced her to a Lord and Lady Somebody, and Rose had put on her friendly face to greet her; their encounter had been brief and at the very least painless.

A delightful and colorful sight had met her eyes when Brienne first entered the gallery. She soon found herself enjoying the tableau of women curtseying and dancing in their intricate figured silks and rich colorful satins. Most of the men, except Avenel, were dressed even more elaborately than the women, and Brienne was struck dumb more than once when Cumberland introduced her to a fashionable dandy clad in a rainbow of silk and embroidery.

They had walked to the eating room soon after her arrival. Her dinner partner had been introduced to her, and Brienne had gratefully sat in the chair he offered. He was Osterley township's minister, a Reverend Trumbell, a shy, fat, aging man with a red face. Brienne thought him kindly, however, and made several attempts to draw him out, but eventually she realized she was even boring herself with her simple talk, and she fell silent, choosing to listen instead to the chatter at the table. She had been slightly unnerved when she first sat down at the dinner table, and perhaps a little hurt that she had not been included with anyone she knew. But her dinner companions proved to be a harmless if gossipy lot.

"My daughter said she met Master Slane in London at a soirée. There must have been a hundred women who set their caps for him at that party alone." An overweight matron eyed Avenel owlishly. She then looked over to her dinner partner and tapped him gently on his arm with her painted fan. "I heard tell it was scandalous! Every party after that where it was even rumored he would attend turned into a mad crush. You should have seen how it pleased the dowagers!"

Brienne looked over to the host's table and saw Venetia familiarly place her hand on Avenel's strong satin-clad arm. It was a simple gesture, seemingly to get his attention, but she knew it held more meaning than that. Venetia looked particularly magnificent in a gown of palest yellow, completely embroidered with ribbons of iridescent light blue and gold. Looking down at her own purple brocaded gown, Brienne wondered if it appeared overly simple; but looking at Lord Culpepper's daughter, she felt relieved that at least it was new.

Suddenly the hairs on the back of her neck prickled, and she moved her gaze over to the Earl of Culpepper. As she had thought, he was staring at her again. Quickly she pulled her eyes from the other table and began on her dinner with renewed vigor. She felt a chill run down her spine and wondered what it was about her that made the man stare at her. It seemed from the moment she had entered the gallery, he had been taken with her. Not that he had begged an introduction; nor had he tried to speak to her. But still she had felt his narrow eyes on her from the start, continually following her across the gallery and now here at dinner from the other table. She had disliked him immediately. There was something to distrust in his pale face and thin figure. He appeared to have imbibed too many spirits before they even had sat down to dinner, and from time to time she could hear his loud, conceited talk from clear across the room.

Cautiously, she looked up from her dinner plate to see if he was still staring. She was relieved to note that he had struck up a conversation with the duchess. Moving her eyes quickly over the rest of his dinner partners, she was caught off guard by Avenel, who raised his head and looked directly at her. Her skin warmed under his gaze. As much as she wanted to show her indifference, Brienne found she couldn't look away. She was lost in the slate gray depths of his eyes, which seemed to pull at her clothes until modesty bade her hand go to her pinkening bosom. She was deliciously trapped under his stare until Venetia spoke to him, breaking the spell. Avenel quickly turned away, but Brienne found herself continuing to stare, unwilling to give up the sight of him just yet.

"How do you find England, little Brienne?" The large matron tried to make conversation, having tired the rest of the table with her talk.

"I find it comfortable," she answered reluctantly, exploring her footed glass of claret as a convenient way to hide her annoyance. She had never used her title before coming to Osterley, but she found it terribly irritating this evening that it was *Lady* Venetia to all and sundry, while she was known simply as *little* Brienne, the backward waif from the Colonies.

The dinner seemed interminable, but when it finally did end, the ladies retired to the drawing room to chat and attend to their toilets while the men remained in the eating room. Brienne followed the women, trying very hard not to call attention to herself by taking a seat near

the wall. Lady Venetia and the duchess engaged in a stir-
ring conversation about the merits of taking or not taking the cure at Bath, which all the women in the room
appeared to find fascinating. It seemed that every
woman had a word or two to add to the discussion.
Brienne was thankful that there was so much going on
that she did not have to converse. She had never actually
been to the fashionable city except to pass by it on her
way from Tenby and to visit it in her dreams during her
first nights at Osterley.

The matron who had sat with her at dinner plopped
down in the settee beside her because she was much too
large for the armchairs in the room. Obviously taken
with the two wealthy young women who were the center of attention, she expressed her opinions of them to
Brienne.

"Lord Culpepper's daughter and Master Slane will
make a lovely couple, don't you think?"

Brienne stared at Lady Venetia, hardly hearing the matron's words. Remembering how the aristocratic co-
quette and Avenel had been conversing happily with the
guests in the gallery and at dinner, Brienne found that
she had to agree. "I suppose they would," she replied
coolly.

"Have you been here at the Park long? I would think a
young thing like yourself would find it very easy to become enamored of its master." The matron eyed her suggestively, hoping she would reveal some newsworthy information.

"I have no fondness for Osterley's master." Brienne
turned away from the old woman and sipped her tea. She
hoped that would end the conversation, but she was not
so lucky.

"You must be blind then, my dear. Even I, in my dotage, admit that I have never seen such a fine figure of a man. Such broad shoulders! Such a trim waist! I hear he even possesses all his own teeth!''

''Well, I find him singularly unimpressive.'' Brienne sipped her tea again and tried to look indifferent.

''I see.'' There was a sly, knowing look on the matron's florid face, and suddenly she stopped asking questions.

Brienne turned away from the gossipy woman and saw that the men were beginning to wander in from the eating room to join the ladies. When she spied Cumberland's familiar visage, her face lit up. He smiled at her also but did not come to join her when he saw Rose sitting near the fire. Brienne watched them greet each other and wondered how soon there would be a wedding at Osterley. Rose had never looked more youthful as she smiled into Cumberland's face and patted a place for him on her settee.

It was strange to feel so alone in the midst of so many people, but watching Cumberland and Rose suddenly made her feel just that way. She looked down at her hands, not wanting them to think she was staring, even though that was precisely what she had been doing. She felt inexpressibly frustrated for some reason, and she found she could no longer tolerate the drawing room. Excusing herself from the matron, she rose just in time to avoid a young fop who was heading her way.

In her hurry to walk out the door before the boring young man could catch her attention, she bumped into Avenel as he entered the drawing room.

''And where are you off to, little one?'' He looked down at her from his great height. He seemed more than pleased by the turnout for his ball; it showed in his lazy smile and relaxed demeanor.

"I—I thought I would go into the gallery and listen to the music in there," Brienne said softly as she felt all eyes in the drawing room turn in their direction. That Avenel commanded attention from this group was plain. It seemed that everyone found him and his curious past a fascinating topic of conversation. Brienne, on the other hand, had wanted to keep her name out of the gossip. She had tried her best to avoid speculation by keeping a demure profile, but Avenel was not helping her cause now, for he stood in the doorway and would not let her pass until they had exchanged familiarities.

"Have you danced?" There was a twinkle in his eyes, and she wondered if he had always been so cold and untouchable.

"I don't know how to dance." She turned away to hide her growing embarrassment. Scrutinizing looks were coming from all corners of the room by now, but none were so pointed as those of Venetia and the duchess, which bored mercilessly into her back. "I've not socialized, you recall. I remember telling you that when you first came here." Brienne motioned to pass him, but still he lingered by her side. It irked her that he had not come to her aid earlier in the evening, at dinner when she had been among all those strange faces, but had instead chosen the present time to offer her companionship. Finally, when she could stand it no longer, she said with annoyance, "If you will excuse me."

"Have I told you how lovely you look tonight, wildflower? Many of the men here must be envious of my position."

"Only because of your relationship with Lord Culpepper's daughter. And I do believe she is waiting for you with bated breath, so . . ." She moved past him out the door, but not before he could whisper to her in passing.

"Is there a note of jealousy in that silken voice of yours?"

She gave him a look of incredulity to prove the ridiculousness of his speculations, but he laughed out loud and watched her go with her head held high.

Brienne stayed in the gallery for a long time, watching the couples dance and declining invitations to do likewise. Quickly running out of excuses, she wandered into the marble hall and found some solitude by the fireside in one of the apses. The Reverend Trumbell generously walked up to her as she stood alone. He nobly tried to start a conversation on the Roman statues of Hercules and Apollo that were placed in the hall, but soon the sinewy nakedness of the ancient sculptures became all too obvious to the both of them, and he quickly excused himself to speak to an old friend.

Another brave young man then appeared at her side, but if there was one thing the evening had proved, it was her newly developed particularity about men. Most of them seemed to be oppressively dull and more than a little self-inflated. So it was a relief when this one's mother called him back to her side so she could introduce him to a more likely candidate for marriage.

Left once again to her own devices, Brienne thought it best to sit out the rest of the evening in the drawing room. When she returned there, however, she found several intense games of loo going on, and she had no way to join in since she had neither knowledge of the game nor the proper funds to play it. She had no idea where Cumberland and Rose had disappeared to, and Avenel also was nowhere to be seen. Closing the drawing-room door quietly behind her, she wandered alone down the south passage and looked out to the well-lighted courtyard from the large aligning windows.

She reached the door to the Etruscan dressing room and thought it would be empty. But the door stood slightly ajar, and she was surprised to hear voices coming from its interior. Her heart skipped a beat when she heard a familiar, coy little laugh and an even more familiar masculine voice.

"Why not, my darling? Just think of the scandal! My father would be apoplectic if he found us in each other's arms amid the splendor of your bedchamber." There was a suspicious rustle of skirts, and Brienne found herself bending closer to the door in horrified fascination.

"Avenel! Kiss me!" she could hear Venetia say in a demanding female voice.

"Lady Venetia, you must know that this is neither the time nor the place." He sounded cool and amused.

"Oh, you cad! You get me so that I cannot think straight, and then you dare talk to me about propriety." Venetia turned deviously and affectedly shy. "Am I not beautiful? I have been called the toast of London. Many surely would have fallen at my feet, begging for my consideration. You should not toy with my affection for fear it will be withdrawn." She could hear the snap of a closing fan and then another high-pitched giggle.

"And if I fell at your feet, also? Would you then find me more to your liking?" Avenel's voice was mocking.

"It's the very thing that has me crazed, your coldness and your distance! But do not be indifferent tonight, my love. Take me now. I offer you everything for your touch." Following that speech there was heavy silence, and Brienne could come to only one terrible conclusion. Not wanting to hear more, she backed softly away from the door and from the couple on the other side; her satin slippers made no sound. Her heart felt unusually heavy in her chest as she moved away. She wanted only to retire from this confusing society and find her room.

But suddenly someone grabbed her arm from behind and pulled her toward the closed mahogany door that led to the state bedchamber. Assaulted with the sour stench of intoxicated breath, Brienne came face to face with the Earl of Culpepper.

"You're as comely up close as you are at a distance." Culpepper swayed and tried to wrap his arms around her, succeeding despite his drunkenness only because of his greater strength.

"How dare you touch me in this manner!" Calmly Brienne pulled away from him, only to find herself being grabbed once more. Her salvation seemed to come quickly, however, for at the other end of the long passage she spied Rose wandering back to the drawing room from the hall.

"Rose!" Brienne called out from the alcove of the doorway. Hearing her name, Rose looked down the passage and then stood very still, watching the Earl of Culpepper place his drunken wiry frame over Brienne's slight one. "Please!" Brienne called to Rose again for help, but hope died in her breast when a frown merely appeared on the woman's angelic forehead and Rose left the passage for the drawing room.

"Your benefactress does not find my attentions objectionable. So neither should you. Don't make me remind you of my nobility." Culpepper smiled lasciviously and grabbed her arm, flinging her into the now-open door of the state bedroom.

"There is a room adjoining this one; I saw it before when Lord Oliver was in residence. We can go there." Again the drunken man swayed under all the alcohol he had consumed. With split-second timing Brienne sized up the situation and made a break for the passage door. But he slammed into her before she could reach it, and the door was soon closed behind her. "Into the other room." He pointed to the tapestry room that could be seen beyond the bedchamber. She turned to see if the other door to the Etruscan room had been left open, but unfortunately it was tightly closed.

He started to push her toward the tapestry room, but then came the joyful sound of footsteps in the passage. She tried to cry out, but a large sticky hand was placed revoltingly over her tender mouth. She heard Avenel's voice grow as faint as the distanced footsteps, and she was again shoved toward the tapestry room. Culpepper closed them off from the bedroom and turned to her. She desperately ran to the other door, which led to the drawing room, but when he caught her, the loud, gay chattering coming from it overrode her moans and cries.

"I shall scream!" she cried at him, watching his jaundiced eyes roam across her face and shoulders. He moved to kiss her, and she promptly started to carry out her threat, but he slapped her hard across the side of her face. Her scream turned into a painful moan.

"I have wanted you from the moment I set eyes on you in the gallery, Brienne. I must have you—and have you now!" He bent to place his salivating lips on her own.

"Avenel!" she called mindlessly, still stunned by the fierce blow.

"Avenel, is it?" He shook her shoulders to make her more coherent. "What is the man to you, sweet cousin of his?" He slurred his S's and sprayed her face with his spittle.

"Get away from me, you monster!" She found her tongue once more and tried with all her strength to pull away from his revolting touch. The stiff embroidery on his coat was pressing painfully into the soft skin of her shoulders, making them raw.

"You dare call me a monster?" Culpepper's face reddened, and he grimaced horribly. "Brienne, the quiet little newcomer from America, who, by my daughter's account, hadn't even the funds to dress herself properly until Slane arrived back from London with some new gowns. Tell me, sweet, what kind of creature allows a man to provide such intimate gifts as the very clothes she wears on her back?" He moved a hand along her scraped and tender shoulders, poking a finger along the edge of her brocaded bodice. "I think only a woman who has whored for the rutting stag countless times would do that." He pulled the material at her shoulders down violently. She flinched and moved farther away.

"Get away from me!" she screamed. "You're a mistaken fool!"

"I am mistaken?" He wobbled in drunken disbelief. "It's you who are mistaken if you think Venetia will allow Slane to continue providing for you. She means to get him by marriage. Then you will be without a home and available for the taking." There was a lustful gleam in his small, beady eyes. "So get down on that floor, my beauty," he said as he raised his hand threateningly, making her cringe back for the descending blow. "And prepare yourself for your new keeper." His hand demanded her compliance as it came down with the bursting of a thousand white stars in her head.

Rose sat still and quiet at the edge of the drawing room; her face bore a distinct frown.

"Are you tired of this, love?" Cumberland's eyes caressed her; he was the picture of concern.

"No, no, I am all right," she said distractedly. But suddenly she burst out, "Where is Avenel? Have you seen him recently?"

"I believe he might be in the gallery. Would you like me to find him for you?"

"No," she said with determination. "It's nothing." She lowered her worried, guilt-ridden eyes and watched her hands clasp and unclasp in her lap. "No, it is something!" she finally said, and she turned desperately to Cumberland. "I must find Avenel. It is Brienne." With new determination she got up from her chair and walked to the door, ignoring the crowds of people in her way.

"There he is now!" Cumberland called to her as he and the ever-present Lady Venetia stepped through the doorway.

Rose let out a sob and ran to him. "God forgive me, Avenel, God forgive me for such doings!"

"What is it?" Avenel looked down at her sharply.

"It's Brienne. Brienne!" She gave a remorseful cry. "I am a wicked woman for harboring such thoughts. I deserve my heartache for what I have just done."

"What about Brienne? You must tell me." He shook her shoulders gently.

"Lord Culpepper has gotten himself drunk. I saw him corner her in the passage near your room. I . . . did . . . nothing." She hung her head contritely in her hands. "Go! I cannot even guess what she must be going through!"

Without even a backward glance, Avenel bolted out the drawing-room door to the south passage. The entire room had fallen quiet during Rose's confession, and soon partygoers began to trickle out to the passage themselves, hoping to glimpse a scandal. Venetia followed

Avenel, calling frantically to stop his hasty action and to avoid one.

Bursting into his bedchamber and cursing violently when he found it empty, he threw open the door to the tapestry room just in time to see Lord Culpepper run his hand up along Brienne's torn bodice and place his mouth slovenly over hers.

Brienne was dazed as she felt Lord Culpepper's body being flung off of her like so much baggage. She took several steps back, and with her arms moving protectively over her bodice, she murmured Avenel's name so softly, it could not be discerned, for her head ached from the effort of trying to speak. But suddenly two safe arms appeared, and she instinctively went to them, comforted by their familiar scent and feel. The numbness began to wear off, and the fear she had felt was relieved in part by sobbing into the white waistcoat before her. While her wracking shoulders were held gently and securely, she felt Avenel kiss her knotted, mussed hair. Her comb was nowhere to be found, but she knew that it lay crushed and broken underfoot.

" 'Tis over now, little one. Rose told me. You will be just fine.''

"He tried to rape me," she cried, and felt anew the raw imprint of Culpepper's hand on her cheek and elsewhere on her violated body.

Avenel looked down, seeing her tender, swollen face, and said, "He cannot now. See for yourself." He opened his arms just enough to let her view Culpepper's body, unconscious on the floor. Venetia was bent over him, and suddenly she sent an accusing look toward them both.

"He is bleeding! You have caused by father to bleed!''

Venetia laid her hand on the earl's head, and it came back laced with red. "I think you have killed him. And for her!" she spat venomously.

Avenel turned to Cumberland, who appeared through the crowds at the door as Rose steadfastly held the on-lookers back. "Have some footmen deposit Lord Culpepper on the other side of the gates. And tell them they need not be gentle."

Cumberland nodded his approval. "I think I spotted a couple of especially burly ones near the breakfast room. I am sure they would oblige," he said before he left the room.

Upon hearing the shriek that vented out of Lady Venetia, Avenel turned to her. "You may go with him, or you may stay. 'Tis as you wish. But he will be out of this house before I return, or I shall call him out and be done with him for good." He then ignored Venetia completely as he turned his attention back to the woman in his arms.

He removed his topcoat and placed it around Brienne's shoulders. He picked her up gingerly in his arms as if she weighed no more than a feather and moved out into the passage through the hordes of curious guests. Brienne was grateful for the black satin that covered the rent near her left breast. She was pale and withdrawn, but her crying had subsided.

One of the guests, a physician, followed them upstairs, and before she had even realized it, she was lying on her bed, swallowing the laudanum he had prescribed. There was no fighting the heavy effects of the sedative that was forced upon her, and she felt her eyes close in oblivion before she could even thank Avenel for rescuing her.

It was no peaceful sleep that she retreated into that night. All sorts of dark, unarticulated specters rose from the recesses of her mind. She tossed and turned to be free of them but could not wake herself up from her drugged sleep.

In one nightmare she found herself back in Tenby. It was a brilliant, clear day, and she and her mother were having a picnic on Castle Hill overlooking both the clear blue waters of the Atlantic and the gray stone walls of the fortressed town below.

"Mama, tell me about the balls. Tell me about the beautiful ladies and all the lovely gowns." She swept a dark red curl from her face as the breezes caught hold of her petticoats.

"They were a magnificent sight. And I had the best of all of it. I had the most beautiful gowns and the most costly jewels. Your grandfather, Brienne, was a generous man. I know he would have loved you dearly."

"Mama, who is the man? Who is the one in your miniature?" Brienne leaned nearer to her mother, wanting so badly to hear the words, the words that would finally free her of a terrible past.

But before she had her answer, her mother's serenely beautiful face grimaced in helpless acceptance as a shadow fell from behind. Brienne hardly dared to look around, but when she summoned the courage, she turned and saw Oliver Morrow towering over them.

"She is too young. Take me," her mother had pleaded.

"Where is my comb, my jewels?" Oliver Morrow had merely laughed, showing yellow teeth and lips that were much too large for his face.

"No! No!" Brienne had cried to her mother. "We will run again, Mama. We will run, and this time I will protect you!" Brienne got off the ground where they sat and took her mother by the hand. Together they both ran up the hill to the free-standing tower, where she had planned to hide. She saw that the earl was running after them. Quickly she shoved her mother into the tower.

A scream tore through the serenity of the Welsh sea-scape as she saw the earl magically appear on the bottom step inside the tower. Before the petrified wooden door slammed shut in front of her, she saw the earl pull her mother's jet black hair violently away from her beautiful face, saying the words, "Someday I will have you both."

"Mama, I will protect you, Mama!" Brienne tore at the rock-hard door with her fingernails until they bled. Mournful sounds came from the top of the tower, and she had to put her bloody hands to her ears to shut out the horrible sound. "I will protect you!" she sobbed helplessly.

But soon heavy footsteps were heard descending the tower stairs, and she pulled away from the door to run. She stumbled down the hill, panicked and sobbing, searching desperately for a place to hide. To her amazement, the cabinet from the Tudor house appeared, sitting starkly on the hill. She slid into the cabinet and hid in its darkness, praying that he would not be able to find her there.

She whimpered softly as footsteps approached. Her nerves twitched and whined in fear, but then thankfully she heard him walk away from the cabinet. In the ensuing quiet, she thought it safe to leave her hiding place and go to her mother. Opening the doors a tiny crack, she saw nothing but the sea, the sky, and the castle tower on the hill. She opened wide the doors, but then with a terrifying jolt the earl's gray-bearded face loomed down from a great height above the cabinet. She let out a scream of pure terror as he grabbed her.

"Brienna love."

"I heard you walk away! I heard you walk away!" she screamed almost incoherently.

"You must wake up. Wake up, little one." Her shoulders were being shaken and her eyes flew open to see Avenel bending over her, wearing the same waistcoat and breeches he had worn at the ball. She was panting and perspiring, and when she looked down at herself, she saw that her night smock was soaked right through. Trembling, she looked out the windows of her room and saw the first dim light of a gloomy dawn.

"Oh," she moaned, "I've got to get out of here."

" 'Twas only a nightmare, my love." She looked up and found herself clutching at his white waistcoat. She dropped her shaking fists back down to the bed and accepted his hand as he softly stroked back her dark hair from her damp forehead.

"He's going to kill me, Avenel. He's going to kill me for being here. I have got to leave."

"And where would you go, wildflower? Your *dinbych*, your fortress, is in ruins and not fit for your return. I've had my men check and recheck for a long-lost aunt or cousin that might come to find you, but you seem to have none. In short, my love, no one has come to claim you, and you have nowhere to go."

"How can I stay? There is only torment for me here. You seem to know more and more about me every day, but still I know nothing about you. Nothing! How can I trust you if I know nothing about you? How can I trust that my father won't be able to—"

"Oliver Morrow is a dead man, Brienne. Believe me. Though he may still walk this earth, I have seen to it."

His voice was as cold and unfeeling as she had ever heard it.

"I want to trust you. I don't know why, but I feel I must. Yet how can I when I know I'm the enemy?" she whispered to him. He was quiet for a long time and did not seem to be able to refute what she said. As his face became clearer in the early morning light, she saw how tired he appeared and how disheveled his clothes were.

He rubbed his unshaven jaw and distractedly ran a hand through his hair. " 'Tis been a long night, wildflower. I cannot answer so difficult a question for you now." On impulse she reached out to feel the scratchy stubble darkening his handsome face, and soon she found she had moved over enough in the bed to allow him to stretch out beside her. He unbuttoned his waistcoat and then she felt him hold her quietly, almost sadly in his arms, until they both fell asleep at dawn.

CHAPTER FIFTEEN

The first thing that met her eyes when Brienne awoke was the soft, dove-gray drizzle that hung on the Park outside her window. She had no idea what time of day it was, but she did feel rested, and her head, which had ached all night even in sleep, had ceased pounding. Turning away from the windows, she snuggled deeper into the bed linens, wondering how she could feel so happy and refreshed after such an awful evening. But when her eyes met the empty place beside her, the realization hit her. There was a distinct round impression in the other pillow, and Avenel's scent lingered on the fine, silken linens.

"So you are awake now, *ma demoiselle.*" Brienne sat up in her bed at the sound of Vivie's voice. She watched as the little woman put down her sewing and got up from the settee, which was pulled up to a roaring, brisk fire. "You have slept well this day, *n'est-ce pas?*" Vivie went to the Pembroke table and got the tray she had prepared for her.

"What time is it?" Brienne asked guiltily. She pushed her tangled mass of auburn hair away from her face and tried to get out of bed. But at the sudden movement the room started to sway; her head still felt the effects of the laudanum.

"Ah! You must stay where you are!" Vivie brought the tray to her bedside night table. She then scurried to get a comb for her hair. "Here, *ma demoiselle*. Let me take this out of your way." The maid untangled the burgundy knots, and soon Vivie had tamed the voluminous strands by putting Brienne's hair into a long plait. That task accomplished, she put the tray on the bed and poured out a steaming cup of chocolate for her mistress.

The hot liquid seemed to clear her head, and Brienne repeated her question. "What time is it? I know it must be late."

"It is past noon, but—"

"Past noon!" she exclaimed fretfully. "I cannot believe it!"

"You were in need of rest. You had a troubled night." Vivie shook her head ferociously and spewed out, "How dare that pig treat you so brutally! I hope the Monsieur has taught him to behave with more respect."

"Have you spoken to Avenel this morning?" Brienne asked, shying away from the answer.

"Briefly." Vivie lowered her eyes, and Brienne guessed that the little woman had come upon them when she had arrived for her duties.

"Yet you have heard what happened last night?" At the little maid's nod, she continued helplessly, "I never should have gone to the ball. I should have known the evening would come to no good. I was so ungainly there among all those wealthy people. I should have seen that it was only a matter of time before someone would take advantage of my lack of knowledge about social situations."

"Why should you speak like that, *ma demoiselle?* Avenel told me you've had a most noble upbringing. You have nothing but to look down your *petite* nose at those others."

"I may have a title, but I certainly lack the other accoutrements associated with the ton. Last night more than proved that. I was a dismal failure. I should have retired to my room after dinner. Then perhaps none of this would have happened."

"It was not a failure! For now you can see that the Monsieur has feelings for you." Vivie looked over as two young girls entered the room and set up a bath by the fire. One was busy setting down a pile of white boiled linens, and the other poured hot water into the tub from a polished copper kettle.

"I will not allow myself to believe that, Vivie." Brienne rose from the bed and stood, holding on to the back of an armchair for balance.

"You must believe it, for he was with you all night long, refusing to leave your bedside until he saw that you slept comfortably. We heard the terrible nightmares, but it was he who comforted you, for he would allow no one else to do so. It is also rumored that he and the Lady Venetia are no longer speaking after her father's display. He cares for you very much." Vivie shooed the little girls out of the room when the tub was ready and started to help Brienne out of her night smock.

"You must not say such things. You must not even think such things," Brienne answered blackly. "Avenel must have had great hopes for Lady Venetia and what she could offer in a marriage—things I could never give. He may have been angered by her father's behavior last night, but should Avenel want Lady Venetia back, he shall blame me for his dissatisfaction." Brienne slipped into the silky water and felt its warmth take away the stiffness in her tense muscles. Leaning her head on the rim, she let her long braid hang down the back of the tub, looking like a red-haired Rapunzel. Brienne refused to take what Vivie said to heart. Even if her words were not wishful daydreams, it was unthinkable that she and Avenel could fall in love. It would be an impossibility, considering the circumstances.

"As you wish, my lady. I will speak of it no longer. But just because things are not identified by the tongue does not mean they do not exist." Vivie handed her a huge yellow bar of soap and went to the dressing room to get her a gown.

"Ouch!" Brienne sucked in her breath. She was looking at the angry red mark on her cheek from her ordeal the night before. It was still very tender to the touch. She had tried to conceal it with some powder, but it contrasted too sharply with the unblemished, creamy skin of the rest of her face.

"The mark still shows. You cannot hide what happened." Vivie shook her head as Brienne powdered the mark. "Besides, the Monsieur does not forget. He will be angry all over again when he sees this." The French maid pointed to the welt.

"I don't want him angry. I don't want to think of the incident anymore." Brienne looked into her mirror with a frown. She looked at herself for a long while, concocting all sorts of schemes for hiding the ugly red bruise. A swift knock on her door made her abandon these thoughts temporarily, however, and she rose to answer it.

Standing penitently on the threshold of her door was Rose. Her red-rimmed blue eyes spoke of little sleep and many tears.

"Rose!" Brienne cried in surprise. She gathered her wits about her and bade her enter the room. Looking up, she saw Vivie quickly depart; she assumed the maid would reappear shortly with a tray of tea and cakes. Brienne asked Rose to be seated on the taffeta settee near the fire; she took one of the satinwood elbow chairs for herself.

"Won't you please sit on the settee with me, Lady Brienne?" Rose patted the empty seat next to her.

Brienne looked at her for several moments but then gladly did as Rose suggested, despite her new-found shyness with Avenel's cousin.

"Can I do anything for you, Rose? I am sure Vivie will be here soon with refreshments, but—"

"No, no, I have no need for that. What I am in need of is your forgiveness."

"My forgiveness?" Brienne asked in bewilderment. "Please don't concern yourself—"

"I must. I've become a heartless woman, one who has taken out her own hardships on an innocent girl."

"You have had your very life shattered in widowhood. And it's natural that you should blame me." Brienne looked guiltily down at her hands.

"He did that to you?" Rose asked tearfully, noticing the mark on Brienne's cheek. When Brienne nodded, Rose wept into the linen handkerchief stuffed into her fist.

"Please don't cry, Rose. It looks worse than it is. Truly, I hardly feel it at all. You were not to blame for last night. Why, anyone at all—"

"My husband, Christopher," Rose interrupted her.

"He was the finest man alive. I know we must have seemed like children when we married. I was only sixteen, and he barely twenty. But I had known them all their lives, you see?"

"Them?" Brienne asked, feeling confused.

"He and Avenel. Christopher was Avenel's brother."

Hiding the shock of this revelation, Brienne allowed Rose to continue.

"What I am trying to tell you is that, although Christopher has been dead for so long and although our marriage was brief and done in the haste of youth, I will always remember him for his great kindness. He had a brutal and early death. Now I've shamed him by the way I've behaved toward you, especially last night." Rose sobbed her contrition.

"Please, you must not say such things. Your husband must have been very proud of you. He must have loved you very much, for I know both Cumberland and Avenel do. You're a goddess in their eyes, and they would not look upon you that way if you were not truly so wonderful." Brienne reached out and put her hand on the woman's shoulders, but then, remembering her place, she withdrew it. Starting on her own confession, she said, "I, in fact, am the one who should be seeking forgiveness. The man you loved was taken from you too early in this life. If it were not for the grievous wounds inflicted upon you by my father, then perhaps you would not be so unhappy, and I would not be here as a terrible reminder of what you have lost." Tears welled up in her eyes, but she forced them back, not wanting to add to Rose's feelings of blame.

"You're a good woman, Brienne. From everything I have seen these past weeks, you've been without fault. Despite your heritage, I've wronged you by my behavior.

I must admit that it has been hard to be cold when all you have offered is genuine friendship. And now if it is not too late, I would like to offer you *my* genuine friendship. That is, if you would be so generous to accept it." Rose looked at her with teary eyes. There was nothing but sincere feeling on her fair face, and when she stretched out her hand, Brienne found herself taking it; her own eyes brimmed with tears of unspeakable relief.

The two women spent the entire afternoon drinking tea and talking. There was so much Brienne wanted to know about Rose's husband, Avenel's brother, that she fairly burst with questions concerning the two men.

"So you are not only Avenel's cousin but his sister-in-law as well?"

Rose nodded. "We all three grew up together."

"In Maryland?"

"Yes. My parents both died of a fever before I was even two years old. So my aunt and uncle adopted me as their own. We three grew up together and were very close. It seems now that I always loved Christopher." Rose smiled at the memory. "Even as a child. He was so handsome and so brave. So much like Avenel is. But of course, there is a difference." Rose's eyes became shadowed. "Avenel has a hardness about him that Christopher never had. But he is still a charming rogue when he wants to be. I must warn you to watch out for him. Avenel has broken many a heart in his day, and I am afraid he could find yours pretty fine game."

"We can hardly hold a civil conversation as it is. I think my heart is pretty safe." Moving to pour another cup of tea from the silver pot, Brienne lowered her eyes from Rose's view. "How did you come about being here in England?"

"I was sent here after Christopher died. Avenel

thought it best." Rose stopped talking and sipped her tea thoughtfully.

"I . . ." Brienne swallowed. Finally she was ready to ask what she had wanted to know since the very first day Avenel came to Osterley. "I know this may be painful for you. But could you tell me why all this has come about? Why does Avenel hate the earl so?"

"Do not ask me that, Brienne."

"Please tell me. I must know," Brienne persisted gently.

"I cannot tell you. Not because it is too painful to bring up; for despite the pain, it is on my mind constantly. It colors every activity of my day, as it does Avenel's and Cumberland's. The reason I cannot tell you is that I have promised Avenel I would not. I cannot break my word to him."

"I see," Brienne said lamely.

"He has protected me and provided for me for twenty years now. His wishes must be my wishes. I cannot be so ungrateful. Do you understand?" Rose lifted benevolent, pleading eyes.

"Yes, I understand," Brienne answered wryly. "It seems that everyone here is in debt to him in some way or another." Her voice began to tremble.

"Do not despair! He has been kind to you, has he not?"

"He has been generous." Brienne smoothed out the rich plum-colored silk of her dress and relished its dusky softness. She looked up with a frown, however, and exclaimed, "But not knowing what is in store for me is hard to bear. What I have imagined must be far worse than the truth could ever be. Avenel has all but told me he will have his revenge." She searched Rose's face to see if she could trust her. Only when she was satisfied that she could did she say, "He is an angry man, Rose, as I'm sure you know. I'm afraid he will make me pay for what the earl has done to you both. Somehow I'm tied to his plan to humiliate Lord Oliver. I fear Avenel for this, but perhaps what is worse, I find I am drawn to him, and that will be my damnation." She laughed sadly and after a rather pregnant silence, she said, "It's like trying to gaze at the sun, is it not?"

Rose put a warm hand over her own trembling one. "He is not as fearsome as you believe. I know he has his moments, but his hatred is for the earl. You must try to forget all else. His hatred is for the earl, Brienne," she repeated, "not for you."

"I hope above all else that that is so." Brienne looked up, and Rose patted her hand comfortingly.

"Leave the past behind you. I am trying to." Rose blushed. "Cumberland has provided ample diversion, I must say."

"I'm happy for you, Rose. I've wanted to tell you. I have a great fondness for Cumberland, and it's been heartening to see how happy you have made him."

Rose gave a youthful laugh. "He is a darling! I almost hope . . . no, I cannot say it, for then I shall be cursed!"

"I can say it then!" Brienne volunteered. "You almost hope he will ask you to marry him! There! It has been said, and you have no need for concern!"

Rose blushed becomingly and said, "I admit I have my hopes."

"Never fear. It will come to pass. It's all too clear in his face. When you enter the room, he is a whole new man!" She laughed out loud. "Like a boy in the first throes of painfully true love."

Both women giggled, but soon Rose grew serious. "I

know this has been hard for you. The circumstances at Osterley are unusual. And you're much too young for sorrow." She suddenly squeezed her hand. "Why, we both are! Promise me you will forget what has gone on before?"

Brienne regarded Rose for several seconds. There was no way to erase the impending doom of her father's arrival, nor was there any way to forget that she was being held at Osterley against her will. But even if Rose's friendship could not last, Brienne knew she would rather live in a temporary truce than in a permanent war. Her voice trembled as she smiled. "I suppose, at the very least, we could try."

Brienne arrived for dinner resplendent in peach-colored satin shot with gold thread. Cumberland and Rose greeted her in the gallery. After several minutes alone with them, Brienne determined that she had never seen two people more in love. Cumberland was his dear self, but every glance, every gesture, and every word seemed to be for Rose alone. And Rose, feeling relieved and at peace, was like a sweet, blushing maiden again under his petting attentions.

As they waited for Avenel to arrive, Brienne sat quietly in an elbow chair, listening to the conversation but happily resigned not to have to be a part of it. It was enough to be among such goodwill, and she reveled in the serenity it brought to her troubled soul.

Soon Avenel arrived, and Brienne instinctively turned her marred cheek away from his sight, hoping she had hidden the mark under enough powder that he wouldn't notice it. He walked around to give Rose a brotherly peck on the cheek, but when he came to her, he stopped dead. Without making a sound he turned her bruised cheek to the firelight and brushed the swelling very lightly with his thumb. At his touch on her tender, battered skin, she tried to hide her involuntary wince, but it could not be obscured. Avenel's jet eyebrows came together in a frown, and his diamond eyes sparkled with unvented rage.

"Don't be angry." Brienne tried to placate him. "Don't be angry tonight."

"That bastard!" he cursed. But his frosty eyes met her gentian ones, and he softened. Taking her hand, he bent to it in a courtly fashion. After placing a genteel kiss on its back, he raised himself and said, "You're more lovely than ever, my lady. Culpepper could never make your beauty less than perfect."

Thankful that the storm had been averted, Brienne took the chair Avenel offered at the table. When they all were seated, dinner commenced in a most amiable fashion. There were a few bland comments about the ball, but everyone skirted the issue of Lady Venetia and her father. Avenel had never been so agreeable, and Brienne found herself basking in his charm and unusual good nature.

It did not seem long before the candles had burned down to stubs and the fire had been reduced to a glowing pile of embers. Dessert had been served and cleared, leaving the four of them sitting with their half-empty wineglasses and quiet talk. It was then that Cumberland's and Rose's faces took on a special glow, and Cumberland stood to make the announcement. He cleared his throat once or twice and then commenced.

"I am a lucky man tonight. I have been blessed with the company of two extraordinarily beautiful women." He raised his glass to both Rose and Brienne, but Brienne hardly noticed, waiting in excited anticipation of the news. "One of them," Cumberland continued, "in her profound humility and grace has accepted my offer of marriage." He smiled, and Rose held out her left hand to show off the ring that he had given her. It was set with a large, square-cut emerald that flamed with highlights of the deepest blue. Brienne exclaimed at its beauty, and it brought them all to their feet to exchange garbled simultaneous congratulations and the thanks that went with them. Avenel quickly rushed a footman off for the best champagne in the cellar, and soon there was toasting and lighthearted laughter.

"We plan to go to London. However"—Cumberland cleared his throat uncomfortably—"considering the immediacy of the situation here at the Park, I should think we won't be gone more than a week."

"I'm sure we'll be back all too soon, for we shall miss you both terribly." Rose took Brienne's hand and squeezed it with new-found warmth.

"You shall not miss us a bit." Avenel laughed heartily. " 'Tis folly to think so!"

They all laughed, and Rose smiled shyly. All too soon, the champagne was drunk, and Rose and Cumberland stood to retire to the drawing room. They walked ahead of Avenel and Brienne, already immersed in their plans for the wedding. Watching them go, Brienne touched Avenel's topcoat lightly to get his attention.

"What is it, wildflower?" He bent down to her and smiled with unusually carefree abandon.

"They need to be alone, Avenel." She nodded in their direction as they disappeared through the door to the drawing room. "So I find I must retire."

He looked down at her and stroked her deep auburn hair. He grew serious as he looked at her, and soon words seemed to flow unchecked from his mouth. "Stay with me tonight, little one. Come to my bed so that I can comfort you. I can make no promises now, but . . ." He stopped talking when he noticed how sad her eyes became with this last sentence. He added, " 'Tis unfair for you to look at me so. Unfair that you make such demands with your eyes."

"I make no demands." She looked down from his face and studied the intricate brocade pattern on his perfectly tailored waistcoat.

"Your demands are as yet unspoken, but still . . ." He dropped his hands from her hair, and they swung lamely by his side. "Go, then. Go to your lonely room, and I will go to mine. But do not expect me to change my mind. And," he added enigmatically, "do not be surprised if you find you have changed yours." She looked up at him questioningly, but there was no answer in his stoic face. She backed away from him and turned to leave. Her head told her one thing and, as Avenel somehow knew, her heart told her another.

CHAPTER SIXTEEN

"Wait!" Brienne laughed, and her breath trailed behind her in frigid little puffs. She ran through the dormant kitchen gardens and headed toward the waiting coach. Beneath her fur-lined cloak, she pulled up the petticoat of one of her finest gowns—a lavender silk lutestring with embroidered bunches of pale yellow flowers—and almost flew over to the pebbled drive in front of the house. Glad that her hair was neatly bound in netting, she held on to the small hat that perched daintily on her head, tied with satin ribbons of butter yellow.

"You will make me late!" Rose cried from the coach, looking happy and beautiful wrapped in several layers of wedding white ermine. Peeking out from the fur blankets was her wedding gown, a lustrous periwinkle with a cream-colored satin petticoat; both were heavily brocaded in gold and silver threads.

When Brienne reached the coach, she allowed the footman to help her into it. Once inside, she reverently placed the well-trimmed branches of orange blossoms onto Rose's lap.

"They are beautiful! Brienne, how thoughtful!" Rose exclaimed and held the flowers, which were carefully bound by a white satin ribbon, to her nose. She inhaled their heady fragrance, which filled Avenel's japanned coach, and looking up, she said, "I wouldn't have believed those old trees in the Orangery could ever blossom again."

"It was their duty to blossom! Every bride needs fresh flowers on her wedding day!" Brienne leaned over to smell them as Rose held them out to her.

"I'm so happy. I never thought I would feel like this again." Rose looked out the coach window as they made their way over Osterley's grounds and through the gates to the small church in the township. It was a beautiful day. Brilliant, powerful sunshine beat down from the azure plain of the sky. With it, even the hard, winter earth was compelled to soften for Rose's wedding.

Brienne let out an unusually contented sigh and looked back at the weeks preceding this day.

She and Rose had spent many a happy hour planning the wedding, and during the evenings the two women, Cumberland, and Avenel had gathered in the gallery to dine and discuss the new arrangements. Brienne had seen very little of Avenel; he had made several day trips to London with Cumberland to make certain purchases, as well as arrangements for the honeymoon. But always, when the two men returned, Avenel was full of good spirits. He beckoned Brienne once again to go riding with him. She smiled secretly as she remembered the day she had first returned to Queenie's back. Avenel had walked over to her and the mare to instruct her in equitation. Placing a lingering, warm hand upon her ankle, he had pushed her heel down into the stirrup, and then, as if embarrassed by the moment, he had told her gruffly to keep it there or she would get into all sorts of trouble. She had tried to behave maidenly and to look away from him then, but it was no use; her feelings for him were growing every day, and they were anything but virginal. They were becoming terrible and magnificent—and harder and harder to deny.

She now sat back in the coach and pondered the future. She had grown to love Cumberland and Rose dearly, but she had to admit that she envied them their security. For as long as she could remember, she had never had that. It was as if she'd been born in a box-wood maze, and no matter what path she took in the topiary, it led to the same dead end, and she could never get out.

The coach pulled up in front of the church, where Cumberland and Avenel stood. All types of townsfolk had seen the posted banns and were there to wish the bride and groom well. After allowing the wedding party to enter, the well-wishers pushed their way into the church, filling every available pew. But a hush fell upon the crowd as the minister started to speak the words of matrimony. Avenel stood by Cumberland, and Brienne watched as his eyes fixed on Rose, who in her happiness appeared much younger than she was. Brienne knew as he watched Rose speak her vows that Avenel was seeing another wedding day twenty years before, and suddenly she could not bear to look at him, afraid she would see that accusing look in his eyes today. But soon she felt his gaze upon her, and Brienne unwillingly lifted her eyes. She expected to see a damning look on his face, but instead there was a look of such open, shameless longing that she found she could not look away. She was held for a long moment spellbound by his compelling, unhooded emotions, which were so rarely unguarded.

The ceremony was soon over, and the spell that had transfixed Brienne was broken by the strange mix of tears and laughter that is seen only at weddings. Rose and Cumberland, now husband and wife, each gave her a hug and then moved over to the other well-wishers. The minister quickly invited the four of them to the parsonage to enjoy a glass of claret, and before Brienne realized it, Rose and Cumberland were sitting in the new coach that would take them to London.

"You take care of him, Brienne," Rose said, referring to Avenel. "He can be such a stuffy fellow at times. He needs you to make him laugh." She bent down from the carriage seat and kissed Brienne on her cheek. Unashamedly holding Cumberland's hand, Rose then took Avenel's jaw in her other hand and whispered something to him that Brienne overheard: "I have forgiven her, Avenel. Today in my happiness I think I could even forgive Oliver Morrow. This is the only advice I will ever give you, love: Forget the past. We can, and you must, or you will never find peace." With that, she dropped her hand from his face. Cumberland impatiently signaled the driver to be off.

Waving at them until they were just a speck on the horizon, Avenel finally said, "I think they have both made a very fine choice."

"They are very lucky to have each other." She looked up at him with serious purple eyes. He frowned as he watched her; he appeared older today than his real age of four and thirty. Perhaps it was the memories that made him so, Brienne thought.

Avenel put his large hand on the small of her back and started to help her up into his carriage. She turned to him and said, "It's such a beautiful day, Avenel. I'd like to walk back to the house."

"You want to walk?" He looked at her in disbelief. His dark head bent down to her so that he could see her face more closely. "This is unheard of! A lady of the realm wanting to soil her satin slippers in the mire of the road-side?"

"I haven't been allowed from the Park for so long, and I thought—" she started to explain, but two strong fingers touched her lips to quiet her before she could go on.

"You needn't give me reasons for your odd behavior, Brienne. I know about the eccentricities of the nobility." He looked up at the cold blue sky and then smiled most charmingly. "Besides, I was thinking the same thing but did not wish to impose my desires on you." He took her by the hand and laughed at the incredulous look she flung at him.

"You? Not wanting to impose your wishes on me?" she exclaimed wryly as they walked through the sleepy township. "That is like King Henry VIII telling his wife he would wish for no divorce!"

"Quiet, you hoyden! 'Tis time you were taught respect for your elders, especially when they are so accommodating." He scowled blackly at her, but when she let out an impudent giggle, she saw a flash of amusement in his eyes.

As they came to the end of the tiny township, they both seemed to slow down. It was as if they both knew their walk would end soon and they were trying to savor each other's company before the realities at Osterley would once again rise between them. As they wandered leisurely along the roadside, they met a shy young girl dressed in indigo homespun. Her mud-water brown hair was neatly tied up in a severe topknot and covered by a dog-eared cap; her face was clear and freshly scrubbed.

"I think she is trying to get our attention, Avenel," Brienne said, pulling on his sleeve irreverently. She smiled at the girl, and soon the waif was smiling back, showing her few teeth.

"Good day to you, Mistress Jill." Avenel looked down at the small, thin girl, and his look made her blush profusely. The girl motioned for them to come into the cottage that stood in front of them. Avenel did not seem surprised by the invitation. "Have you been taking care of your charge?" he asked the girl when they entered the thatched cottage. Dutifully the girl nodded her head and gave another uneven grin.

As Brienne stood by Avenel's side, she spotted an old woman sitting in the darkness of the windowless mud-frame, cottage. She turned toward the light from the door and Brienne almost gasped at the woman's appearance. The woman looked like a witch out of a child's nightmare. Warts disfigured her chin and nose, sprouting gray hairs like grass on a hillside. With a shapeless, toothless mouth, the old woman drooled when she smiled, as she did now. Having grown accustomed to the darkness, Brienne saw that the hag's eyes were unnaturally white and probably sightless.

"Mistress Blake. How do you fare today? I see you have your new roof," Avenel said in a loud, firm voice. Yet he refrained from shouting at the old woman.

"Aye, 'tis such a pleasure, what having me dry and toasty." The old woman cackled, and drool slid down the corner of her mouth. "Sit with me for the bye, will you? And take me thanks in a cup of brew." Mistress Blake waved in the direction of a large black kettle that steamed slowly over a small bed of coals. The girl, Jill,

who still hadn't spoken, went to the kettle and stirred
the brew. She ladled it into earthenware mugs that she
graciously handed first to Brienne and then to Avenel.
After completing the task, Jill bowed back into the dark
recesses of the room.

Brienne looked anxiously at Avenel, but he merely
stood by the fireside, drinking the witch's brew. Not
wanting to appear ungrateful, Brienne timidly took a
taste of the liquid, hoping she wouldn't gag. But when
the brew touched her tongue, she was surprised to discover that she liked it. It was made with smooth cider,
fresh cream, and mysterious spices. In no time she was
sipping on it happily.

"You come not alone, Lord Oliver?" old Mistress Blake
questioned.

Brienne gave a confused start at the name. She turned
to Avenel and whispered, "Why did she call you that?"

Forbiddingly, Avenel shook his head. " 'Tis a young
woman with me, Mistress Blake. She hails from the Colonies in America."

"And a winsome one, no doubt! For you were always
one for the ladies, Lord Oliver. I remember well." The
old woman cackled again.

"Avenel, correct her!" Brienne whispered. "How can
you allow her to call you that despised name?"

"Come here, lass! I canna see you but for my fingers."
Mistress Blake beckoned.

Brienne's eyes darted toward Avenel, who gave her a
reassuring look. Timidly, she moved closer to the old
woman and knelt down beside her. Ten gnarled fingers
touched her face, thoroughly examining Brienne's features. Then Mistress Blake grabbed a lock of her hair and
turned in the direction of Avenel's voice. "What be the
color?"

" 'Tis the color of dark red, but more so. I have never seen anything like it." Avenel gazed at Brienne's hair, taking in the magenta highlights that gleamed even in the faint light of the burning coals.

"You tell this old woman tales, my laird. She is not from the Colonies, for I know this one, do I not?" Mistress Blake released the lock of Brienne's hair. "Her eyes be the fairest and strangest color." She turned toward Brienne. "You, child, are not an easy one to forget. You came from Osterley with the false one."

"With Master Slane?" Brienne questioned her, but there was no answer. "Lord Oliver is gone now—" She tried to correct the befuddled old woman, but Avenel took her by the arm and pulled her up from the floor.

"We must take our leave," he said. "If you find you are wanting again, send the girl to the Park." Still holding her arm tightly, Avenel ushered Brienne out the door before she had time to thank the two women for their hospitality.

"Why did we leave so abruptly?" Brienne cried as they walked briskly toward the estate. Avenel was silent until they were a safe distance from Mistress Blake's. Then he turned around and gazed at the roof of the distant cottage.

" 'Tis a fine roof, is it not?" he said, ignoring her question. He stood looking at the tightly bound thatch that was three feet thick in some places. The dry, golden grass was shorn in a diamond pattern on the pitch but was smooth over the two dormers.

"I don't care about the roof! You were rude to interrupt me when I was trying to help the poor old creature. Mistress Blake is living under a misconception, Avenel. How could you not correct her?"

"She is old, Brienne, old and befuddled. She finds solace not in corrections but in a warm place to live and in companionship. That is all the help she needs." He grasped her arm, and again he walked rapidly, forbidding Brienne to appreciate the rare and glorious winter's day.

"So answer me this. When she touched my face, did she recognize me, or was it again merely a trick of her poor, confused mind?" Brienne persisted, growing angry at Avenel's forced lack of interest.

"She was mistaken."

"Ah, mistaken. Of course. There are so many women at Osterley with my color hair, and my—"

"Your inquiries may turn against you one day, Brienne. Don't read more into a situation than is there." He cut her off.

Her frustration mounting, Brienne took a new tack as they crossed the gates into Osterley. "You gave Mistress Blake the new roof, did you not?"

She noted Avenel's affirming grunt and continued. "It was a kind gesture." She then became more sly. "Perhaps it was done in repayment for a debt? The old woman seems to believe you're a Morrow. No doubt she is very loyal to my family and could provide you with all sorts of information, befuddled and otherwise."

"I gave her the new roof for the simple reason that she was in need of it. She is blind and alone. I cannot sit at my board every night when there are old women in the township without a decent dwelling place." He slowed his pace as they passed by the finger lake.

"Why do you say Mistress Blake is alone? There is the girl, Jill, who takes care of her." Her ire was mounting, but still Brienne spoke civilly. Watching Avenel stop, she thought she would burst from frustration. Would he ever give her a satisfactory answer to even one of her questions? The wind picked up, but she hugged her cloak around her. This might be her last chance to wheedle some answers out of him before her father arrived. She could not miss the opportunity simply because she was growing cold. While she waited for Avenel to speak, she leaned back on the trunk of a dead elm.

"Jill takes care of her now." Avenel rested his hand on the trunk near her shoulder. He looked up at the brilliant blue sky, and his dark hair gleamed in the powerful sunshine.

"I suppose you provided the girl for her, too?" Brienne studied him, uncomfortable with his closeness. Her eyes, helplessly appreciative of his fine, masculine form, quickly turned away. Instead, she focused her attention on the lake.

"Jill's family was living near starvation. Her parents are elderly, and their only child, Jill, was hardly employable. Not only is she deaf and dumb, but she was listless and withdrawn as well. However, the family would not consent to accepting charity." He looked down to where Brienne's cloak parted. The satin bows that held her stomacher in place peeked out. Slowly he fingered the last of them near her busk, seemingly in innocent amusement. He distracted her by continuing to talk. "I thought it the best way to handle the situation. I pay her to care for the old woman, and now she is the provider for her family."

"It was a generous offer." Brienne forced herself to be gracious. Quietly, she added, "I know the earl would never have been so kind, nor would he have taken the time to see that his people's needs were met." She watched the chill gray waters of the lake flow to the shallow shore like ruching on taffeta.

"The girl has a purpose to her life now. And 'twas simple enough to give her one." His eyes were lowered

to her *échelle,* and his lashes, thick and black, fluttered
with the calculated movement of his eyes.

"What purpose have you given me then, Master Slane?
I bid you tell me, and do not leave me in this void created
by you and my father." Now seriously in pursuit of his
answer, she took the undone ribbons from his inquisitive
hands. Indignant, she noticed that all but one bow had
become untied. She ineptly tried to tie them once more.

His hands free, Avenel thoughtfully rubbed his jaw.
"Your purpose, little one?"

"If that poor, cowed little girl deserves a purpose to
her life, then surely I deserve one, too." She tried to
keep her voice even, but there was so much emotion in
her breast that she could hardly contain it all. Her *échelle*
seemed impossible to handle, and with a vengeance she
dropped the ribbons and confronted him. "You're so
kind to those around you—just look what you've done
for the girl, Jill, and for Vivie. Can't you give me that
kindness also and let me go?" She tossed her head and
looked him in the eye. This time, she vowed, she
wouldn't let him go without answering. After seeing the
deaf girl, Jill, maybe he would see the comparison as
clearly as she did. And perhaps he would finally prove
that his feelings for her ran deeper than he showed.

"You have a purpose at Osterley, wildflower."

How bitter tasting the resentment was in her mouth! It
was not fair that he could use her so! It had appeared
that with the advent of Rose's and Cumberland's wedding there might have been some small seeds of consideration growing between them. But now all she could
feel was the return of full-blooming, passionate hatred.
Avenel cared not a whit for her. His only concern was to
make sure she would be useful in his schemes. He

treated even the paupers of the township with more respect.

"I see," she said coldly, and made a move to go.

"No, you don't see." He gripped her arm and forced her back against the tree trunk. Placing each of his hands against the trunk on either side of her head, he leaned all his weight onto his arms. When he had positioned himself, she was trapped by his large frame.

"I won't be mauled again, Avenel." She looked up at him defiantly, but he just smiled, his sensuous lips baring clean, white teeth like a hungry wolf's.

"I've given you a purpose, little one. Make me happy. Make that your job here at Osterley."

"That would be a wife's duty, not mine!" she cried out, still glaring at him. Pulling on his muscular arm, she was determined to go back to the house. But he only leaned closer and put a stop to her physical resistance.

"But I have no wife. And never shall, I suppose. What then?" he reasoned harshly. It was clear that her aversion to him only fueled his own anger and passion. Lowering himself upon her, he forced her gaze to lock with his.

"I cannot bring you happiness. If anyone knows this, you do!" She spurned him, even though, as his lips moved closer, her own burned with longing. Struggling to be out of the prison of his arms, she found that her opposition was no match for his. Her physical strength appeared inconsequential when he desired to prove his dominance.

"You can make me very happy, my love," he whispered as he closed the gap between them.

"I don't want—" His mouth finally descended on hers, and it seemed that not an inch of her body was free from contact with him. Before his attack had even begun, Brienne knew where he was leading her. She also knew, that at that moment she should have been kicking and screaming like a fishwife to be free. But as his lips sought her traitorous ones so compellingly, she found herself responding and with a ferocity she had never dreamed possible, not even in her most impassioned reveries of romance.

He demanded from her a desire equal to his. But beneath his ravenous kiss she had the insane desire not only to conform to his wishes but to exceed them. So instead of fighting him off, she allowed his hand through her cloak. With strong, experienced fingers, he undid the last bow of her *échelle*. Her breath was released in a long, burning sigh as his hand finally slid by her pinned stomacher and took possession of her breast, still encased in the silk of her stays. With renewed passion, his mouth delved deeper with his kiss, and she was jammed against the tree. Her hat fell off, and her netting ripped against the roughness of the trunk. But she didn't care.

Shamelessly, her hands went up to touch his face. His cheeks were scratchy and hard, and in the back of her mind she thought that he would have to scrape his face with a razor again before dinner. She heard his breath quicken as his thumb brushed across her nipple, and she trembled when the sensitive peak hardened. Placing her hands inside the warmth of his cloak, she desired to feel his chest, too, his that was hard, hair roughened, and broad. With shy, awkward movements, she wove her way through the layers of waistcoat and neckcloth to find the ties to his shirt. She pulled on them and was immediately rewarded by the touch of his lightly furred chest. As if struck by an uncontrollable madness, she found herself sweeping her fingers along his muscular front. At that moment she thought nothing would please her more than to see him naked and to explore every part of his forged, muscular body.

A cold metal object dangled by her hand. The brass key implanted itself in her palm, and she pulled it to her as if by instinct. Feeling the tug around his neck, Avenel lifted his mouth from hers. Pausing, he waited for her to speak.

"Avenel," she whispered, her breath heavy and labored, her eyes dark and impassioned, "can we forget this crazy scheme? Is that at all possible?" She held the brass key out to him. She knew he felt the tremors of her heart, for his hand was still enclosed around her breast. "Give this to me. Give this to me freely, and I will make you very happy. I promise."

There was silence, as if he were thinking over her proposition. But then, very assuredly, came a negative shake of his head. "You cannot have your freedom."

"What if I give you what you have been asking for?" she bargained, somehow feeling disappointed that it had come to this. "What if I spend this night warming your bed?"

"Then I see no reason to wait for nightfall." He bent his head and began the madness again. This time he kissed her throat, moving lower and lower, until she released a shudder of delight.

"And then you will give me my comb?" she panted, lacing her fingers through his dark hair. He bedeviled her to no end with his lovemaking. He fogged her thoughts, and clouded her goals. But shaking her head, she fought for the sanity to ask again, "And then you will give me my comb?"

"Perhaps then," he answered aloofly, and there was the tiniest shard of insincerity in his voice. Immediately she stiffened and seized her hands from his hair.

"And perhaps not, eh, Master Slane?" she cried bitterly, pushing his hand off her stays. Feeling more empty and unfulfilled than she had ever felt before, she retorted, "You would have me comply with all your wishes, I think, but then you would deny me my payment. What a shame we have spent so much time together, for now I can tell when you are lying. You bastard!"

"If I lie or not, what does it matter? You have little choice but to accept my dictates," he snapped.

"Never!" She pulled her bodice together, already feeling the heat of humiliation staining her cheeks.

"What pretty disdain, my lady! You weren't feeling quite so repulsed a moment before." He snatched her hands and forced them to her sides.

"I loathe you, I loathe your house, your touch, your kiss!" She raised her eyes to his in battle.

"Shall I prove otherwise?"

She felt his breath on her lips.

"No!" She suddenly found the strength to break away from him. Stumbling away from the elm, she watched as he taunted her with the brass key and placed it calmly back into his shirt, where she could no longer see it. "I hate it! Do you hear me? I hate that key and everything it stands for! And God willing, it will not be long before I completely hate you!" She backed away and scooped up her hat and netting, which had come off with their kissing. Spinning around, she ran to the great house in the distance, feeling, for some strange reason, mournfully sad.

When she got to the steps of the house, she saw that an unfamiliar carriage had been pulled almost out of view into the stable block. But running up through the portico and through the courtyard, she dashed into the marble hall without thinking of her appearance or the visitors.

"Well, well, if it isn't the little American cousin." Lady Venetia Culpepper's voice echoed through the hall as she and the Duchess of Hardington entered it from the gallery. Venetia was coldly beautiful in a round gown of chardonnay-colored silk. She examined every facet of Brienne's appearance, from the pieces of tree bark clinging to her unbound hair to the bows still untied on her bodice. Speechless and angry, Brienne saw Avenel storm through the doors behind her. He ignored the old footmen and flung his coat onto one of the scroll end stools. He then gave Brienne the blackest look she had ever seen.

"I will not stand another outburst like that, or I'll give you something to be truly angry about!" he bellowed.

"So the little beggar has been unwilling, has she?" Venetia walked farther into the hall. Avenel finally saw both women, and he forced his gaze from Brienne. "And after all she has put you through. Tsk, tsk." Venetia shot Brienne a malicious look and gazed contemptuously at her undone *échelle*. But Brienne vowed not to tie them until she was safely out of the woman's view. She would not give Lady Venetia the satisfaction of seeing her embarrassment.

"Lady Venetia. Duchess." Avenel tersely acknowledged the other women's presence.

"We've come for a visit, Avenel. But perhaps we've arrived at an inopportune moment." The duchess shot an amused look at Brienne and then modestly patted her brilliant sapphire-colored skirts.

"I shall join you both in the drawing room momentarily," he said. Then, putting a finely tempered iron hand on Brienne's arm, he turned to her decisively. "Brienne, go upstairs to your room."

Rebellion raged within her, and she snapped her arm away from his grasp. "I will not!" She jutted her chin out.

Avenel's jaw seemed to throb with agitation. "Go upstairs now! I can take care of this without you."

"I will do no such thing! I'm not a child, and I will not tolerate . . . !" Brienne gasped as he flung her carelessly over his shoulder and removed her like so much excess statuary from the hall.

"You despot! You blackguard!" she screamed, and her voice echoed down the passage as she beat her fists into his hard, muscular back. "I will never forgive you for this humiliation! Do you hear me? Never!" She bit her lip in impotent fury.

"I will not have you in your angry state near Venetia," he whispered hotly. "She has all but said she wants compensation for her embarrassment at the ball. Don't you think she would love to know why you're really here? Not only would she get even with me, but I'm sure her father could have Morrow here in a moment to claim you!"

He dumped her unceremoniously onto the Deccan counterpane in her bedchamber and then left her without another word.

"Afraid that tongues will wag, eh? That the Duchess of Hardington will say you've been dallying with someone not quite up to snuff?" Spewing and sputtering unladylike expletives, Brienne vented her anger by throwing the nearest porcelain figurine at the closed door. She then allowed her heart to rage uncontrollably with fury and embarrassment—and worst of all, jealousy.

CHAPTER SEVENTEEN

It was nearing March before Cumberland and Rose were expected back from London. Brienne counted the days like soldiers, waiting for each one to fall before looking ahead to the next. Avenel spent most of his time riding about the estate; it was an infrequent day that Idle Dice was in the stable block. But on those occasions when Avenel was in the house, Brienne chose to stay in her room; she would have tea and sit by the fire, trying to ignore the footsteps that paced below her in the library and the cursing that wafted up from the hall. Of late Avenel was in a foul mood, and his temper ran short in the presence of a lax footman or a fumbling maid.

The only respite from her boredom was her new-found ability to ride. She, like Avenel, rode regularly; she went out on Queenie every afternoon. Although she was not allowed to go without one of the grooms, Brienne found a great release in galloping madly across the clearings and meadows and in freely jumping the crumbled stone fences in between.

She rode now and caught sight of Orillion trotting ahead into the woods beyond; his white fur stood out among the golden groundcover and sunlit evergreens of the forest. The animal's presence was a sure indication that his master was near, and Brienne fumed since his presence was forced upon her today. After several minutes of riding in silence, she finally turned to Avenel and said in an almost surly manner, "I do not like being the American cousin any longer. That woman"—she eyed him dourly when she referred to Venetia—"has done nothing but make me feel like a peasant."

"You mean there was a time when you did like being thought an American?" He pulled Idle Dice nearer to her and relaxed the reins, allowing the bay to toss his head and prance tightly around her.

"Never! Those rude, boorish—"

"You forget that they are not all like me, my love." He laughed and tried to pull at her small velvet hat, which was angled on top of the curls so painstakingly arranged by Vivie. She swiftly trotted out of his reach, giving him a look of utter boredom.

But strangely he brought his bay to a halt and then became very still. He looked behind them sharply as if he expected to see someone.

"What is it? Is there someone there? This is the third time . . ." She looked over to his back, where he kept a loaded pistol tucked into his buckskin breeches. She saw his gloved hand twitch for it and then resist the urge. There was also a large, rather deadly looking knife tucked into the top of his right boot. He didn't know she knew about the weapons; she'd once spied him in the stable block hiding them on his person. It was strange, his compulsion to pack an arsenal on these innocent romps through the countryside. But it was a habit for him, and she was used to seeing the concealed bulge at his backside.

" 'Tis nothing, I suppose." He brushed it off as he had thrice before. "Just the sounds of the woodlands." He smiled and again reached for her saucy hat, but she chose to continue their previous conversation, ignoring his attempts to make her laugh.

"It is Cumberland's misfortune to be American. But you'll never convince me that Rose fared well in that godforsaken land. She is as English as I, and I'm sure she is glad that she left."

"Maryland is not anything like you picture it. In many ways it resembles England, with its sown fields and country estates. There is a city named after Lord Baltimore that has many fine homes, buildings, and cabinetmakers who are almost as skilled as Osterley's John Linnell." He smiled at her in a preoccupied manner and then said, "Come, I will take you there some day and prove to you that the United States is far less heathen than that *dinbych* you grew up in."

"I will never go there." She cantered ahead in defiance. Concentrating on keeping her heels down and her hands in their proper position, she forced herself to ignore him.

"But you would go back to Tenby, wouldn't you? 'Tis all but sow fodder now. Yet you would return to it rather than stay here with me." There was a hard edge to his voice as he cantered beside her.

"Tenby was a nice township. It has been forgotten. But it will be nice again, and I cannot help but want to go home." She set her mouth in a firm expression but slowed Queenie down to a walk so that she could talk to him. "How did you find out I was from Tenby? I've wanted to know ever since the night of the ball. I never told you where—"

"I had someone find out. Once I knew you could speak Welsh, I simply inquired about the hired coaches. My fortune was that you are not easily forgotten." He slowed down beside her.

"And you? You speak Welsh. How is that?"

"My mother was from Wales."

"Your mother? Now, that is hard to believe. You never had a mother." She looked straight ahead, watching Orillion, who was still ahead of them, going deeper and deeper into the woods.

"Not for long, 'tis true. And I suppose it does show— that I will grant." He laughed; her dry comments obviously bounced off him like so many leather balls.

"She died young?"

"Aye."

"I am sorry." She paused and then gave him a mildly taunting look. "However, lack of maternal care does not explain every aspect of your rude personality." Playfully, she turned to canter away once more, daring him to follow. But before she could start, she looked back and saw he had stopped again. "There is nothing there, Avenel. What do you expect to find?" she asked, becoming worried over his behavior. But before she could question him further, he seemed to brush aside his premonitions and took a chance. His hand snaked up and grabbed the hat from her curls. "Oh!" she cried furiously at his back as he galloped off.

Squeezing Queenie into a canter, she followed him deep into the woods. Orillion had circled back and was now at Idle Dice's feet, which moved along at a well-controlled speed. When she finally got to Avenel's side, he held the hat out to her, teasing her in the hope that she would reach for it. But he only laughed when she turned up her nose to his unspoken dare and galloped ahead.

They were now very far from the Park; she was not at all familiar with this forest. The sky was becoming overcast, and soon deep, dark shadows revealed themselves underneath the evergreens. The air was also quite cold, making her serge riding jacket seem inadequate.

"Your boyish pranks have amused us all," she said as she stopped Queenie in a small clearing. "But I think it best if we turn back now. Nightfall is coming, and I'm afraid I haven't the slightest idea which way is Osterley." She looked around the clearing, brushing her dark windswept locks from her eyes.

Avenel rode up to her side. "Aye, and 'tis cold enough. There's an old hunter's cottage that I know of, not far from here. Perhaps it would be wise to go there . . . and get warm." There was a silver glint in his eye as he pulled up beside her, but she refused to reply to his wicked suggestion. Instead she looked away and muttered vaguely about certain people's bad upbringing.

"How far is the Park from here, Avenel? I am not sure—" She turned to look back at him but was struck dumb by the expression on his face. Orillion let out a low growl, and when she looked down, she saw large, tufted hackles raised along the dog's neck and back. "What is it?" she asked in rising terror. Looking back at Avenel, she saw every muscle in his body tighten; his shoulders were visibly raised for combat.

"Go!" he said quickly to her, pulling out the pistol from his waistband.

"What?"

"Go! 'Tis your chance! Get out of here, I tell you! I give you your freedom." He looked off to a dark, thickly evergreened niche in the clearing, and his eyes narrowed from tension.

"Avenel, I cannot—" Suddenly her ears drummed from the horrible sound of a shot coming from the thicket that he had been watching. The horses reared in fright, and several moments were lost as both riders attended their mounts. Before Brienne finally brought Queenie down onto all four legs, Avenel had already grabbed her reins and was forcing both animals out of the clearing. They found meager cover behind a mass of holly bushes, and Brienne noticed that Avenel's face had gone white. Soon the reason for this became apparent. Several bright red streams of blood ran down Idle Dice's belly and trailed off onto the needle-covered forest floor. "My God, Avenel, you've been shot!" she whispered, edging Queenie over to him.

"Get out of here, Brienne!" he rasped at her through clenched teeth.

"Avenel," she pleaded with him, "we've both got to run." But he did not listen to her. Instead, he jerked out his whip and furiously beat her mare's delicate rump.

"Get out of here!" he said, each time giving Queenie a stiff welting. It didn't take much more to make the animal rear, but miraculously Brienne was able to take control and steer clear of Avenel's whip.

"I can't leave you here." She winced at the blood streaming from his thigh. Another shot rang out, and she saw Orillion dash madly into the thicket where the attacker must have lurked. From Orillion's growls and snarls, she knew that the dog had turned dangerous because of the smell of his master's blood that was spattered on his brilliant white coat.

"Brienne, this is your chance. Orillion will rout the

bastard. Go now! There might be others lurking about—"

"You're right. There might be others about. Come, we've got to get back to Osterley." She put an end to his speech; it was pointless to talk of her abandoning him. Looking off into the battleground clearing, she shivered, knowing somehow that her father was behind this attack. Turning to Avenel, she saw the pain he was in as he tried to stanch the flow of blood with his hand. "We can't hide here forever, Avenel. Whoever's shooting out there will come looking for us. You must try to follow me. We must get back to Osterley." Again she ran terrified eyes over the clearing.

"Go on, then. Lead the way." He gripped his leg and clenched his teeth. Brienne prompted Queenie into a trot. Without waiting for Orillion to return, they began the route back to the Park.

After picking their way through the dark forest for almost half an hour, it soon became apparent that they would have to bind Avenel's leg if he were to make it back to Osterley. Blood dripped a trail on the forest floor, and even the strength of his hand upon the wound did little to inhibit the crimson stream. Seeing the vulnerable state Avenel was in, Brienne forced herself to be brave. Her heart leaped to her throat every time there was a sound behind them, and the merest rustle of forest creatures was terrifyingly loud in the stillness of the twilight forest. But she took courage in the fact that they'd been able to travel this far without being followed. She only hoped that Avenel had been right and that Orillion had found his target.

"Avenel, I think we must rest," Brienne said. "Your leg—"

"Go on to Osterley. I'll stay the night at the hunter's cottage." His words were thick with pain.

"Where is the cottage?"

"Not far." Unexpectedly, he handed her his pistol. "It's still loaded, Brienne. Take it and go. But do me this one thing: tell them at the Park to fetch Cumberland from London."

"Show me the cottage, Avenel. We'll make sure Father's minions aren't nesting there, and then we'll return to Osterley in the morning."

"Wildflower, your fondest dream has come true. You—may—leave." He obviously thought she didn't understand him.

"Where is this cottage?" She tried to sound commanding, but seeing his ashen face, her words came out as a whisper. "Please, Avenel. I won't go back alone."

He took a minute to think about what she'd said; then, as if he already knew it would be harder to convince her to do otherwise, he nodded in the direction of the cottage. "I think it's less than a mile from here."

Brienne took note of his labored breathing and his pain-racked posture. She gave him a trembling, fearful smile. "All right, then. Let's be off."

They reached the small woodland cottage in a matter of minutes. Brienne dismounted and made her way up the path, taking the pistol with her. She was not exactly sure how to fire it, but she held the heavy weapon in front of her and hoped that would keep away any attackers. Behind her, Avenel's shadowed form could be seen, weaving sickly on his saddle.

After making a quick assessment of the area, Brienne was comforted by the fact that the place looked utterly abandoned. She walked up to the cottage threshold and peeked into the dark, open doorway.

Then she had the fright of her life. From out of the cottage there leaped at her what seemed to be a four-legged ghost.

"By all that is holy!" She gave a quick sob, relieved that she didn't know how to shoot the pistol. "Orillion! How did you know to come here?"

"He's been here before," Avenel answered behind her. Having dismounted, he now grasped his wounded leg, wavering on the brink of collapse. "I tied the horses." He talked like a drunkard; his loss of blood already slurred his words.

"Good." She walked over to him. Gently she put her arms about him and helped him into the cottage. She swallowed her revulsion as two large rats eyed her from the windowsill. Noting a straw-covered pallet on one side of the room, she walked Avenel over to it and helped him lie down. With every movement, he groaned, and Brienne couldn't help but feel faint herself in sympathy with his agony.

"Let me get us some light. Then I will bind your leg." Before turning to the dusty fireplace, she went over to the soot-blackened door and shut it. A shiver ran down her spine when she thought of what, or who, might be lurking outside the cottage in the darkness. But she forced herself to ignore her fears. She had to be brave; there was no other choice.

Finding a small stack of wood in one cobwebbed corner, she piled a few logs under the flue. Then, blessedly, a flint was found on the mantel, and soon a cheering fire crackled in the hearth. When that task was completed, she went back to Avenel.

"Let"—she swallowed, seeing the dried blood on the hand Avenel had placed over his wound—"let me know if I hurt you."

"How ironic that *you* should be tending my wounds," he said with a grim smile.

Smiling tremulously in return, Brienne bent down and grasped the hems of her particularly fine batiste petticoats. She tore them into strips to use as bandages. In the soft firelight she slid the knife from Avenel's boot and started cutting the leg of his breeches. It took a painfully long time for her to cut through it, but when he was finally free, she took the strips of cotton and bandaged his wound. The shot had seared the muscular flesh of his thigh. It was an ugly wound, and Avenel moaned several times during her ministrations. With each sound he made, her heart skipped a beat. When she was finished, she dropped her shaking hands and gratefully moved to the hearth, seeking the fire as a balm to her overwrought nerves.

She stirred up the fire with a stick, quickening the flames. Hearing a rustling noise behind her, she nervously looked around and saw that Avenel had slid over to the side of the pallet nearest the wall. He patted the straw beside him, indicating that she should join him. He watched her with an intensity she had never before witnessed. If she hadn't known better, she would have thought it was tenderness.

"There's hardly enough room for you," she whispered. "I might hurt your leg."

"You're small enough, my love. You can do nothing worse than keep me warm." Again, he patted the empty place beside him.

Brienne left the hearth and slowly walked over to him. Feeling awkward and not a little bit reluctant, she lay down beside him, but she quickly found she could not avoid touching his body lest she fall onto the floor. Avenel laid one well-muscled arm around her and forced her to relax against his broad chest. Quickly his breath deepened in slumber, but Brienne found sleep elusive. She attributed this to the hardness of the grass pallet, but deep down she knew the sensual warmth of the hard, masculine body next to hers was what kept her awake.

CHAPTER EIGHTEEN

"Christopher!"

Brienne awoke at the cry, abruptly rising from the pallet. Although the fire had died down to red embers, she was drenched in perspiration. Looking down, she found the reason for this. It was Avenel, and he seemed to be burning with fever. "It's all right, please," she whispered to him in the dark. Hoping he was simply having a nightmare, she tried to wake him. But her efforts were to no avail.

"Christopher, my God!" He cried out his brother's name with agonizing clarity. Then his body went rigid upon the pallet, experiencing anew the excruciating pain that gave him such a terrible dream.

"Avenel, Avenel!" Touching his arm, she made a tentative move toward him. But then to her surprise his ice blue gaze met hers squarely. It was dim in the cottage, but nonetheless Brienne could discern the glazed-over appearance of his eyes. It frightened her.

"Who are you?" he demanded in a surprisingly strong voice.

"It is I, Brienne." She brushed his damp black locks from his forehead and frowned at the alarming heat emanating from his skin.

"You are some peasant girl?" He looked at her tattered, dusty skirt and the grass clinging to her bodice. Self-consciously she brushed some of the straw off her garments and then pulled and twisted her hair from her face.

"I'm Brienne, Avenel. Don't you know me?" Her eyes grew wide with concern.

"I know of no woman named Brienne. How is it I know you then, maiden?" He cocked an eyebrow and looked at her intently.

"I am the earl's daughter," she began again, twisting her hands in nervous agitation. "We met at Osterley Park." Hesitating, she whispered, "You do not recall?" She bent down, failing to conceal the worry lines on her forehead.

"You are the earl's daughter?" Avenel laughed madly. "In those rags you have done yourself up in? I hardly think you should be impersonating Lady Venetia when you cannot even dress the part."

"I do not claim to be Lord Culpepper's daughter," she said sharply. Looking down at his feverish visage, she softened. "I am afraid I'm the daughter of the Earl of Laborde."

"You? The daughter of the Earl of Laborde? How is it you are so old, then?" He laughed as if she'd made some hilarious jest. Then he tried to sit up against her gentle, restraining arms.

"I am not so old. Perhaps in my disheveled state I give that impression." She pulled him back onto the pallet but found him amazingly strong to grapple with.

"What are you? Eighteen if you be a day." He laughed

loudly. "Now, how could the earl have an eighteen-year-old daughter?"

"I am nineteen. But please do not concern yourself with these frivolous matters now. You must rest—" She pulled him down again, frightened by his ramblings.

"Frivolous matters?"

"It's all right. Everything will be all right," she said, mostly for her own reassurance; Avenel was raving like a madman.

"You are a lying, little wench, aren't you?" He sat upright, scaring her so badly that she jumped back.

"No. I only want to help you."

"You care for me, then?" He turned his glassy eyes upon her. "Are you perchance my mistress?"

"No." Her voice caught in her throat, and she made a courageous attempt to get nearer to the pallet. "I am who I said. I'm Brienne."

A crazed half-smile was on his lips. "You are my mistress. We have been familiar with each other." He caught her hand and gently started to pull her on top of him.

"Nay, stop this! You are wounded and ill. This will not do!" She forcibly backed away, wondering how she would handle him in this state if he chose to force himself upon her. He was strong—amazingly strong—despite his present affliction. While he labored his movements, the wild, hot gleam in his eyes would not leave.

"Admit we have been lovers!" he demanded, still gripping her hand. "I know I find you more than desirable. Tell me I haven't let you pass me by."

She looked down at him and saw his expression become mournful. He seemed to want so badly for them to have been lovers that she finally gave in to his wishes, hoping then that he would be satisfied and find his rest.

"You have not passed me by, sir. We have exchanged some—"

"I am your lover then. Say it," he demanded.

She paused and then lied with a pensive frown. "You are my lover."

"Aha!" He shot up, grabbing her with two very powerful hands. "Then you were lying! You are not related to the earl!"

"I am not lying." She swallowed hard and attempted to pry his fingers from her arms, for they were bruising her.

"You're a beautiful, lying piece of baggage! How can we be lovers when you claim to be my daughter? What kind of father would I be?" He lay back on the pallet, triumphant and exhausted, obviously waiting for her confession.

"Your daughter? I am not your daughter, Avenel. Look at me, at least. I am much too old." Chiding him, she wiped down his brow with an extra piece of her petticoat.

" 'Tis as I said. You lie." He mumbled this tiredly, and she saw his eyelashes flicker. "You are not the earl's daughter! You are not the earl's daughter, because I am the Earl of Laborde." As soon as the words left his mouth, he fell back into a tormented sleep, leaving her utterly confused.

The next morning when Brienne opened her eyes, several moments passed before she could remember why she was sleeping on a hard pallet in a beggarly abode. With stiff, cold motions she raised herself up on her elbows and saw in the unnatural darkness a man sleeping on the pallet next to her. Then she remembered where she was and what had befallen herself and Avenel. She walked over to the hearth to rebuild the fire. Next, she tentatively opened the oaken door and was delighted to find Orillion sitting on the threshold. He saw her familiar face, and his tail drummed against the door in greeting.

"There you are! I had almost forgotten about you!" She bent down to give him a couple of reassuring strokes on the head. "Let's see how the patient is doing." She stood up, allowing the dog to enter, and then she anxiously walked over to the mean little bed now bathed in the orange glow of sunrise.

How still and pale Avenel was as he lay upon the straw! For a second her heart twisted in her chest, for she thought him dead. But then to her unspeakable relief his lips moved in undecipherable, feverish whispers.

"Avenel?" She touched his arm.

"Am I dead, then?" His lips parted dryly with the words, and he raised his head. His eyes were still glazed, but the madness in them of the previous night seemed gone.

Brienne gave him a tired little smile and said softly, "On the contrary."

He sighed and rolled his head back onto the pallet. "Good. That's good."

"Are you in much pain?"

He shook his head.

"I don't know how we're going to do it, Avenel. But we have to get back to the Park." Tenderly, she wiped his brow.

"I know. Get the horses." He closed his eyes as if preparing for the ordeal to come.

"I'll be right back."

"Brienne?" He called to her before she could go.

"Yes?"

"Take the pistol."

"Yes." She clutched the walnut-handled weapon to her breast. "Of course."

It was late in the day when they arrived back at the Park. Avenel had begun bleeding again halfway through the ride. By the time they reached the edge of Osterley's formal grounds and were spotted by some of the grooms in the stable block, he had nearly fallen unconscious from the loss of blood.

"Take him!" Brienne cried as Cumberland and the two burly Norwegian gatesmen ran up to her from across Osterley's courtyard. They pulled Avenel down from Idle Dice and laid him on the grass.

"Hans, get the physician from the township. Tell some of the lads to come here and give us a hand getting him back to the house!" Cumberland called out orders, ignoring Brienne for the time being. Hans took off, and soon an army of young footmen showed up; they took their master into their charge and quickly removed him to the house.

"I didn't know if he would be able to make it." Brienne hugged her grimy green riding jacket to her. Chilled and shaken, she was worn out from the ride. Cumberland, noticing her state, put his arm around her and tried to comfort her. As they walked back to the house, she was able to gather her wits about her somewhat. "I thought you and Rose would still be in London."

"Yes, yes. Well, we had a delightful time. But neither of us felt easy about leaving the Park. In London, we received news that the Earl of Laborde had returned to England. I'm afraid I suspected something like this would occur." After Cumberland spoke, Brienne noticed the deep lines of worry that were etched on his pleasant face.

"Then it was my father." Her whole body seemed to quake with the statement; her fears were confirmed. "Every time I'd see Avenel leave the house, he always carried a pistol. But there was no way he could defend us. We were just attacked. . . ." She couldn't go on. Gratefully, she felt Cumberland's arm tighten around her.

"When you didn't return from your ride, we sent out a search party. I'm glad you were both able to return on your own. Rose and I are not very brave. I'm afraid we feared the worst."

"Perhaps I should have waited at the cottage for help. I don't know if I did the right thing letting Avenel ride." Thinking of the way the footmen had had to carry him off, Brienne suddenly found tears in her eyes. She wiped at her muddied cheeks; her eyes glowed like two sparkling amethysts in her soiled face. She knew she looked terrible, but she didn't care about that now. Seeing Avenel almost unconscious had been more than she could take after all they had been through.

"You did exactly the right thing. Avenel will recover. He's been through worse."

"Worse?" Brienne stifled a sob and looked at Cumberland. She couldn't imagine anything worse than what had happened in the clearing.

"Let's not speak of such things now, my lady. I think it's time you were attended to. I might add that Vivie has been worried sick. We all have been." He hugged her before they mounted Osterley's steps.

"Is there s-something I can do to help Avenel before the physician arrives?" she stuttered once they were inside, not wanting to retire to her room. Although she desperately needed food and a bath, she felt she would go mad if she were forced to wait upstairs for news.

"No, no, my dear. You've done enough. Rose will take

care of him now." Cumberland paused and studied her face. "It seems that you have acquired a fondness for Avenel in the days we've been away."

The statement caught her unawares. But there was little need to argue. She knew her feelings for Avenel must show. Her very heart had fallen, torn and bleeding, with him when they'd pulled Avenel off his horse.

Seeing her stricken face, Cumberland nodded in resignation. He then murmured enigmatically. "I don't know if that is good or bad. But your feelings for him have at least kept him alive."

Before Brienne could question him, Rose met them in the hall. She ran up to them and placed her gentle arms around Brienne.

"How is he?" Brienne asked her.

"He is in the bedchamber," Rose replied. "I'm waiting for the physician, for I dare not remove the bandages without the doctor's approval. I fear he will bleed further."

"I—I tried to help him. Truly I did." Brienne shivered.

"Avenel owes you his very life. But never fear! He may look bad, but he's as strong as an ox. No doubt it would take more than a flesh wound to put him away. I am sure he will be all right." Rose took Brienne's icy hand. "Come along. I'll take you to your chamber. I think it's time someone took care of you for a change. Cumberland?" Rose turned to her husband.

"I will let you know as soon as the physician arrives." Cumberland looked at both women, and Brienne noticed how old and gaunt he had grown since the wedding. That had been less than a week before, but it seemed as if years had passed since the morning she and Avenel had watched them leave for London.

Rose nodded to him and then led Brienne up the

grand staircase to her room. But during the evening, Brienne was only dimly aware of the care she received from Rose and Vivie. Her mind was far away in the state bedchamber, where Avenel lay. The physician from town arrived promptly, and when he left, she was told that Avenel slept comfortably and that she must also. But as she sat in the yellow settee watching the crackling hearth, she knew it would be more difficult to sleep tonight than it had ever been.

CHAPTER NINETEEN

A week had gone by—a week of hearing news from the state bedchamber. A week of waiting to see Avenel. But no request for Brienne ever came from the resplendent green velvet room.

Every day, Brienne watched people go back and forth from Avenel's chambers. The florid-faced village minister, Reverend Trumbell, came once, nodding to her in brusque greeting before he disappeared down the passage. The physician was a common sight now. But there were, strangely enough, no other outside visitors. At Avenel's request, security was tightened around the Park. Cumberland informed the gatesmen and groomsmen of the looming threat of the earl, and although Brienne ached to ask Cumberland why Avenel hadn't asked for her, she stayed clear of the troubled man; her guilt became unbearable every time she looked upon his pleasant, endearing face. Then all she could think of was how much she hated her father.

Rose seemed to be the only one who understood her sufferings. Every time Brienne said she was sure that Avenel loathed her and refused to see her because of all the damage her father had done, Rose quickly came to her aid, reassuring her that this was not so. But even Brienne knew Rose was perplexed by Avenel's unexpected refusal of her company. Left with nothing but frustration, all Brienne could do was roam the halls and passages of the great house and wait for the moment when Avenel would say he missed her.

But there seemed no desire on Avenel's part to seek her out. The days trudged on, yet not once did Avenel make any effort to see her as he recovered. As Rose and Cumberland had predicted, Avenel was quick to heal. Although Brienne was relieved by this, she was also disheartened, for this only made his rejection of her even more puzzling.

Every evening when Brienne, Cumberland, and Rose sat down for their meal in the eating room, the dear couple would try and make light of the situation, relating stories of Avenel's strange fancies throughout the years they had known him. There had still been no response from his bedchambers concerning Brienne; but Rose would toss it off as one of his odd quirks. She would make excuses, each day adding a new one, until they all realized there simply were no excuses. For some cursed reason, Avenel was shunning Brienne's company. She had saved his life, and yet others who finally had been allowed to call, such as the Duke and Duchess of Hardington, were the ones he entertained as his bedside companions. Brienne felt as tossed away as his old bandages. And that very fact seemed to drive the green dowel of jealousy right through her heart. Even the winged sphinxes that supported the chairbacks in the state bedroom had more of his time than she did. Brienne found herself envious of the mere sheets that he lay upon.

By now the last vestiges of clear weather had left. Snow dusted the grounds, and though it was late, winter finally descended on the Park. The grounds grew too slick and icy to ride. Because of this, Brienne sat up in her room and watched the dismal fields grow heavy with wet, white flakes. Dusk had fallen early today, and the day seemed to mirror her spirits exactly—it was dark, cold, and miserable. A tray was set up by Vivie for her dinner, and the little maid, ever sensitive, now bustled quietly about the chamber, giving her a bit of company with her discreet presence yet not intruding upon her thoughts.

Standing up from the tray, Brienne roamed her bedchamber, restless and unspeakably agitated. She forced herself to settle down to read a book of poetry that she had borrowed from the downstairs library, but once she was sitting comfortably on the taffeta settee, her attention wandered to the flames licking up from the fireside. She stared into the fire and sought out its orange and lapis-tipped warmth as solace for her inexpressible feelings. She was in a particularly black mood this night, for Rose and Cumberland had spent the entire evening with Avenel.

Putting down the book of poetry, she couldn't help but wonder what they were doing now. She bit her lower lip, deep in thought, trying desperately to understand what was going on. Why would Avenel behave this way to her? Although her guilt was still upon her, she knew she could not be considered merely the daughter of Oliver Morrow any longer. She had saved Avenel's life. Why had he turned his back on her after she'd proved how much she cared for him?

Because it was your father who shot him. The words could not be stopped from entering her mind. Moaning, she acknowledged the possibility that Avenel hated her now more than ever. With every ache and pain of his recovery, she knew he thought of the earl—and then he thought of her.

Shaking off her despair, she told herself that the situation had now become a matter of pride. She would not force her company on him if he had no desire for it. But she knew, as the days had passed, so had her anguish over his rejection.

"Tout de suite!" Vivie called out as someone knocked loudly on the bedchamber door. Brienne looked up from the settee; the knock brought her temporarily out of her melancholy. *"Oui?"* the Frenchwoman inquired. Brienne saw that a young footman stood outside the door, giving Vivie a message. Then the maid closed the door and ran up to Brienne in a flurry of excitement.

"Ma demoiselle! The Monsieur has called for you in the tapestry room!"

Her nerves jumped but Brienne tried to exude a false calm as she inquired, "What answer did you give Toby?"

"I told him that you would be there." Vivie looked at her in wide-eyed amazement. "You wanted me to tell him that, *non?*"

"That's all right, I suppose," Brienne said reluctantly; her ire was raised not by Vivie's mistake but by Avenel's unparalleled gall in issuing commands.

"But, my lady, I did tell the boy that Master Slane would have to *wait* for your appearance." Vivie let out a sly smile, which Brienne now returned.

"I see. So tell me, Vivie, since I have all this time, I think I shall have . . ." Brienne thought for a moment, wondering what activity would take the most time and would therefore cause an irritating wait downstairs. "Why, a bath!" She laughed out loud, unpinning her gleaming hair. "I do believe my hair could use a good washing. After all, we've just gotten it dry from this morning's bath!"

Both women laughed mischievously, and Vivie took her time calling for the housemaids to bring up the tub.

Two hours later, Brienne stood in the drawing room by the mahogany door that led to Avenel's private apartments. Her vigorously brushed hair gleamed with highlights of magenta. It was artfully dressed, and one glorious, swelling curl rested on her bosom. She was simply gowned in a hyacinth satin brocade. The dress's stays laced up the front over a stomacher of the same material. There was not a stitch of embroidery to be found on the plain but vastly becoming material. She felt fresh and pretty, and this gave her the confidence to open the door after she heard Avenel give the disagreeable command, "Come in!"

Quietly she stepped into the tapestry room. Vulcan courted Venus in half-naked elation, and Cupid and Psyche played as well in Boucher-inspired medallions that were woven *trompe l'oeil* into the rich crimson needlework; they represented the loves of the gods. Amid them, Avenel sat on the richly hued Moore carpet with one leg bandaged and straight and the other bent at the knee. His back rested against a settee upholstered in needlework from another Boucher design, *"Les Amours Pastorales."* He stared away from her into a blazing fire that chased away the draft and actually gave the elaborate room a cozy atmosphere.

Brienne was forced to take several steps farther into the room to see his face. When she did have a full view, Avenel's visage appeared unusually hard and strangely desolate. It was not the face of a man who had just spent the evening in the company of his friends. She noted that his hand was wrapped around a crystal glass filled with fine aromatic brandy.

"You wanted to see me?" she asked, moving softly to him until she could be seen in the distant ring of fire-light. She noted that the dark red wallcoverings made the edges of the room disappear. As there were no candles lit in the farther reaches, the room was deliciously warm and intimate.

"How dare you order a bath after I called for you!" He shot her a glaring look and spoke with tight, forbidding lips. He picked up an apple from a plate of fruit and started peeling it exactingly with a sharp steel fruit knife.

"I was not aware of my servitude here at Osterley. Must I now run to the master at his every beck and call?" She did not move or flinch underneath his baleful gaze. She was still very angry with him, and she vowed that she would let him know it.

"You've kept me waiting for over two hours!" he yelled at her, dropping the fruit knife and crossing his dark-haired, muscular forearms over his robe. He was obviously waiting for her apology.

"Yes," she said, taking time to note every sorely missed aspect of his appearance. His dark locks gleamed in the firelight, and she took a particularly long moment to appreciate the way his thick, green-blue robe fell open at his chest. This left to her view a magnificent male torso that rippled down to a taut abdomen and finally disappeared suggestively underneath the folds of a silk and velvet sash. "Yes, I suppose two hours is a very long time to wait," she finished, letting all the bitterness she'd felt during the past week fill her voice.

He looked at her sharply. "I see. You're angry with

me, are you not?" He let out a mirthless laugh. "Sit down, little one. I will ease your tensions."

She complied, taking an armchair directly in front of him. "What was it you wished to see me about, sir?" she asked sarcastically, feeling the heat of his eyes on her more intensely than that of the flames that burst up through the chimney.

"I have come to a decision where you are concerned, my beauty." His returning sarcasm forced her gaze to his arrogant face. "It has taken me a week, but at last I have made it. It will be finalized tonight."

"A decision?" She frowned.

"Yes." He looked away momentarily and took a long draught of his brandy.

"I don't understand—"

" 'Tis not for you to understand!" he snapped at her. Suddenly he tossed a golden object to her that landed in the lap of her gown. She looked down at it and swallowed the dread that had caught in her throat.

"What is the meaning of this?" She held the gold key in her hand.

"You've earned it. I should have given it to you a week ago, but I needed the time to think." His eyes glistened and then chilled to a solid frost as he watched her reaction. Finally he snapped out ferociously, "Take it then, and be off with you!"

"It's worthless," she gasped, reeling from a sudden, inexplicable pain in her chest. "I have no comb any longer. It was broken here in this very room. If you will recall, the Earl of Culpepper crushed it."

"I've had it repaired. Along with the bag of gold I plan to give you, you will have enough money to go anywhere you like. And the coach will be at your disposal to take you there in the morning." He moved the knee of his wounded leg stiffly and then grimaced as he relaxed it once again. He looked up at her and made her jump with the harshness of his voice. "Go! I tell you, leave this instant!"

"You don't—" She found herself choking on the words.

"Find some lost relation and live there, Brienne." He softened, seeing the torn look on her face. "You've more than earned your freedom. And it's my duty to urge you to get away from this mess."

At Avenel's words, Brienne envisioned the two of them at the little cottage. She remembered with heart-twisting clarity how warm his arms had been when she had lain in them that night. She remembered, too, the deep regret she had felt that it had probably been her father or one of his henchmen who had attacked them in the clearing. In the morning, when Avenel had been forced into the torturous mounting of Idle Dice, she recalled how she had felt compelled to apologize for all that had happened to him. But she knew that "I'm sorry" wasn't enough to make up for all his pain. She had stood by searching for the right phrase that would be a balm for both their spirits, one that would help them make the journey back to Osterley more pleasant, one that best expressed what she felt in her heart. But then, quickly realizing the insanity of her thoughts, she had mounted Queenie and they were off before she had uttered those terrible, irretrievable words, "I love—"

"Are you listening to me?" Avenel demanded, pulling her attention back to him.

"I am." She swallowed hard, not knowing how to handle the situation. Only weeks ago she would have glee-fully taken the key and the money and not given him a second glance. But now she felt as if her whole world were coming to an end. The burning anger she'd felt when she had entered the room now turned into cold desolation, and there seemed to be nowhere to turn. "You want me to leave."

"I want you to leave." He refused to meet her searching eyes, but his words were more than clear. "You must leave."

"That night . . . at the cottage—" she began stupidly.

"Forget that night! Forget that place!" he interrupted her. "We're back at the Park now, and we must live by Osterley's rules and Osterley's past. There is no choice."

"I see," she said, her voice wavering. Numbly, she stood up to go but then realized that the key had fallen to the carpet near where he sat. She knelt down to pick it up, and her hand trembled as she reached out for it.

"Tell me one thing, Brienne, before you go." His fingers caught her delicate wrist as she reached for the key.

"Yes?" She looked at him, her face pale and drawn.

He took a long time before he finally asked, "After I'd been shot, why did you not leave me altogether when I told you to go?"

"You . . . you were hurt."

He shook his head. "Is that the only reason?" He searched her violet eyes; his own narrowed. "I think not."

When the words came to her, they were not the words she wanted to say. "You already know why," she whispered, looking away from the dark triumph shining in his eyes.

Avenel lowered his gaze to where his fingers were clamped around her tiny wrist. The tone of his voice held many contradictory emotions. He was commanding her, she knew, yet for the first time, there was a slight hint of uncertainty in his order. "Tell me to let you go, Brienne. Say the words. Say them now. Then you'll be free. If not . . ."

Hesitating for one fatal second, she knew she could not bring herself to go until, bending near to him, she placed a long, sweet kiss on his distrusting lips. It was a kiss for remembrance, one to last her the rest of her life. When it was over, she would have to comply with what she knew was a rational decision. It was best she get away from this crazed personal war he and her father were fighting. It was best she leave this man who openly declared himself her enemy.

Before her gentle kiss ended, she had unconsciously dropped the brass key once more. Yet she heard its thud on the carpet more clearly than she would have cannonfire. Her mind shrieked a warning, but her heart refused to heed it. She felt Avenel's hand release her wrist, and then, in the brief interlude when their only contact was between their lips, she had her last opportunity to go.

She stayed.

Allowing Avenel to pull her into his arms at that moment was like allowing a lion to eat her alive. Gone was the gentle, chaste kiss, and in its place was a raw, starved devouring that left her senses skittering on the brink of ecstasy. His lips moved roughly and claimed every part of her mouth as his; his tongue licked like flames over her own. Enveloping her in his strong arms, he pulled her so close, his robe opened. Only when the soft hyacinth brocade of her dress met his hard, naked flesh did he tear his lips from hers. Although the kiss had ended, she could tell from the look in his eyes that they had just begun.

"You should have forced me from you. You should

have fought to get away. If you had an ounce of self-preservation, you would have done this, my love," he gasped desperately. "It took me seven days and nights to allow you to go."

"I wanted . . ." she whispered, suddenly desiring him with every inch of her body and soul.

"You know if you stay here tonight, you will never be rid of me or Osterley. My mark will be permanent—I'll have it no other way." He took her face into his large, powerful hands, searching for her answer. And she gave it immediately, not with words but with her lips, which moved of their own volition over his.

Deep inside him she heard a groan, and soon she felt her laces being severed one by one with the sharp edge of the fruit knife. His hands forced the dress apart, and it fell in satin folds around them as they both half-sat and half-lay on the floor. With one uncontrolled movement, he shoved aside her slashed shift and claimed both her breasts with his hands. His beard-roughened jaw left a trail of blush-colored marks along her shoulders and chest until his roaming mouth nipped at each crest of her bosom. The inside of her belly burned as his teeth grazed her sensitive skin. Mindlessly she ached for more; recklessly he gave it.

His hands moved down the creamy smoothness of her thighs and roughly pulled at her silk hose. With two sudden rips, her stockings and her green slippers lay in a fluffy pile at her side. As if drowning in the whirlpool of his frenzied demands, Brienne could only look on with eyes sultry and dark as he released his arms from the robe. Once free of his clothing, he abruptly pulled her into his arms, and then, as if forcing the animal in him to perform a more civilized ritual, he carried her into the state bedchamber and flung her onto his ornately domed bed.

Something related to fear made Brienne pull the torn edges of her shift together as she tried to get to her knees. Her whole body trembled with fearsome, unexplored desires, yet looking up from the bed as Avenel stood over her, she wondered if she would be trampled by her own inexperience. How would she keep up with this man tonight? Had she been foolish to think she would fare well against his raging passions? Almost dazedly, she watched as he folded his arms across his chest. She was allowed a tantalizing glimpse of his maleness as he stood with his powerful thighs leaning against the mattress, and her thoughts turned to those few times she'd overheard talk of what went on between a man and a woman. "The first taking is painful. . . . It must be suffered through. . . . The lucky ones don't bleed much. . . . But you must submit, submit, *submit*!"

Nervously she backed toward the headboard. Perhaps she should have gone. Perhaps she had made a mistake. But even now, as Avenel towered over her, naked and magnificent in the dark, ember-lit bedchamber, she knew she had made the right choice. Her gaze wandered over him, and she saw how terrifyingly beautiful he was. His body exuded masculine dominance with every flex of the most minute of his muscles. She was crazed, she concluded wildly—she had to be. For how could she want so badly something that seemed destined only to hurt her?

As she battled her doubts, Brienne saw that Avenel had paused; the firelight revealed a tormented expression on his face. His eyes raked up and down her body until they settled on her face. He seemed to be searching for something, and his unnatural stillness unnerved her.

"What is it, Avenel?" Brienne whispered to him from the dark recesses of the bed. Had she gone this far, only to feel the sting of his rejection? Clutching at her bosom, she wondered self-consciously if he were seeing her now not as a vulnerable woman ready for love but as her father's daughter. As she prayed that whatever traits she'd inherited from Oliver Morrow wouldn't show, she lifted her eyes, only to find Avenel pensively staring at the burgundy spill of her hair.

"It's beautiful," he murmured almost to himself. His hand reached out and grasped several locks. "You're beautiful."

With that, the spell of indecision that had come upon him was broken. With new resolve, he pulled her to the edge of the mattress. His face became taut and unreadable, and Brienne felt a new tremor of fear and excitement. Avenel was ready. To get what he desired now, he looked as if he would embrace the devil.

"Untie this," he said, nodding at the ribbon that held together the remaining shreds of her sleeveless shift.

Showing her trepidation, her hands trembled as she raised them. She clutched at the single tie that so tenuously held the tattered garment to her; it took her a long time to finally pull the silken ribbon between her breasts. But before she had even released it, Avenel was tearing the filmy shift over her head, letting her dark red curls fall around her with the motion. He stared at her in the firelight as she knelt on the huge bedstead. Again her hands instinctively went to her lush breasts to hide them from his view, but he would have none of it.

"Don't," he said, pushing her arms to her side. Gently he entwined his fingers in her hair, and he bent to kiss her.

"Avenel, wait—" Her words were lost as his lips took

possession of hers. His arms dropped to her supple waist, and before she could catch her runaway senses, his kiss grew more demanding. He seemed to want more from her than she knew how to give. Breathlessly, she tried to ignore his persuasions, for she was reluctant to taste him. But when his hand slid to grasp her bottom, she found herself growing more brazen. The wildfire he was creating in the nether regions of her belly made her act without thinking. Every time he moved his hand, the flames licked higher and higher. Finally, when she could stand it no longer, a soft moan escaped her, and she did as he desired. Her tongue slid timidly into his mouth, and with that she became all too aware of what he thought of her lovemaking. They were so close, she could feel every muscle tense along his front. Avenel stiffened, and Brienne soon discovered that the deeper and longer she kissed him, the greater his response grew. Although she was shaken by the force of his reaction, she at least knew he was pleased.

"Avenel, we're going so quickly," she gasped when he tore his mouth from hers. His scent, rich and masculine, one that no amount of soap could wash away, lingered on her skin, and his mouth burned along her neck. Drowning in its heady influence, she fell silent before he roughly laid her back on the bed. She felt his weight upon the mattress, and soon he was next to her, cupping her breasts and making her own hand move down his broad, muscular back. Anxiety and delight made her vision dim. His hand was warm and gentle on her flesh, but she felt flashes of fear whenever she looked at him. He seemed possessed by his desire for her. Because she couldn't understand his urgency, she was frightened by it.

In an effort to slow him down, she placed her hands

against his chest. With his body pressed against hers, she could feel how the hair of his chest made a fine stream down his rock-hard belly and finally thickened once again below his navel, where he was pressing urgently against the softness of her stomach. Her palms grew damp, and she wondered madly how she presumed to control a man like Avenel Slane when she couldn't control her own body, which was arching against his like a moth to a flame.

She tried for the last time to regain her self-control before Avenel's hand forced her to abandon the effort. He began by stroking the curve of her waist, then swept his palms over her hips, and finally explored the intimate sweet flesh of her inner thigh. His teeth nipped at her shoulder and moved down to her breasts.

"I want you, Brienne, do you know that? I want you like no other woman I've ever known. But are you my curse or my charm?" He groaned and didn't wait for her to answer. Expressing his desire perfectly, he took each of her breasts and brushed their creamy roundness with his fingers until each rose-colored nipple blushed and strained for more of his touch. Fire raged within her then as his mouth possessed them, and she felt as if she were being swept away in the rampage of Avenel's desire. Panting and utterly helpless, she felt his tongue trail down the gentle curve of her breast, and with that he edged between her thighs. When his hands wove themselves into the unbound glory of her hair, she knew it was time for his fiery need to be satisfied.

Yet his desire was too demanding and too ferocious. Seeds of panic lodged in Brienne's breast when his strong body came to rest between her legs. Choking on her words, she made one last attempt to explain her own needs to him: "Avenel, you know I'm not wise in the ways of love."

He paused, just as she'd hoped he would, but only to whisper very firmly in her ear, "I know that, my love. A wise woman would have left."

He kissed her then and moved farther between her thighs. Yet with his every movement, Brienne felt her panic grow. "Avenel, wait . . ." she cried softly, but he seemed not to hear. Instead he roughly took her hands and held them over her head. Stunned and disoriented, Brienne wondered if he even realized who she was at that moment. His movements had become so calculated and practiced, it seemed almost as if he were making love to another woman, a woman with experience that she had yet to gain. He was breathing hard, and she knew he was anxious to enter her. His body had gone rigid, and his heart was pounding heavily in his chest. Although she believed it was impossible to stop him, she knew she had to make him realize what he was doing to her.

Releasing a sob as he moved nearer, she suddenly clamped her legs together and felt hot, burning tears glide down her cheeks. Horrified at what she'd done, and then more so when she saw the shocked look upon Avenel's face, she turned her head away to hide her hurt and her fear.

"Brienne, Brienne," Avenel gasped above her. He hadn't released her, but his hold loosened. Over her head, his hands clasped with her own, and he asked very slowly, "Brienne, what is it?"

"I don't want you to hurt me," she cried against the pillow.

"I've frightened you." His voice was harsh but understanding. He seemed to be fighting off some terrible pain, and it took him several moments before he spoke again. When he finally did, she noticed that his breathing had slowed down and his body seemed more relaxed. Kissing her forehead, he still refused to let her go, but he soothed her by saying, "Remember that tonight is a first time for us both, my love. You've never had a man and alas, I've never had a virgin."

Even though she still felt frightened, with Avenel lying on top of her, her tears began to dry. "I do want to be close to you, Avenel," she whispered.

With that he seemed to laugh and groan in one breath. Stroking her hair, it appeared that for the first time in his life he was at a loss for words.

"Teach me how to do that, Avenel. I know you can." Brienne stared up into his handsome face. "Teach me how to love a man. Teach me how to love you." She dropped her eyes. She was baring her soul to him. She could only hope that Avenel would understand what she was saying so artlessly.

"No," he answered so swiftly that she thought her heart would break.

A silent cry sounded in her head. A tear slid down her cheek. *He doesn't understand. He doesn't—*

"My love," his voice broke into her thoughts. Her eyes lifted to his, and she took a deep breath, readying herself for his rejection. But it never came. Instead he kissed her eyelids and said, "I would have it the other way around. Tonight you must be the teacher. Tonight you must show me what to do, how to love a virgin."

"I don't know how to teach you anything, Avenel. I don't know—"

"Well, does one please a virgin by kissing her here?" Slowly he bent his head and pressed his lips to hers.

Their hands clasped more tightly; feeling his new tenderness, Brienne found herself relaxing.

"Or does one kiss her here?" He moved lower, reaching the fragrant hollows of her throat. He took his time kissing her there and appeared to savor the way her pulse quickened with his touch. He lingered for a long time before he made his way lower.

"Or here?" he finally asked as his mouth reached her breast. But this time she was ready for him. This time, she was the one drinking in sensations. Her fingers combed through the thickness of his hair, and she melted beneath his practiced lips.

A long time passed before he raised his head, yet his magic was working. She moaned shamelessly, "Avenel, give me what I'm missing." Her loins this time didn't rage with fire but smoldered in a slow, urgent burn. But he was not through. He was not ready to satisfy her yet.

He turned her on her stomach and cupped her smooth, rounded bottom. Her spine took the heat of his lips, and he kissed her in places she'd never been kissed before.

"Is this what a virgin seeks?" he teased her, his voice husky and promising.

"Avenel . . ." She moaned the rest of her answer when his tongue wound lazily down the small of her back. Before she could articulate another word, he pulled her on top of him, kissing her breasts, her shoulders, her waist. He paused only once to brush the burgundy strands from her eyes and whisper urgently, "When I look at you like this, do you know how I feel?"

She shook her head and delighted in the gleam of his eyes.

"I feel greedy. So overwhelmingly greedy that I would rather die than see you in another man's bed." With that he gave her a long, slow kiss that took her breath away and made her weak.

When he laid her back on the bed and again moved over her, she found no more fear in her breast. When he whispered possessively into her ear, "My beautiful, sweet woman. My beautiful, sweet Brienne," she knew then without a doubt that it was the most natural thing in the world for them to form a union. And finally, when she felt the searing tear of her maidenhood as it was lost forever to his lovemaking, she took him willingly, ready to pay the price in exchange for the pleasure he'd given her.

But unknown to her, there was more. She moaned and felt a sparkling tremor move down her thighs as her hips and Avenel's moved in rhythm. With Avenel's every thrust, Brienne felt her body loosen, and she took more of him into her arms and into her body. Soon a delicious tightening between her thighs began, and she looked up at him, touching the handsome planes of his face. Although she was almost blinded by the feelings he aroused in her, she could see how he watched her. His eyes, usually icy blue, had become smoky and passionate. With every movement, the expression in them grew hotter and more possessive, until Brienne finally could stand it no more.

Shuddering, she felt her entire body writhe beneath his movements, at once trying to get away from his excruciating, tantalizing rhythm and at the same time move toward it, desperate for more. When her release came, she whispered almost inaudibly, "I love you, Avenel." But she didn't know if he heard her, for as she said the words, he closed his eyes and unleashed himself, giving out a low powerful growl from seeking and receiving his pleasure to the fullest.

When they both lay breathless, still entwined in their intimate embrace, Brienne swept one hand down his thigh; her emotions showed clearly on her face. Avenel had taken her to a place where she thought she'd never go. It had been a place where even the coldest and most sinister of men could learn to be loving and giving. All her days of loneliness seemed to dissipate before her like mist with the dawn. She had become close to Avenel, and with him, for the first time in her life, she had had her first taste of true happiness. Closing her eyes, she vowed to cling to it as she had never done before.

As she lay quietly with her thoughts, Avenel brushed her hair back from her brow. But before either knew what to say, Brienne felt warm blood permeating the bandage on his leg.

"You're bleeding," she whispered.

Avenel studied her for a very long time, not moving, not leaving. He kissed her then, deeply, and startled her by biting her full lips. Then, as if they were words he almost hated to say, he said, "I'm afraid, my love, your father has seen to it that we both are." With this enigmatic statement, he finally extricated himself from her and enfolded her protectively in his arms.

CHAPTER TWENTY

Someone was knocking at the bedchamber door, softly at first, then more insistently when no one answered. Avenel opened his eyes; his gaze went immediately to Brienne, who lay next to him. Her hair fanned out across his chest like an exquisite ruby-colored counterpane, and she lay sleeping in his arms, her lips reddened from their passion of the night before and slightly parted in slumber. Slowly he moved away from her, hardly making her stir underneath the warm creamy linens and heavy green velvet coverlet. He bent, kissed her enticing lips, then covered her tender breasts, before moving naked to the door.

"What is it?" he asked impatiently as he opened the door to the passage. Seeing Cumberland standing in the threshold clad only in his red banyan and hat, he cocked one jet brow and said, "The sun has not yet risen. What could be so important that you must come here now?"

"A letter, Slane, from Satterlee." Cumberland's mouth was a grim line, and he didn't even seem to notice

Avenel's lack of clothing. "I am afraid it's been delayed getting here. The messenger told me it was on a frigate sunk by the Americans. Do you see the date? It was written five months ago, the day after we left." Cumberland shot him a nervous, foreboding glance and watched as Avenel forced open the wax seal with the Satterlee crest. He read the letter swiftly, and when he was finished, he too looked grim. "What is it, Slane?" Cumberland asked in a voice that implied he was not sure he wanted to know.

"Staples is dead," Avenel answered in a lifeless voice.

"How?" The elder man swallowed.

"Morrow's handiwork. It seems he left his signature on Staples's body."

"Oh, God, no!" Cumberland gasped. "But what about the boy? Is he dead, too?"

"No, apparently Nob was out hunting at the time. When he returned, he found his father, and then ran to Satterlee for help." Avenel ran a shaky hand through his dark, untied mane. "He's been staying at Satterlee, but they said that if they hadn't heard from me after a few months, they would ship him here. It seems they think I'm the best keeper for the boy. He needs to be looked after, and . . ." He gave a great, mournful sigh and refused to finish.

"He is all right, though, Slane. He should arrive in a matter of weeks, safe and sound. Things could be worse."

"No!" Avenel lashed out through clenched teeth. "Things could not be worse! Staples saved our lives when he found us swimming ashore, bloody and maimed as we were. Look how he has been repaid! Because he helped me regain Osterley, Morrow has butchered him." Suddenly his face contorted into a mask of murderous rage. "God help that beast," he said low and hard. "God help him if he ever sets foot on Osterley soil again. Though he caught me off guard in the woods, I swear he will never get a second chance!"

"Aye," Cumberland assented. But suddenly the old man's mouth dropped open, and he stared beyond Avenel to the domed bed. There could be no mistaking whose auburn head rested on the pillows.

"It's early, Cumberland. Go back to bed. I shall take care of her." Avenel spoke in a flat monotone. His eyes shone with vengeance like rays of icicles, and Cumberland shook with fear for the young girl who now slept so peacefully in her lover's bed, unaware of the storm brewing around her.

"What are you going to do, Slane?" Cumberland asked, desperate to reason with him. "She has had no part in this." He pulled the letter from his friend's grasp. "She is innocent—"

"No longer, my friend. And 'tis just as well." Avenel took the letter from the old man's hand.

"Don't do this to her, Avenel. She loves you. And this will kill her." Cumberland licked his dry lips.

"I gave her her chance to leave, and she refused. Now she is a part of this. Whether by her own hand or not, I tell you, my friend, she is now a part of this." Slowly Avenel backed into the room, closing the door behind him.

"For God's sake, Slane! She saved your life! Don't do this!" Cumberland whispered desperately at the door.

"Then she is playing the fool. For perhaps 'twas not worth saving." The door closed with a thud, and not another sound could be heard from behind its reaches for a very long time.

Gradually Brienne's sleep-heavy eyelids opened, and two gentian irises peered out from the encircling dark lashes. She breathed in deeply and became heady with the scent of Avenel and their lovemaking that clung to the fine Egyptian linen surrounding her. Raising her head, she looked to the other side of the bedstead for him, but the bed was empty. Soon, however, she spotted him standing naked at the window, awash in the predawn light. His back was to her, and he appeared almost stern. His arms were folded neatly across his chest, and his finely hewn thighs, one still bound with white linen bandages, were spread apart in a stance of superiority. Her eyes caressed his body, from the wide, scar-nicked shoulders to the firm, small buttocks that finally melded down to two, dark-haired, muscular legs. These sights brought on memories of the night before as time and time again, he had taken her to him and they had tumbled helplessly about in the bed. They had made love ferociously all night long, as if there would never be another time for them. Now, feeling wonderfully sore and utterly satiated, she sat up in the large, columned bed, draping the linen modestly across her full bare chest.

"Avenel, love," she greeted him, feeling for perhaps the first time in her life fully glad to be alive. She smiled and waited for him to turn around and wrap his strong, warm arms around her. But there was no response from him at all. "Avenel? What is it, my love?" Lines of concern marred her smooth forehead. He still did not turn around to face her, and perhaps that was what disturbed her most of all. "Please?" she whispered, and he answered her in a harsh, merciless voice.

"I've received a letter today, *Lady* Brienne." He suddenly seemed to take pleasure in reminding her of her title.

"A letter? But it's not even dawn." She pulled the covers to her, feeling a quickening desire for protection.

" 'Twas sent by special messenger. It was lost in the war we are having and just recently was found."

"What—what does it say?" She moistened her lips with her tongue and vaguely wondered how they could be so dry after so much kissing the night before.

"It says," he began, this time raising his voice. "It says that my friend has been murdered by your father."

"Murdered?" She frowned. "He will be tried for the crime, will he not? When they find him guilty, they'll hang him. Lord Oliver will be dead, and we'll be left alone," Brienne reasoned, desperate for him to change the hard-edged tone of voice.

"How can your father be tried when the authorities do not know it was he?" He laughed bitterly.

"But you know it was the earl."

"Yes, and do you know how I know?" He was deadly calm now.

"No, Avenel," she whispered, suddenly fearful.

"Because he left his calling card." She listened to the hatred in his voice and then watched as he slowly turned around to face her. Suddenly she let out a horrified gasp, and the morning bloom left her face as she gazed below his waistline. Dimly she recalled moving her hand down his abdomen the night before. But never did it occur to her that the smooth flesh she had touched there was the result of so many scars. His entire belly below the navel was flecked with a starburst of razor-thin scars. A particularly mean one ran down one side of his groin, just missing his manhood, it would seem, by a hair's breadth. "Do you know what castration means?" Avenel forced her eyes back up to his angry face.

"I—I do. You are marked, but surely—"

"Ah, but I am not referring to myself. There was a botched attempt on me, to be sure. But I speak about your loved one, Brienne. I am talking about Cumberland." His eyes flashed coldly.

"No!" she cried at him, refusing to listen. But soon his words seemed to find their way to her ears, and he spoke without regard for her delicate senses.

"We were on a ship bound for England, my brother and I. That was when it happened to Christopher." He paused, and his entire body seemed to burn with vengeance that was now directed completely at her. "Your father had him disemboweled, *my lady*"—he spat at her —"disemboweled and castrated. When he and his band started on me, Cumberland attempted to fight them off. But by the time we jumped into the Chesapeake Bay, he had left all that made him a man in a bloody heap on the decks."

"He is still a man. Rose loves him very much." She wept bitterly, thinking how dear Cumberland had become to her and how brutally the earl had treated him.

"You may be right there. But think of the humiliation! Think, will you?" He walked up to her, grasped her unbound mass of hair, and jerked her face painfully up to meet his. "Think of the pain of hitting the salt water with your body half-butchered. And watching your own blood make the clear blue waters of the Atlantic turn red." He tossed her violently back onto the bed and then walked over to the window, now not moving a muscle except the one that twitched in his lower jaw. "I was thirteen then. It took me twenty years to find retribution.

And the day after I found it, he killed and castrated the man who helped me."

"Why does he hate you so?" She wiped her tear-stained cheeks with the back of her hand. Unmindful of her unclothed state, she shivered and sat back on her slim haunches to look at him.

"You will find that out in good time. For now, let it suffice to say that greed has been his motive." He touched the ancient lapis urn displayed so proudly on the tripod pedestal before the window. In the early morning light the piece shone almost black. He skimmed the polished surface with his palm and watched it wobble precariously. "Your father has a great love for beautiful things, has he not?" He looked back at her with an evil glance.

"Yes," she said flatly. "My mother was one of his things."

"Ah! Then you know how it is." He looked back out the window. The only sound in the room came from the heavy, wobbling urn.

When it finally came to a stop, he stood quietly, and she took this moment to assure him. "I will help you, Avenel. Whatever it is that I can do to help you, please know that I will do it. Together we will find some way to—"

"We have already found a way."

Suddenly the hairs stood up on the back of her neck. There was a stance about him so utterly void of emotion that she could have sworn he was some sort of satanic being. Reluctantly she breathed the final question, knowing the answer was not what she wanted to hear: "And what is that way?"

"I planned this for you all along." He laughed harshly and then started to speak as if she were not even present in the room. "From the very first moment I'd heard Oliver Morrow's daughter was stranded at my blessed Osterley, I asked myself, how could I use her to get to him? What would be the one humiliation no father would stand for?" Inch by inch, his eyes trailed to the magnificent rumpled bed. "I'm afraid the answer was obvious. After all, how could the earl stand by while I made his daughter prisoner in the house he believes to be his? While I not only forced her to live in servitude and submission, but also"—he paused as if he were struggling with what he had to say next—"but also made her my willing whore as well."

Something inside her died when she heard his words. It was not her love for him that seemed to wither and fade, for that, she knew, was destined to remain strong and tormented. But her reason for living and this hoped-for, fresh new beginning was swiftly killed by his shrewd words. She saw now that their wonderful night together that had brought her love for him to the surface had been nothing less than a calculated and immoral act. And now all he could relay to her was his consuming hatred for her father and his contempt for her.

Cold, mad laughter seemed to come from her throat, and she suddenly spat out at him, "What a pathetic creature I must seem to you! But the little plan you've devised for my downfall will come to naught—of that I can assure you. For I will not go along with your scheming. And it will do no harm to the earl for you to torture me. You see, Oliver Morrow despises me. He despises me almost as much as you do." She stopped and watched as his eyes moved worriedly over her face, as if he wondered about her sanity.

"He may hate you, my lady. But he will not stand by while I—"

"While you rape me? Despoil me? But that is not so! For rape is one of his favorite pastimes," she spewed at him.

"But were you raped last night?" He moved to the bed and grabbed her arm, demanding her answer.

"Don't touch me." Violently she pushed him away and got off the bed.

"You see? That is where I'll get him. I have his precious house under my hand and his only daughter, who'll willingly take everything I can give." Now it was his turn to laugh mirthlessly. "Aye, that will do it. Whether he hates you or loves you, that will bring him to his knees."

"How wrong you are!" She pulled her arms across her bare chest and looked for her shift, which was nowhere to be seen in the bedchamber. "I'll leave before that comes to pass. I have the means now, and I'll use it."

"You have the means? Pray tell, and what are they?" He cocked his brow wickedly.

"The money . . ." Her voice trailed off, seeing his taunting smile. "You would go back on your offer?" she demanded.

"The offer was withdrawn last night, love. You chose to stay."

"But that was when I thought you . . ." She looked down, hiding her vulnerable, expressive eyes from his sight. She tried to think, but her head pounded from a wretched headache. All she could say was "Then I shall leave without any means."

"You will never leave here. You're mine now because the price for you was extracted from my own flesh and blood." His words were tightly spoken, as if he were fighting for self-control. But then he suddenly shoved the priceless lapis lazuli urn off the pedestal. A moment's flash of anger and the three-thousand-year-old urn lay in worthless shards before her feet. A stifled sob racked her body and she quickly ran to the tapestry room to get away from this unfeeling, brutal man who was bent on torturing her. She gratefully saw her hyacinth brocade laid out on a chair near a newly built-up fire and she quickly flung the fabric over her head.

When she had the dress on, she pulled it together with her arms, looking down for her laces. Then she saw the gold key sparkling in the light from the hearth. She knew Avenel was behind her, stalking her like some magnificent, naked carnivore, and she knew she would have to be quick if she were going to win her freedom. She grabbed the key, but her cry soon went from triumph to defeat as he came upon her. He almost broke her fingers as he wrenched the gold key out of her hand. Without an ounce of remorse on his face, he then flung the precious key into the fire. Instinctively she reached for it, moaning from the sharp pain that the flames inflicted on her. But when he grabbed her to get her hand away from the flames, she thrust out her fist and beat mercilessly on his bandaged thigh, knowing from her experience with his wound exactly where her small hand could hurt him most. When he was helpless and groaning, she calmly walked out of the room the victor. Yet she felt bitter with the knowledge that, despite his aching wound, she had left him feeling less pain than she felt—not from her burned hand, but from her ravaged heart.

Everything was ready. Her brown cloak lay on the counterpane with a coarse cloth bag that held all her worldly possessions: two dresses, an extra linen shift, and the miniature of a young man painted on a wafer-thin sheet of ivory. Stepping into her pattens, she momentarily rubbed her forehead. Her head ached pitiably from the tears she refused to shed. Taking a deep breath, she went over to the bed to grab her cloak and bag. Then she moved to the door, somehow feeling anxious about her departure, which seemed to be going too smoothly.

But then she encountered the locked door. Pulling on the brass knob, done in arabesques and etchings, she struggled with it for a long time, hoping against hope that it was just stuck. She hadn't heard the quiet click of the lock when she had first entered her bedchamber, for she had been too involved in collecting her things and getting out of the hyacinth brocade. But there was no mistaking it now. The door was locked, and she could be sure there was no key left behind for her.

She gave up on it and looked around the yellow taffeta room, seeking another way out. There was only one other door. Going into her dressing room, she went to the wall where the jib was placed. She ran her fingers along the edge, seeking the spring lock, but she quickly realized it was no use. The door could only be sprung from the other side by the servants, and for the moment it was tightly shut and locked, too.

"Damn," she whispered, holding her head, which now pounded unmercifully.

Late that afternoon, Avenel sat by the blazing fireplace in the gallery just underneath the painting of Oliver Morrow. A glass in his hand was filled with amber spirits. He held on to it tightly, keeping the tension of his fingers on the beaker just below the breaking point.

"You've been drinking all day, Avenel." Rose walked over to the armchair in which he sat. She kneeled down beside him, taking his free hand in hers.

"So I have." His eyes were red and tired from the drink, but his speech did not show its effects.

"Perhaps you would like me to help you into your bedchamber? You could try to rest." She placed her head gently on his knee and looked over to the side where her husband stood.

"That sounds like a good idea, Slane. You look worn out." Cumberland moved closer to them.

"No, no. I'm not tired. I've been thinking. Remembering times past." Avenel lifted the glass to his lips and took a long sip of the expensive liquid. "I was recalling that terrible fever you had. It seemed to me and Staples, 'twould never cease. Do you recall?"

"Not hardly. It all seems a bad dream," Cumberland said.

"I do, though. Staples had me up and about in no time after we jumped ship. But you—you were laid up for a long while." Avenel squinted as if he were pulling something from the back of his mind. "I remember how I went to work with Staples. 'Twas in the tobacco fields with that fresh shipment of African flesh. We were hardly better off than the slaves that toiled alongside us. By the end of the summer, Staples and I appeared as black as they from the sun beating down on our backs. To this day I still cannot abide the stench of dried tobacco leaves. It reminds me too dearly of the cost in blood and sweat."

"Staples was a dear friend. I mourn him too, Slane. But we moved up, didn't we? And we moved him up with us," Cumberland reassured him.

"It was mostly your doing. We never could have gotten him such a plantation if you hadn't taught me how to gamble." Avenel sipped again and frowned. "As it was, it took years before I thought I could win. Those wealthy, impetuous fools!'' he scoffed. ''How easily they threw away their gold, when they didn't have the vaguest knowledge whence it came! Nor how hard a man must work to earn the most meager of livings.'' He laughed now, his mood as changeable as mercury. ''But look at the three of us! We're all three rich beyond our wildest imaginings and back at Osterley Park. We have them to thank for it!''

''We have you to thank for it,'' Rose said softly, looking at his pain-filled eyes.

Avenel took notice of her now, and he found comfort stroking her corona of faded blond hair. ''You must tell me, Rose. Why did I not marry you when Christopher was killed? You're still lovely, though you be years older than I.''

''Hush your musings, my lord!'' she exclaimed with a playful smile. ''For my husband is near, and you will force him to call you out!''

''But tell me, why did we not fall in love and—''

''Because, my lord,'' she answered gently, ''you were not Christopher and you are not Cumberland. And I, alas, am not Bri—''

''Do not!'' Avenel warned her before she could say the name.

''But it's true, is it not, Slane?'' Cumberland forced his way into their conversation.

''No! You're both mad if you think I would fall in love with Morrow's daughter!'' Avenel sat up straight in the armchair, causing Rose to jerk her head abruptly from his knee.

''Why don't you admit it? We cannot go on fooling ourselves that the girl upstairs is to be used and then cast aside. She is a person, Slane. It's true we had our plans to do that to her, but that was before we came here. We thought she'd be a vile, selfish creature, well used to a soft, indulgent life. But Brienne is not like that, and you cannot abuse her like a London strumpet." Cumberland looked over to him with imploring blue eyes. "She loves you, Slane. And God forgive me for saying this, but you love her too!"

"Damn you for saying that!" The glass that Avenel held so forcibly now shattered in his hand. Tiny rivulets of crimson started down his palm into the crisp, snowy lace of his cuff. Rose jumped up off the floor to get a cloth from the tea table, but he violently waived it away, choosing instead to vent his anger on her husband. "Are you crazed, old man, for speaking such things?" Avenel stood up and shouted at Cumberland. "Why not be quick about it and simply put a knife in my back? Or are you both hoping Morrow will do it for you? I daresay, he would love to attend to that task! Just look what he did in the woods!" Avenel looked up, his eyes as mean and white as a wolf's. "But I vow to both of you, and heed my words well," he spoke in a tightly controlled whisper. "Oliver Morrow will not get to me through Brienne. He will not get me that way!" He kicked out at the fine elbow chair and then stalked out of the room, leaving Rose and Cumberland behind, their faces full of shock and helpless disbelief.

Brienne paced the pale wool carpeting in her bed-chamber. The waiting was driving her mad. She knew someone, whether it be Vivie, Cumberland, or Avenel himself, would have to enter her room eventually, and when they did, she would make her escape. But now it was all she could do to fight the compulsion to bang wildly on the door and beg to be let out of her yellow-silk-hung prison. But she forced herself to pace quietly and wait, to ease her aching head in the peaceful solitude of her bedchamber. There had been a lot of time to think as the early evening sun descended into the surrounding forests. A plan had formed in her mind as to how she could get past the guards and gatemen, who by now had surely been informed of the possibility of her escape. She did not doubt Avenel's thoroughness in this matter, but she knew that with the plan she had in mind her greatest obstacle was getting through the locked door before her and not by the burly Scandinavians at the Park's entrance.

Her ears pricked at the sound of a key in the keyhole. There was a click, the lock was sprung, and she backed from the door to meet whoever stood on the other side of the thick mahogany.

"Get out!" she whispered vehemently at Avenel as he stood in the threshold. But he did not heed her words; instead he closed the door behind him and relocked it. Brienne noticed the stark, glazed appearance of his eyes and knew he had been drinking, although his calculated and controlled movements belied this fact.

"Leave me, I tell you!" she demanded, horrified that he nonchalantly placed the key on the mantelpiece and then sat on the settee. He removed his tall, black boots and his fine knitted stockings. She watched in absolute silence as he pulled each of them off his legs, noticing for the first time his cut and bleeding palm. But she felt no sympathy for him, only fear, as he pulled off his waistcoat and tossed that elaborately embroidered garment onto the floor. Then he looked straight at her with dispassionate eyes and pulled off his white linen shirt. Bending his head to his front, he slowly unlaced his doeskin breeches. She watched from her place at the window like a frightened red vixen caught in a trap. The scarred flesh of his taut, lower abdomen was exposed, and then his manhood, large and unfettered, was revealed. She looked away as he tossed the last vestige of his clothing over the settee; her mouth went dry, and her heart beat desperately in her chest.

Slowly and deliberately, he walked over to her; his naked male flesh swung with every powerful step. All too soon he was upon her, and she expected a violent assault on her body. But there was none save the soft brush of his skin as he positioned her against the wall.

"You will have to force me this time." She jerked her head to the side in refusal, breathing in his brandy-laced scent. His darkly furred chest skimmed the bare skin that was exposed at the top of her bodice, and against her will she found it pinkening and tingling beneath him.

"I think not," he whispered into her mass of auburn, honeysuckle-scented hair. He inhaled her fragrance deeply and then paused to admire the sweet, kiss-starved curve of her lips before his own descended on them.

Her eyes squeezed shut as if to force from her mind the overwhelming memory of their lovemaking. Her hand pushed against his well-muscled chest to announce her reluctance. But there was no pulling away from the proud, naked man as his hips pressed into her soft belly, proving his desire again and again with his hard and swelling manhood. She dared not look down in fear of its very size, and so she looked up, thereby allowing her mouth to be opened and explored by his hard, thrusting tongue.

"Nay," she moaned deliriously as she felt her bodice open underneath his experienced fingers. Soon his palm was overflowing with the rose-crested fullness of her breast, and a bittersweet feeling came over her as she noticed how generously she filled his large, bronzed hand. "Nay, I tell you!" She pulled her bodice to her and then ran over to the mantelpiece, seeking the key.

"I can make you want me, Brienne. With just one finger I can make you." He stalked her at the mantel. In panic she sought the key, but before she had it within her grasp, she was pulled by the waist to the settee.

"Oh, God, how wrong you are!" she spat at him, elbowing and kicking at him to free herself of his iron embrace. He forced her down onto the cushion, but she swore she would not give up until she was free, not this time. "I don't want a man who hates me! I tell you, I want no part of you!"

Before she could cry out another protest, his mouth clamped over hers. He kissed her long and hard, and by its end she found she was no longer struggling with him. But it was not the assault of his mouth that she could not deny. Instead it was his hand as he moved it along her leg and up between her smooth, inner thighs. She felt his fingers touch the dewy softness that hid in the silken wine-colored triangle. In moments he had her panting and so very hot, she thought she would be consumed by the fire burning within her.

She groaned as he pulled her down onto the floor. Pushing on his bare chest, she said in a broken voice, "Cease this madness, Avenel! Stop. Stop!" Her nails raked at his skin.

But he appeared to feel nothing but the devil at his tail. He shoved aside her bodice. Her dress unfastened, her shift proved no barrier at all.

"Take me within you"—he bent down and placed a nibbling kiss on her taut, sensitive nipple—"or live out the rest of the day with the ache that only I can satisfy."

"You can satisfy nothing in me, you heathen!" She spurned his kiss over and over again. But when his lips finally caught hers, she became almost pliant beneath their caress. When they had drunk of her mouth, he used them to trail down her throat. He bit her and licked her until she was forced to let out a helpless moan of desire. He then moved lower and lower and pushed away her shift, which had caught at her elbows. When his rough velvet tongue met the peak of her breast, she thought she would surely go mad from the emotional and physical war that raged within her.

"Take me." He positioned himself over her and waited for her choice. She writhed beneath him; her screaming, demanding senses seemed too great to fight any longer. She made one last incoherent plea for sanity, then his dark, handsome head bent over her breast once more. Desire rushed through her soul like water through a dam, and she knew she was lost. Wordlessly, mindlessly, her head nodded in helpless assent.

"Say it, then," he demanded. "Say you'll take me."

"I will take you!" she cried just before he entered her. In her frenzy for appeasement, her hands clutched at his back, wanting to feel each muscle as it flexed and slackened. Her traitorous mouth reached up for his, and she took it with the same demanding force that he had used on her earlier. An unbearably short time later, she began to shudder. As Avenel's hard body rocked between her quivering thighs, the torment and pleasure instilled within her was too much to control. With a gasp, she surrendered to the dizzying eddy they had created, and she found what she had so carelessly sought. In a world of right and wrong, she felt as if she were perfectly suspended between the two, grappling with her heart and her body. When Avenel spent himself into her, she moaned. But whether this was from pure ecstasy or complete heartbreak, she was never sure.

When they finally broke free, Avenel lay back on the floor and peered at her with sleepy eyes. He seemed more relaxed than before, but she could almost believe there was remorse in his eyes for what he had done. There was a softness about him now that he had not possessed when he'd first entered her room. It was as if the demons that had held him in their grasp had been expunged by his actions. But she wouldn't wait for their return.

Quietly she rose from the floor; her hair fell over her expressionless face like a veil. He watched her, waiting for angry, spiteful words. But there were none. Instead she walked naked up to the mantel and took a large green *Sèvres* vase from it. Then, with great calculation, she crashed it over his dark head before he could move to avoid her onslaught.

"You bastard!" she hissed at him. A flicker of surprise at her retaliation crossed his handsome face. But it was tempered by a gleam of respect that shone briefly in his eyes. Then he slumped backward onto the floor, out cold.

It was almost evening when she approached the ragged children who were playing unlawfully on the grounds of the Park. Brienne was small, and any womanly curves were painfully bound to her chest with large strips of fine batiste. She was dressed much like the children, in a torn and dirty overdress that boasted no warm petticoat underneath and no protective shoes. Carrying a large, coarsely woven bag slung over her hips like a pocket, she shivered in the chill.

"Would you like some pigeon pie?" She held out the small meat pastries she'd stolen from the kitchen before sneaking out of the house.

Wary of strangers, especially of those from the Park, the children eyed her distrustfully at first. But she did not appear to be one of the grand, satin-clad figures they had seen from afar. In her rags, she was more like a child herself than an adult; her creamy soft skin and her persuasive amethyst eyes were unhidden by adornment. Softly they stepped nearer to her like ragged fawns, to seek out what she held in her palms.

"Truly, they are quite fine. And not even one day old." She trembled with anxiety, but it did not take many words to convince the children that she was sincere. The starved, homely creatures were enraptured with the beautiful pauper whose uncommon magenta-streaked hair was almost completely hidden underneath a soiled gray mobcap, and whose violet-blue eyes seemed to speak of the treachery and deceit cast upon her.

"Them's fine, you say?" A skinny boy came the closest to her. "Where'd you get 'em?" He cast doubtful eyes upon her.

"I stole them," she said. "They're for the master's dinner at the Park. But now he has none."

A hoydenish laugh came from the circle of children, and soon they were all laughing. They had a great appreciation for the truth. One by one, each child claimed a pie until they were all gone.

"Get away with you! Before I have your hides!" The larger of the blond giants from the gatehouse came into view and yelled at the children. Snarling at the ragamuffins, he ordered them away from Osterley. As Brienne had hoped, he paid no special attention to the dirty girl who kept her eyes on the ground and wore a tattered pink polonaise.

The children quickly dispersed along the fence line, laughing at their mischief and at the giant's irritation.

Brienne saw a boy disappear beneath the fence where a depression had been dug in the earth. She followed him, but because she was larger, she was almost afraid she would get stuck. But with one last push she was running past the other side of the fence away from Osterley.

II

Bath

A fine slope to the grave . . .
—James Quin

CHAPTER TWENTY-ONE

A heavy mist began to fall just as the last vestiges of daylight were disappearing and darkness settled upon the countryside. Shivering and damp, Brienne sadly watched the raggedy children scatter into the night; each headed for his or her hovel. She wished she could repay them. They would never know how much they had done for her.

She looked down at the wet and muddied polonaise and shook uncontrollably from the cold in spite of the tightly wrapped strips of linen that bound her bosom. Even though it was spring, the chilly night air descending around her made her think it was a winter's eve. Aching for the warmth of her woolen dress and heavy cloak, she stole across the quagmire of road and ran for the eaves of the nearest cottage, where she sought shelter to change into her traveling clothes. She felt the cold more intensely than ever when she stripped her body of the desecrated pink silk and linen bandages and searched through her burlap bag for her brown woolen dress. She

pulled this over her damp shift and hooked it down the
front, instantly feeling less cold. Shoving on her coarsely
knitted woolen hosiery and the oxblood riding shoes for
which she vowed to repay Avenel, she wrapped herself
snugly in her cloak and gathered up the evidence of her
departure. She wanted to hide the ratty material in a
place where Avenel would never find it.

"Oh, my God!" She spun around and found herself
staring directly into Jill's catlike yellow eyes. The girl was
spotlessly clean, and her harshly combed-back hair was
tied severely to her nape. She was dressed in a fichu and
blue woolen round gown, and to her waist was tied a
pair of yellow linen pockets—a sign that she had finished
her work for the day and was returning home.

She watched the girl, not sure whether she should try
to explain her circumstances or whether to immediately
flee from her because of her loyalty to Avenel. She soon
made up her mind, for at the far-off gatehouse of the
Park, both girls saw a commotion and a band of men
riding anxious and furious horses. Someone called out
instructions to them, and the horsemen started off in
every direction imaginable. Standing just under the dark
shadow of the eaves, Brienne needed little prodding to
escape. She imagined the bloodthirsty look on Avenel's
rock-hard face when she heard him shout orders from
the road. In a split-second she looked at Jill and saw a
traitorous gleam in the girl's amber eyes. That was all she
needed.

As soon as Jill ran out from the eaves of Mistress
Blake's cottage to flag Avenel down, Brienne dropped
the evidence of her escape and took only her brown
burlap bag. With this in hand, she frantically set out
across the cold, black nighttime pastures, assured at least

that he would never find her this night, for even the moonlight had abandoned his cause.

"She's gone to Wales. She must have. Where else would she go but to that eyesore of a town, Tenby? She knows of no other existence."

"There could be other avenues for her. Perhaps she has gone to London to find solace. It won't take her long to realize there are many wealthy men who would give their souls to take care of a woman as unique and lovely as she," Cumberland answered.

"Damn you! Mind your implications, sir!" Avenel beat his fist on the library table, making the Vitruvian scroll at its satinwood edge waver.

"You pushed her too far! You pushed her until she broke under the strain. I daresay, it's my fault. I should have helped her leave that night she spent in the stable block, just as I helped you twenty years ago on that ship. But back then I was a mere shiphand and not the rich man I am today." Cumberland confronted Avenel, his blue eyes full of worry and guilt.

"I did what I had to do," Avenel answered, his voice low and distant.

"Did you, now?" There was an edge to Cumberland's voice.

"Enough of this!" Rose entered the library from the passage. "I'll not hear you argue any further!"

"Stay out of this!" Avenel snapped, unmindful of his regard for his cousin. He fingered the precious bit of tattered gray-pink silk in his lap.

"I shall not. I'm afraid I must be blunt. For while you are at each other's throats, Brienne is wandering about the countryside, completely alone and with no funds to spare her from begging for her dinner. And since she has already been with"—she paused and gave Avenel an accusatory stare—"we must at least try to prevent her from having to resort to—"

"Enough." Avenel swept an anguished hand through his unkempt hair. Giving a heavy sigh, he rubbed his tired eyes with his thumb and forefinger. "I accept the responsibility for this. 'Tis no other's fault but my own. I shall leave tonight for Wales. I will find her before she wants for anything, I promise." He stood up, looking quite haggard, and started out the door. Cumberland grabbed his sleeve.

"You know, of course, Slane, that I never had any children." He paused. "I never had a daughter. I'll never have a daughter." Cumberland looked straight at him, almost pleading with him. "When you find her, you must forget about Morrow. Treat her as you would my daughter, if you can. She deserves that at least." He let go of Avenel's sleeve and sat down heavily in one of the honey-colored elbowchairs, looking beaten and unutterably worn.

Avenel looked at him and then nodded his head rigidly, staring ahead at the darkened windowpanes. It was already the second night.

Numbness was all around Brienne, even in the trees that stood motionless with frost clinging to every branch and nub. She had been walking for three days, hardly stopping for sleep and not once for food. Her feet seemed almost separate from the rest of her body as they trudged onward through the damp spring countryside to the west. The only cheerful sight she beheld was the countrywomen, dressed in bright scarlet cloaks, taking their daily walks through the small old villages that dotted the Cotswold Hills. The day before, she had walked up to one of these women who had held a basket of warm, braided, honey-brown bread on her arm. Steam rose from the folds of cloth that covered the loaves, and the temptation had been too much for her. Hungrily, she had approached the woman; her eyes were like great, purple saucers and her stomach was tightly knotted.

"Hello," she had said, unmindful of her soiled hemline and her dirty, knotted hair. "The bread—it truly smells wonderful."

"Aye, does it?" The woman smiled benignly at her, her attention taken with greeting some neighbors as they passed on a wagon.

"It's irresistible." Brienne licked her dry lips, which were bleeding from the cold and wind.

"Have you any coin, then? I'll not be handing out to beggars." The woman eyed her doubtfully. "And I must say, you don't look as if you possess—" She gasped when she met Brienne's unusual violet gaze. There was a moment of quiet, and then the woman burst out, "Your eyes are most uncanny. Are you a witch come to curse me?"

"A witch? I'm no witch!" she defended.

"Even the color of your hair is unreal. Mistress Crocker has been claiming all along that a spell was put on her when she lost her two boys. She said they were fine until a witch passed her on the road. She claims the witch and her black deeds turned them around in her womb and then had them strangled as they were born." The scarlet cloaked woman backed from her; Brienne watched as the loaves moved farther away.

"Please don't go! I am sorry for the Mistress Crocker, but I am so hungry. I must have some of your bread."

"You'll curse me and poison my loaves, you will!" The

woman ran from her; the flaming cloak rippled behind her.

"No, no!" She watched in panic as the coveted bread was whisked away on the woman's arm.

"Go away! I'll not be seen with a witch!" were the last words Brienne heard as she was left devastated on the barren road to Bath.

But now the whole incident didn't seem to matter much. Hunger was a distant and deniable need; of late she had been able to refuse its demands with little effort. There wasn't a great deal of feeling left anywhere in her body as she trudged up yet another steep, snow-patched hill, only to find still another waiting for her as she looked down from the top. The only thing that spurred her on was the thought of Avenel.

After her last encounter with him, all Brienne wanted, all she thought about, was putting more distance between herself and Osterley. Even the possibility of meeting up with her father in Bath seemed tolerable in order to get away from Avenel's grasp. She knew she was taking a great risk going to Bath; she prayed that the earl was staying in his London town house, as the solicitor had said. Still, Brienne knew she had to prepare for the dangerous possibility that the earl might be in Bath.

So during the long, wretched hours of her trip, she had devised a plan. She told herself she would go to the house in Bath and pose as a servant in need of employ. After making inquiries as to whether the earl was in residence, she would proceed to leave or to stay, depending on the situation. She hadn't decided what she would do if it was necessary to leave Bath to avoid the earl. No matter how hard she wracked her brains to remember a long-lost relative of her mother's or even a kind friend who would take her in, she came up with nothing. If the earl was in Bath, her only salvation would be to return to Wales. Yet that plan hinged on her ability to get enough money. But there, at least, she would be safe. The earl knew nothing of that place. Suddenly she blanched; her carefully laid plans fell to wrack and ruin: Avenel knew of Tenby.

Avenel. The name echoed through her weary mind, producing a fearsome headache. For the past few days as she walked, her thoughts had spun with self-loathing, hatred, and disgust. She wondered how she could ever have been so dim-witted as to allow a misspent colonial gambler to take her to his bed. After the earl had raped her mother, she had vowed never to let anything like that happen to her.

But Brienne knew, deep down, that there could be no comparison. For as much as she had learned to hate Avenel's manipulative ways, she had wanted him with a desire that had rivaled his own. She knew she had loved him, although her mind rebelled at the thought now. Even that last evening when he had shown up in her bedchamber, angry and half drunk, she had wanted him. He had shown to her pleasure that could be at once sin and salvation. No matter how much she had wished to kill him when he had rolled off her that last time at Osterley, the worst she'd been able to do was smash the green *Sèvres* vase over his head. It had sent him into blissful unconsciousness while she dressed in her tattered pink silk and ran from the house. She had uttered her last words to him as he had lain at her feet, naked and beautiful in his defenselessness; in a voice fraught with anger and pain she'd said, "You demented beast! You'll no longer use me in this vicious war! From now on, let Osterley be the battleground!" With that she had knelt beside him and placed a bitter kiss on his lips. But she had felt more pain than she could express at the thought of never seeing him again or at the thought of why that must always be so.

The stone-colored Georgian city lay nestled in the golden hills above the river Avon. When Brienne first saw Bath she was awed by its wealth and grandeur. She avoided the main road into town, where a parade of personages were going into the city; she felt too self-conscious about her shabby appearance to join the ranks of poets, wits, and society patrons. Therefore, she reached Bath through various sheep fields that graced the higher elevations of the town. Now, along busy Milsom Street, where the smart lending libraries and bookshops were located, she found herself aghast and wondering how amongst the many streets would she find her father's house.

She wandered about in her raggedy apparel, feeling completely out of place. The gentry, bedecked in peacock-colored satins, velvets, and brocades, rode alongside her, carried about in their square black chairs. One or two of the chairmen glanced her way, but she was too afraid to ask them for directions. Walking down Milsom Street, she felt dizzy, the hardships of the past few days finally caught up with her.

A man dressed in garnet velvet rudely bumped into her. Taking note of her impoverished appearance, he said harshly, "Out of my path, trollop!" He moved away and entered a milliner's, whose window was delightfully filled with every color of satin ribbon possible, from parrot green and fiery orange to the deepest shades of sapphire, ruby, and emerald.

She stared after the man, too tired to feel more than slightly affronted by his abuse. She knew she was not going to last long without some food, and now she only wanted to find a resting place sans Oliver Morrow.

Walking farther down the hilly street, she spied a wizened, poorly garbed old woman hawking fresh flowers on the corner. Hoping she could give her the directions she needed, she patted her tangled and matted hair and approached her.

"Pardon me. I am looking for—"

"We 'ave no need for another beggar in this city." She laughed, showing her lack of teeth. "Away with you, 'afore you cause ruination to the business." The ancient woman spat a thick, greenish sputum and pulled her greasy, gray skirts back from Brienne.

"Please, you misunderstand. I am in need of directions. The Crescent—if you would but tell me where it is?" she said in an overwrought voice.

"The Royal Crescent? The scullery help there is in better shape than you, missy." She gave her a jaundiced eye. "But you're a pretty creature! Would you be wantin' a posy for your trip there?" She smiled, showing blackened gums, as the heavy, sickly-sweet odor of rotting violets wafted from her basket.

"No, thank you." Brienne swallowed her nausea.

"Then be off with you! The welfare of the business, you see." The woman was apologetic as she picked up her baskets of violets and multihued tulips and walked away to find a less competitive corner.

Placing a shaking hand over her mouth, Brienne frowned; the cloying scent of violets in the seller's wake made her feel ill. Suddenly she seemed overwhelmed by the problems that had plagued her since she'd left Osterley. Her birthright she felt forced to deny, but it was galling to her that, she, the daughter of a powerful earl, was reduced to an impoverished existence on the streets

of Bath with no one civil enough to give her directions.
If she weren't accused of witchery, then it was begging.
Suddenly she felt as if she'd been an outcast her entire
life. Only at Osterley, where she should have felt least
welcome, had she ever really belonged.

This irony made her feel almost like giving up. Perhaps, she mused, she could find a meadow where only
the black sheep grazed and lie down in the sparse, grassy
field and close her eyes, never to reopen them again. She
would see her mother again, the only person who had
ever loved her. Her lips trembled at the thought of her
mother, and quite unbidden, her thoughts grew as dark
as a thunderstorm.

"I couldn't help but overhear, pretty maiden. You are
looking for The Crescent?"

She was startled out of her morbid thoughts by a kind,
masculine voice. Looking up, she saw an appreciative
pair of brown eyes, and as she gazed into their soothing
depths, she wondered if she might make it after all.

"You seek The Crescent?" the young man asked her
again. Though his manner was polite, his gaze was warm
and intimate. At first glance he seemed to overlook her
dirty, travel-worn state and instead see the woman underneath.

"Yes," Brienne began warily, lowering her eyes from
his appraisal. Quickly she pulled up her hood to cover
her hair. The man seemed to pay an unusual amount of
attention to its strange color, and this unnerved her. She
wanted to be as inconspicuous as possible, on the
chance that the earl was in town.

She began an assessment of the man. Although not
particularly tall and broad, his figure was muscular and
well proportioned. He possessed a handsome face. It
wasn't dark and fierce, but it was still handsome and

could have graced one of the Roman statues in Osterley's hall. His blond hair was neatly bag-tied onto his nape, his eyes were drawn with fine golden brows, and his nose was straight; the slight flare of each nostril gave him an air of unmistakable integrity. Brienne instantly found herself wanting to trust him, but she reminded herself, she had learned hard lessons at Osterley. Finally she answered, "Yes, I am looking for The Royal Crescent."

"Then may I be of some assistance? You're going in the wrong direction. The Crescent is up Milsom Street and then through King's Circus and—" The man suddenly frowned, as if noticing her weary state for the first time. "Perhaps I'd best take you. Quite frankly, you do not look as if you could make it there alone." He nodded at the high-sprung, lacquered carriage that waited for him at the bottom of the street. "Allow me." He graciously offered her his arm.

"I'm afraid I cannot." Brienne stepped back; her sudden movement made her dizzy. She didn't know what to make of this stranger's generous offer.

"Please, princess. You look as if you're ready to drop." He grasped her arm and steadied her, and she found his fingers warm and pleasant.

"Princess—what a name to be calling me," she murmured, finding his name for her at odds with her appearance.

"It's not so strange. Not when one considers how you speak. You speak like nobility, princess." His eyes examined her gently. "And if you didn't have that dirty cloak to hide behind, I daresay, you would look like nobility, too."

"I am going to The Royal Crescent to find employment as a servant," she said quickly. "I'm afraid you are mistaken."

"Mistaken or not, allow me to take you there." He smiled a beckoning, boyish smile.

She hesitated, but when he began steering her toward the carriage, she decided a real servant wouldn't refuse the generous offer of a ride. She would only make herself more conspicuous by refusing it.

Once inside the large black carriage, she began to doubt the wisdom of her decision. She wondered if she should have insisted upon directions and then, after doling out hearty thanks, trooped up the hill on her own.

But the stuffed leather seat of the carriage's comfortable interior compelled her to believe otherwise. As soon as she was seated, she realized how bone tired she was. She was as tired as one could be without dropping in the gutter. She watched the young man take the other seat and knock on the door for the driver to be off, and she returned his smile, praying that he would truly take her to The Royal Crescent and not to his apartments.

As they lurched forward through the streets, the young man peered into Brienne's muddied, delicate face.

"Is The Crescent very far?" she inquired politely.

"No, but I cannot promise a quick ride. Carriages are inconvenient in Bath." He smiled at her, but she only dropped her eyes again, finding his curious stare highly unnerving. She then noticed the slow pace they were taking to avoid collisions with the numerous chairs being towed in front of them. She finally looked out the window to ease her discomfort.

They had just left King's Circus with its three curved Palladian buildings, encircling a large cobblestoned center. Her delight was tempered with exhaustion, but the buildings were undeniably magnificent with their three orders of capitals—Doric, Ionic, and Corinthian—and with the sandy, acorn-carved finials that alternated above roof level.

"This ride is an unusual kindness." Her smile wavered. Examining the interior of the massive coach and the man's fine purple embroidered worsted topcoat, she was sure the man had wealth. She wondered if he were titled, too, but remembering the absence of a crest on the carriage door, she decided he was not.

"It's of no consequence whatsoever."

"Do you often offer rides to lost beggars?" she asked pointedly.

"No. Only when they are exquisitely beautiful."

His comment and his dark brown eyes left her dumbstruck until the carriage came to a halt on Brock Street.

"Is this The Crescent?"

"My coachman needs the house number." He looked to her, but she was able to hide her consternation.

"The house number?" she echoed in a desultory manner.

"Well, there are at least thirty residences. Which one do you claim, princess?" he prodded gently.

"I cannot recall." She racked her memory for the number. She was taking too many risks already today to show up at the wrong house. "I have heard it spoken of as the first one. Could there be a first one, perhaps?"

"There's Number One. Shall we stop there?"

"Yes. That will be fine." She bit her lower lip as he instructed the coachman through the window. They began to move again.

Suddenly Brienne was plagued by doubt. What if the earl were in residence after all? Could she then make it to Tenby? What if Avenel had somehow outmaneuvered her and were waiting for her here? What if the earl were not in residence but the servants didn't believe she was Oli-

ver Morrow's daughter? What if . . . ? Her mind was
pelted by questions, but all too soon they stopped at
Number One, The Crescent.

"Allow me." The young gentleman jumped from the
vehicle and extended his hand to help her down. Nervously she looked up at the house that faced Brock Street
with its two-story Ionic columns and rusticated ground
floor. She couldn't see the rest of the building as it
wound around the corner, and so, feeling a bit less intimidated, she turned to thank the young man.

"You have been very kind."

"Not as kind as I could be, princess." He smiled down
at her although he was only a few inches taller than she.
"Is someone expecting you here? May I call on them for
you?"

"No, no," she answered hastily, not at all sure of her
reception. "Please, I must not take any more of your
time. I am sure you have many pressing obligations, and I
have made you late as it is."

"May I see you to the door?" He looked at the stairs
that curved below the ground floor and led to the service
entrance. She looked at them also but was determined
that, if she did enter her father's house, it would be
through the main entrance as Lady Brienne.

"No, thank you," she said, eyeing the stairway that led
to the pedimented front door. "I've not been here for a
very long time," she lied. "And I'm afraid it may take
some time for me to reacquaint myself."

"Does your family work here? Will you be here
awhile?" he pressed.

"I cannot say," she evaded.

"Well then, at least will you bestow upon me your
name?"

"My name is Brienne," she faltered.

"Just Brienne?" His fine brow lifted.

"Yes, just Brienne."

"A simply beautiful name for a simply beautiful maiden. When will I see you again, Brienne?"

"I am sorry. Thank you for everything." She shook her head and started ascending the steps, obviously much to his surprise. Her forehead wrinkled with worry as she came closer to the front door, and she knew the young man was staring at her from the street. And she was feeling ill again—there was no doubt about it. She dreaded the next few moments, dreaded them with all her heart. Just thinking of her father made her mouth dry with fear. The possibility that he might be in the house before her, that he might even be watching her now from the drawing-room window, made her feel faint. But then, forcing herself to think of Osterley and its dark, demanding master, she raised the beautiful brass door knocker and let it fall.

The door opened immediately. "Yes," a footman answered dourly.

"I—I—" She swallowed and prayed that the wind would shift from the kitchen at the back. Her senses were suddenly overcome by the heavy odors of beef and lamb cooking. The onslaught was too much for her empty stomach and light head.

"Speak up, wench! You've got enough nerve coming to the door like this. You should be downstairs." The footman shook his gold braid on his red topcoat and watched her suspiciously. "Did Mallorey send you here, trying to get me ousted from the one decent bit o' living I've come across?"

"No, no one sent me. I . . ." She held the iron railing alongside the door, trying to keep her balance. "I have come to seek employment. Is the earl in residence?"

"The earl?" The footman seemed taken aback. But then with a jovial, sly smile, he exclaimed, "Ah, Mallorey did send you! But you tell him I have no taste even for your fair flesh, lass, when I've been as good as gold for nigh a fortnight! Hrumph!" The footman snorted and began closing the door.

"Wait! You must tell me!" she gasped through her increasing delirium. "Is the earl in residence?"

"The earl? Now, what would you be wantin' with him?" He opened the door again and looked at her curiously.

"I have no business with him, except that I am seeking employment," she whispered. "Is he here?"

"Bligh' me!" The footman slapped his knee and laughed out loud. "That whoremongering Mallorey has one bit o' humor in his old bones. The earl can't oblige you, lass, so take your sweet fanny back to his'n and tell him it just won't work." He stiffened at a noise coming from the depths of the house. "Look! You've got Mrs. Whitsome a-coming! Be off with you now! And tell Mallorey no more games."

"No, do not! I must know, is the earl in residence?" She watched as the door moved closer to its frame. She reeled suddenly, but whether this was from hunger, from the tantalizing scents wafting from the kitchens, or from the entire agony of the past three days, she didn't know. All she knew was that her eyesight was dimming, and as yet she still had no idea if the earl was in Bath. Gripping the wrought-iron bannister, she tried to back down the stairs. It was better to faint in the street than to pass out on the earl's doorstep.

But she was too late. Her endurance was spent. Stumbling backward, she fell limply into two waiting arms. Her eyelids fluttered shut, and she missed seeing the horrified expression on the housekeeper's face as she came to the door.

Watching as Brienne's tattered, limp figure was lifted up into a man's capable arms, the housekeeper cried out to her rescuer, "God bless you, Mr. Harcourt! It's Brienne Morrow! Why, no one could mistake that hair, not even when she was a babe!"

CHAPTER TWENTY-TWO

The restorative scent of ammonia under her nose made her jerk her head back violently in repulsion. Her eyes opened, and Brienne looked around the Prussian blue room and at the wool flame-stitched settee that she was ensconced upon. But she saw no one and nothing familiar.

"Rest your head. You must not get up now," a soothing, maternal voice whispered from behind her. Brienne's violet eyes shot to the doorway, and she saw a white-haired, mobcapped woman standing near her. "Here, my lady. It will only do you good." Aged, lily-white hands held out a silver mug, and the mild scent of warm milk and honey filled her nostrils, tempting her empty stomach.

"Am I at The Crescent?" Brienne frowned.

"Yes, my lady. You're at Number One."

Panic made her eyes grow wide. "Is—is the earl—?"

"The master isn't in residence now, my lady. Please, you must drink this."

Hearing the words she had longed to hear, Brienne relaxed a bit and took the mug. Ungraciously, she gulped down its contents, and then she lay back on the settee, exhausted.

"I told Mr. Harcourt that it was not too likely you'd remember this old woman." The mobcapped matron sat down on a stool near the settee, careful to position her bum roll discreetly under her lavender Spitalfields silk.

"If ever it is within my power, I shall remember your kindness for not turning me away from the door. You don't know how many days I have been without sustenance," Brienne answered, misunderstanding the woman. Closing her eyes, she fought off exhaustion.

"It's payment you think I want?" The woman laughed and then grew serious. "Ah, Lady Brienne, I see what has become of you, and it's a sorry state indeed. But what, may I ask, has become of your mother?"

"My mother?"

"The good Lady Grace."

"She's dead," Brienne said blankly. "May I ask how you—?"

"Yes, love. I was your nurse at Osterley from the day you were born until you and your mother left the Park. Mrs. Whitsome is my name, although I know you'd hardly remember it."

"I suppose then you know why we left the Park." Brienne looked down at her trembling hands. "Is the earl expected anytime soon? You must know that I came here only with the hope that he was not in residence—"

"I'm afraid we've more to worry about than a confrontation with your father, child. The truth is, Lady Brienne, that the earl has been ruined. He no longer lets this house. Another took it awhile ago, but we were instructed to stay on. After you left Osterley so many years back, Lord Oliver bade me come here. I am Number One's housekeeper now."

A terrible feeling rose from the pit of her stomach, and Brienne forced out the question even as she dreaded the answer. "This new tenant. Is he, perchance, an American? With queued black hair and—?"

"A Colonial? You're joking, to be sure! Have you no idea the rents that are paid here at The Crescent?" Mrs. Whitsome laughed in bewilderment.

"But this one happens to be particularly wealthy."

"Never fear. The American you speak of could not be the one. I deal with his estate manager and have yet to set eyes upon the new master, but I've been told that he's a peer with a title as old as they come."

Brienne breathed a bountiful sigh of relief. For a moment a possibility too awful to contemplate had entered her thoughts.

"But we've got a bigger problem now, my lady." The woman stood up from her stool and walked closer to the settee. "You've come here expecting to find a home, and the truth is, there's not one here to be found."

"Yes, I see." Brienne lay back on the armrest and reflected on this new development. She had been in Bath but a few hours, and her life had already taken another turn for the worse.

"This is much too kind of you." Brienne looked at herself in the mirror wearing a matronly dark blue gown of Mrs. Whitsome's.

"Pooh! This woolen isn't nearly grand enough to be worthy of thanks. Stand still, child." The matron carefully placed some long steel pins in tucks made in the waistline and then turned her around to see the final effect. "That should do it, my lady."

Brienne eyed Mrs. Whitsome affectionately. "You must not be addressing me so. It's Brienne or nothing at all for this servant."

"Ah, that will take some getting used to. Especially with your carriage, my lady—oops." Mrs. Whitsome put both wrinkled hands to her lips and then hid a rosy smile. "Well, all I can say is that it's hard to believe you were raised in that tiny town in Wales and not in the finest salons of London. Your mother would be very proud of you."

"I'm afraid she wished better for me." Brienne shrugged out of the unaltered dress. "But she at least left me with a friend, and all the gold in Versailles cannot purchase that." She smiled timidly. "Shall I start by helping in the kitchens, or—?"

"No! No! I would deem you my assistant. I've already informed the household of your position, and perhaps, if you're still determined to find your own employ at a bookshop, then I daresay, I can allow you to stay here until the master arrives. You can be a relative of mine if it comes to that. But who's to say? Bath could turn unfashionable, and then we'd not have to worry about his visit at all!" The woman took the fallen garment in hand and swung the material over her arm.

"It's funny," Brienne mused. "If I'd truly had all the relatives that people have recently claimed I have, I would not be in this position." Pensively she tied the worn laces on her stays and slipped into her old, raggedy but now clean round gown.

"Has this to do with the American you spoke of the day you arrived?"

Brienne stiffened. Mrs. Whitsome had been a blessing and a true angel of mercy. She had cared for her for almost a week after she had arrived and had devised a scheme by which she could remain at The Crescent. But not once had she questioned Brienne's straightened circumstances, and not once had she mentioned her father after their very first conversation.

"I have not told you very much about myself, have I?" Brienne said.

"And what explanations are there to give? You told me you grew up in Wales, and you told me Lady Grace seemed to be happy there." Mrs. Whitsome bustled busily about the immaculate bedroom.

"I was at Osterley before I came here," Brienne burst out before she could stop herself.

"Your father was an evil man." The matron shook her head as if she feared what Brienne might tell her. "I want you to know, we were glad to be rid of him. I and the entire household could find nothing redeeming in his character."

"I didn't see my father at Osterley. The Park is in other hands now, just as this place is."

"How wonderful!" Mrs. Whitsome brightened.

Brienne sighed. "Not so. For I am afraid the new master is my enemy."

"The Colonial?"

Nodding her head affirmatively, Brienne answered, "He didn't want me to leave Osterley. You see . . ." She tried to find an explanation that the good housekeeper would approve of.

"Those things don't matter, love. You're here now. So it's best to forget the past." The woman patted her hand, then moved to the jib door at the rear of the room, which was papered in a French lily-of-the-valley print that matched the wall.

Brienne smiled wryly and nodded her head. She then turned to the window, hoping the pastoral scene below would help her do just that. Horses clip-clopped along the newly paved cobblestones and among the greening fields and trees; the river, Avon, swung a path through it all, still gray and icy from the last freeze. Staring at it, Brienne found herself thinking of a certain pair of eyes, similar in color to the thawing Avon, and also of the one night she'd seen them melt.

Three days later, wearing the ill-fitting, scratchy blue woolen, Brienne ascended the stairs from the servants' entrance and walked out to Brock Street. The late morning was nippy and bright, and it put her in an optimistic mood as she looked about her. It was her first journey from the house since her arrival there, and she was determined to make the best of the gorgeous blue-skied day and see the magnificent city she had heard so much about during her long and lonely childhood.

Rounding the corner, she gazed at The Royal Crescent that arched in an elliptical curve across the great lawn; it rose in Palladian grandeur with not less than one hundred columns marking its presence.

"How some people live," she mused as she watched a lovely bewigged young woman dressed in pink-and-green-stripe satin over stupendous collapsible hoops being helped into a waiting carriage from Number Fourteen. As the carriage passed her, Brienne saw the woman seated between a spinsterish chaperone and a ladies' maid, while a young man courted her from the opposite seat.

I love you. The words clung to her like cobwebs to a chandelier. Slowly her hand rubbed the headache from her forehead. "Forget! Forget! He's not worth crying over," she whispered to herself as she watched couples stroll along the green. Chiding herself for allowing her thoughts to stray to Avenel, she bitterly pushed away her longing and reminded herself that she would never return to Osterley. Avenel's warmth and charm could be a powerful opiate for one starved for both, but she wouldn't permit herself any sweet remembrances. She only needed to remember that last afternoon in the taffeta bedroom to make her blood boil. After that, humiliation and anger had become her constant companions. But at least they had kept her going after that terrible last day at the Park. She bit her lower lip and frowned. Pain pulled heavily at her chest, and she was forced to wait until it was gone. She would never forgive Avenel for that day! Never!

"Mind you, bide what I say, child." Mrs. Whitsome, still in her mobcap, came to the top of the servants' stairs and called to her.

Brienne walked from the corner and met her. "I'll remember. No talking to strangers, especially well-dressed men. And keep my head covered." She smiled sheepishly as she pulled the hood that had fallen back in the breeze over her locks.

"These things are important, miss! If you insist on looking for employment, you cannot be too careful." The matron eyed her with misgiving. "I wish you wouldn't go, love. You should wait until I've heard from the estate manager. I've already posted the letter to him, you see. I'm sure that when he sees I need the extra help—"

"I know, I know. But what if he does not answer your letter right away? And then he could say he doesn't feel extra servants are necessary at a house that his master has yet to see. You couldn't find fault in that logic."

"How will you ever find a husband working in a bookshop?"

"Perhaps I will find one who loves me dearly."

"And with not a tuppence to his name, no doubt," she scolded.

"A spinster's life would not bother me. I'm living a spinster's life now, and I say, I am happy."

"Pooh." Mrs. Whitsome frowned. "You hardly ever sleep. I hear you tossing and turning all night. And you've a measly appetite at best."

"Please—" Brienne tried to stop her.

"Stay here where you're safe." The housekeeper made one last attempt.

"Let me at least inquire into the possibility of working in the bookshops. I can't be a burden on you just because my father no longer lets The Crescent." Brienne gave the old woman a peck on her wrinkled cheek and then waved her small cold hand as she watched the woman descend the stairs to the warm servants' rooms.

The Circus was behind her now, and she walked by the new Upper Assembly Rooms, in which she could hear a pianist practicing. The townsfolk—if that was what one could call the dukes and earls, painters and poets who hobnobbed between rides in their chairs— were beginning their promenade through the bookstalls on Milsom Street, their hands full of expensive, fashionable bound volumes. She took a deep breath to still her suddenly jangling nerves and approached the first shop, trying to imagine what it would be like to work in this place. The huge painted door creaked as she opened it, and a young man, well outfitted in a forest green topcoat, came to the counter.

"But have you worked before, miss?" He looked at her with a doubtful, kindly glance as he answered her inquiry.

"No," she answered truthfully.

"Well, the fact is, I would like an assistant who has experience."

"I am very well read." She looked up with hopeful eyes.

"I am sorry." He seemed to shrug with genuine regret.

"I see. I thank you anyway." She gave a half smile and then left the shop, refusing to feel the least bit defeated. There were other bookshops along the busy, congested avenue, she assured herself. She would just have to continue until she found one with a more willing shopkeeper. With rekindled enthusiasm, she inquired along the hilly fairway. Her hood had fallen off her head after she'd left the first shop, and she didn't heed Mrs. Whitsome's warning until two wealthy men started following her down the street, trying everything imaginable to get her eye. When she finally noticed them, she quickly pulled her brown hood over her locks, silently cursing her hair for attracting so much unwanted attention.

Well after four o'clock, she reached the last shop. All day it had been one rejection after another. The shopkeepers either found her appearance too shabby, or refused to hire a female, or were simply not hiring at all. Soon she would have to give up her independence and hope that the mysterious master of Number One would allow her to stay on as extra household help. But how she pined for an existence of her own! After months in captivity at Osterley, she longed for a little cottage of her own in the hills that overlooked the city, perhaps one that was old and solid like the one she and her mother had lived in in Tenby. She closed her eyes and pictured it in a daydream. Well, it wouldn't remain a fantasy if she could help it! She gritted her teeth and entered the last shop.

It was a small one and rather out of the way, near

Abbey Churchyard. Through the door came the familiar and much-loved scent of tanned leather and foxing papers. She waited quietly among the tomes as a middle-aged man, obviously the owner, spoke with a customer —a quite distinguished-looking one. The customer looked about fifty years old. He could have been older, but his vibrant good looks seemed to disguise his true age. He had gray-white hair that was curled and fashioned without powder and grease. He possessed a straight nose and a firm mouth. Despite the wrinkles that circled his lids almost until they reached his cheekbones, the man had dark piercing eyes that were quite arresting.

"Fanny Hill. Bawdy, you say?" the customer said to the shopkeeper and laughed as he flipped through a plain cordovan-bound book. She noted how incongruous his oddly stained hands were with his finely embroidered golden waistcoat.

"Quite so, but don't let on to that sister of yours that you got it here! That Mrs. Gibbon—if she can't hover over you as if you were a child, she's just not happy." The shopkeeper cracked a smile.

"That she does," the handsome man agreed. "Mary's a fine woman, but I admit I'm content to just visit now. Seven years I've been away from the Circus. And you see," he added slyly, "I have found in London that there are advantages to be had—such as not having to worry about letting the family come to call at certain critical moments!"

Both men broke out in laughter. Suddenly the shopkeeper noticed her presence and raised a respectful eyebrow to the customer as he asked Brienne, "Can I be of assistance?"

"I . . . ah . . ." Suddenly she was nervous. The customer was looking straight at her, and she found she could not meet his eyes. They seemed to scrutinize every aspect of her appearance, from her creamy wind-chapped cheeks and the faint lavender crescents under her eyes that proclaimed her exhaustion to the way her breasts were held tightly under her stays. His inspection did not aid her deflated self-confidence. Brienne began haltingly, "I am seeking employment. Naturally, I can read and write. I've read all the great volumes, such as . . ." Droning on with her well-rehearsed speech, she detached herself from the words and was then able to steel herself for the rejection that was sure to follow. When she was through, the shopkeeper's rejection was quick and complete, and she headed toward the door, feeling completely disheartened.

"Wait." She heard the command and abruptly stopped near the door. The voice was not that of the shopkeeper but that of the aging customer. When he walked toward her, she did not know what to expect. He took her by the shoulder, and as if she were made of stone and alablaster, he swept his stained hand across the smooth flesh of her face, examining every plane and hollow. "Hold still and let me look at your eyes." He turned her face to the dimming afternoon sunlight that came through the shop's window. Receiving no help from the owner, she glared at the older man balefully.

"Do not touch me!" she demanded, feeling overly sensitive to a man's touch, any man's, after her experience with Avenel. She backed away from the eccentric gentleman and reached for the door handle.

"Will you sit for me?"

"Sit for you?" she questioned, her hand on the oak door.

"Would you like me to paint your picture? Perhaps in a meadow, sitting under a willow? No! That wouldn't be

right for you. Perhaps then . . ." Brienne suddenly realized that the dirt on the man's hands was not dirt at all
but the pigments that the man handled in his profession.

"What is the salary? Would it be adequate?" she asked.

At this question the bookseller laughed. "Oh yes, the
salary, Tom," he interjected. "You wouldn't want the
poor child to starve to death right on the canvas!"

"Salary! What an abomination!" The customer turned
to Brienne, goaded by the other man's teasing. "Look,
miss. You cannot expect payment! After all, it's you who
should be paying me! Here now, since I have taken a
fancy to you, I shall do the portrait for free if you just
give me your time."

"I'm afraid that I haven't the time or the luxury to sit
for you. But if there were a salary—"

"God, no! I have never had to stoop so low as to pay
for a model. You flatter yourself! Do you know I can
easily exact one hundred pounds a head?"

The figure left her amazed, but she knew it was futile
to speak of the subject further. She needed to be inde-
pendent; therefore, she needed to work. She was not a
well-heeled lady but an impoverished spinster. She'd had
no job offered to her today, and she couldn't spare the
time to sit for a painter when she had work to do for
Mrs. Whitsome. "I am sorry." She opened the door and
walked out to the street.

"By damned, you will be!" the painter shouted at her
rashly, making her flinch with embarrassment. She
turned the corner to go home and didn't see the painter
reenter the shop and slam his hand onto the bookseller's
desk. Remorse showed on his weathered visage, and he
ran out the door to find her. But she wasn't privy to the
regret that softened the man's stormy eyes when he saw
that she was nowhere to be found.

CHAPTER TWENTY-THREE

"Love! Get up! Mr. Harcourt is here!" It was late in the morning before Mrs. Whitsome came into her bedchamber. The housekeeper peered as Brienne sat up, startled from her nap.

"My God! I am such a chit. What time is it? You must surely want to beat me!" Brienne cried remorsefully as she scrambled from the mussed coverlet and frantically tried to smooth it. "I haven't even raised the blinds in the drawing room yet!"

"No, child. It's already been done."

"Oh," she answered in a small voice. "Never mind the beating, then. I shall give myself one for you."

"Now, that just wouldn't do."

"I'm truly sorry. I don't know what came over me. I was just going to the drawing room when I suddenly felt tired. I only meant to rest a minute." Brienne rubbed her forehead. She didn't understand the illness that had been plaguing her. It was erratic and unwelcome. At times she had never felt worse; she felt so very tired, she thought she would drop where she stood. But then, only yesterday, Cook had told her she never looked better.

"Don't worry yourself, love." Mrs. Whitsome stared at her oddly.

"Nonetheless, you must tell Mr. Harcourt that I haven't time to see him, for I am so very busy making up my extra work." To the housekeeper's delight, the gentleman had called several times since she'd first arrived in Bath, and although Brienne found Mr. Harcourt quite pleasant, she felt too guilty about her undone tasks to take time for a visit.

"Now, that especially wouldn't do." The matron patted her curls, which were held securely beneath the frills of her cap. "It's tired you've been these days, love. How so?"

"I really haven't a clue. Perhaps it's the weather. It's been a cold spring." Looking into a small baroque mirror hung over a kidney-shaped table, Brienne straightened her mussed hair.

"But I've noticed the evening brings you into fine form. I daresay, it seems the morning is the worst time for you."

"Aye, it does." Brienne finished in the mirror and smiled sheepishly. "What's to be made of it?"

"Oh, nothing! Nothing, I'm sure! So come, let's see your gentleman caller." The housekeeper whisked her out of the room, but Brienne noticed lines forming on the matron's already wrinkled brow. Her stomach tied in a knot, she followed the housekeeper down the stairs, trying all the while to shrug off a sense of foreboding.

"Mr. Harcourt! Please, sit," Brienne greeted him in the servants' main room. With the roar of the huge fireplace in the background, they sat together on an Irish pine bench. Acting as chaperone, Mrs. Whitsome, as custom had it, lowered herself into the portly, blackened Windsor chair.

"Good day, Brienne, Mrs. Whitsome." Ralph Harcourt nodded to both women, but his eyes were for Brienne alone.

"The weather—is it quite cold?" Brienne asked, noticing his spruce velvet topcoat was wet.

"Yes, it's a bloody miserable spring we're having." Suddenly, he reddened at his unintended coarseness, but then winked at Brienne. She stifled a giggle, thinking that their stiff, proper behavior in the company of Mrs. Whitsome contrasted so sharply with the way they'd met.

Trying to turn the conversation away from his faux pas, Brienne asked, "So, pray tell, what have you brought for me today? Do not plead innocent—you've already given me an indecent amount of gifts, and I fear propriety will soon force me to hand them back over." Brienne laughed as she took his proffered package, wondering if it contained another book of Shakespearean sonnets or perhaps some satin ribbon for her hair. His gifts had always been in the best of taste, yet were always spare enough in expense that she and Mrs. Whitsome both felt she should feel no discomfort in accepting them.

Handling the package, Brienne noted that the box was too small to hold a book. Since it was relatively light, she supposed it might contain dried rose petals to be placed in the famille rose bowl in her room or perhaps some steel pins, of which any woman would be happy to have more. When she untied the bow, the lid of the box tumbled to her skirt. Inside, nestled in several pristine wads of cotton wool, something caught the light from the fire. She gasped at the brightness.

"The Lord in his wisdom—" Mrs. Whitsome was

heard to sputter, and then she abruptly left the room to give them privacy.

"Mr. Harcourt." Brienne swallowed.

"Ralph, princess. My name is Ralph." He took the huge blue-fired emerald ring from its nest and held it out between his thumb and forefinger.

"Uh, Mr.—Ralph . . ." Brienne stammered, trying to gather her wits.

"Yes?" He smiled a warm, tender smile. Gently his hand went about her tiny waist, and he placed a kiss on her cheek.

"I don't know what to say."

"Say you'll be my wife, princess. All you have to say is yes."

"I'm a servant. I haven't even a dowry."

"The Harcourts have been Bristol merchants as long as there's been an England. We've more gold than we know what to do with. I have no need for my bride's dowry." He slipped the ring onto her left hand.

Brienne stared down at the magnificent jewel, yet all she could think of was how happy this was going to make Mrs. Whitsome. Silently she berated herself. *This will make you happy too,* she thought. Studying the magnificent emerald, she tried to picture herself as the wife of the man before her. She was sure that they would make a good marriage. Ralph Harcourt was generous and honest. He would give her a home. And there she would be secure and well loved. They would have beautiful children, blond and fair. So what was bothering her? She frowned. Why had she had a vision that her children would be dark, with stormy gray eyes, just like their father— She gave a start. What could she be thinking of?

Nervously, she glanced at Ralph, who was gently turning her face toward his. *He's going to kiss me,* she thought distantly. *Oh, please, let it be wonderful.* Feeling his lips upon her own, she moved her body closer, wanting a more soulful kiss. She wanted to feel the fire in her loins that she'd felt whenever Avenel had kissed her; she wanted to feel desire coursing through her veins like molten silver. Opening her mouth to him, she desperately deepened the kiss on her own, trying with all her heart to kindle a desire that had been repressed since that night in March. She felt Ralph's surprise as his hand tightened around her waist. He kissed her fully, letting his tongue search the sweet recesses of her mouth until his sense of propriety finally seemed to tell him to stop.

When they broke apart, he leaned his forehead against hers. "Who are you, princess?" He took a deep breath. "You kiss like—"

"I'm a servant. Just a servant." Brienne turned from him to hide her stricken face. The kiss had been nice, but it had been nothing like— Suddenly anger flared in her eyes. Why did she have to think of Avenel Slane at a time like this? *Damn him!* she cried to herself. *Damn his soul to hell!* Had his lovemaking ruined her so that she could never find pleasure in another man's arms?

Ralph interrupted her thoughts; his deep voice demanded an answer. "Brienne, you are no servant. Although you dress like one and perhaps have the duties of one, I know it's a facade. From the very first day I looked at you, all I could see was your gentle manner and your noble beauty. You have a past, my love. I know it. Just tell me what it is, and on my honor I will not judge you."

"I can't think now." She put a hand to her head.

"All right, then." He stood up. "You may tell me after we are wed."

"No, wait!" She bit her lip. "You would dare marry me, not even knowing what is in my past?"

"I would dare anything for you."

"But my past could be . . . terrible." She dropped her eyes.

"Then we would bear it together." He forced her chin up and placed a sweet kiss on her lips. "I love you. Do you doubt me?" When she shook her head, he continued. "That won't change, no matter what."

"Please, Ralph, you must let me think." Her hands shaking, she pulled the ring from her finger. "Your offer is more than I deserve. I must have time to think."

He took the ring back. Sadly, he nodded his handsome golden head and retrieved his hat from the bench. "Send me a note when you have your answer, then. I'm at The White Hart."

As she watched him depart, she felt her heart fill with sadness. What had gone so wrong in her life that she hadn't jumped at this wonderful man's proposal? she asked herself. Avenel Slane, that was what. With grim frustration, she sat down and hung her head in her hands.

CHAPTER TWENTY-FOUR

A fortnight passed before Brienne saw Ralph Harcourt again. It was a cold and rainy day, but she had promised Mrs. Whitsome that she would go to the market and buy some aniseed for Cook. The housekeeper had been crestfallen for days after Brienne refused Ralph Harcourt's proposal of marriage, and Brienne had tried to cheer up the elderly matchmaker, but it had been to no avail. Gossip had it that the wealthy merchant's son suffered greatly from the rejection of an unknown young woman and was now seen in the company of a Mathilda Geddings at the Lower Assembly Rooms. So with Mrs. Whitsome's heart broken, Brienne had left for the market, promising to keep her hood about her along with her wits.

The market along the Avon was spilling with goods. Everything from caged green monkeys from Antigua to an even greener hogshead cheese from Chester could be had for the quibbling There were makeshift stalls fragrantly laid with salted pork, dried jerky, and sausages.

Wily hags freely bartered their summer-dried herbs, hiding their potions smelling of prohibited gin under the counter until a gent with a "sickness" came to call.

Brienne procured the aniseed easily, bothering neither to haggle the fee down nor to shop the other stalls for a better price. Her trips to the market had always seemed a small adventure to her, distracting her from the bothersome headaches that had plagued her ever since she had run from Osterley. But today the stalls seemed to wreak of strong, offensive odors. Whereas before the sweet smells from the taffy man and the winery had always tempted her, now they made her head feel light. Watching the rabbit cart pass by, her stomach turned uncomfortably.

Walking away from the stall, she bade the seller a hasty farewell. She turned to the edge of the sprawling market near the waterfront and walked quickly to the embankment, hoping the chilly river breeze would steady her senses enough so she could endure the walk back home. There were people everywhere; some built makeshift fires to cook their suppers and others just wandered along through the crowds, searching for a wealthy, wayfaring gent whose purse they could lighten. As she passed the back of the harnessmaker's, she heard a female giggle and then some cooing.

"Lovey, not to worry. You'll be taking a bite out of him soon."

"And you'll cling to me, won't you?" a man's voice rasped sarcastically. "When I have everything back, you will expect to be my queen."

"I'll stay with you, lovey. 'Twas a sign I knew when I found you here, keeping watch on The Crescent. If my brother hadn't been kicked out of that fair in Bristol, we'd never have—" There was a great moan and her voice was muffled.

"Do not remind me of it!"

"But, lovey, when you get the house back, you'll come around. I know it. And then I will be countess." Brienne heard a lewd sucking noise.

"I'll come around. And you'll beg for it, painful though it may be."

"I'll beg for it now, if that be what you want, lovey." The woman cooed again, and the man laughed unpleasantly.

Thinking the rather obscene conversation to be of no concern—just a maid's dalliance—Brienne had almost turned away from the stall when two bodies showed themselves amongst the new pieces of a leather hackamore.

Fear rose in her like poisonous, liquid mercury. The man was dressed like a commoner, with a once-fine, soiled, and patched topcoat, threadbare hose, and worn-out gaiters. The last time she had seen him, he had been wearing the heaviest of satin with the most elaborate embroidery. But there was no mistaking him, from his laugh, which she had heard a thousand times in her nightmares, to his hands, long and completely white from his nails to his wrists. Horrible, effeminate hands, hands of death, she thought as she held back a sob. The man she saw in the harnesser's was none other than her father! And the woman he was caressing publicly through her loosened stays was none other than her former maid at Osterley, Annie!

The man looked up as a snake does when it senses a mouse. Seeing this, Brienne quickly backed away and screamed silently. Her breast beat wildly with her terror-stricken heart. *God, oh God, oh God,* she whimpered as she stumbled along the embankment, trying to put distance between her and the earl. Suddenly, despite her churning stomach, she ran and ran as if for her very life.

"You've changed your mind, princess?" She stifled a scream as she slammed into a solid, masculine form. Looking up, she shed tears of relief when she saw the handsome, boyish face of Ralph Harcourt. "What is it, love? Why are you running?"

"My hood!" she cried in terror.

"Your hood?"

"My hood! Cover my hair! My God! You must cover my hair!" She clutched wildly at her back, trying to snatch the hood up. Ralph quickly helped her pull the material over her locks so that the startling burgundy color was completely hidden from view. "Take me away from here. Please, Ralph. Take me away!" Brienne sobbed into his cuff.

"But what is this?" he said, bewildered. Taking one look at her terrified visage, he uttered, "Of course! Of course!" Stopping a passing hackney, he helped her inside and firmly shut the door behind them. "Where to, my lady? Back to The Crescent?"

"No!" she gasped before she could stop herself. She forced herself to calm down and remind herself that the earl no longer held claim to Number One. She took several deep breaths, and wondered if her father had come to Bath uninformed of his loss. Thinking more rationally, she said, "Yes. I'm afraid I was mistaken. I suppose I should go back to The Crescent."

When she was safe inside the kitchen of Number One, drinking a beaker full of warm milk, Brienne asked Ralph, "How does it feel to have made your offer to a coward?"

"A woman need not be brave, especially when she has

been so terribly frightened." Ralph bent down to her, concern hardening his beautiful, Romanesque face.

In the background Brienne heard the comforting squeal of whirring iron as the dog-wheel spit went around and around, powered by a small, gray-muzzled mongrel that Cook pampered and called "my precious."

"What has made you so frightened, princess?" Ralph asked sharply.

"Please, I cannot tell you." She looked away; terror rose in her violet eyes.

"Then get away from here!" With a look of exasperation on his face, he turned and looked around the kitchen. "You deserve better than this, Brienne. You deserve protection and a fine home. I have wonderful homes in London and Bristol, and I vex myself every day that you are not mistress of them."

"Please, just give me some more time," she pleaded.

"And what do you need all this time for?" Gently, he lifted her chin.

"I don't know." She looked into the fire; misery shone bright on her face.

There was a long, soul-wretching silence as he pondered her. Finally he said in a bleak voice, "You don't love me, do you?"

"It's not that!" She denied it, but she could see he didn't believe her.

"I suppose I'd guessed as much." He stood up, angered, and yet for the time being resigned. "You don't have to answer me right away. But when you do, princess, you know where I live. Call for me at any time. I mean that." He tilted her head up and kissed her passionately on her mouth. "I'd make you love me. Know that."

"I think you could," she answered truthfully. "Just

give me a few more days. I'm sure I'll give you the answer you want then."

After his departure, Brienne sat on the kitchen bench and watched the mongrel run its wheel, around and around. Cook had told her of dogs that had been forced to run by having the pads of their feet burned. They ran the wheel in hope of finding relief from the pain. But of course, "my precious" wasn't the type to run away on slaughter day, not having undergone such mistreatment. But as Brienne watched the dog perform its arduous task —a mongrel of less than two stone roasted a side of beef that was near five—she couldn't help but note similarities between the mongrel's situation and her own. Both of them had arduous tasks to perform. Around and around in her mind spun the questions, what should she do now that the earl was in Bath? How could she stop him from carrying out his nefarious schemes?

When the body was found, the servants at Number One indulged in all sorts of morbid speculation. Mrs. Whitsome sent the footman out at dawn to get the edition of *The Bath Chronicle* that held the details of the gruesome murder and the description of the unknown body.

It seemed that the mysterious girl had common enough features, a large, full figure, and indistinct coloring. There were unusual markings on the body—a cluster of three black moles of various sizes on the girl's upper lip. A sickening sensation came over Brienne as she read about the body's brutal rape with a harness tanner's knife.

Completely subdued, she gave the paper back to the other curious servants and left for her room, now knowing the ugly truth. All she could think about was Annie back at Osterley, when she had wickedly thrust herself into the pink polonaise. The maid's upper lip had twitched sensuously when she talked; Brienne recalled how proud Annie was of the fact that she required no patches to look lusty. Annie possessed natural markings that created the effect—three moles.

Brienne bit her upper lip, thinking hard. Perhaps she should write to Avenel. He could handle the situation. But her head started to pound when she seriously considered the possibility, and she knew she wouldn't do it. She remembered the scars that the earl had viciously produced on him, and suddenly a fierce protectiveness came over her. Hardly believing it herself, she pictured Avenel actually vulnerable when put up against such unholy evil as her father. No, she would not ask him to come. She would not involve him.

She now knew she had to find a way of dealing with her father before he sought his revenge on the new owner of Osterley. As much as the idea of being the earl's spawn repulsed her, she felt that if she could put him away, perhaps it would absolve her of her heritage. But the only way to do that was to go to a man more powerful than the earl himself. She would have to go to the Duke of Degarre.

That had been no easy task, she told herself several days later. First she had had to convince the coachman to take her to Castle Coombe, where the duke lived. Then she'd had to convince Mrs. Whitsome of the necessity of the trip without alarming her. Finally she had claimed that the entire outing was a rendezvous with Mr. Harcourt, so she had been allowed to go. It was Brienne's luck that the housekeeper was so busy that she couldn't serve as chaperone and sent a young serving maid in her place.

Now riding in the carriage, as a spring rain began to let up, Brienne felt as nervous as she had the day she left Tenby, perhaps even more so. For this was a nasty business. She looked out the rain-washed window and saw the first towers of the aged castle. Before she knew it, she was gathering her cloak about her to descend to the ground, not bothering to awaken the tiny maid who had drifted off to sleep before they'd left The Crescent.

Swallowing her fear and then her pride, she walked up to the huge medieval door and knocked on it loudly enough to awaken the dead. "I have come to see the duke," she said to the silver-haired footman who answered the door.

"The duke?" The tall, thin man opened the door wider, allowing her to enter.

"He is in?"

The man cocked his head and smirked at her.

"I realize this must seem extraordinary. But I must have an appearance—"

"No explanations are necessary. The duke resides in the morning room at this hour. Follow me."

She followed him through the maze of dusty halls and steep, crumbling stone stairways and finally was let into a large room with high, soot-stained gothic windows and dingy tapestries. The first thing she noticed about the room, however, wasn't the duke himself nor its cathedral atmosphere; rather, it was the sickly sweet odor of the room. It made her want to retch right there on the stone floor. But she swallowed her bile as she walked toward the thronelike chair on which the duke was seated, praying that his action against her father would be swift and her trip worth the risk.

"Your Grace, my name is Brienne M-Morrow," she stuttered, suddenly fearing the large bulky man who was

the Duke of Degarre. She was surprised that he appeared
so unkempt and lifeless—and dirty. His knee breeches
had yellow egg stains dried upon them, and his hair—or
what was left of it—was shiny and greasy. He certainly
didn't look like a man with much authority, and when
she finally met his faraway gaze, her hopes sunk into a
quagmire of despair.

"Morrow, speak to me of the young Morrow," the
duke mumbled incoherently. His eyes wandered across
her face.

"Your Grace, you must help. Oliver Morrow has—"
she began.

"The Younger will help. Speak to me of Morrow."

"I shall speak to you of Morrow," she said, her voice
trembling with hopelessness and anger. This man could
hardly hear her words, much less understand them. No
wonder the footman had looked upon her with such ridi-
cule. She continued, "It is because of you that he has
been able to commit these heinous crimes unchecked. I
know now why. It is all because of you—all because of
you and your vile Chinese drug."

"Who are you?" he asked, only half aware. Then he
adjusted his fat, wavering belly, which was covered with
matted velvet and looked like the underside of a cur. He
seemed to want to stand up but his drugged body could
not complete the motion.

"I am Brienne Morrow! I am the daughter of the Earl
of Laborde!" She raised her voice, despite the man's high
rank in the peerage. "I have come here in hopes of stopping my father. I had hoped that you would be able to
. . . Damn you!" She fought back tears of misery. "You
worthless man! You probably can't even stand up by
yourself, let alone control your dukedom!"

"Speak to me of Morrow. The Younger will save us all.

Then my guilt will be assuaged," he whispered euphorically.

"You want me to speak of Morrow? Then so be it. The Earl of Laborde is the devil. He is a murderous, evil Satan. And he will be stopped from his mad desires, even if I have to be the one to do it." As she turned to leave, she knew the trip had been a failure. But then, she should have known. Her father had had free rein to perform his evil deeds, and now, glancing back at the slothful, drugged duke, she knew why.

"You've not spoken of Morrow!" The man laughed mildly at her fleeing back. "Come back, wench! Tell me who you are!"

"I am Brienne Morrow!" she screamed at him futilely. "The daughter of the Earl of Laborde!"

"Nay, nay!" He snickered in his delusions. "The earl has no daughters!"

She stopped in her tracks. No daughters! Was the man telling her something about her past? In his drugged state, would he make some grand revelation—perhaps that she was illegitimate after all? Her interest piqued, she paused at the door and said, "The Earl of Laborde— Oliver Morrow—is not my father, then?"

"The earl? Your father?" he whispered, now inexplicably coherent. He smiled with almost painful regret, and then he disclosed something she had never expected. "How could he be, wench? Lord Oliver Morrow has been dead longer than you've been alive."

CHAPTER TWENTY-FIVE

"Are you contemplating paying a visit to Degarre?" Cumberland coughed into his hand as he watched Avenel greet a flurry of new faces. They had been to seven soirées in less than five nights, and the hectic pace was beginning to wear on both of them—especially Avenel, who was developing a sharp edge in his already intimidating countenance. He did not look as if he were enjoying London society, and at times Cumberland wondered why they socialized at all. But then when he was reminded of who Avenel was, he ceased wondering.

"And what for? To watch a child being entranced by a poppy plant? 'Twould be more than useless," Avenel sneered.

"I daresay the old addict has caused a mound of trouble through the years. Sometimes I wonder what would have happened if the old bird had been different. You know—"

"Have you seen her?" A woman rushed up to a small

group nearby, her excited voice carrying over to the two men.

"Seen who?" a young man in the group interjected.

"The painting! In the library! They say she's an unknown. Oh! But to be so beautiful! It just isn't fair!"

"Whatever is the commotion? I haven't seen these people so excited since the Princesse de Lambelle was rumored to have visited," Cumberland said a little contemptuously. "You know, Slane, I must admit that they are a dull bunch. So proper and witty, they could put you to sleep in mere seconds. And now—who was it, a Mrs. Montagu or somebody—wanting you to join her poetry group? The man who took the daughter of the last Maryland governor, and right underneath his very nose practically—"

"Enough said." Avenel's face twitched with suppressed laughter. "Who knows? Maybe Mrs. Montagu will find me a poetic gentleman after all."

"Poetic, maybe. A gentleman? Never!" Both men laughed until certain dignified ladies peered at them over their fans, quietly demanding that they stop.

"Let's have a look at the old gal, shall we?"

"The painting?" Avenel laughed again. "Another pastoral scene of a young miss who looks vaguely like a brown Guernsey? No, thank you."

"I suppose you've hit the nail on the head. I'm afraid the evening may be a long one, so let's have some more spirits."

"Amen to that." Avenel led the way.

It was a long evening. Both men willingly imbibed too much. Although it was unusual for them to do so, neither seemed to want to stop. Dinner was interminably long, and they were grateful when it was time to retire to the viscount's library. Walking ahead of the party after dinner, Avenel went straight to the marble-topped mixing table and poured another couple of brandies. He turned and deposited one in his friend's hand; he himself had already taken his in two long gulps.

"Easy, old boy," Cumberland said to him, noticing that the drink was taking some of the sharpness out of the younger man. He also noticed how miserable Avenel was. Perhaps it was time they returned home; perhaps they should be back at Osterley.

"And now what do we talk about? Another session against the Colonies? Or do we trample the French this time?"

"Look, Slane, we don't have to do this. These social events won't make as much difference in your final acceptance as we thought. Truly, to look at these people now, all they really judge is one's purse—and yours is lined with gold and silver. You have nothing to prove." Cumberland noticed that men were wandering into the library and gathering about a large painting over the blazing marble fireplace.

"I'm beginning to believe that." Avenel palmed his empty glass in his hand and looked up. "But we've just got to do everything right. It has taken so long, and we've tried so—"

Cumberland waited for him to finish, but Avenel's words never came. When Cumberland looked up at Avenel's face, he was awed by the powerful display of emotion that he saw there. Relief, joy, and even love could be seen, but Cumberland also saw a foundation of red-hot anger that seared each of these passions. Confused, he followed Avenel's shocked gaze to the place over the mantel. There he found a typical pastoral painting of a girl. But then he, too, felt the sudden jolt of surprise. Although weeks had passed since she'd left, he had yet to forget that face. Dressed in an ill-fitting gown and poised in unbelievably idealized surroundings was the beautiful face of Brienne Morrow. Everything was hers, from the wind-touseled locks of deepest auburn hair to the haunted blue-violet eyes; she was as real in the painting as she had been the last time both of them had seen her.

"You say it's by a man named Gainsborough?" Cumberland said thoughtfully over his teacup. "You're quite sure?"

"Oh yes, the viscount said so himself." The pigeon-breasted viscountess sipped from her cup. "I must say, I find it strange that you haven't heard of the man. He has made quite a name for himself since his days in Bath. Have you been away to the Continent, perhaps?" She peered at him, and for a second Cumberland actually thought she would coo.

"Ah, no. I mean—yes! The Continent, of course."

"I had rather guessed, you see. I'd have known if you'd been in England. Especially since you have such a handsome companion." She blushed deeply.

"Yes. Of course."

"Not that you aren't, mind you."

"Aren't what, my lady?" Cumberland asked distractedly.

"Handsome! Perhaps a little on the small side, but altogether you do make up a fine figure." She pulled her fauteuil closer to him.

"How thoughtful you are, my lady." He stood up in a flash. He knew he was being rude, but he was bent on self-preservation. "If this will suffice for the picture, I am afraid I must be off." He tossed a heavy purse of gold on the inlaid tea table.

"So soon! But you must stay for breakfast! I had thought that when you left your card with my footman this morning, wanting to see me, you would—"

"All true, all true, my lady." He coughed. "But I am afraid I've an unexpected appointment with Master Slane."

"Yes, that one," the viscountess said slyly. "Perhaps you could give him my regards?" She narrowed her eyes meaningfully, and he did not lose her message.

"Of course, and I am sure he will be utterly flattered." Cumberland was unspeakably relieved to see the viscountess stand.

"I do hope so. I am of the peerage, as you know. You must make it clear to Master Slane that it will do him well to have friends in high places. Remember, one cannot buy good bloodlines."

"No, my lady."

"My footman will show you to the library. The viscount will be furious when he discovers that I have sold his painting, but I say good riddance! The chit is rather attractive, and it doesn't do having her grab all the attention, now does it?"

He furiously nodded his head in agreement and kissed one of the woman's pudgy hands. Then he was finally free to go to the library down the hall and retrieve the canvas from its frame.

Thank God that's over, he thought as he was led to the front door, canvas in hand. It was a good thing he had come. If Avenel had been the one to do this job, he might have been eaten alive!

"Here she is." Cumberland stepped into the waiting carriage and handed Avenel the rolled canvas.

"Did the viscountess know anything about the model?"

"No, only that the girl was making her exceedingly jealous." Cumberland swallowed hard. "But she does send her fondest regards, Slane. And when I say fondest, I do mean it!"

Avenel laughed as he hadn't in weeks. Cumberland noted that it was a deep and joyful laugh, quite a change from the dark, brooding grunts that had been the man's response to every question or problem that had arisen since Brienne had run away.

"I've already told the driver to take us to the painter's house. He's apparently quite well known, which is a blessing. Name's Gainsborough."

"Does he live far away?" Avenel questioned anxiously.

"Again you're in luck." Cumberland sat back satisfied. "Did you get the package?"

"The rider delivered it near daybreak" was all he could say before the carriage stopped at its destination.

"Mr. Gainsborough does not receive guests without prior notice. He is very busy, and the morning light is best for his eyesight these days." A small, dour young man stood in the front doorway and blocked their passage.

"Will this make for a better reception?" Avenel tossed three gold coins into the man's palm.

The footman inspected the money and then allowed them to enter.

"Who is at that blasted door?" a voice boomed out from a back room. The young footman pursed his lips and stared at the two visitors accusingly.

"We have come about a painting," Avenel said quietly, waiting for the painter to appear.

Gainsborough came into the hall wrapped in a blue silk banyan and cap. "A painting, you say? All right, tell me who you are, so that I may deem you worthy of my canvas or not."

"We have no desire for you to paint our portraits. Rather, we've come for information about a painting you've completed," Avenel explained, trying to control his impatience.

"Information? Whatever is this about?" the painter asked.

Avenel turned the canvas in his hand and almost flung the portrait at the elder man.

"The Street Chatelaine! She's come back!" the painter exclaimed.

"Is she here?" Avenel's eyes narrowed.

Cumberland placed a restraining hand on his arm.

"Here? No. Who is she?" Gainsborough asked him.

"You're telling me that you've painted her portrait but you don't know who she is? I find that utterly unbelievable!" Avenel pushed forward.

"Still yourself, sir. I am telling you that I painted that portrait from memory. I don't do it often, but beautiful as she was, she was simply unforgettable. Still, I feel I haven't quite done her justice." Gainsborough became sidetracked as he looked at the limp canvas. "The face is correct. But the rest of her—well, there's just something missing."

"This, perhaps?" Avenel took the package Cumberland was holding. When he ripped open the brown paper, out flowed yards and yards of hyacinth silk. Shaking it, he gingerly laid the dress against the back of a chair as if its scent and its very presence held bittersweet memories for him.

"Beautiful gown, I must say. Was it hers?" The painter touched the brocade reverently as if already intent on transferring its lush fabric to the canvas.

Avenel merely nodded his head. "Tell us, how did you come about meeting her? Was she"—his voice caught with uncharacteristic emotion—"was she all right?"

"She was a strange creature," Gainsborough talked freely, sensing the man's distress and understanding it. "But in good enough health. Why, she fairly bloomed! It was the damnedest thing. There I was in a bookstore, and not a very proper one at that." He smiled at the men rather jovially, but neither smiled back. "Well, you see, I didn't expect to turn around and see such a beauty. But there she was in the flesh and, of all things, seeking employment! That's why I call her my 'street chatelaine.' She had everything that seemed to make her a great peer —beauty, intelligence, and manners—but there she was looking for a job. It was quite extraordinary. And when I asked to do her portrait, she refused because I wouldn't give her funds for sitting for me. Can you believe it? We had quite a bickering session for never having been introduced. Then the chit up and left. I was never so disappointed in my life when I couldn't find her again."

"She needed funds, then." Avenel went white. "So this was in London?"

"Certainly not. I was visiting my sister, Mrs. Mary Gibbon, you see. I used to have a place there, but one grows tired of—"

"Where?" Avenel demanded sharply, ignoring the painter's conviviality.

"Good heavens! Why, this was all in Bath, of course."

"Bath!" Cumberland exclaimed. "My God, she's been right under our noses all the time! That damned letter from Mrs. Whitsome at The Crescent! The new girl, Slane—that must have been Brienne. Oh, how could we have been so stupid?"

Angrily, Avenel dropped some gold onto the commode

in the hallway and said to Gainsborough, "The painting
is mine now, and I would have the girl dressed in this."
He tossed the hyacinth brocade to the painter. Then,
leaving behind the money, the canvas, the gown, and a
stiff thank you, Avenel led Cumberland back to their carriage, where his face took on the look of a madman.

CHAPTER TWENTY-SIX

The Crescent was indeed a lovely house, Brienne thought as she waxed the great desk-bookcase that stood in the study. She arched her back almost unconsciously, looking about her, comparing her present surroundings to Osterley. Granted, the rooms were not nearly as large, nor as fashionable. At the Park, the rooms were done in the latest pastel colors, whereas the study at The Crescent, with its deep blue verditer pigmented walls, had the old-fashioned look of an earlier time. But the sturdy Kentian pier tables and the Axminster carpet gave it a warmth and intimacy that Osterley lacked.

But was it her state of mind that made it so? She had been frightened of everything back then, of Osterley and its master. Number One carried no such anxieties for her; perhaps that was why she did not see it as so threatening.

Unwillingly, her mind remembered back to when she had first seen the master of Osterley. There couldn't have been a more fearsome room than the gallery in which to meet him. She could almost laugh now at how terrified she had been. What a pathetic little creature she must have seemed to that large, dark, awe-inspiring man!

The vision she'd summoned of Avenel made her thoughts wander into forbidden territory. What was he doing now? she mused over and over again. Did he ever, in some long, lonely night, think of her? She shut her eyes to this painful question and tried to rid herself of all remembrances of him. It mattered little to her what he was doing, she forced herself to believe. He didn't care for her. Rather, he hated her. So she couldn't waste her energy on what might have been. She was better off without Avenel, she thought with rock-hard determination.

"Ah! Look at you, miss!" Genny, a young maidservant with a nervous twitch, exclaimed from the trompe l'oeil marbled hall.

"I guess I am a sight." Brienne looked down and saw that umber wax soiled her dress.

"Mrs. Whitsome said you were not well, miss. You should not work so hard." The maid's cheek twitched, and she gave Brienne a nervous, admiring gaze.

"I'm fine," Brienne insisted. "But the old desk was desperate for wax; perhaps I overdid it." She wiped her hair from her cheek, leaving a dark streak of wax across it. "I'll go and clean up so Mrs. Whitsome will be none the wiser." She grinned at the young girl and disappeared up the servants' stair across the hall.

It was a tedious chore to have a bath. But when Brienne got to her small room and peered into the polished metal that was her mirror, there was no doubt in her mind that she needed one. She had wax smudged in her hair, on her face, and even in the cleft of her bosom after she removed her fichu. With a great sigh, she donned her brown cloak and made her way through the chilly, covered walkway to the kitchen. It was the only place where the servants could bathe.

"Love, you're a mess!" The housekeeper greeted her from her Windsor chair.

"I know. I'm afraid I've gotten wax all over myself."

"Well, there'll be no lifting heavy water pots for you! I'll get you your bath!" Mrs. Whitsome placed her tatting in the chair and went to heat the water. At Mrs. Whitsome's odd remark Cook gave both of them a vaguely curious look, but then, as if she'd spent years minding her own business, excused herself from the kitchens.

"Please, Mrs. Whitsome, I can prepare my own bath water." Brienne tossed the housekeeper a quizzical look.

"No, love. It's no bother, really." Mrs. Whitsome was firm; she gestured for Brienne to remove her clothes.

"Cook is marketing today? Isn't that rather strange? She usually goes at the beginning of the week." Brienne stood near the fire, having stripped herself of her clothing. She unconsciously rubbed the gentle curve of her belly and watched as the tub was pulled out and filled.

"The reason is that we're to have a visit. I just received a note to prepare the house."

"The master is coming here?" Brienne shrugged off a misbegotten shiver of apprehension. She had nothing to worry about, she reminded herself staunchly. After all, Mrs. Whitsome had gotten the new owner to approve of her employ. She remembered the housekeeper telling her about the letter from the estate manager. Considered a mere servant at Number One, Brienne told herself, she would probably not even have to see this man.

"The new master will be arriving from London today," Mrs. Whitsome informed her.

"So soon? Why, that's hardly any notice at all."
Brienne thanked her for her help and eased herself into
the steaming tub before the large kitchen fires. She was
more worn out than she had supposed, so instead of
scrubbing herself clean, she lay back and closed her
eyes.

"It's their way, these upper crusts. But the house is
presentable. I have no qualms." The housekeeper picked
up her lacemaking from the Windsor and put it away in
her sewing bag. "I've got to check the linens. Will you be
all right?"

"Of course. Why wouldn't I be?" Brienne frowned.

"Have a nice long soak, then. No one will have need to
come by the kitchens, so worry not. I'll be back in a few
minutes." The housekeeper smiled, ignoring Brienne's
question. She then donned her cloak for the chilly passageway and left.

Quiet settled into the kitchens, and Brienne almost felt
herself doze off in the soothing, warm water. Soon, however, she heard barking from the yard outside the kitchens, and she opened her eyes.

Now that was strange, she thought. She looked down
and saw "my precious" lying close to the fire. The little
honey-colored mongrel's ears were pricked up with
alertness, and she was growling softly. Knowing there
was only one real entrance to the yard and that that was
from the house, Brienne was curious about how another
dog could have entered the back.

She sat up in the tub and looked out one of the small
windows that faced the house. Sure enough, there was a
dog in the yard, bounding in the damp gardens and barking happily at the closed door, where it heard Cook's
mongrel respond. Yet this dog was special. Her face grew

pale as Brienne saw that the animal was not only large and beautiful but also as white as snow.

Forcing herself to remain calm, she lay back in the tub. She knew she was just imagining it. She had to be. The dog that barked at the door could not be Orillion.

Eyeing again the uncanny look-alike, doubt and apprehension descended upon her like a plague. Was it possible that the dog was Orillion? She bit her lip. Was it possible that Avenel had taken over Number One, as he had the Park, and was now coming for a visit? No, no, she told herself. That could not be. Hadn't Mrs. Whitsome told her that the new master had a title as old as English soil? Avenel Slane had no title. He was American.

But her thoughts were not put to rest. Suddenly, Brienne heard heavy footsteps coming down the passageway, and panic flared through her like wildfire. The small kitchen seemed to shrink in size like a closing trap. She groped for a towel. But before she could reach the stack of linens on the pine bench, she heard the door crash open behind her. Gasping, she threw her arms over her bosom and sank low into the tub to hide her nakedness. Then she heard from behind her what she dreaded most in the world: an angry, accusing silence.

God, did she dare to turn around? She knew with utter certainty that everything she had run from was back there in full force and that soon she would again experience the anguish she had felt at Osterley. It was painful to turn around. But it was not nearly as painful as when her violet eyes met the silver-gray ones, and she was all at once filled with feelings of anger, bitterness, and love.

"How could you be here?" she accused him, wanting desperately to sound cold and heartless.

"I could ask you the same, wildflower. Ah, but finding you here at all has answered that question for me."

Avenel's large, splendid frame filled the doorway. Slowly he moved to close the door behind him. Shivering from the cold air that touched her damp skin, Brienne clutched her breasts more tightly.

"So you've found me." She tried to put on a brave front but wondered how she could reach for the towels without removing her arms from her chest. "But it signifies nothing, for I mean to leave at the first opportunity."

"Fine. Have it as you will, ragamuffin." He walked toward the tub and ran his hand over her wax-soiled cheeks and hair. "But where will you run next? Your father's house in London? You'd still be living under my roof. Consider it another one of my conquests." Avenel looked down at her; his eyes smoldered with furious desire as they raked up and down her water-clad figure.

"I am not one of your conquests. I left you, remember? And I shall do it again, even if I must live in the streets," she answered vehemently.

"You'll never be out on the streets, my love. I'll see to that." With his hard hand he stroked the satin skin on her back, although she suspected that in his angry state he would have preferred to whip it instead. Not daring to move, she closed her eyes and hoped that darkness would dispel the magic of his persuasive touch. The water was still warm, but she was shaking and she desperately wanted him to leave. She wanted him gone so she could dress and escape.

"I shall choose the streets over you." She finally pulled away from him, fearing that he would advance farther upon her. She would never repeat that last afternoon at Osterley. She would hate herself forever if she did—hate herself for lying with a man who didn't love her and never would. It would be unbearable.

"You would leave the comforts of a home? Sometimes

I think you are touched in the head, love—just as I was told when first I arrived at the Park." He laughed, and his mouth twisted into a painful grin. "But then, I pride myself on knowing you as no other has. And I see your motivations very clearly."

"So you see why I would assume a life of hardship. I think it would be a far greater pleasure to be out on the streets whoring for all men than whoring just for you." Her eyes locked with his, and she could almost feel the sting of a slap on her face. She was surprised when it didn't come. Instead, she saw his eyes narrow. It was almost admirable, the way he controlled himself. Still, she decided, she was not willing to test him again soon.

"Get out of the tub. Put on your clothes. We're going back to the house," he ordered, this time obviously expecting no retort. But she didn't move to comply. "I said—"

"I heard you," she replied slowly. Was it modesty that gave rise to her sudden anxiety in her breast? She didn't think so, but the thought of exposing her body to his scrutiny unnerved her beyond reason.

"Come along, my love. As much as I enjoy the view" —his eyes dropped to the bath water, which only partially hid her voluptuous body—"we must talk. And I think we'd get more said if you were wearing your clothes." He smiled a wicked, tormenting smile.

"Turn around," she ordered. "Turn your back. Then I'll get dressed."

"What maidenly shyness! But you know you have nothing to show me that I've not seen before." Insolently, he took a seat on the pine bench before her. "Get up now." He held out a towel for her to step into.

"No." Quickly she reached for the stack of towels, but

he merely slid them out of her reach. She was forced to reclasp her arms over her chest.

"Let me assure you that I can control my lust in the presence of your naked body. Get up," he ordered again.

"Please turn around." She made another attempt to save herself; from what, she wasn't exactly sure.

"Brienne"—he bent and put his hand firmly on the nape of her neck—"I said I can control my lusts. Don't make me not want to."

"Please."

"What are you afraid of? It's as if you have something in that naked body of yours to hide. . . ." His words dwindled. Suddenly a gleam appeared in his eyes, and he growled, "Get out of that tub."

"Avenel, don't." She knew what he was thinking.

"Now!" Before she could fight him, he placed his strong hands under her arms and forced her up. Bath water sloshed up on his waistcoat and breeches, but he seemed not to notice. All he did was stare at her body and at the slight changes that had taken place since he'd seen it last.

"Let me go!" She began to struggle, and immediately he put her down. Scrambling out of the tub, Brienne grabbed the nearest towel and pulled back from his tall, lithe body, covering herself with the linen.

"The child must be big, if already—"

"There is no child!" she screamed at him.

"Brienne!" He stood up and went to her. "Tell me. I have a right to know."

"Damn you! Damn you!" she cried out and backed away closer to the fire. "Why did you have to find me?" Twisting beneath his gaze, how she wanted to deny what was happening! How she wanted to scream and cry that it was not so! But deep down she knew it would be for naught. The absolute demand for truth on Avenel's face told her he would be relentless.

He walked closer, and she stepped back until she felt the scorch of the fire at back. His hand, sure and strong, reached for her belly, but she brushed it away. She tried to hide behind the towel, but he grabbed it from her and tossed it across the room. Gasping in shock, she glared at him and watched him rest his hand on her naked abdomen.

"It's true," he whispered to her, and suddenly she too was caught up in the unbearable realization. She had refused to come to terms with what was happening to her body until now. But now she knew it was obvious. Although her belly still looked young and sleek, a slight curve to it now was making her laces harder and harder to tie up each morning. Her breasts had become tender and fuller.

And she knew Avenel missed not a detail. The changes were just that much more dramatic because he had not seen her for so many weeks. Although she had been able to hide the small changes from the servants who saw her every day, looking up at his face now, she knew she wasn't hiding it any longer.

For a long moment every possible emotion seemed to cross his hard, angular face. There was a brief flash of guilt, followed by amazement and then by doubting fury. But when he spoke his voice was calm and reflective. "You, of course, claim I am the father."

"I claim no such thing." She tried to grab her cloak, which was flung over the back of the Windsor, but he kept her from it, easily holding her by the waist.

"Ah, I see." Avenel narrowed his eyes; his face revealed nothing. "Well then, were you raped, or were you forced into this state by your need for coin?"

"Rape? Surely it was not so after such great efforts of seduction," she said to him bitterly.

Feeling her jab, his jaw began to twitch with anger. "I hope at least you were well paid. In bed, love, you're worth your weight in gold."

"Paid well? Look at me! You can see how well I was paid, you bloody—" she cried in anger.

"Shall I kill him for you then? This mysterious lover of yours?" He pulled her against him. "Or do you have a fondness for the grunting ox that did this to you?"

"You are the grunting ox that did this to me!" Seeing smug satisfaction in his eyes after she had confessed, she then hissed, "But believe me, I have only hatred for the father."

"You have good reason to, wildflower." His hand once again touched the swelling curve of her belly. "But I'm not such a fool as to believe your words, when your eyes look at me with an emotion very different from hatred."

"Leave me alone, Avenel. You have no need for me or a child in your angry existence."

He laughed out loud. "No need for you?" Moving back, he suddenly kicked at the pine bench so forcefully that it collapsed in a dusty heap on the stone floor. Then, looking only slightly relieved by its destruction, he circled her as if he simply could not make up his mind what to do. "I've had every need for you! Oliver Morrow has seen to that!"

"Avenel"—she kept her voice calm in the wake of his fury—"in truth, Mrs. Whitsome and I talked about leaving Bath for her widow's cottage in the country. I thought she could teach me how to make lace so we might open a shop." She stopped and swallowed the lump that was forming in her throat. "I have neither the need nor the desire to make demands on the child's father.''

Avenel was quiet for so long that Brienne was beginning to wonder if he had heard her. When she could take it no longer, she picked up her cloak and hid her nakedness.

"Don't you know how rich I am?" he asked. "Don't you know what comfort you would live in as the mother of my child?"

"I will not be a prisoner of yours ever again."

"You would not deprive our child of its true father."

"Then the child is . . ." *Not yours!* she wanted to cry out, but when she met his searching gaze, she found she could not speak the lie. "Damn you! You cannot have me!"

"I will. I did," he stated, his face full of vengeance. Grabbing her up, he said, "Have you any idea what this child means to me? Twenty years and more, Brienne, there have been no children. I tell you there have been no children! And I have not lived the life of a saint!"

"Those scars you carry were not a hindrance when you took me to your bed. Now you see they are not a hindrance to any part of your manhood. Through me, justice has been served. You have discovered that the wounds my father dealt you were not as deep as you thought." She pulled at his iron grasp.

"Justice will be served when I have the earl's daughter and his grandchild back at the Park."

"Never," she vowed, freeing herself. "Now I must speak with Mrs. Whitsome so that we can leave today."

"You are not leaving." The words were low and ominous.

"You must prove yourself on another woman, Avenel.

For I am leaving.'' She turned to the door. Her eyes almost showed her tears.

''A baby! Good God!'' Cumberland's eyes nearly burst from their sockets. He was in the study drinking a warmed brandy when Avenel found him. He put down his glass in the stunned silence. ''Is it possible? Could it be yours, Slane?''

''If it is possible, then it must be mine.'' He leaned both hands on the scagliola tabletop and hung his head, looking very much like an expectant father.

''This is the greatest of blessings! Your father must be laughing from the heavens!'' Cumberland raised his glass excitedly. But then, seeing the scowl that it brought to Avenel's face, he lowered it at once. ''Slane, don't tell me you aren't delirious with happiness, because I know better.''

''And if she's lying?''

''About being pregnant? Don't be absurd! How could she? You saw it yourself!''

''Not about the baby. About the father.'' Avenel scowled again blackly. ''The child must be mine. But, my God! I thought I'd have a child before now. And I've never produced one!''

''Brienne wouldn't lie.'' Cumberland pondered it further. ''No, the girl wouldn't. She's just not the devious kind.''

''Not devious! She knocks me over the head, she runs away from Osterley in the dead of the night, and despite our efforts she has evaded us for weeks! Don't tell me that the girl isn't devious!''

''She had her reasons for leaving, and well we all know them, especially now.'' Cumberland gave him an accusing look, and all Avenel could do under his perusal was run an agitated hand over his unshaven jaw. "She was *virgo intacta* when you—?"

"Of course!"

"Then there is no dispute. I have spoken to the housekeeper, and she gave me the exact date when Brienne arrived. The girl walked, and it would have taken every five of the missing days just to get here."

"But in the meantime?"

"Meantime? Jibberish. She isn't the sort, and you well know it." Cumberland eyed him closely. "I see the gleam in your eye, Slane. You know it's your child."

"And Oliver Morrow's grandchild."

Cumberland got up and patted him on the back in an age-old congratulatory gesture. "Forget that, Slane. It's not important now." He took a deep breath. "So what shall we name him, eh?" He winked. "But perhaps we should be thinking about marriage before names. When will the wedding take place?"

" 'Tis not in the near future, I assure you." Avenel banged a fist on the scagliola.

"You are going to renege? Don't you remember the vow you made? Let me see, we were in Baltimore, were we not?"

"Yes, yes," Avenel answered hastily.

"And you were a cocky jackanapes back then, if my mind isn't failing me. And pretty damned drunk at the time, too. You'd been whoring along the wharves all day, and I remember you said you'd marry any girl who got pregnant with your child, even if she was a tart, walking the streets. That's what you said, Slane, word for word— you said even if she was a tart."

"That does not apply here."

"Brienne's no tart, to be sure. But nonetheless, it still applies. And better than we had ever dreamed! Brienne

Morrow will be the perfect mistress for Osterley. But more important, she will be the perfect wife for you."

"She is the worst choice imaginable!"

"All that matters is that you love her. I know I am not to speak of it, but it cannot be helped just this once. We've spent weeks looking for the girl with a vengeance I have rarely seen in you. Admit it—you can't live without her, and if that isn't love, what is?"

"I can't marry Brienne. You know that."

"You would have your only child born a bastard?"

"Better a bastard than not born at all!" Avenel cried.

"Come now, Slane, his own grandchild? Surely the earl wouldn't harm his own grandchild," Cumberland said with doubt in his voice.

"And if it isn't his grandchild? What do we really know of Brienne's parentage? He is the only one who knows for sure. I'll never take that chance. We must lie low. There cannot be any posting of banns for a marriage. The fewer that know of Brienne's relationship with me, the safer she and the child will be."

"And the housekeeper here? She must have a strong guess as to the babe's paternity. What to do about her?"

"We shall take her with us back to Osterley."

"I suppose it's the best thing. But what's to become of us, Slane? Especially now that our numbers are increasing?" He added this last part as an afterthought.

"I don't know. But whatever does become of us"—he looked at his companion, his eyes glittering with bloodlust—"it will happen at Osterley. Of that I assure you."

CHAPTER TWENTY-SEVEN

"Genny, you promise not to breathe a word to anyone?" Brienne nervously folded the vellum note and handed it to the little maid.

"No, miss. I'll deliver it right now to The White Hart. I'll present it to Mr. Harcourt myself."

"Thank you." Brienne gave a wry smile. "I just hope Mr. Harcourt can get here first thing in the morning. I cannot stay any longer than that."

"Yes, miss." Genny looked sad, and then promptly left with the note.

A little while later Brienne heard Avenel at her door. He stood in the open threshold; Brienne watched him anxiously as she sat before the fire combing dry her long mane. She was in the lady's bedroom now, Mrs. Whitsome having shown her to it promptly after finding out who the master was. The two serving maids had set up a bath, and with great awkwardness she had accepted it, if only to finally remove the wax that still clung to her hair and skin. It was an impossible situation for her now, one that seemed inexplicable to Mrs. Whitsome. The house-keeper had ordered about the two little maids, keeping an eye on Brienne but behaving more formally toward her than she had before. Avenel's arrival had changed their relationship, and Brienne resented it.

"Come along, wildflower. Let's take a short walk, shall we?" Avenel said.

"Darkness has fallen. It does not seem a pleasant time for a walk." Brienne turned from him and faced the fire. It was almost miraculous, but already some of her clothes had arrived from the Park. Now she was dressed in a sack-back gown that, being pleated in the back, had been simple to let out in the bodice. There was a light green satin quilted petticoat to go underneath the rustling rose taffeta, and with two penny-size lead weights under each sleeve, the gown hung perfectly in every way. Feeling unusually pretty, Brienne continued to untangle her hair. She sat quietly on the soft rug and tried her best to ignore her keeper, telling herself the arrangement would only last until Ralph arrived.

"Pleasant or not, we must talk. Come along." Avenel entered her room and grabbed a fur-lined cloak that had been tossed onto the painted four poster. He held it up to her and before she knew it, her hair had been tucked into its collar and she was being led down the stairs.

Cumberland greeted her in the hall with a kiss and a hug, but Brienne's greeting was a bit more reserved. She loved Cumberland, yet she couldn't quite remove him from the situation. To her, Cumberland was still part traitor, and she couldn't resolve her warring emotions about him.

"Rose has missed you, child," Cumberland said.

"I have missed her, too," Brienne whispered glumly. "She and Vivie—are they both well?"

"Rose has been fine. It seems marriage agrees with her. However, Vivie, with that French temperament of hers, has been utterly unmanageable since the day you . . . ah, shall we say, disappeared. Have you been faring well, child? I must say you look extraordinarily lovely. Your color is quite high."

"I have been fine." Before she could say another word, Brienne felt Avenel's touch at her elbow, and she was bundled out into the night air.

The Crescent took on an ethereal quality in the foggy nightfall. Candles twinkled from windows; their light brushed the cobblestones and softened all the hard edges of the building. Despite her problems, Brienne was taken in by the beauty and the grandeur. Stopping before the wrought-iron gate to the lawn, they both stood listening to the ramble of a distant hack and the soft whispers of passing cloaked pedestrians. Brienne felt Avenel's arms slowly go around her, and together they listened to the tinkling of sheep's bells lost in the mist.

"I missed you, wildflower. Can you believe me?" Avenel pulled her hood down and nuzzled her hair.

With his strong arms around her, she felt so secure that she had to bite her tongue not to agree with him. "I'm sure you found companionship in my absence."

"Not so. No one has quite your touch, little one."

She laughed bitterly. "Nor my addled brain, I'm afraid." She tried to pull away from him, but he held her fast. "I'm not going to stay with you. I am not going back to Osterley."

"And where will you go, if not with me? Where else will you find safety from your father? Here?"

"No, I don't want to stay here. Apparently even Bath is not the place for me. I saw him here, Avenel. I saw my father here in Bath." A tingle of fear ran down her spine at the memory of Oliver Morrow in the harnessmaker's stall.

"I know. He was here looking to get Number One back. I've got trackers following him, Brienne. I know where Oliver Morrow goes and what he does almost every minute of the day." He gently shook her shoulders. "Can't you understand how I must have felt when I found out you were here right under his nose? You ran from me only to almost end up in the enemy's arms."

"My father didn't see me. And I'll not take the chance of meeting up with him again," she stated resolutely.

"So you'll go back to Osterley?" Avenel sounded pleased.

"No, I'm going to the widow's cottage with Mrs. Whitsome in the country. There I won't be bothered by you or the earl."

"Mrs. Whitsome has already agreed to go to the Park."

"You're lying. She would never abandon me," Brienne replied indignantly.

"She never would, 'tis true. But because you are going back to the Park, she has graciously offered her services as housekeeper there."

"I'm not going. I have a right to my own life. And that does not include being your prisoner and your pawn."

When Brienne pulled away from him, she saw a brilliant flash across the frozen night sky. It was like nothing she had ever seen before; a great star with a long white tail was making its way through the heavens. Frightened, she stepped back into Avenel's embrace, but as soon as the phenomenon disappeared, she felt foolish and struggled once again for her release.

"A bad sign," she heard Avenel whisper to her. " 'Twas Christmas when a star such as that appeared in the Maryland sky, the year of our Lord 1758. That was what made my father want to return to England. Two weeks later he died from pains in his heart." He held her so tight, she was almost afraid she would break in his arms. "You must come back to the Park. You carry my child, and you need protection. Do you understand me?"

She understood his words, but what he implied was hard for her to accept. Refusing to think of the maid, Annie, Brienne spoke in irritation and denial. "You Americans! Are you always so superstitious? Surely a fallen star does not warrant such concern!"

"Do you understand me?"

"No! Damn you! I don't understand anything! I don't understand the monster who claims me as his child. I don't understand you and your claims to Osterley. I want to be alone. I want to go back to Wales. This is my baby, not anyone's but my own. And he shall not be raised in captivity!" She choked back a sob.

Seeing her distress, Avenel softened a bit. "Shh. I don't want to fight you, wildflower. I've spent weeks looking through every town in Wales just to find you. But you've got to see my position. The babe is my flesh and blood. He must be raised at Osterley."

"You speak as though the child had value to you besides as a tool to get back at my father."

"I don't intend to abandon the babe after the earl has met his maker," Avenel shot back at her.

"No? But then what use is the child to you after that?"

"I claim the child, Brienne. And a child of mine will not be raised anywhere but in its rightful home."

"You have no claim to this child, Avenel. It was begotten out of trickery. And because of that, I would rather the child had no father than know of the circumstances of its conception."

"Tell me those circumstances! Tell me how awful it was for you that night in my bedchamber!" he almost shouted at her.

"It was awful!" she cried. "I went to your bed for one reason only. But I was tricked! In the morning I found out my part in your dastardly scheme. I found out what a fool I had been." A slow, hot tear fell on her cold cheek. Not wanting him to see the depth of her emotion, she backed away from him.

"You've never been a fool, Brienne. But to fight me now would be foolish. You're going back with me to Osterley."

"No! No! I'll be leaving you! My child will be told he was born out of love, even if I must lie for an entire lifetime!" She ran from him, hating herself for allowing her cold heart to melt even a little bit in his presence.

"Brienne!" He caught up with her, but not before she'd slipped on the slick cobblestones and tumbled onto the wet road. "My God!" She heard Avenel's horrified gasp and saw Cumberland running toward them from the stoop at Number One.

"Are you all right?" Avenel asked urgently.

"I'm fine. I'm fine," Brienne answered, feeling foolish. She looked down and saw that the entire front of her gown had been soiled by the fall.

"If you ever do something that utterly stupid again, I'll lock you up and throw away the key!" Angrily, Avenel got her to her feet.

Hurt by his harsh words, Brienne brushed away his assistance and refused to see the worry in his eyes. "Tell me this." She turned to him and vented all the anger in her breast. "Am I the object of your concern, or is it your precious new captive, the earl's grandchild?" Getting no response from Avenel other than a cold, shocked silence,

Brienne was hurt further. Her tears turned to sobs, and she ran up the steps to Number One, not paying heed to the shouting behind her. Speeding past Cumberland, she entered the front door and mounted the steps to her bedchamber, grateful that for once Avenel hadn't followed her.

But before long he walked into her room, still looking angry. "Get out of those wet clothes. I've sent for your dinner."

"I don't want any," Brienne snapped while trying not to shiver. Her dress was thoroughly soaked down the front, but she was not about to remove it at his orders.

"Fine." He pulled at her wet laces.

"What are you doing?" She tried to move away from him, but it was useless. As always, he took command, and this irritated her no end.

"Treating you like the child you want to be." He made to remove her dress.

"I'll do this!" she protested, pulling back from him. But still he kept his hands on her, ignoring her wishes. Angrily watching him pull down her soaked bodice, she asked, "Why did you have to find me? Why did it matter so much to you?" How she wanted answers to these questions! He was mystifying, traveling all the way to Bath just to recapture her. Hadn't he gotten his revenge on them all that last night at the Park? Didn't he have bigger battles to wage than the one with her? Glaring at him, she waited for his reply.

Yet he hadn't seemed to hear her. He'd undressed her down to her shift, which was wet and nearly transparent. Only after his fingers accidently brushed over her breast and his hand began to shake did he finally step back and allow her to finish.

"Put this on." He tossed her a purple velvet dressing gown.

Catching it, she waited for him to avert his eyes. When he failed to do so, she turned around, pulled the white cotton shift over her head, and hastily donned the robe. When she turned around to face him again, she realized she had not been modest enough. For she saw in his eyes the familiar gleam of naked, unfulfilled desire.

Silence filled the room, and Brienne stiffly settled herself in a chair. Dwelling morbidly on the future, she hardly took notice of her meal when it arrived. The little maid, Genny, who had taken Brienne's note to Ralph Harcourt, served them both from a huge silver tray. The young servant made no reference to their earlier encounter, and Brienne watched her leave thankfully, trying not to think about what she would say to Ralph so that he would take her away from The Crescent.

Along with dinner Genny had also brought a glass of brandy for Avenel. He sat leisurely in an armchair, drinking his brandy and frowning. The fragrant steam that rose before her from the roast lamb and hot fig pudding made Brienne realize how hungry she was. Using her meal as an excuse not to acknowledge Avenel's presence, she ate her dinner. Only when she had completely finished did she notice that Avenel had stopped frowning.

"Leave that. You're not a serving wench." He scowled when he saw her pick up her tray.

"It's awkward now. Don't you see that?" Her eyes flashed angrily as she put down the tray. After resettling herself in her chair, she watched the fire and soon grew sleepy.

"Do you remember the night we spent at the cottage, wildflower?" Speaking to her softly, he, too, stared at the fire's mesmerizing flames. The sadness in his voice brought a lump to Brienne's throat, but she reminded herself that it was she who loved him and not he who loved her.

"No," she lied.

"I recall that I awoke that night and didn't know who you were. With that beautiful face, I thought you were a peasant girl brought in for my salvation. But when I awoke from the fever back at Osterley and knew who I'd really been envisioning, I was so sorry that you weren't that other girl, the girl with no past." He looked at her intently. "Why do you think that was?"

"You were delirious with fever. It's the only answer," she forced herself to say. Why was he torturing her like this? Was he trying to give her another lesson in humiliation? Violently she forced all her thoughts to Ralph Harcourt and to how she would be free tomorrow, at last.

Seeing her pensive face, Avenel walked up to her and stared at her until Brienne could no longer stand his piercing gaze. Giving him an angry, repudiating look, she expected him to back away. But instead Avenel bent and kissed her, innocently taking her soft mouth to his.

She should have refused him. She should have turned her head away and clearly shown him the distaste she had for his touch. But then his kiss should have repulsed her. It should have made her feel victorious in her decision to flee, victorious in her feelings about him.

She moaned. *Oh, but it didn't.* Instead, a wild, reckless yearning leaped up in her. Desperately she tried to deny what was happening to her, but all too soon she knew she couldn't help herself. Avenel was dangerous, even more so when he was quiet and gentle. Opening her mouth to him, she saw herself falling back into the net he had cast upon her at Osterley. She would have to get away tomorrow; her thoughts whirled around her in a frenzied manner. Tomorrow she would have to get away. . . .

She felt a jolt of surprise run down his body when he recognized her needy response, and she was surprised when he stopped kissing her. He moved to leave her, but Brienne clung to him with hunger that exceeded his own.

"What is this?" He looked down at her after the kiss had ended. "Has my lovely young virgin grown lonely in the past weeks?" His gray eyes mocked her.

"I am no virgin," she stated, feeling shame at her response to him. She had tried to sound accusing, but somehow her words just came out low and husky.

"And perhaps 'tis a good thing, too." His warm, hard knuckles moved down her breastbone until they were lost inside the velvet dressing gown. With a shiver that ran up her spine, she felt him brush her nipple with his thumb until it became hard and sensitive. Looking up at him, she saw invitation in his face, but still she was hesitant and doubtful.

"I can almost see love in your eyes, Avenel. But when you're through with me tonight, what will be there in its stead tomorrow?"

"If you think you see love, then believe it is there, wildflower." He bent to kiss her once more, and then slowly he picked her up from the chair and placed her on the turned-down bed. With a strange mixture of gratitude and shame, tension and relief, she let him remove her dressing gown. Then, bare and lovely, she placed his palm over the softly rounded part of her belly that was their child. He seemed enchanted by that little curve, and he stroked her and then moved down to kiss her. His lips left a trail of liquid desire wherever they touched her silken skin.

"I've missed you, little one."

He rid himself of his clothes, and before she could fathom what was taking place, he was holding her next to him, worshiping her like a goddess with his large, masterful body. His kisses were long and unsettling. They left her weakened but at the same time greedy for more. She moaned beneath his caressing hand, saying over and over again, "I want this, I want this." Yet when she moved to say, "But how can this be?" his lips ferociously covered hers, not allowing her to finish, as if to say that tonight there were no contradictions. And even though she knew better, she believed him.

Hearing him groan, she felt the ultimate proof of his desire along the smooth satin of her inner thigh. His hands went possessively to her breast, and after filling his palms with her sweet flesh, he lowered his mouth to taste them. Sighing with fulfillment, she reveled in the moment; her mind, body, and soul ached with love for this man. He was her dark-haired lover, and it was so easy to forget everything when he worked his particular magic on her.

Only when he strove to mount her did reality intervene. Her concern must have been evident when her hand went to her belly, but slowly he moved it away, reassuring her that the baby would not suffer from their lovemaking. She watched as he balanced himself on his corded arms, being careful not to unduly rest his weight upon her. She opened herself to him, letting his thrusts push her to a pinnacle of unbearable pleasure.

"Never leave me again, Brienne. Never leave me again." Avenel groaned above her. Though she tossed her head back and forth, unable to come up with an answer, in the end she was able to ease her lonely ache only by pulling him onto her and finally holding him so close that she feared his back would show her marks in the morning.

In the time that followed they lay side by side on the white feather mattress in peaceful silence. Even with the dim light of the candles, she knew he was near. Her softly tapered leg fit intimately between his own. With every breath she took she thought only of him. Her senses reeled in the aftermath of their pleasure, and she resented the sound of servants' voices that even now rang through the house. The sound was too intrusive. They reminded her of the real world with all its contradictions and complications.

"Brienne."

"Must you speak?" She raised herself to her elbows and kissed Avenel full on the mouth.

"Listen."

"I cannot." She kissed him again, hoping they could once again succumb to the hushed, dreamlike state of their lovemaking.

"Love, come back to Osterley." His voice was strained. "For that I'll give you anything you want, anything I have. Just don't fight me anymore, little one. Come back to Osterley with me, and whatever you want is yours."

Brienne paused a moment before speaking. "I will go back with you for one thing only."

"Your price?"

"There is no price. Not even your wealth can buy me what I desire." She took a long, deep breath to still her trembling breast.

"So what is it you want?" He raised one jet eyebrow mistrustfully.

I want to be the girl with no past, she thought, looking back into the fire. *I want you to love me.*

"Brienne? What is it you desire?" his voice prodded low and gentle.

She closed her eyes. Was it pointless to tell him of her true feelings? Would she again look pitiful, once more revealing her love for a man who couldn't love her?

"Say that you love me, Avenel." She moved from him slightly to look into his handsome face. His eyes were shadowed in the flickering light, and she wasn't sure how to read them. "Just say the words to me." She hesitated and then whispered, "As I have spoken them to you."

"There are things you don't understand, wildflower." Thoughtfully he stroked her rich hair, which spilled over his chest.

"I understand everything. My father is between us." Suddenly she felt herself panic. "Just say the words, Avenel. If you told me you loved me, I would gladly go back to the Park. For that I would even gladly be your whore."

"Never say that word to me again!" He shot up from the bed. His body, outlined by the fire, was sleek and fit. He paced the room like a lithe African cat held in a cage.

"Avenel!" she cried out. "Please don't be angry! It's not your anger I want."

"Then don't say that word. It does not become you."

"I won't. Just tell me you love me." She clasped at the velvet robe that lay by her side. Nervously she waited to hear the words, but he did not speak. "I know marriage was not good for my mother. But I'm not asking you for that now. Right now I don't care a whit for my reputation. Just say the words, Avenel. It's all I ask. Please." She looked at his large powerful back, now turned to her to hide the expression on his face. *And it must be terrible indeed,* she thought half-heartedly, wondering how she would ever win back her pride if he refused her request.

" 'Tis not a matter of love. I'm afraid it never has been," he said dismally. "There's so much you don't understand, Brienne, things even about yourself."

"Then tell me! Make me understand!" Anxiously she placed her dressing gown over her bosom, as if by hiding her nakedness she could hide her vulnerability. She then watched as he fingered a small Meissen figurine on the mantel. It was so fragile and delicate next to his strong hand that the two seemed incongruous. But she was not going to be the porcelain girl, she told herself. She was not going to wait for a knock of his hand to shatter her very existence. He had not said the words. So from now on she would force her emotions to become as hard as the diamonds on her comb. It was the only way she could survive.

"This is very unwise." Avenel grappled with his decision to talk to her. "The situation is already dangerously out of hand. But I will explain." He turned to her, but she scooted back on the bed, refusing his seductive touch. After he noted her reaction, his mouth formed a mean, hard line, and he said spitefully, "You belittle yourself one minute, and the next you're once again Lady Brienne, estranged daughter of a make-believe earl. Make up your mind, little one. Are you beneath me or above me?" He went to her and grabbed her in his arms.

"I am above you, you rutting beast," she spat at him, feeling hurt, beyond repair.

"Then play out your part." He tossed her gently but angrily back onto the bed. "But remember—everything lies with me, *Lady* Brienne. Everything. And words of love won't change the circumstances except make them

even more bloody complicated than they already are."
He gathered up his clothes to retire from the room.

"Everything does not lie with you. You believe you've
such control. But even with all your colonial money and
your precious Osterley, Oliver Morrow still has the one
thing you lack. He still has the power of his title and with
it the power of fear."

"Oliver Morrow has nothing, I tell you. Nothing! I
have made sure of it! But if it's the power of the Labordes
you fear, then cower before the last, lovely maid, for I
possess all their power and more." When he stopped
speaking, Brienne was silent. He seemed puzzled by her
reaction to his sudden announcement. "What, are you
not going to refute what I have said? Or denounce my
earldom? I have now relieved you of all vestiges of your
infamous, yet useful, heritage, and I hear no sound coming from your lips."

"I don't believe you," Brienne finally said, wondering
even herself if she didn't.

"And what don't you believe? That my name is actually
Avenel Slane Morrow? That a ruthless ship's captain
named Quentin Spense could have the acting ability to
last for the run of a play for twenty years? That he, who
looked enough like the true Oliver Morrow, was able to
kill my father before he could get back to England, the
and he had left many years earlier? Or is this what you
cannot bring yourself to believe." He looked spiteful.
"That he could do enough damage to the earl's offspring
that they would hardly present a threat to his masquer-
ade? Are my scars not real enough for you?"

"Don't say another word. My mother wouldn't marry
an imposter! She was beautiful and wealthy! She would
not have been a party to such trickery!"

"She did not know. She was young and perhaps be-

lieved herself in love. But she did leave him eventually.
My guess is she found out the truth but was too power-
less to do anything about it."

"No! She wanted me to be the daughter of an earl! She
wanted me to have my title, at least! And my comb! That
proves that what you say is false! It is part of the Laborde
jewels!"

"Think, love. Who has the piece that matches the
comb? Not your father." Brienne thought back to the
night when Avenel had brought her the beautiful amethyst necklace. Then she hadn't seen the connection, but
now she knew that if she looked at the two pieces
closely she would see that they matched. And the
Laborde seal was probably even stamped somewhere on
the necklace, exactly as it was on her comb.

"You're mad. Crazed. My father won't relinquish his
title to you." She held fast, despite her doubts.

"He never had a title to relinquish," Avenel said dis-
gustedly.

"But he'll never give it up." Brienne felt her insides
turn to ice. "He'll see us both die before he'd do that."

"So you understand."

She nodded her head slowly; her realization grew out
of fear for her child.

"Then you can understand why I must hold you at a
distance."

"Yes," she said numbly.

"I'm sorry," he said. He walked up to her and placed
his hand on her hair.

But Brienne's mind cried out for time to sort out the
meaning of his words. "I have no need for the company
of an earl," she whispered. "Please go."

"*Avec plaisir.* Just be ready to return to Osterley in the
morning," Avenel snapped, and he stalked out of the

room without even bothering to button his breeches. Watching him go, Brienne felt sorrow for them both. They were struggling so hard, and there seemed to be no end to their troubles. But when Avenel closed her door behind him, she felt the frost melt inside her. When she wept, she wept for herself alone.

CHAPTER TWENTY-EIGHT

The next morning, after a painfully restless night, Brienne was in her room packing her belongings. Genny was helping her, and amidst the sounds of sliding drawers and swooshing silks, she asked the little maid, "How long did they say they'd be gone?"

"Mr. Cumberland and the master were to see about fixing the carriage. It seems they made such a mad dash to get to Bath that the master feared they might have sprung something in their wake." Genny lovingly folded several aprons.

"Mr. Harcourt did tell you he would be here this morning?" Brienne asked for the hundredth time.

"Oh, yes, miss. Most assuredly he did." Genny nodded, a frazzled look on her face. Brienne knew something—or rather someone—had made the girl jump.

If only Ralph would get here before they return, Brienne thought as she quickly packed her last gown. She wasn't taking much—only the clothes she'd acquired while at The Crescent. She was leaving to Genny the care of the other gowns that had been brought from Osterley. She wouldn't be needing those any longer.

Anxiously, Brienne thanked Genny for her help during the hours since Avenel had arrived. She then took her willow baskets and waited for Ralph in the drawing room, knowing from there she would more easily hear his carriage pull up than from her room. How she hoped and prayed he would be here soon!

Brienne had hardly believed her good fortune when Genny brought her her morning chocolate and told her about Avenel's absence. Taking fate by the horns, she'd wasted not a moment and had quickly packed so she would be ready for Ralph's arrival. Brienne was still not sure what she was going to tell him, but she knew she had to take her chance while she had it. Although at first she'd scoffed at the idea of Avenel's daring to stop her if she chose to go with another man, she had taken pause, thinking of all the things in the past that Avenel had dared to do. It was then that Brienne knew it was better to sneak out of Number One like a thief than to try to leave openly.

As she waited in the drawing room, she tried desperately to ease her jumping nerves. She gazed at the painted ceiling, letting her eyes follow the curves and plumage of the wreathed honeysuckle and husked festoons. It was a calming sight and in marked contrast to the street noise that seeped through even the tightest window frames. Outside the sedan chairs carried the rheumatic and the gout-ridden. Morning was the time to take the cure, and the convalescents spent it in the baths. Then, wrapped up like babes in swaddling, they were carried right to their beds in the black sedan chairs. The only good thing about the odd Bath traffic was that the sound of a carriage could easily be distinguished from it. And Brienne was certain that Ralph would want to take his bride away in his carriage.

Swallowing the lump in her throat, Brienne heard wheels creak to a halt in front of the house. She stood up and descended the main stairs, clutching her willow baskets. There was knocking at the front door, and she stood in the empty, faux marble hall, watching as the footman answered the door.

"Brienne! What is it? Have you changed your mind?" The door opened, and with a wretched start of indecision, Brienne acknowledged Ralph Harcourt as he stood in the threshold.

"I—No. I mean, I need your help." She moved forward to greet him.

"What is it, princess? You can't imagine how alarming I found your note. What is it?" He caressed her cheek gently.

"The master of the house is . . . in residence." She gulped and looked behind her, afraid she'd see those condemning silver eyes. "I cannot stay here. I hoped that you would help me leave."

"We can be in Gretna Green in a matter of days. Is that what you desire? Marriage?" Ralph's eyes sparkled, and she knew without a doubt that he loved her very much.

"I think . . ." Brienne murmured, looking away from his soul-baring gaze. She couldn't bear to hurt him, but somehow, she knew she must. She carried another man's child, and suddenly she realized that marriage to Ralph Harcourt was too dishonorable to think of. He was a good man, and she couldn't use him to extract herself from Avenel's grasp. If she did, she would be no better than the ones who had used her.

Her eyes wandered over the hall while she tried to think of a gentle way to let Ralph know how she felt.

Seeing the empty staircase and the tall clock that ticked away her few precious moments, she felt no answers coming to her, only a tearing bout of indecision.

Her hand flew to her mouth. Her heart thumped in her chest, and her knees weakened beneath her. In the study to the left, she spied Avenel sitting quietly in a wing chair, staring not at her but at Ralph Harcourt. One shuddering look into those stormy eyes told her everything she needed to know. Avenel had overheard their entire conversation.

"What's this?" Ralph's eyes trailed in the direction of her shocked ones. He frowned when he saw the large, dark man watching them from the study.

"The carriage is ready, Brienne." Avenel rose, nodded to the footman, and stepped into the hall.

"I am not going with you to Osterley." Brienne fairly shook in her boots, seeing the beginnings of a situation she had wanted to avoid.

"No?" Avenel's smile was nasty. "I'm afraid you must not have heard me. I said the carriage is ready to take us home. Now, let us go. We cannot keep Cumberland waiting." He grabbed her elbow. "If you will excuse us," Avenel said to Ralph unpleasantly.

"I say I will not!" Ralph stepped up, showing what Brienne believed to be extraordinary courage. "The girl you are ordering about is going to be my wife. She is not traveling anywhere with you."

Suddenly Avenel stopped and stood deadly still. "I see. Your wife." He gripped Brienne's arm almost painfully. "Brienne? Is this true?"

"I don't want to go with you, Avenel. No matter what happens." She bit her lip to keep it from quivering.

"Well, let me tell you what will happen if you choose to dupe this gentleman into marrying you," Avenel growled. "I will never give you a moment's peace for the rest of your life. There will be no place on this earth where you could go to be free of me. And even if you insist upon ruining your own life in this fashion, be wary of ruining his, too." Avenel nodded at Ralph.

"Here now, unhand her!" Ralph commanded, stepping forward.

"Brienne, don't you have a little news for your fiancé?" Avenel tormented her.

"No, don't make me say it." Brienne closed her eyes, knowing how much her answer would hurt Ralph. She was being left with no choice, but Ralph wouldn't understand this. He didn't know of her child.

"Unhand her, I say. She's coming with me!" Ralph spoke with unruffled confidence.

" 'Princess'?" Avenel goaded Brienne, his eyes burning with vengeance.

"Ralph, you must understand—" Brienne started but he interrupted her.

"It doesn't matter, love. I need no explanation. I told you that before." Ralph's voice was calm and reassuring. It was as if he already knew her troubles and had forgiven her. How she ached to go with him! But deep down Brienne knew her destiny lay with Avenel. Her entanglement with the master of Osterley was too complex to unweave with one simple exit.

"Ralph, I'm sorry. Terribly sorry." Her voice broke, and she felt shame enough for them all. "I don't know how to explain this. . . . You see, I've a past. . . . I'm tied to this man because of it. There's no other way but for me to go with him. Oh, Ralph . . ." She couldn't go on.

"I see." Ralph's beautiful brown eyes filled with pain.

"Ralph, you must understand. I didn't want it to be

like this!" Brienne tried to pull free and console Ralph, but she knew from past pain and pleasure that Avenel's arms were as strong as steel.

"Get to the carriage, Brienne," Avenel ordered.

"No! I must explain!" Again she turned to Ralph. She would beg him to understand if she had to! Anything to get that look out of his eyes.

But she was never given the chance. Suddenly furious, Avenel grabbed her by the waist. Sweeping her legs into his arms, he had her out the front door before she could utter another word. Demanding to be let go, her cries fell on deaf ears, and he mercilessly dumped her into the waiting vehicle.

"I won't leave like this, I tell you! I won't leave like this!" Brienne cried, unable to bear the sight of Ralph's golden head hung in defeat.

"I think he understands, my dear." Avenel smiled, but his eyes looked hard. "We are leaving." He sat next to Cumberland and swiftly shut the door behind them.

The finality of the situation weighing upon her like a board and stones, Brienne jumped up and attempted to leave the carriage. She would spare Ralph's feelings even if it meant exposing her illegitimate pregnancy for all the world to see. But Avenel held her fast.

"Please let me tell him, Avenel! Don't let me leave him like this! He was kind to me!" She finally found herself pleading with him.

"And why not leave him like this?" Avenel answered maliciously. "After all, you don't love him. If memory serves, I recall that you love me."

Avenel sat back while she absorbed this blow. But it wasn't long before she had her retort.

"Yes, and my soul will burn in hell for allowing my love to be so misspent!" She leaned forward and slapped him viciously across the face. Yet he never flinched, nor did he seek retribution. Rather, he spent the rest of the trip in cruel silence, purposefully ignoring the glare in the violet eyes next to him.

III

Fools rush in where angels fear to tread.

—Alexander Pope

CHAPTER TWENTY-NINE

Spring came with a vengeance in 1781. It was April 10, and the Park's grounds were saturated with rain. The damp cold foreshadowed a dreary week, but there were times when Brienne wondered if it foretold something else as well, something more sinister.

She tried not to linger on such matters, for it was not good for the child, who was growing by leaps and bounds inside her. Fighting her constant fatigue, she moved about the great house, trying to keep busy with some needlework that never succeeded in holding her attention, and with her friendships with Rose and Mrs. Whitsome. It was good to see Vivie again and be back in her yellow taffeta bedchamber. But it had been a bittersweet homecoming, and she was reminded of this every time she saw Avenel.

She fairly burned with anger whenever she thought of their departure from Bath. She'd written a long letter to Ralph explaining her circumstances as best she could without mentioning the child. She'd entrusted it to Vivie, and she knew the little maid had posted it without delay. But not even that could assuage the bitterness and anger that had descended upon her. She vowed to shun Avenel's presence as long as she could.

However, it amazed her that in a house the size of Osterley it was difficult to avoid seeing him. In the hall, in the passages, in the library, their eyes would meet for the briefest of moments and then Brienne would find some implausible excuse to leave his presence. Any words they might have spoken remained unuttered. She refused to allow him to hurt her further.

There was a new addition to the household, aside from the one whose arrival was due in December. A young Colonial boy had arrived. His name was Robert Staples.

At first glance, Nob was a quiet, skinny lad. It was not unusual to find this melancholy boy sitting in a corner of the gallery, gazing awestruck at the huge sixteenth-century paintings that lined the walls.

But Brienne found herself spending more and more time with the boy, especially since she'd learned what had happened to his father in Maryland. She was grateful that Avenel had not told the boy of her relationship to Oliver Morrow, for she knew Nob looked upon her with adulation; his eyes always shyly sought hers in the room and then glistened with delight if she arose to keep him company.

Their friendship grew with the long, wet days spent indoors. One time, when Brienne felt a twinge within her belly, she found Nob had turned ashen with concern. Feeling he needed reassuring, she had looked down at his thin, little face and said, "There's nothing to fear. I'm going to have a baby. Here, see?" She had taken delight in allowing him to feel her stomach, where her baby was growing. It was a motherly thing to do, she had decided. It made them both feel as if they were part of a family.

But Avenel did not play a part in their make-believe family. He remained as distant as ever. Sometimes Brienne would sit in the drawing room and listen to him pace back and forth in the closed chambers of the tapestry room. Even her breathing would hush as she focused all her thoughts on the other side of the door and the man behind it. They were waiting, Brienne knew: she, for the birth of their child; Avenel, for something more.

They were all at dinner when the news came. It was the first dinner Avenel had attended since they had returned to the Park. Rose and Cumberland were there, as was young Nob. Brienne said hardly three words during the meal, feeling distracted and uncomfortable in Avenel's company. The surprise came when Hans bolted into the eating room, mindless of his jackboots that were covered with dirt from the road.

"Slane, he's disappeared. The messenger has just delivered this." A mud-spattered note was quickly handed to Avenel and just as quickly torn open. Frowning, Avenel read the scrawl and then lifted his eyes.

"Good work, Hans. I suppose this is what we've been waiting for. Get some extra footmen to patrol the grounds. You and your brother take the gate. But be careful! Spense is a cocky bastard, and I don't doubt he'd prefer to enter the Park like an earl." Avenel dismissed the huge Norseman and turned to Brienne.

"Quentin Spense has slipped away from my trackers. He can now show up here without warning."

"Then I would like Rose to leave." Cumberland stood

up nervously. "She should to to London, where she will be safe."

"Exactly." Avenel paused as if he were going to make an announcement to which he had given great thought. "And I want Brienne to go with her."

Brienne gasped "Now?" she asked incredulously. "You've gone to great lengths to get me here for this moment. Now you want me to go to London?" She began to laugh. "Don't be absurd!"

"Your condition, Brienne. You can't stay here—" Rose said.

"Of course I shall stay here! He's my father! He's ruined my life! He's ruined all our lives!" Brienne turned to Avenel. "And I've paid the price of your revenge. So I've paid the price to stay." She stood and stared at both men, who seemed acutely uncomfortable under her determined gaze.

Avenel shook his head. "Now that the time has come, I won't take the risk. You will go with Rose."

"But I could be your lure, your bait. Isn't that what you've wanted all along?" Brienne crossed her arms in front of her.

Ignoring her, Avenel turned to Cumberland. "Tell them in the stable block to prepare the coach for the morning. I would have them go now, but I don't like the idea of Rose, Brienne, and the boy traveling at night."

"Yes. I'll go right away." Cumberland wrung his aged hands.

"No, I am not leaving! I have my own desire for revenge!" Brienne said irately.

"Revenge will be had," Avenel assured her. "And better so if you're in London. Remember, you care for two lives now, and you cannot endanger one without endangering the other."

At this quiet reprimand, Brienne paused. It was a difficult decision to make. In the back of her mind, she knew he was right. But she also knew that she needed to confront her father with all the misery he had caused her and her mother. And was there also the possibility that something might go wrong at the Park while she stayed in London and that she would never see Avenel again. Brienne hastily pushed this idea aside. That would mean she still loved Avenel, and she had been determined to deny that ever since they'd returned from Bath.

"Let me see you to our chambers, Rose. You should start packing," Cumberland said gently.

Brienne looked up just as he started calling out instructions to the footmen. She watched as he and Rose walked out of the room.

Avenel turned to the boy. "Nob, since you will serve as protector to Mistress Brienne, why don't you retrieve one of my pistols, and I'll show you how to hold one for your ride tomorrow." Hearing these words, Nob's eyes brightened, and he shot out of his seat ready to go.

" 'Twould be my pleasure, Master Slane . . . uh—my lord." Nob stumbled over the words, not yet used to Avenel's title.

Avenel laughed. "Well then, search under my bed. The pair you'll find there should be unloaded. Bring them to the gallery, and I'll meet you there in a little while."

The boy quickly nodded and ran from the room gleefully.

Quiet settled over the eating room when Brienne was alone with Avenel.

"Why don't we all go to London?" she suggested. "We could wait until my father's whereabouts are known and then come back."

"And continue in this manner forever? No, wildflower.

'Tis best to get this over with. He means to kill me. He has for twenty years. I'll not go another score, waiting to be ambushed.''

"Then perhaps if I went to see him, perhaps if I told him I was going to have a child, your child, his grandchild, he would feel differently."

"Come, now." Avenel walked up to her and stroked her glossy hair. "Do you really think that would make him change his mind? He has no fondness for his own daughter. I can't imagine how little he would care for his own grandchild—especially one begotten by me."

Brienne felt sadness well up within her. She moved to the window, but all she could see was damp darkness. "Yes, my father doesn't care for me. I suppose that has been the cruel irony of this whole scheme."

"So you see, little one, that's all the more reason why you should leave."

"No," she laughed morosely. "That's all the more reason to stay. He hurt me and my mother. I'll see this through to the end. I want a hand in bringing him to justice, too."

"Brienne, I will not fight about this. You've got the child—"

"Yes! The child!" Brienne turned around and faced him. "Let's talk about this child. This poor child, who will only know its mother's love."

"Brienne, stop," Avenel commanded, but she brushed it aside.

"I am staying, Avenel. My child would want me to. He would want the one person who loves him to fight for his heritage."

"What do you mean?" He snapped.

"I'll be here when Spense arrives, if only to put to rest for once and for all the question of who my father is."

"He isn't your father," Avenel insisted angrily.

"Oh, no? And what proof have you? None. Only my mother and Spense know the truth, and now it's up to Spense to tell me."

"Who your father is doesn't matter!" Avenel fairly shouted at her.

"Doesn't matter? Doesn't matter?" She lashed out at him. "How dare you say such a thing to me! When my child asks me why his grandfather detested him so, I'll have to say it was because of his father. And when he asks me why his father detests his mother so, I'll have to answer that it was because of her father." Suddenly unleashing all her pent-up fury, Brienne started to beat on Avenel's chest. "So don't you tell me that fathers don't matter! They matter in every way!"

"My God! Brienne!" Avenel took her fists into his hands. He tried to calm her down, but she would not be quieted.

"Just know this, Avenel: there isn't a reason in the world that could keep me from staying here to the end! My safety be damned! There isn't a reason in the world!" she ranted.

"Yes, there is!" He caught her and pulled her against him.

"No!"

"Yes, there is! I have the best reason of all. You will leave on that coach tomorrow!"

"Why, then?" she cried. "What can you say to make things different? What can you say to make me different?" An ominous silence filled the room, and Brienne saw myriad emotions flicker across Avenel's face.

"I love you," he said fervently. "I love you, Brienne. And all I want is to see you safe."

"You? You?" she stuttered, unable to believe what she was hearing.

"I love you. So much that the question of who your real father is will have to remain a mystery so that I can keep you out of harm's way."

She touched his face, a face she knew so well, and loved so deeply. Even though he had hurt her, she still loved him. But had she heard him correctly? Had she? Softly she asked, "How can this be, Avenel? How can you be saying this to me of all people? You despise me."

"I love you," he refuted with a whisper. "I've tried to fight off my feelings for you with more vengeance than I've ever used before, but there's no denying it any longer. I love you, wildflower. I love you beyond flesh and blood, I love you beyond everything."

"You don't care even if I am Quentin Spense's daughter?" She held her breath.

"I don't care. You're the most beautiful, loving woman I've ever met. And I'd give up everything I've fought for just to keep you looking the way you do now."

"And how is that?" she whispered.

"As if you love me much more than I've ever deserved." His voice caught with emotion.

"Avenel," she moaned. "I do love you, Avenel. I have for longer than you know."

"Then come." He kissed her so ferociously, she was left breathless. "We'll go to my chambers. Show me how much you love this Colonial beast, Brienne, and let me show you how sorry I am that I've put you through so much."

"But Avenel, Nob is waiting in the gallery." Brienne stood in indecision.

"Nob will wait." Avenel smiled a beautiful rakish smile.

It was a long time before they finally met Nob in the gallery. Avenel closed them in the state bedroom, and time seemed to shudder to a standstill. Clothes rustled and dropped. Sighs mingled with whispers as Avenel undressed Brienne tenderly, taking his time to see that no part of her body yearned for his caress.

"Is this really happening?" She kissed the palm of his hand.

"Oh, little one, it's really happening." He groaned and took her to his bed.

"Have I all of you?"

"All that you'll take." His smile was almost lost in the contours of her breast.

"Then I'll take all of you."

He rose atop her, and her eyes widened.

"Wench, you're as greedy as I am." His laughter rumbled in his chest, but then he grew serious. Kissing her brow, kissing her eyelids, he murmured, "I'll never give you up, Brienne. Never. I'm a selfish man. Can you live with that?"

"I can" was her answer.

Taking him inside her, she let him make love to her with an intensity she never thought possible. His touch was explosive, his kiss devouring. Wrapped in the security of his love, she abandoned herself totally in their union, and finally with a gasp of sharp pleasure Avenel touched her soul.

Kissing his warm lips, Brienne pulled the linen over her breasts and snuggled deep into his embrace. Thoughts of tomorrow were banished from her mind, and she tried only to think of the man who lay by her side, the man she loved with her whole being. With the flicker of a candle, a pensive look came upon her face. In the quiet of the evening, she murmured, "How can one be so happy and yet so sad."

"What has you so sad, my love?" Avenel lay on his back, softly petting her hair.

"You've said all along how you needed me in order to exact revenge against my father."

"Mmm . . ." He turned thoughtful.

"So if I leave tomorrow, you'll not have—" He put a finger to her soft lips.

"I don't know if I could have ever really used you, wildflower. I thought it a glorious coincidence when I procured the house and found out that the earl's daughter was still in residence. Before I met you, I made many a cruel plan for you to be my means for revenge. But these plans were all dashed the very day I arrived."

"But how was this?"

"Well, you see"—he smiled lazily—"the simpering, self-indulgent maid I hoped to find here did not exist. Instead in her place was the most beautiful creature I had ever seen. She was fair and gracious. And even with her elbows sticking out her sleeves, she was proud. When she fought, it was not for her father or for her station; it was for herself. She was more than I could handle."

"If this was so, why did you force me to stay here?" Brienne's eyes looked serious.

"I knew you'd leave if I didn't force you to stay. And I think, in the back of my mind, I still had delusions of using you against your father. But as the days passed, I knew more and more that I'd never be able to do it."

"So why didn't you let me go then?"

"When you had that terrible dream the night of the ball, I found out how afraid you were of Oliver Morrow. I knew I had to protect you, even if it meant forcing you to stay here." He rubbed his jaw in agitation. "My God! You don't know how frantically I was looking for you when you left back in March. I searched every *dinbych* in Wales, along with Tenby. I was sure you'd be there somewhere. It was a terrible blow not to find you. The thought of never seeing you again ripped my insides apart."

"But you hated me. You all but said so that morning in the state bedroom." Her whole body trembled, waiting for his answer.

"I was angry. So angry over Staples's death, I could hardly think straight. He was one of my dearest friends. His death was as hard to bear as Cumberland's would have been. Can you ever forgive me?" He turned her face to his and stroked her cheek with his thumb. "Could we start anew? When you return to Osterley, after—"

"There will be no returning to Osterley. Please let me stay here with you." Brienne clutched him, trying to hold him close.

"Shh . . . my love." He held her tightly. "It must be. It must be."

"I'm afraid. I'm afraid for you. You know I love you."

"Then stay with me tonight. Let me finally hold you without anything coming between us. Just for this night, let there be no past."

"Nor future." She began to cry. He loved her now. He loved her! But was it all for naught?

"There will be a future, wildflower." Avenel put a warm hand to her belly. "There will be a future."

CHAPTER THIRTY

Nob watched as Orillion stalked a gray-furred animal near the stable block. From the breakfast room, he couldn't make out whether the dog's intended prey was a large rat or a field rabbit that had yet to darken its coat for spring. But both boy and dog were captivated by the hunt as the small bright-eyed creature popped its head out from the hole in the bricks and then as quickly disappeared through it, after perceiving its predator.

Laughing at the dog's antics as it pawed the hole and pricked up its white ears, the boy soon gazed with longing at the play, obviously lusting for the same activity. Rose and Cumberland had just left to go to their apartments at the other end of the house. Now alone, Nob began to wonder if he would be missed in the short time it would take to join Orillion. It had been a tedious voyage from America to England. There had been long stays in the ports of many tiny Caribbean islands where sugar was taken on board and dark African flesh unloaded. The stifling cross-Atlantic sail was a lot for an active young body to endure, so it was no wonder that young Nob soon found his way to the ground floor, vowing to make the most of his free time before he had to undertake another journey. The Mistress Brienne would be busy with the travel preparations, and his disappearance, he rationalized, would not be noticed before he returned to the house. Besides, he grimaced, it would be another day of sitting in a carriage like the one that had brought him from Liverpool. He would have to get out now or never.

Pulling his worn three-cornered hat more closely over his head, he opened the door that led to the outside. It took less than a minute to reach the stables. Looking about, he saw the hole where Orillion had cornered the animal, but now, strangely enough, the small gray bunny that had been hiding in it was scampering off to the trees near the Temple of Pan.

"Orillion! Here, boy!" He gave a sharp piercing whistle, but there was no response in the silence of the morning. "Orillion!" he called again, and walked closer to the stable block. A streak of red caught his eye near one door, and he said to it, "Have you caught a rat then, Orillion? I suppose the rabbit was too quick for you." He sauntered over to inspect the patch of blood.

With a thud his small body was jerked off the ground and pulled across the courtyard into a dark doorway. The breath was knocked from his lungs, but grappling with a meaty forearm, he still was able to beat wildly at the man in front of him. He was knocked back, however, and two blows to his head made stars appear before his eyes.

"Keep yer mouth shut, an' you'll not end up like the dog."

Nob saw the bloody, shaking form of Orillion lying near him in the threshold. Then, gasping and reeling, he was pushed into the stable. There he found the brute was not alone. He had three companions, only one of whom Nob recognized—the tall, gray-haired one. His eyes widened with shock, he gazed at the earl from the violent card game in Maryland.

"Where is Lady Brienne's room?" the earl questioned.

"I'll not tell you. You killed my father!" Nob shouted back bravely.

"Listen, lad"—the earl smiled and pointed to the stairs —"we're going to toss you out the window if you don't cooperate." He came closer, and Nob drew back. "Where is Lady Brienne's room? Is it the yellow one?"

"No!"

The earl wasted no time deliberating, and Nob paled. "Take him upstairs and drop him from the top. That'll get someone out here."

"No, wait!" Nob was being pushed up the stairs by one of the henchmen. His eyes grew accustomed to the dark of the stable's interior, and he looked down and saw Kelly bound and gagged in one corner, helplessly watching the proceedings. Swallowing his fear, Nob finally cried out, "Lady Brienne is staying in the yellow room. But you can't get her out here! Slane will keep her away from the likes of you!"

"Oh, he will, will he?" The gray-haired earl laughed viciously. "I think we have a way of coaxing her out." Turning to the burly henchman who held Nob, he said, "Take the boy upstairs and hang him from the northwest window!"

"No!" Nob began to protest, but before he could, a foul, urine-soaked rag, was stuffed in his mouth.

"Nob!" Brienne poked her head into the boy's chamber next to her own. "Are you ready? We've got to leave

now, or Avenel will be furious. Nob?" She bit her lower
lip in puzzlement at the empty room. She walked into it
and eyed the boy's things that lay in a neat bundle on the
side of his bed. But the lad himself was nowhere to be
seen. Picking up one of his gaiters, she noted its shabby
appearance and promised herself that they would get
some proper clothes for him in London. Putting the
leather down, she started to walk out of the room, but a
waving motion from the stable across the way caught her
attention.

She walked to the window, and to her surprise she
saw Nob waving to her from the uppermost floor of the
stable. He was leaning out of one of the abandoned
rooms, arching his arm unnaturally in the air. He hung
precariously from the window frame. Her breath caught
in her throat when she saw the spire below him that
jagged upward from the ancient gables of a lower level.

*If this is what little boys do for pranks, Robert
Staples, then I can see Avenel will be breaking in his
hand on you!* she thought snappily. Without giving a
thought to Avenel's warnings of the previous evening,
she quickly went down the stairs to the ground floor,
grabbed a servant's cloak and pattens, and started for the
stable.

"Brienne! Brienne!" She stopped walking. Now, that
was odd. The boy should be in the window, but he was
nowhere to be seen. Looking around, she spied his
worn, three-cornered hat lying on the wet ground nearer
the Temple than to the block. "Brienne! Brienne!" Nob's
voice called to her. It seemed forced and unusually high
pitched. She couldn't believe he was actually taunting
her, but growing annoyed, she made her way toward the
stable.

If he thought he was hiding from her, she contemplated grimly, he was wrong. Nob would have to be disciplined for this silly and dangerous behavior, she fumed.

"Brienne! Brienne!" She looked up toward the voice. Expecting to see the boy's jaunty face undone with mischief, she pursed her cold lips to form a reprimand. But when her eyes met eyes that were not Nob's, Brienne stopped dead in her tracks. Comprehension and regret rushed through her.

Avenel paced the gallery; every sinew and muscle was tensed and ready. Occasionally he would stop near the fire but even its warmth couldn't alleviate the bone-deep chill he felt.

"Go see what is keeping Mistress Brienne!" he snapped at the nearest footman, one of the elderly gents who stood in the hall. After the footman withdrew to do his bidding, Avenel paced the gallery once more and moved ever so slowly to the window. He saw the misty, green fields through the panes, and their serenity beckoned him. He perched on the sill to wait for Brienne, but out of the corner of his eye he saw a fustian cloak move below him on the grounds. A curl of deep, unmistakable auburn hair lay outside the hood. He inhaled sharply when he recognized who it was.

"Damn! . . . What?" His anger at her foolishness quickly gave way to fear for her safety when he switched his gaze from Brienne to the man she looked at with such trepidation. A large, unfamiliar, burly man stood by the stable block waiting for her. The man smiled meanly at Brienne, and Avenel felt he could kill just for that smile alone. Swiftly he turned to claim his revenge—but then his body froze with shock.

"What a compliment to my taste! Why, the place looks

the same!" A horribly familiar laugh rang out, and Avenel came face to face with his enemy.

"How did you get in here?" Avenel asked through clenched teeth.

"You see? I *am* the true earl! I know Osterley better than you!" Quentin Spense smiled. "Of course, it doesn't hurt that the grounds are so vast that it would take an army to patrol them effectively. Nor does it hurt to have one or two servants in the household who've never lost their loyalty to their true master."

"And who is that?" Avenel's eyes glittered vengefully.

"Naturally, I'm speaking about Fergie McInnis and his good wife, the cook. I thought of poisoning you one night at your own table, but that was too subtle. And I so want to be present when you meet your end."

"Where are the McInnises now?"

"Why, I believe they're upstairs locking old Cumberland and Rose in their apartments! I'd like to keep our tête-à-tête as quiet as possible. No need to roust your army of footmen—that is, not until I've reclaimed your earldom."

"You'll never reclaim my earldom." Avenel crossed his powerful arms across his chest.

"Invulnerable, are we?" Spense stepped forward. "Well then, look out the window and see how invulnerable you actually are."

"I'll kill you if Brienne is touched," Avenel said with deadly calm. His eyes blazed with hatred for the man who stood before him.

"My daughter is quite lovely, is she not?" Quentin Spense walked to the sill. He watched with glee the drama being played out below the window. Brienne slipped on the soggy ground and failed miserably to regain her freedom from the man holding her. In the background of the stable block, Nob watched, trussed up like a pheasant ready for the spit, his hands tied painfully through his crotch.

"You're already carrion, Spense." Avenel's fury reached a fever pitch, and he lunged at the other man. Swiftly and brutally, however, a pistol butted him in the neck, and he was taken by surprise by two men who would have dwarfed Hans. His vision swirled from the blow; but shaking his head several times, he was able to come back and land several good blows on each of the henchmen.

It was almost flattering that the earl had refused to underestimate him, Avenel thought dimly. Still, the two giants were too much even for his powerful size. Eventually he was pulled into an elbow chair and forced to remain there as they tamed his rebellious movements with the pistol butt.

"Slane, Slane, what am I going to do with you? You've been a thorn in my side for years. And there's even been talk about my own daughter bedding down with you. Have you turned her head?" Spense laughed demonically.

"Stay away from her, Spense. If she is harmed—" For this retort Avenel was again butted in the head, but quickly the earl raised his hand to stop his henchmen.

"Never fear for her comfort, Slane! My man has instructions that she is not to be *touched*." Spense's comment met a bone-chilling silence. "You've developed quite a fondness for little Brienne, haven't you?" Again there was silence. "Yet you assume I haven't any fondness for her. But let me assure you, I do, I do! It's been a long time since I saw her last, and I must say, she's breathtaking. But then, I knew she would be. You should have seen her mother. My question to you is, have you enjoyed riding her, mate?" Spense bent his tall frame down near Avenel to hear the answer to his question. However, there was none. "Come now, you must have some comment to make, some criticism of her, some praise. Spit it out, Slane."

"I'm glad you're here," Avenel said with deadly calm, "so I can finally—"

"No! No! I don't want threats! I want opinions! Like how about this?" Spense went over to the long sofa and slouched his older but well-built frame into it. "Can you see me here, Slane? Is the view advantageous? Then all we need is to get Brienne to give a leg over, and off we'll go, eh?"

A deep furious growl escaped from Avenel's lips, and soon he was out of his seat. The other men effectively beat him back down once again, but this took some time, and afterward Quentin Spense looked a bit more nervous than before.

"She must be your Achilles' heel."

"She has no part in this. Tell your man in the stable to let her go."

"By association, she has everything to do with this, Slane. What would you give me to leave her alone, eh?"

"I would give you everything I have to leave her out of this. But then, there are no assurances, are there?"

"You're an intelligent one." Spense's lips curled into an evil smile. "And it's unfortunate that the only way to deal with you is to finish the work left undone twenty years earlier." He pulled out a polished steel blade that caught the dancing light from the fireplace. He walked up to Avenel, and with lightning speed, he flicked the tip at Avenel's cheek, making a small nick that nonetheless bled profusely.

Barely flinching from the pain, Avenel looked steadfastly into Spense's face; his hatred was tangible enough to make Spense step back.

"Watch him," Spense said to one of the brutes. Turning to Avenel, he said, "I'm going to get your lover, mate. When I've broken her in enough to bring her back here, you can prepare yourself for a show. Then you can prepare yourself for the grave." He laughed and accepted his cloak from one of his minions. Avenel watched him and his burly helper leave the gallery; each stepped over the unconscious old footman who was sprawled in the marble hall.

When they had finally gone, Avenel studied the sweaty hulk before him. After several moments, Avenel suddenly laughed out loud madly.

"Shut up, you!" The henchman hardly wasted a second before lumbering over to Avenel to force him to be quiet. But the huge, slow man never knew what had happened. Avenel pulled a blade from his topboot. Effortlessly yet with studied revulsion, he slid it across the brute's large, heavy throat.

"Nob?" Brienne whispered in the dim light of the stable room. It was the one where she had spent the night when Avenel first arrived at Osterley. "Nob, are you all right? Where are you?" she called to the dark corners of the room; her voice was frightened. Rain was beginning to fall outside the dark mullioned windows, and she huddled in the cold room, waiting for Nob to answer.

"I'm sorry, Mistress Brienne," the boy blurted out. Soon she heard sniffling and the boy's moan. It was all she could do not to cry herself.

"Hush, Nob," she tried to comfort him. Inching over on her buttocks, she made her way to him, cursing her hands and feet, which were securely bound with a chaffing hemp. Soon she felt the warmth of his thin little body next to hers. But she was horrified when her eyes grew accustomed to the darkness, and she saw how Nob was bound. Circling the boy's neck was a rope that went down his back and then tied his hands through his groin. It was a complicated knot, and every movement the boy made caused more tightness for him below. Nob had to be still or suffer excruciating pain.

"I wanted to protect you, Mistress Brienne. I tried, truly I did. But then I saw Orillion laid out cold on the cobbles, and then the man—he was the one who killed Father!" He held back his tears in as manly a way as he could, but he could only last so long.

"Avenel will think of something. It was not up to you to take care of me." She soothed him, letting his head rest on her bosom. In the silence of the room, she wondered how her father had gotten past all of Avenel's precautions. But then she thought of the vastness of the Park and how well her father knew it, and she thought, too, how difficult it was to stop a man as evil and determined as he.

"It hurts," Nob quivered, making the rope tighter.

"Yes, I know." Her voice caught in her throat. "But you must relax. Just relax. Think of how brave you've been, and don't think of anything else."

"I haven't been brave," he chastised himself.

"Not brave? I only hope the child I carry now will be as courageous as you."

"Really?"

"Really. Now just relax. If you can, then perhaps I'll be able to untie you. I want you to run from here. Run as far as you can go and don't stop—not even in the village. I don't know who you can really trust."

"But you must come too. I'll untie you."

"I'm afraid not. You'll have far to go, no doubt. With the child I would not be up to that."

"I cannot leave you! What would Master Slane—?"

"He would want you to go, Nob."

"Where is he, Mistress Brienne?"

"I—I don't know." Fighting back hopelessness, she worked on the boy's knots. Her own wrists were tied in front of her, but her fingers moved as swiftly as they could despite this. Yet it was hard to concentrate. Where was Avenel? she wondered time and time again. Had her father caught him unawares? Was he already—? No! She refused to think of it. All she wanted, all she could think of, was to be with him. She and their child—they wanted to be with him, wherever he was now.

CHAPTER THIRTY-ONE

"There!" Brienne cried in triumph as the complex bindings fell from Nob's small body. Quickly the boy started in on hers, but when they heard laughter from downstairs, she whispered quickly, "Someone is coming. You must go now. Out the window there is a small ledge. Be as careful as you can and take all the time you need. Beware the spire below. You must not slip, but get to one of the gables, then to the ground."

"I cannot leave you," Nob whispered urgently.

Hearing footsteps trodding menacingly up the stairs to the room, she implored him, "Someone must go. Along the way you can find help. But I'm of no use in this condition. Go!" She thrust her head toward the large window. Outside she could see the mist and the rain swirling about and the sky filled with heavy, dark clouds.

Nob stood indecisively for another moment, but finally her persuasions were enough to convince him. "I'll go for help! I'll get you assistance, Mistress Brienne!" He hugged her tightly. She held her breath as he pulled his skinny body through the little window out onto the outside ledge, and her heart skipped a beat as he almost slipped twice on the slick, wet surface. Closing the unlatched window behind him, he got away just before the footsteps reached the landing.

"Hullo, Papa's here," a voice droned from the top of the stairs. Jolting at the sound of it, Brienne shivered.

"I'll light a fire, Spense." Two men entered the room. One, thick and slow, knelt by the small hearth and quickly made a fire with old mildewy kindling. The other man, her father, merely stood in the threshold and stared at her. He was dressed in lavishly embroidered white silk and a waistcoat of deep, blood red.

"Hey! Where's the boy?" the giant asked her stupidly.

"He's gone," she replied, defiant despite the cowering fear she felt inside.

"No matter. Leave us, Bilikins," Spense ordered.

"But the boy!" the large half-wit almost whined.

"Leave us!"

The hulk obeyed his master's orders, looking like a kicked mongrel.

"You're a beauty, Brienne love. Give your father a kiss." Spense picked her up from the floorboard as if she were a doll and placed her on the pallet. She tried to struggle, but his hands, held her down. She gasped when she felt a knife ruthlessly cut her feet free.

"Where is Avenel? Where is he?" She was not sure if she could stomach the answer.

"You want me to tell you he is dead?"

She lashed out at him with her bound wrists, trying to keep him away from her. "No," she whispered, horrified.

"Your lover also misses you, Brienne love. What say

we give him something to be jealous of?" Spense tried to put his lips on hers, and she kicked him, groaning with revulsion.

"Don't!" she screamed.

"I've wanted you. Even when you were a child, you were so exquisite. So lovely." He attempted to kiss her again, but she kicked at him once more. This time her foot found its mark in his groin, and Spense pulled back with a jerk. "Rough is how you like it, eh?" He pulled her to him.

"Let me be! Let me be!" She struggled in vain.

"I'll let you be. I'll let you be. Just have a tumble with me like you've done with Slane." He dragged her, kicking and struggling, across the rough floorboard to the fire grate. The fire was already beginning to dim, but the heat was still intense near the source. The earl pulled a half-burned stick from it, which he held dangerously close to her face. "Have a care, girl. I don't want that lovely face marred by an accidental burn."

"It scorches! Please!" She felt the heat on her cheeks.

"You'll be a good girl? Who knows? Maybe I'll even spare that gelded lover of yours." He tossed his gray head back and laughed.

"He is no gelding," she defended despite the fear of being burned.

"Not so, eh? Where's your proof then, girl?" He laughed again. But this time she couldn't hide the triumph in her face. Seeing this, Spense stopped laughing. He scanned her body for signs of her pregnancy and she knew he found them by the murderous glint in his eye. "With child, are we? My little whoring daughter." His tone changed, and he spoke softly, drawing the burning stick even nearer. "I'll not hurt you or the babe. If you be the obedient thing you can be, know that I'll not hurt you by far."

"Please," she gasped as he pulled her head up.

"Take me. Bite me if you want." He began to unbutton his breeches.

"Please," she sobbed. Her fear was so real, she could taste it.

"Come on, Brienne love. You've done it for him, now do it for me."

"God, please, no!" she screamed, pulling her head back, but the burn she expected never came, for the door burst open behind them.

"Come alive, Spense!" Avenel stood in the passage. He saw that she was all right and watched as she scrambled away from Spense's hold, then he began to laugh. But it was laughter that lacked sanity. With his white linen shirt drenched with fresh blood that was obviously not his own and his buff-colored buckskins also splattered with blood, he made a terrible sight indeed. "Where are your cutthroats when you need them? Tsk, tsk." Avenel finally entered the room, calmly refusing to meet Brienne's overwrought gaze. She watched him, and relief poured over her seeing that despite his previous battle he appeared unharmed.

"I'll be rid of you yet, Slane. Bilikins! Bilikins!" Spense yelled as he rebuttoned his breeches.

"Bilikins and your other idiot sit below with their throats slit." Avenel smiled. "You're alone, Spense. You're alone with me."

"Stay away, or I'll kill Brienne." Spense took her by the throat and pulled her toward the back of the room. It was getting very dark in the little stable room; the fire had spent its last flame, and the rain was falling heavily outside the window. In the dimness of the room Brienne could make out Avenel's body as he stalked them, but his face was now indistinguishable.

"Stay away from me, I warn you. Stay away!" the earl cried to Avenel's moving form.

But Avenel refused to stay away. He came closer and closer until, with a last grasp for self-preservation, the earl thrust Brienne toward Avenel and made a break for the door.

Gently Avenel lowered Brienne to the pallet and then went for the door.

He grabbed Spense back into the room and started punching him down. Brienne watched, helplessly, as the men tumbled from one corner to another, unable to do anything with her hands, which were still tied. At one point Avenel had the earl on his knees and was doling out painful kicks to the head, but then the earl rose, and they were once again knocking each other about.

"I'm going to kill you! Not for my father, not for my brother; I'm going to kill you just for touching Brienne. 'Tis enough just for that!" Avenel shouted at Spense.

"She's my daughter. I would not harm her," the earl whined in reply, trying to save himself.

"That's a lie! She can't be your daughter! Admit it! Tell her once and for all who her real father is, Spense!"

"She is my daughter! I say she is!"

"So help me, I'll slit your throat if you don't tell her now!" Avenel grunted and landed a heavy blow to Spense's jaw. "Admit it, and I may spare your life!"

"Her mother was carrying on behind my back, and when I found out I swore I'd make her pay! Grace was a whore, I tell you, a whore!"

"No!" Brienne cried out from the pallet. "How could she be expected to be faithful to a man who was cruel to her?"

"She was an adulteress, and after her aristocratic lover died from consumption, she was never the same." Spense looked at Brienne. "And I see she's got a whore for a daughter, too."

Letting out a fierce cry, Avenel threw himself on Spense, and again the two men grappled. But this time Brienne found it harder to tell who had the upper hand. Both men possessed the same build, and it was getting more and more difficult to tell them apart in the dark room. Furniture crashed as the two men fell to the floor, and when they righted themselves, there were more crashes as one tried to claim victory by tossing the other against the wall.

When the final crash came, Brienne heard a man's shrill cry and a great shattering of glass. Screaming herself, Brienne heard the thump below, more with her body than with her ears. Without thinking, she ran past the slumped body on the floor to the broken window, needing to see the destruction herself. She leaned over the sill into the driving rain, and through the heavy mist she saw a body impaled on the medieval spire below. Her heart seemed to stop beating from the shock and horror of it all, for she saw Avenel's blood-stained shirt front.

Screaming her disbelief, she clung to the jagged edges of the broken panes with her bound hands, which now bled profusely. Behind her, it was all the man could do to pull her away from the window.

"Take me with you, Avenel," she pleaded hopelessly to the fallen figure. "I love you. Take me with you," she sobbed. But soon her cries were muffled, and she was pulled struggling into the victor's strong arms. Soothing words were whispered in her ear, but she paid no heed to their meaning. All she noticed was the man's red waistcoat coming toward her, nearer and nearer, until she could stand it no longer. Her mind rebelled from the strain, and she sank into blackness.

CHAPTER THIRTY-TWO

Her whole world was full of sunshine when her eyes opened again. Brienne looked about her yellow taffeta room where she lay, adjusting her eyes to the bright, beautiful surroundings. She looked at everything, wanting to remember every detail. That the fire sparked happily in the fireplace was as important to her as that the cupids, plump and gold, were prettily carved into a chairback.

Avenel. She closed her eyes from the pain that stabbed within her. Curling on her side, she ignored the sun's bright rays from the window, which made square patterns of light on her bed. She sobbed softly and refused to think of the future or to try to answer the questions left from the past. It was only Avenel that she cared about, and his child who would be born in December. She felt her belly and found solace in its comforting curve. But despite this, she continued crying out of bitterness and regret.

"Crying, are we? And on a beautiful day such as this?"

she heard a distant voice say. Afraid that it was Quentin Spense coming to take his revenge, she sobbed even harder.

"Go away! Please, go away!" she whispered miserably, closing her eyes.

"Now, that's gratitude for you. Have my bloody head nearly knocked off my neck, and what for?" She felt the mattress dip as the visitor sat down comfortably on the side of the bed.

"Can it be? Good Lord in heaven!" she exclaimed and backed away, holding on to the bedcurtains. It was Avenel sitting at the edge of her bed! His face appeared tired, and he had a great, ugly bruise along his temple. *But it was Avenel.*

"Don't faint again, wildflower. I say, the child has a stake in this, too, and he is decidedly against it." He smiled and reached for her. "Come, love, don't look so shocked. 'Twas not me who took the fall, I promise you."

"But I saw . . . I saw with my own eyes." She held back a sob.

"It was dark, and the rain and mist blurred your vision. Feel me, touch me—I'm real enough."

"I want you to be real," she whispered. "But I'm afraid. So much has happened, so much has been a nightmare. When I looked out the window in the stable block, I thought I saw my worst fears come true."

"That's exactly what you saw, little one. You saw your fears, nothing more. You must have been so over-wrought that when you saw Spense dead, you thought you saw me. But touch me, let me reassure you. He's the dead one. Not I." He held out his hand.

Slowly, she took Avenel's strong, bronzed hand. Soon she was entirely enveloped in his embrace and in every aspect of him. His scent, the feel of his queued hair against his neck, and the way his lips touched her so demandingly convinced her that he was indeed all right. When they finally parted, tears of joy streamed down her cheeks, and she saw the happiness that lit up his own gray eyes.

"I thought I'd lost you."

"And was that so terrible? You would have had your precious freedom then."

"Do not speak of such things!" She grabbed him and held him close.

"I love you, little one. Do I say that too often?"

"Nay, you can never do that." She pressed her mouth against his and kissed him desperately. All that mattered in the world was sitting before her.

"Where is Nob?" She lay back on the pillows sometime later. "I untied him, and he escaped. But last night how did he fare?"

"He's fine. I found him climbing down one of the gables in the stable block before I got to you and Spense. He and Orillion are both a bit stiff, but they could have been worse off." Avenel's eyes narrowed with the thought.

"I see Orillion's master is a bit sore, too, this day." She touched the bruise on his cheek tenderly. "Why has all this happened? Can you tell me now?"

"I shall tell you. You'll need to become used to your title."

"I no longer have a title. Legally I've been the daughter of a commoner I loathed, and now I find out I'm the bastard of an aristocrat I'll never know. But tell me, Avenel, how could the earl fake a thing like that? How could he steal your father's title and for so long go undetected?"

"Because the real earl, my father, had been away for a long time. He'd been in America."

"Your father left his title?" she asked incredulously.

"Yes. He left Osterley to find adventure in the Colonies, planning to return after a few years. But there he met my mother. She had two sons by him, and after that he could not bear to take her away from her beloved American home. When she died of fever, I was thirteen. My brother Christopher had married, and my father thought it best to return to England and give his sons back their heritage. Unfortunately he died on the first leg of the voyage."

"But it wasn't until you had set sail that—?"

"We were docked at Annapolis. A man named Quentin Spense was the captain of our ship, the *Rosalie*. He had a motley bunch of cutthroats working under him. The cruel twist of fate was the remarkable likeness he had to my father. The same build, the same age, the same coloring. There were differences, of course, but my father had been gone from England for twenty years, so those who were close to him had either died off or were getting too old to trust their own instincts. And of course, there was the Duke of Degarre."

"It's all his fault. A shabbier excuse for a man—" she said vehemently.

"And how would you know, love?" He grabbed her small hand, and she relished the warmth of his touch.

"I called on him when I was in Bath. I wanted him to do something about the earl—Quentin Spense, I mean. He was pathetic. This trickery has gone unnoticed for years because of him."

"Fortune has not smiled upon the Morrows—until now." He touched her cheek.

"But Avenel," she looked concerned. "Everyone believes Spense to have been the earl. How will you ever prove otherwise?''

''Never fear. Already I have been accepted into the peerage with my vast amount of coin. With a claim to a title, I'll be even further venerated. And of course, if anyone doubts my claim, I have the Laborde jewels to prove my bloodline.''

''The stamp on my comb, QE. Is it somehow a part of these jewels?''

''The Laborde jewels were given to us by Queen Elizabeth when she traveled to Osterley to escape the Black Death that was the scourge of London at the time. The amethysts and diamonds were part of the royal jewels, and she had the necklace and comb made before her trip.''

''But how did my father get them?''

''He didn't. Before I jumped ship with Cumberland, my brother's dying words were to take the Laborde jewels. I was able to escape with the necklace but not the comb. Spense then gave the comb to your mother as a wedding present and as partial proof of his false title. But my guess is that when you turned four or five, your mother realized she had married an imposter. She took you and the comb and fled.''

''The title is rightfully yours, Avenel. I'm happy for you. I only wish I could take back my words when I insisted you call me Lady Brienne. I feel quite foolish.'' Her cheeks turned pink.

''Spense was not your father. You're no commoner,'' he said adamantly.

''There is the miniature, I suppose, but that's my only proof.''

''The miniature?''

''Yes.'' She leaned to the bedside table and opened the

drawer. Holding the priceless slip of ivory, she took a long, wishful look at the portrait and then handed it to him. Avenel studied the handsome young man.

"There's your father." He tossed the miniature onto the bed. The young man stared back at them with bright green eyes. He was dressed in a simple linen shirt and bottle green topcoat. His hair remained undressed, and his deep auburn locks appeared so dark as to be shot with magenta highlights.

"He must be. But I'll never be sure. All three people who knew the truth are dead." She chewed her lip anxiously. "Believing I was the earl's daughter was terrible. But now I have no heritage at all, and no name. Am I to be called Brienne Spense now?"

"I think Brienne Morrow suits you quite well," he said softly, watching for her reaction.

Brienne paused. "Avenel, are you asking me to marry you? Do you mean—?"

"I mean that you need to rest for now. But I shall not let you go without a title for more than a few more days. How does a week suit you, my countess?"

"I think a week is a very long time to wait." She laughed and hugged him tightly, her eyes shining with happiness and love.

EPILOGUE

In a dream it did seem—
But alas, dreams do pass
as do shadows—
I did walk, I did talk
With my love, with my dove
through fair meadows.
Still we passed till at last
We sat to repose us for our
pleasure.
Being set, lips met,
Arms twined, and did bind
my heart's treasure.

—Attributed to Shakespeare

The long gallery was silent except for the clinking of French porcelain and silver. As Mrs. Whitsome set up for tea, a pair of beautiful, haunted eyes looked down upon the scene from the mantel, where the portrait of Quentin Spense had hung for more than a decade. The girl in the Gainsborough portrait looked regal in the hyacinth brocaded dress she wore, and she smiled an enigmatic smile that spoke of love lost and love found.

Outside, laughter rang from the Temple of Pan underneath the spray of falling cherry blossoms. Summer was upon Osterley. Brienne sat on a brocade cushion, having just fed Lord William Cumberland Morrow. Now on her lap, the babe slept. She tried to relace herself, but her husband intervened.

"No pap for my child, I see," he mocked.

"I was not fed pap—nor I wager, were you," she said, smiling.

"Aye, no pap for this Colonial beast. But what of this one?" He stroked the child's fragile head.

"Are you saying I'm not a good mother?" Her hand went to her chest in mock denial.

"No pap, no swaddling. The babe enjoys too much freedom. Already he appears far too healthy."

"Yes. He is too much like his father. Lusty, spoiled, and self-indulgent."

"Aye, that and more." Avenel placed the sleeping dark-haired boy on a pillow near them, then sat down next to her, claiming her mouth in a possessive kiss.

Giggling, she tried to push him away, but it was of no use. He was too demanding. *Just like the babe*, she thought. Closing her eyes, she relived the birth of their son.

Avenel and Cumberland had sat on the steps of the great staircase like two bandy urchins, orphaned from their cause by their very masculinity. They had listened to Brienne's cries all through the morning. But by the afternoon her cries had ceased, replaced by the throaty yell of their son.

"Please, is it a son?" she had whispered, exhausted from the ordeal of giving birth.

"He is a son, my lady!" Vivie and Mrs. Whitsome had gasped as Rose held the babe in her arms.

"Is he beautiful?" Brienne smiled weakly. In the moments following, Avenel burst into the room as pale as she had ever seen him. He rushed over to the bed, as if to assure himself that she was all right.

"It's a son, Avenel. But does he look like you?" Brienne had pulled on his waistcoat.

"Hush, hush." He placed a bittersweet kiss on her lips.

"We must change those damp linens, love, before you catch your death." Mrs. Whitsome scurried over to her.

Slowly she was raised in Avenel's arms as they bathed her and changed her bedclothes. Her legs shaking from the strain, she had been placed back in the bed. But still she was adamant.

"Avenel, go see your son. Tell me if you approve."

Cumberland was allowed to enter the room next. As the older man walked over to the child, he gave a gasp of amazement.

"Oh, what is it? Is he ugly?" Brienne had cried, becoming distraught.

"Come along, Avenel. I'm afraid this is something you must see." Cumberland shook his head. "I never thought I'd see the day."

Avenel had stood and walked over to the crib near the Etruscan room. The elaborate baby's bed was swathed in blue silk, and the child cried from among the folds.

"Lord Avenel, your son." Rose had presented the infant to him. Peering into the crib, Avenel had blinked to hide the emotion that roiled within him.

"My lord, what is it? Is the child flawed?" Brienne had cried desperately from the bed, unable to hide her disappointment.

"His only flaw is that he takes after his father. He will be a handful, no doubt." Cumberland laughed and patted Avenel on the back.

"He pleases you then?" Brienne rested back on the pillows thoroughly exhausted.

"Aye, he pleases me, wildflower."

With this, she had promptly fallen asleep, so great was her need for rest. Her dreams had been pleasant, full of blue silk and baby's laughter. She had yet to see the child that she had borne. But she already knew what he looked like. Just as she imagined—a baby with hair as dark as coal lay in the Linnell crib, and he stared back at the world with crystalline blue-gray eyes.

Opening her eyes, now at the Temple of Pan, she sought out her son, who slept on the cushion.

"Lady Brienne, you have too much need to be a doting mother," Avenel said gruffly when she left him.

"He is so precious. Our only son—how can I not spoil him?" She returned to her husband's arms.

"Methinks he needs some competition." Intently, he opened her loosened bodice and touched her breasts. He kissed the top of one that peeked out from her shift, and raising his head, he grinned. Six months had passed since the boy was born. Brienne had let him treat her like a madonna ever since then. But with his touch today, she knew she didn't want to be one any longer.

"Are you saying we should provide him with a sister?" She ran a finger down the length of his thigh.

Watching his hand as he slid it beneath her petticoat, he answered her question without saying a word. There among the soft summer breezes and the scent of orange blossoms, he showed her exactly what he thought. Brienne's happy laughter floated out among the gardens and to the far reaches of the Park. She simply couldn't have agreed more.